PENGUIN BOOKS

MISS JUL

Ann B. Ross is the author   pular
Southern heroine Miss Juli   *Luck
Day*, a novel about one   ...oken
residents: Etta Mae Wiggins. Ross holds a doctorate in English from
the University of North Carolina at Chapel Hill, and has taught
literature at the University of North Carolina at Asheville. She lives
in Hendersonville, North Carolina.

* * *

Praise for *Miss Julia Inherits a Mess* and the Miss Julia series

"A charming, fun adventure with new relatives, old secrets, and a will
putting Miss Julia and the Abbotsville regulars in a true Southern
mess. I loved it!"

—Duffy Brown, bestselling author of
the *Consignment Shop Mysteries*

"The memorably droll Ross has a gift for elevating such everyday
matters as marital strife and the hazards of middle age to high com-
edy, while painting her beautifully drawn characters with wit and
sympathy." —*Publishers Weekly*

"Ann B. Ross develops characters so expertly, through quirks, names,
and mannerisms, that they easily feel familiar as the reader is gently
immersed into the world Miss Ross has created. . . . A delightful
read." —*Winston-Salem Journal*

"Miss Julia is one of the most delightful characters to come along in
years. Ann B. Ross has created what is sure to become a classic Southern comic novel. Hooray for Miss Julia, I could not have liked it more."
—Fannie Flagg, author of *The All-Girl Filling
Station's Last Reunion*

"Yes, Miss Julia is back, and I, for one, am one happy camper."
—J. A. Jance, author of *Cold Betrayal*

Also by Ann B. Ross

Miss Julia Weathers the Storm

Miss Julia Lays Down the Law

Etta Mae's Worst Bad-Luck Day

Miss Julia's Marvelous Makeover

Miss Julia Stirs Up Trouble

Miss Julia to the Rescue

Miss Julia Rocks the Cradle

Miss Julia Renews Her Vows

Miss Julia Delivers the Goods

Miss Julia Paints the Town

Miss Julia Strikes Back

Miss Julia Stands Her Ground

Miss Julia's School of Beauty

Miss Julia Meets Her Match

Miss Julia Hits the Road

Miss Julia Throws a Wedding

Miss Julia Takes Over

Miss Julia Speaks Her Mind

Miss Julia
Inherits a Mess

ANN B. ROSS

PENGUIN BOOKS

PENGUIN BOOKS

An imprint of Penguin Random House LLC
375 Hudson Street
New York, New York 10014
penguin.com

First published in the United States of America by Viking Penguin,
an imprint of Penguin Random House LLC, 2016
Published in Penguin Books 2017

ISBN 9780525427124 (hc.)
ISBN 9780143108658 (pbk.)

Printed in the United States of America
1   3   5   7   9   10   8   6   4   2

Set in Fairfield LT Std
Designed by Cassandra Garruzzo

Acknowledgments

Last year, the Blue Ridge Literacy Council of Henderson County, North Carolina, offered at auction to the highest bidder the naming of a character in a Miss Julia book. This is that book.

Although I do not know Diane Jankowski, whose most generous bid won her namesake a prominent role in *Miss Julia Inherits a Mess*, it was a pleasure to work with my version of her. I have given that character a professional background as an accredited furniture appraiser and, as such, she is a great help in extricating Miss Julia from the mess in which she finds herself.

Through the many months of working with "Diane Jankowski," I have come to know that character quite well. I can only hope that the real Diane likes her as much as I do.

My thanks to you, Diane.

Miss Julia Inherits a Mess

Chapter 1

"*Julia!*" Barely catching her breath, LuAnne Conover started talking as soon as I answered the phone. "Have you heard? Everybody's talking about it—it's all over town. I can't imagine what she's been through, can you?"

"Well, no, LuAnne, I can't. Who're we talking about, anyway?"

"Why, Miss Mattie Freeman, of course. Who else would we be talking about? I *mean*, Julia, who else do we know who fell and broke her hip and couldn't get help no matter how long she cried and screamed, and had to lie sprawled out on the floor all night long?"

"Oh, my," I said, abruptly sitting down. "No, I hadn't heard. Is she all right? What happened?"

But LuAnne wasn't finished with what she'd started. "It's beyond me to understand how you miss everything, Julia. It's not as if you live out in the sticks or anything. In fact, I live farther out than you do, and *I* heard about it more than an hour ago. I would've called you sooner, but my phone's been busy."

Yes, and I knew why—she'd been on it. But I said, "Well, I don't get out and around like you do."

"That's because you have Lillian to run your errands and do your shopping and everything else, while I have to do everything myself."

Every now and then, LuAnne had to take a little jab at those of us who had household help. Not, I assure you, that she couldn't afford it herself, although I concede that she might've had to compromise on other things. But still.

"That's neither here nor there, LuAnne," I said, unwilling to apologize for my good fortune. After all, I'd had to put up with Wesley Lloyd Springer for forty-some-odd years to get it. "Tell me about Miss Mattie. Is she all right?"

"*Who knows?*" LuAnne said, almost in a shriek. "Nobody'll tell me anything! I've called the hospital and I've called Dr. Hargrove and they won't tell me a living thing! They ask if I'm a member of the family—they're the only ones they'll talk to. And, Julia, I've known her for *years,* which I think ought to count for something."

"Well . . ."

"I even called Sue, and would you believe she said I knew more about it than she did. Now, I just don't believe that, because she's the doctor's wife. Who else would know something if not her?"

"When did this happen, LuAnne?"

"Not fifteen minutes ago. And she said she had something on the stove and couldn't talk. Hurt my feelings, too."

"No, LuAnne, I mean when did Miss Mattie fall?"

"Oh. Well, sometime last night or maybe yesterday afternoon. I can't get a straight answer out of anybody. Do you think the EMTs would tell us anything?"

"I don't think I'd bother them. They're probably under orders not to give out information. But does that mean they were called out for Miss Mattie?"

"Julia," LuAnne said with just a touch of impatience that meant I was being uncommonly slow. "Who do you *think* they'd call? Miss Mattie had been lying on that floor in horrific pain all night long. She had to have somebody who could get her on a stretcher or whatever, and somebody who had an ambulance to get her to the emergency room."

"Oh, of course. But who found her?"

"The postman! You know how they have all the tenants' mailboxes in the hall of her building? Well, he was delivering the mail right beside her door, and he heard her moaning, so he called for help. And thank goodness he did. But I can't believe her mail comes so early in the day. Can you? If it'd been me, I would've been lying there till suppertime, practically."

"So she's in the hospital now?"

"Surgery. They're still operating on her."

"Oh, my," I said again. "Should we go over? I mean, maybe a group of us could sit in the waiting room to show our concern. She doesn't have any family, does she?"

"Not that I know of," LuAnne said, slowing down as she thought about it. "It's strange, isn't it, to know someone so long, yet know so little about her? But I'll tell you something else," she went on, gathering steam, "If you get a group together to go over there, don't bother calling Helen Stroud."

"Well, she's probably busy."

"Busy, my foot. She's just not interested, and I don't think she gives a flip about Mattie. When I phoned to tell her what happened, all she said was, 'That's too bad. Thank you for calling.' Now, is that cold, or what?"

"Well, you know how Helen is. She expects people to do what they say they'll do, and Mattie . . . well, Mattie's not the easiest person to get along with."

To tell the truth, Mattie Freeman could be downright disagreeable—abrupt and outspoken—with little thought of the feelings of others. She also had a tendency to volunteer for anything that came up, then to either forget it or just not do it. Helen, on the other hand, was the most efficient and organized person I knew—when she said she'd do something, you knew it would be done. She'd probably washed her hands of Mattie years ago and felt no need to manufacture a great concern for her now.

Not wanting to discuss those thoughts with LuAnne, though, I picked up on her earlier comment. "I think it's strange, too, that no one seems close to Mattie. I've known her since I first came to Abbotsville as a bride, yet I can't really say I *know* her. But what do you think? Should the two of us go over?"

"Well, I will if you will, but Leonard will want his lunch before I go. And there's really not much use in our just sitting around if she's still in surgery. Why don't we think about it for a while?"

I agreed, knowing that Miss Mattie would spend some time in the recovery room after the surgery anyway, and would be unlikely to feel up to receiving visitors anytime soon.

I put down the phone after LuAnne's assurance that she'd keep me up to date on Mattie's condition. I had no worries on that score, for LuAnne kept everyone up to date with anything and everything she heard, knew, or even thought of.

I sat down on the leather Chippendale sofa there in our library, which had once been the downstairs bedroom, to think about what had happened. Miss Mattie Freeman, bless her heart, what would she do now? As far as I knew—and I knew enough— she wouldn't have too many options. It was a settled fact, though, that she would need round-the-clock care for some time to come. Whom did she have to make those decisions and those arrangements if she was unable to do so herself? Which, at her advanced age, was highly likely to be the case.

Thinking of Miss Mattie's present, uneasy situation, I recalled the day a few weeks after Wesley Lloyd's passing—this was years ago now—when Binkie, my curly-headed lawyer, called me to her office.

"Miss Julia," she'd said, holding out a frayed, much-used ledger, "you may not know about this, but you should take a look. It's a list of people who owe money to Mr. Springer—well, to the estate now. It shows how much they borrowed and how they're repaying it."

"Oh, you mean bank loans?" Wesley Lloyd had been the owner of one of the last independent banks in the state, a situation in which I'd wanted no part. I'd sold out as soon as I profitably could.

"No, not bank loans—personal loans. You'll forgive me, Miss Julia, but Mr. Springer was running his own operation and charging a pretty penny for it, too."

I hadn't needed to forgive her for anything she had to say about my first husband. I'd had plenty to say about him myself.

As I glanced down the list of names in the ledger, I realized that I knew most of the people who were indebted to my husband, and now to me. I smiled to myself as an idea began to form in my mind. Hazel Marie Puckett, my late husband's paramour and mother of his little son, who up to that point had been thoroughly snubbed by the town, would, I decided, soon be welcomed in some of the finest homes in Abbottsville. Or else I would see that a certain number of loans on that list would be called in forthwith. Then I saw Mattie Freeman's name. I closed the ledger and handed it back to Binkie, feeling as embarrassed as I would've if I'd walked in on Miss Mattie in the act of disrobing. I told Binkie to cancel that debt, but none of the others.

It was days later that Binkie told me that Mattie had been highly offended at the cancellation, saying that she didn't need charity from anyone, much less from someone she had to see in the Lila Mae Harding class every Sunday that rolled around. I'd left all further decisions about Wesley Lloyd's loan sharking up to Binkie after that and never mentioned the matter to Miss Mattie. For many people who run out of funds, pride is the only thing left, and I respected that.

Chapter 2

When the phone rang again, I hurried to it, hoping there would be news of Mattie's condition.

"Julia, it's me," Mildred Allen said, although I instantly recognized her voice. Mildred lived next door in what was the largest house in Abbotsville or, if not the absolute largest, pretty close to that distinction. "I guess you've heard from LuAnne about Mattie Freeman."

"I have, and I was just sitting here wondering what Mattie will do, now that she probably won't regain her mobility anytime soon."

"Well," Mildred said, "I say it'd be a good thing if she doesn't. Julia, she can't hear and she can't half see, yet she drives that old car like she's the only one on the road."

"Oh, I know. I pull to the side when I see her coming." We laughed a little at the thought of Mattie's age-old Oldsmobile barreling around town. "I don't think they make those things anymore, and I keep hoping it'll die on her. I doubt she'd be able to get parts for it, so she'd have to park it."

"We'd all be safer if she did, but let me ask you something," Mildred said. "I've had her on my mind all morning and started wondering about this. Have you noticed how Miss Mattie's teas keep getting smaller and smaller? I can remember when she'd have about a dozen guests every spring to repay her obligations for the past year. Her teas were always lovely—especially those luscious finger sandwiches she served. But last year there were just a few of us there. Are people turning down her invitations or is she just not inviting many?"

"Oh, Mildred, I finally figured that out. It took me awhile, but I think I know the answer. You're right, years ago she always invited eleven ladies, making twelve counting herself. That's about all her living room will hold at one time anyway."

Miss Mattie had lived in a two-bedroom apartment in an old but substantial building near town for as long as I'd known her. The tall, spacious rooms with medallioned ceilings, designed by an architect unaffected by modernism, were filled with furniture of a size and quality that indicated a decline from more gracious surroundings. She entertained once a year—always in the late spring when it was warm enough for her guests to expand into the sunroom through the French doors in her living room.

"Yes, I know," Mildred said, "but what I'm saying is that she hasn't had that many guests in a number of years. Last spring there were only five of us, six counting her."

"Well, hold on. I'm telling you why. You know that lovely china she has?"

"Meissen, isn't it? I don't know the name of the pattern."

I started laughing. "I don't think anybody does. Remember the time LuAnne raised her cup over her head to look at the mark on the bottom?"

"And tilted it so she spilled tea on herself? I sure do—funniest thing I'd seen in ages."

"Well, anyway," I went on when we stopped laughing. "It's a beautiful set—so thin you can practically see through it and quite old. It's probably been discontinued by now. But that's the problem. Mildred, I think that over the years, Miss Mattie has suffered some cup and saucer breakage, and as they break, she's had to cut down on the number of guests she invites."

"Why, that's right. I should've figured that out myself. I remember thinking—what was it, three years ago?—how strange it was that Mattie had invited only seven guests. Such an odd number, but that meant she was down to eight cups and saucers. And last year she must've been down to six. Oh, bless her heart, that's so sad."

"It is," I agreed, "but you have to admire her for keeping up appearances in spite of it."

"She certainly does that. And woe be to anyone who leaves her off a guest list. Ever since she started using that walker, though, she's a danger to have around."

"Oh, I know. She almost crippled a visiting preacher one time when a rubber-tipped metal leg of that walker landed on his foot. How old do you think she is, anyway?"

"Older than we are, that's for sure."

"I guess that makes her fairly close to ancient—speaking for myself, of course."

"Of course," Mildred said, laughing. "But, Julia, do you think she'll have to go into a hospice or a retirement home or what? She won't be able to stay by herself, will she?"

"I wouldn't think so, and the way hospitals discharge patients so quickly these days, something will have to be decided fairly soon. Does she really have no family at all?"

"I've never known her to mention any, although generally there's a distant cousin crouching in the background somewhere just waiting for a death notice."

"Oh, don't even think that. Besides, I expect that even if a distant cousin shows up, he'd be sorely disappointed." We let a few seconds pass in silence as we thought of Miss Mattie's dire straits. "Mildred, you and I may have to step in if it comes down to it."

Mildred sighed. "I was thinking the same thing, although I don't want it to get around that we're providing Social Security supplements. No telling where it would end with all the impoverished widows in this town."

"I'm in total agreement with that. But let's just wait and see how she gets along. For all we know, we'll be dodging that Oldsmobile again in a few weeks."

After hanging up the phone, I walked to the window overlooking the backyard. It was a beautiful spring day—clear skies and a warm breeze stirring the leafed-out ornamental fruit trees we'd planted a few years back. The forsythia, jonquils, and tulips were about gone, but the wisteria over the arbor and the crape myrtles beside it were just before their full blooming stage.

It was time for Miss Mattie's annual tea party, but there wouldn't be one this year. *Maybe I should do it for her.* That was an inspiring thought, and I congratulated myself for thinking of it. I sat down to think it through.

I would have it here at my house, of course, and Mattie would be the guest of honor. And I would invite more than five or seven or even eleven guests because I had thirty-six unbroken and un-chipped cups and saucers. And they would be constantly washed and replaced on the silver tray as guests came and went.

I would seat Mattie in one of the large wingback chairs, not in the living room, which would create congestion at the front door, but here in the new library, where the ladies could line up to be greeted in style. And I'd keep that perilous walker far from Mattie's chair, so she couldn't get up and down, posing a danger to every foot in the room.

Mattie would be in her element—she loved parties and never missed a one. If, for some reason, she did not receive an invitation to a party that she knew someone was giving, she wasn't above calling the hostess with the news that her invitation had been lost in the mail.

But thinking of all that, my mind eventually came back to the question of what was to become of her now. There were at least two large complexes near town that catered to well-to-do couples, widows, and widowers in their declining years, offering both excellent living conditions and lifetime care. One of those would be ideal for Miss Mattie—she would revel in the attention—but I doubted she'd be able to afford either one.

The alternative, as far as I knew, was some crowded government establishment where she'd have a roommate who'd keep her awake by moaning and crying all night, and aide workers who would do the best they could, but which in the final analysis wouldn't be good enough. Shunted aside, that's what it would come down to, and I hated the thought of that.

I might as well be honest here and say right up front that Mattie and I had never been close. She'd been on the fringes of my acquaintances throughout the years, and neither of us had made any effort toward a closer relationship. She had always been so *old,* even years ago when we were all younger. Her hair had always been up in a bun, and her clothes had always been gray or black. For years, she had been a tall, big-boned woman—not particularly overweight, but in the last several years her frame had broadened and become more hunched as her legs bowed from the weight. You wouldn't want to go through a doorway with her.

I smiled to myself recalling the first time Lloyd had seen her not long after he and his mother had come to live with me. He'd thought she was the witch from *Hansel and Gretel,* and he'd kept his distance from the oven as long as she was in the house.

It had been a natural progression for Mattie to go from a limp to a cane to a walker. And now, perhaps, to a chair or a bed for the rest of her life.

I got so sad thinking about it that I had to get up and walk around.

And a convenient move that was, because I could walk right on out of the room as Lillian called me to lunch.

Chapter 3

"Tuna fish salat," Lillian said, motioning to the plate on the kitchen table. "I always think of it when springtime come rollin' 'round."

"It does look good," I said, sitting at the table. "Have you eaten?"

Lillian laughed. "I been eatin' all mornin'." She scrubbed a spot on the counter, then rinsed the cloth under running water. "Miss Julia, did you hear 'bout pore ole Miss Mattie Freeman? Everybody at the grocery store wonderin' what gonna happen to her now."

"Yes, I have heard, and I've been wondering the same thing. It's so sad to be all alone in the world, which is what we think she is. I can't imagine what she'll do. I don't even know what her choices would be in the way of getting the help she'll need."

"Well, they's lots of nursin' homes out in the country," Lillian said. "But they all crowded up with cranky ole people that can't do nothin' for their selves. I wouldn't put my dog in a one of 'em."

"Oh, dear," I said, lifting a fork full of tuna salad. "Well, I hope she's had the foresight to designate someone to make those decisions for her if it comes down to it. But," I went on, "for all we know, she could get over this and be her old self again. Lots of people do."

"Yes'm," Lillian agreed, but with little conviction. She busied herself with pulling out various pans and pots in preparation for dinner. "Oh, I forget to tell you," she said, turning to me, "I run into that nice Miss Etta Mae in the coffee aisle at the store today. She ast me how you doin'."

"Well, how sweet of her. I haven't seen her for a while. Is she getting along all right?"

"Yes'm, I guess. She smilin' an' talkin' like she always do. But, I tell you, she have that long, lonesome look 'round her eyes—you know what I'm talkin' about. So all that talkin' an' carryin' on don't fool me. She a sad young woman."

"Oh, I hate to hear that," I said, putting down my fork, troubled by Lillian's insight—she was rarely wrong. "I hope nothing bad has happened to her." I put my napkin by my plate and stood up. "I think I'll call her and see how she's doing. I've been thinking of her anyway, wondering if she might be available to help Mattie when she comes home."

"Yes'm, Miss Mattie gonna need lots of help, an' maybe Miss Etta Mae could go stay with her like she did when Miss Hazel Marie have her twinses."

"Well, I don't know about that," I said, rolling my eyes just a little. "You wouldn't believe what her employer—Lurline Somebody—charged for letting her do private duty. I wouldn't have minded if Etta Mae had gotten it—I mean, she was up and down all night every night with those babies, then taking care of them and Hazel Marie during the day. She earned every penny, but she only got her regular salary."

Lillian smiled. "I 'spect you make up for it, though."

I smiled back. "A workman is worthy of his hire, I always say."

I stood by the table for a few minutes, lost in thought. Then I said, "You know, if anybody else could hear me I wouldn't say this—I'd probably be strung up by wild-eyed feminists. But I think what Etta Mae needs is a man."

"Law, Miss Julia," Lillian said, laughing as she cut her eyes at me. "From what I hear, she already have a bait of 'em. I 'spect that the last thing on her mind."

"Well, I'm talking about a decent, hardworking man who'd

love her and support her as she deserves to be. She's all alone in the world except for Granny Wiggins, who seems healthy enough now, but how long will that last? And it'll be Etta Mae who'll be taking care of her."

"Well, you know what they say. You spend the first part of your life taking care of chil'ren, an' the last part taking care of your mama an' daddy. An' your grands, too, if you got 'em."

"That's the truth," I said, then had to smile because it wasn't the truth for me. "I guess that's the bright side of having no children and outliving all your relatives. I tell you, Lillian, I don't think I'm cut out for taking care of an old person. Not enough patience, for one thing."

Lillian grunted. "You didn't think you was cut out to take care of no chil'ren, either, and look what been happenin'."

"Well," I conceded with a smile, "Lloyd is a different matter altogether. And the little Pickens girls, too. And I guess Coleman and Binkie's Gracie as well. But I'd rather deal with children than with some sharp-tongued old person who's never pleased with anything you do."

"You got that right, 'less," she said, stopping to laugh, "it Latisha you got to deal with. She a handful."

I smiled at the thought of Lillian's talkative great-grandchild. "Well, it's said that the Lord never gives you more than you can handle, but I thank goodness that Sam and I are the oldest in both our families. I don't have to worry about having someone in declining health on my hands for the rest of his or her life."

"Yessum," Lillian mumbled as she began peeling potatoes. "The Lord, He know what He doin', all right."

"Etta Mae?" I said when she answered her cell phone. "It's Julia Murdoch. I hope I'm not calling at an inconvenient time."

"Oh, Miss Julia! How nice to hear from you, and, no, it's not inconvenient. I'm in my car, on my way to the next patient."

"Well, good. You're so busy that I always hesitate to call."

"Oh, don't do that. You can call anytime you want to. I can always stop what I'm doing if you need anything."

"That's very thoughtful of you, Etta Mae. But what I'm calling about now is to see if you could add another patient to your list."

There was silence on the line. Then she asked, "Are you having trouble, Miss Julia?"

"Me? Oh, no. My goodness, I'm as healthy as a horse. No, I'm calling about a friend who might need some help." And I went on to tell her about Mattie Freeman, although emphasizing that I was simply exploring the possibilities.

"Well, sure," Etta Mae said, although with markedly less enthusiasm than I'd previously heard. "Lurline would have to rearrange the schedules with the other girls, but if you ask for me, I expect she would."

"Understand, though," I said, "that I'm not talking about round-the-clock care from you. That would be entirely too much to ask—and I'm not that close to Mattie. And it may not come to needing you at all. For all I know, she's made her own plans, and I hope she has."

"Maybe so, but you can let me know."

"Thank you, I will. But, Etta Mae . . . ?"

"Ma'am?"

"How are you doing?"

"Oh, I'm okay," she said with a sigh. "Just a little disappointed, I guess. I thought maybe you were calling about taking another trip to West Virginia or Florida or somewhere." She laughed at her dashed hopes.

"I tell you what, Etta Mae," I said, about to promise something that I'd never thought of before. "When this business with Mattie is settled, we ought to take a trip. But not for the reasons we took the other ones. Let's think about just going somewhere for fun."

"I would love it," she said, and from the way she said it, I knew she meant it.

Chapter 4

"Julia," LuAnne said when I answered the phone later that afternoon. "Mattie is out of recovery and in her room. I just checked, and she's doing fine. Do you want to go visit her?"

I glanced at my watch. "Why, yes, let's do. It's not quite four, so we could go and be back before supper."

"I'll pick you up on my way. Fifteen minutes?"

"That's fine," I said. "I'll see if Mildred wants to go with us."

Mildred didn't. I called her as soon as I'd hung up with LuAnne, and Mildred had said, "Just give Mattie my best, if you will. It's too late in the day for me. I'll try to go over tomorrow."

I wasn't surprised, because Mildred had become less and less active lately—a matter that concerned me. But how do you point out to someone that they need to exercise and lose weight without losing a friendship in the process?

After telling Lillian where I was going, I slipped on a cardigan—hospitals are always cold—and hurried out to LuAnne's car when she pulled to the curb.

The Pink Lady at the front desk gave us Mattie's room number, then we followed the painted lines to the surgical ward on the second floor. Stopping at the nurses' station on the ward, LuAnne asked about Mattie's condition.

"She's still a little groggy from the anesthesia," the nurse responded, "but the surgery went well." Then she smiled warmly. "She should have no problem with a full recovery."

Well, that was encouraging, I thought, marveling again at the wonders of modern medicine.

We proceeded down the hall and entered a room with two beds, a partially pulled curtain between them giving a semblance of privacy. There was a patient in each bed. Mattie was in the one closest to the window, but it took me a minute to recognize her. Her hair was loose and stringing across the pillow, and the wrinkles on her face were deeper than usual. No wonder, of course, considering the night she'd spent on the floor, as well as the hours of surgical intervention that she'd endured. I hated to think what I would've looked like if I'd been through the mill as she had.

We walked past the first bed, courteously averting our eyes from the woman who lay there engrossed in a movie magazine. She paid us no attention.

"Mattie," LuAnne whispered as she leaned over the bed, careful to avoid the lines and bottles and beeping machines that were hooked onto or into Mattie. "How're you feeling?"

Mattie's eyes opened, then she stared at the ceiling as if LuAnne's words had come from there, but she didn't respond. I lingered at the foot of the bed, hesitant to get close for fear of disturbing the medical paraphernalia.

"Mattie! It's me," LuAnne said, no longer whispering. "And Julia. We've come to see how you are." Turning to me, she urged, "Say something, Julia. Don't leave me to do all the talking."

I edged along the side of the bed so I wouldn't have to raise my voice. "Mattie," I said, leaning over, "we're so concerned about you. Is there anything we can do? Anything you need?"

Her eyes blinked, then she turned to look straight at me. In a hoarse voice, she reached toward me and croaked, "Oh, Mother, has it come?"

I took a step back.

"What?" LuAnne said. "What are you looking for, Mattie?"

Mattie's head turned toward her. She blinked several times and frowned in thought.

"My gown!" she said, her head rising from the pillow with the forcefulness of her answer. "It's got to get here or I won't be able to go."

Tears suddenly welled up in Mattie's eyes, and I said, "Lu-Anne, we're disturbing her. Maybe we should go."

Mattie immediately turned back toward me. "Yes, go see about it. Call Neiman's, Mother. Tell them it has to be fitted and everything, and it has to get here." Tears streamed down her face. "I'll just die if I can't go."

LuAnne and I looked at each other across the bed. LuAnne's mouth was open, reminding me to close mine.

"We'll go see about it," I said, hoping that was enough to reassure Mattie. "We'll be back later." I motioned to LuAnne that we should leave, and we started for the door.

As we passed the other patient in the room, she lowered her magazine and said, "I hope you find that dang dress. That's all I've heard ever since they moved her in here."

"Well," LuAnne said as she drove toward my house, "the nurse said she was still groggy from the anesthesia."

"Uh-huh," I said, slightly shaken from the state of Mattie's mind. "Reliving the past, I guess."

"But you know," LuAnne said as she stopped at a red light, "I don't think she knew us from the man in the moon. Why, she thought you were her mother, which is pretty funny when you think about it."

"More like pitiful," I said somewhat drily, "considering the fact that Mattie's well over ninety, and I'm nowhere near it."

For once, LuAnne didn't pursue the subject of age differences, even though she was uncommonly proud of the fact that her birthday was six months later than mine.

Chapter 5

"Sam," I said as we settled into our usual places in the library after supper that evening. Lloyd was with his mother's family and Lillian had just left, so the house was quiet and settled. Occasionally, a low rumble of thunder rolled around in the distance, heralding a spring shower.

He lowered the newspaper, looked at me over his reading glasses, smiled, and said, "What's on your mind, honey?"

"A couple of things. First, I had all good intentions of going over to Mildred's after supper and enticing her to take a walk around the block with me. I'm worried about her, Sam. She's gaining weight instead of losing it, even though she's constantly on a diet. Or says she is. And here lately all the exercise she gets is walking from one chair to another."

"Why don't you get her a pedometer? That might encourage her to move around a little more."

"A pedometer? What does that do?"

"It counts steps. You wear it or carry it in a pocket or wherever, and it counts the number of steps you take in a day. The idea is to increase your steps by a thousand or so each day until you reach an optimum number—about ten thousand, I think."

"Ten *thousand*! Why, Sam, you'd be walking from sunup till sundown all day long and getting nothing else done. I don't think Mildred takes much more than a hundred steps a day. That's why I thought a walk around the block would be a start, at least.

"I knew it was no use asking her, though, at the first sound of thunder. She would no more take a walk with rain threatening than she'd fly."

"You could try early in the morning before it gets too hot." Sam, like a lot of people, had plenty of suggestions for what somebody else could do.

"Oh, Sam," I said, smiling, "Mildred is a late sleeper, and when she does wake, she has breakfast in bed for another hour or so."

He lowered the paper again. "Really?"

I nodded. "Yes, she's getting less and less active. And speaking of that, who knows if Mattie Freeman will ever be active again? So that's another one to worry about. I just don't know what's to become of her. I told you how her mind was wandering all over the place when LuAnne and I visited this afternoon. It just stunned me how far out of it she was."

Sam reached over and put his hand on mine. "That may not be permanent, honey. Tomorrow, when you see her, she may be her old self again. The anesthesia will have worn off and she'll be feeling better."

"Well, I hope so. She's going to have decisions to make. I doubt she'll be able to live alone in that apartment for some time to come, if ever again." I turned to him. "Oh, Sam, I'm so glad to have you. If I ever get in that situation, I know you'll take care of me."

Sam smiled his sweet smile. "You can count on it," he said. "But remember, it may be the other way around and you'll be looking after me."

"Oh, don't even think it." Then a second later, I added, "But if it happens that way, I'll gladly look after you."

"I tell you what," Sam said. "Let's go downhill together, and let Hazel Marie, Lloyd, J.D., Binkie, Coleman, Etta Mae, Lillian, and I guess Latisha, too, have us both on their hands. How would that do?"

I laughed. "It would do just fine and serve them right, too."

"Well, you know, it's interesting," Sam said, in a musing way. "I was thinking about this the other day and about the fact that neither of us has children to call on. But then I realized, sweetheart, that you've gathered various children along the way, so I don't think either of us has anything to worry about."

Now, that was an intriguing concept, and as I thought about it, I couldn't help but congratulate myself just a little for being so prescient. Although I hadn't realized that was what I was being when I began collecting the unrelated family members who now surrounded us.

We sat in silence for a few minutes as a glow of well-being settled in. Or, at least, it did for me. Sam, on the other hand, obviously had his mind on other things. He frowned as he folded the newspaper and put it aside.

"Maybe," he said, a serious look on his face, "we shouldn't count on others to do what we're unwilling to do for ourselves. I'm wondering if we should begin thinking of moving to a retirement community. Sign up for some of that perpetual care they advertise."

I stared at him. "I can't believe you're thinking of that. Why, Sam, we've visited people at Halifax Gardens—supposedly the best of the best—and all you see are gray heads and stooped shoulders and walkers and wheelchairs and wrinkled faces everywhere you look. I don't want to live where I see myself staring back at me in every face around. It's unnatural to live without young people and children around to—I don't know—equalize things, I guess. Besides," I went on, smiling at him, "I think that perpetual care you mentioned refers to cemeteries, not retirement homes."

We laughed, for Sam rarely misused a word, although it occurred to me that he'd done it to amuse me.

"Anyway," I went on, "just so you know, if you're really serious about that, you'll have to go by yourself. The last time Clarice Miller invited me to lunch to meet some of her friends out there, the main topic of conversation was how many shrimp each person had gotten in her shrimp Creole."

Sam laughed as he picked up the newspaper again, but the

memory of six elderly women stirring piles of rice with their forks while they counted shrimp saddened me. I let him finish reading an article that he seemed especially interested in, then I went back to what was foremost in my mind.

"Sam?"

"Hm-m?"

I waited until he looked at me over his glasses. "I spoke to Etta Mae Wiggins this afternoon just to feel her out about taking care of Mattie for a few days when she comes home. Now I'm wondering if I stepped on anybody's toes or pushed myself in where I wasn't wanted. I mean," I hurried on, "I'm concerned about having a backup plan if Mattie's not made any provision for herself. Or if she doesn't have the means for any kind of plan."

"So you're asking what I think about your shouldering the expense of Mattie's care?"

"Not exactly, because Mildred said she'd help. I just mean looking around at the possibilities at this point. Etta Mae might not be able to do it or want to do it. I sort of hope she won't."

"Why? That's pretty much what she does, isn't it?"

"Yes, I guess it is, except her regular schedule as a Handy Home Helper gives her the freedom to come and go from one patient to another. She doesn't stay cooped up all day and night with one crabby old woman. See, Sam," I went on, trying to explain my hesitancy, "I'm concerned about Mattie, but I'm more concerned about Etta Mae. She could use the money, I'm sure, but she needs to be out and around people her own age."

"You mean men her own age?"

"Well, yes. And what's wrong with that? I worry about her— Etta Mae, that is. She does nothing but work, and I keep thinking I should have her over for lunch or something to meet somebody nice. Except there's nobody nice for her to meet."

"I tell you what," Sam said, as if he'd just thought of it. "If you just want to get her out and around, why don't you ask her to stay here with you while I'm gone? I'd feel better if there was someone in the house with you."

"Hm-m, now that's a good thought, because I'd feel better if there was someone here, too." Sam, Mr. Pickens, and Lloyd were leaving for a trip to Biloxi for a week of deep-sea fishing the day after school let out for the summer. It had been Mr. Pickens's idea to have a three-man vacation with Lloyd and Sam, and thank goodness for that. Mr. Pickens was proving that he could easily step into stepfatherhood, and I was delighted that the three men would be off on their own with no women around—especially me. I wouldn't have gone deep-sea fishing on a bet.

"Of course," I went on, picking up the conversation, "I wouldn't have anyone nice for Etta Mae to meet, but it would be a change for her to have company after work and Lillian's good cooking, too. I may just do that, and, Sam, while I'm thinking of it—don't forget to pack some sunblock. And a hat. You'll need a hat out on the gulf."

"Yes, ma'am," Sam said, grinning. "I won't forget. You won't let me."

"Oh, you." I smiled and reached for his hand. Then I went on in a more serious vein. "But back to Mattie, Sam. Mildred and I are just trying to think ahead. It'll be a big responsibility on somebody to determine what Mattie needs and where she should go, especially if she stays mentally eighteen years old for any length of time."

"Well, look, honey. If she doesn't recover her mental capacity, it may be that she'll have to go into hospice care. But you don't need to worry about that. Her doctors will decide what's best for her."

"Well, that's true, and thank goodness for professional experts. I don't want to make any such decisions for Mattie or for anybody, and Mildred most assuredly doesn't. We don't mind contributing financially, but neither of us would want the burden of deciding what's to be done with her."

"You're worrying for nothing, sweetheart. Think of this: Mattie Freeman has lived alone for as long as we've known her. She's always known that she'd have to look after herself. Don't you think she has a contingency plan? Something legal that'll kick in if she's incapacitated?"

"Like what? I've never thought I'd need anything like that."

"That's because you've always had plenty of people who would step in for you. Actually, though, in spite of that, you do have something legal. You and I gave each other power of attorney right after we married."

"We did?"

"Yes, and I told you to read it carefully and be sure you understood it."

"Well, I guess I just signed it because you told me to."

He laughed. "Don't make a habit of that. Anyway, chances are good that Mattie has everything lined up to take care of whatever happens. I'm not sure who her attorney is. She never came to me, so it's unlikely she went to Binkie, either. Maybe Ernest Sitton— he's been around forever. He may be looking after her affairs."

"I hope so. I truly hope somebody is. You know, Sam, Mattie's always been a part of our circle, but she's been on the fringes, so to speak. So much so that even Helen Stroud, who's the most socially correct woman I know, upset LuAnne with her lack of interest in Mattie's situation. But then," I said, pausing to smile, "LuAnne was upset with Sue Hargrove, too, for being less than forthcoming with inside information."

"It seems to me," Sam, the least judgmental of men, said, "that LuAnne is fairly easily upset."

"Oh, you can say that again," I agreed, then returned to the more pressing subject. "You know, Sam, I don't think Mattie has ever had a close friend. And that is really strange when you think about it, considering how long she's been around. But," I went on with some complacency, "that shouldn't stop us from doing the Christian thing if we have to."

Sam nodded. "That's true, but it wouldn't surprise me if some lawyer doesn't pop up with a list of just-in-case instructions signed and sealed some years ago by Mattie."

"I hope you're right, not because I wouldn't want to do my Christian duty, but because I can hardly make my own decisions, much less have to make somebody else's."

"Julia, honey, you worry too much."

"Maybe so, but if I don't, who will?"

Chapter 6

I made another hospital visitation the following morning. Alone this time, for LuAnne had other things to do and Mildred was still in bed. I went not because I wanted to but because I was hoping to find Mattie mentally sound so I could stop fretting about having her care on our hands.

I just hated feeling guilty about the possibility of having to do something I not only didn't want to do but also didn't feel I should have to do. But that was the quandary I was in. So if Mattie showed any signs of being in the present day, rather than in another era, I was going to ask her about that contingency plan that Sam had mentioned.

How much better it would be to know exactly what she wanted, given her present inability to know not only what day it was but what year. Some people plan ahead, but most of us don't, assuming, I suppose, that we'll live forever. I've even heard of people who go so far as to plan their own funerals years before the need arises, even down to the particular hymns they want sung at the service. They say they do it to take the burden off their families, but I think some of those preplanners enjoy the thought of still being in control. LuAnne's husband, Leonard Conover, for instance, had already planned his funeral. He'd gone to the Good Shepherd Funeral Home, selected his casket, bought a cemetery lot, specified a vault, and paid for it all up front. But that made sense for him, because who would want to leave such arrangements to somebody like LuAnne?

But such thoughts were too far in the future for Mattie. There was no reason in the world to think she wouldn't recover from a broken hip—many did and had a lot of good years ahead. Although, I conceded, most of them weren't burdened with as many years behind them as Mattie had.

I walked down the hall toward Mattie's room, swerving around empty gurneys and wax polishers and the occasional robed patient shuffling along. As I neared her door, a short, paunchy man in a three-piece suit swung out into the hall, almost running into me.

"Pardon me, madam," he said, without a glance but with a brief nod of his head as he strode with authority on down the hall, a briefcase swinging at his side.

Now, that looks like a lawyer, I thought, and felt immeasurably better. Unless he'd been visiting Mattie's roommate.

As far as I could tell as I leaned over Mattie's bed, there was no marked improvement in her appearance. In fact, she looked worse. Her face was sallow and gaunt, the wrinkles deeper, and her hair in tangles, but this time her eyes were open.

"Mattie," I whispered, "how're you feeling?"

She frowned as her gaze flitted around until it landed on me. "Did you find them?" she mumbled.

I frowned, too. "Find what?"

"My gloves," she said somewhat sharply. "I have to have them."

Now, what do you do in a case like that? Go along with whatever was on her mind, or tell her she had no use for gloves in a hospital bed?

"Well, Mattie," I said, temporizing, "I'll try to find them. What do they look like?"

One hand—the one with a needle stuck in it—grabbed my arm. "My *kid* gloves, the long ones that go up over the elbow.

They're required." She released my arm and turned away. "You know that as well as I do."

"You're right, I do." Deciding to humor her, I pulled a chair close to the bed and sat down. "Our youthful days were exciting, weren't they?"

"Maybe for you," she mumbled, trying to turn over. "But not for me unless you get busy and find my gloves." Then she slung herself over in the bed and in a loud voice said, "I do my curtsy better than any of the other girls, and don't tell me I don't!"

"Oh, no, I wouldn't for the world. You do it beautifully, Mattie, so deep and graceful." I stood up, deciding that I'd visited long enough. "Is there anything you need? Anything I can bring you? Besides your gloves, I mean."

She glared at me. "Don't come back without them."

"Yes, well, I'll look for them." I backed away from the bed, turned, and started out of the room.

The woman in the other bed lowered her magazine as I walked past. "Good luck with that," she murmured, but I hurried past, anxious to be on my way.

Seeing a nurse busily writing at her station, I stopped for a minute. "Excuse me, but can you tell me how Mrs. Freeman is doing?"

She looked up, frowned, and said, "Well, her surgery went quite well. We'll be getting her up later today and she'll soon begin physical therapy. There's every reason to believe she'll fully recover,"

"That's good to hear, but somehow she doesn't seem quite herself. Mentally speaking, that is."

The nurse pushed back her bangs and sighed tiredly. "That's another problem, but fairly typical for her age. Perhaps you should speak to her physician. I really can't comment on that."

"I understand," I said, "but, I declare, it's distressing to hear a ninety-something-year-old woman go on and on about a debutante ball."

———

By the time I got home, I'd decided that I had done all I could do for Mattie and I could strike her off my list. I had no authority nor any particular desire to make arrangements for her, and all I can say about what I'd done so far is that I had felt *burdened* to do it. Pastor Ledbetter was often led to preach on the topic of bearing one another's burdens. It seemed, according to him, that the Lord puts these burdens—which I would call *worries*—on us so we'll do something about them.

Well, I was ready to have the burden of Mattie lifted from my shoulders because I couldn't figure out why the Lord would choose me to bear it. I mean, I wasn't any closer to her than a dozen other women I could name, so why had I been selected to worry about her?

I decided right then and there that other than visiting occasionally and taking the odd gift now and then—as others would also do—I'd done all that I was being called upon to do.

So by putting aside my fretting over Mattie, I decided that I should concern myself with more current problems—possibly those that I could do something about. To that end, I did what I'd been meaning to do for a day or so.

I phoned Mildred and asked if she wanted to take a walk with me.

"What for?" she asked.

"Why, just to get out for a while. It's a beautiful day, Mildred, and everything's in bloom. Besides, I need the exercise."

"Well, you can get it without me. But why don't you stop by here when you're through and have a snack with me?"

I had to laugh, but that meant I'd have to come up with some other way to get Mildred moving. Maybe a pedometer would be just the ticket.

Just as I finished putting that on my shopping list for the next time I was downtown, the phone rang.

"Julia? It's Helen Stroud. How are you?"

Surprised at the call, considering how infrequently she was in contact these days, I responded warmly. "Helen! How nice to hear from you. I'm doing well. And you?"

"Oh, I'm fine. I'm calling to see if you're still interested in a flower-arranging class. I remember your mentioning it at one time, and I'm getting a few people together to go over the basic elements of form, composition, and so on."

"Well, I guess I'd about forgotten about that. To tell the truth, Helen, the only time I really think about it is in the fall when the garden club has the flower show. That's when I realize how little I know. Will you be teaching it?"

"Yes, but only because a couple of people have asked me to. I'm not an expert by any means."

"Why, Helen, you're more of an expert than anybody else in this town. You've won more blue ribbons and best-in-shows than anybody I know." Actually, Helen was an expert at anything she attempted because she studied and experimented with whatever took her interest. Take flower arranging, for example. She had a natural flair for anything artistic, and had trained herself to such an extent that she had become an accredited judge of flower shows.

And there was no telling what else she'd become, not out of personal interest, but rather out of personal need. Once a leading matron in town, wife of a successful businessman, keeper of a perfect home, and the serene and capable ideal of many of us, Helen had suffered a great downfall. Richard, her husband, had had money problems—not that he'd lost it, but that he'd taken it. Other people's, that is, and he ended up in one of those white-collar prisons in Florida after a very public arrest in Mildred's backyard. It had taken every cent the Strouds had to repay what Richard had stolen, and the shame of it all had taken the heart out of Helen. She had quickly sold their home, moved into a small apartment, taken whatever part-time jobs she could get, dropped out of or off all the clubs and committees that had counted on her leadership, and divorced Richard. I admired her more than ever.

All of this flashed through my mind as I realized that Helen might be indicating that she was ready to be sociable again. And far be it from me to stymie her efforts. "So, yes, Helen, I would be interested in learning something besides how to cram a bunch of flowers in a vase. And if you're teaching, then all the better. Just let me know when you want to meet. And, oh," I went on, "let me know whatever the class will cost, because I do hope you're charging for your expertise."

"Thank you, Julia. I regret that I have to, but it will be a minimal charge. I'll let everybody know what they're to bring to each class, but it'll be mostly things you already have. A particular kind of container, for instance, or a piece of driftwood and one or two flowers will be all you'll need."

"That sounds easy enough. I'm looking forward to it. Maybe I'll even put my name on my next flower show entry."

I hung up feeling uplifted—not so much about learning to arrange flowers, but because I had missed Helen and was glad that she seemed to be coming out of her self-imposed exile. And if I was going to cut down on worrying about everybody and his brother, I would need other things to occupy my mind. Learning to arrange flowers in a formal manner could be just the thing to keep me busy—even though Japanese minimalism was not exactly my cup of tea.

Chapter 7

In spite of my good intentions to lay aside the problems of others and tend to my own business, the Lord still had me in His sights. Before I knew it, there I was again—in spite of the prospect of taking ten thousand steps a day and placing one chrysanthemum on a piece of driftwood—with not only Mattie but Etta Mae and Mildred as well weighing heavily on my mind. Did that mean I was supposed to be doing something for them or to them or about them? If so, I wished to goodness I knew what it was.

I knew that there was a fine line between helping and meddling, and far be it from me to meddle in someone else's business. I would have to watch that and curb my impulse to jump in and help.

I had to double down on my intention to stick to my own knitting and let these so-called burdens roll right off. My first responsibility was to Lloyd and Sam. Then came Lillian, Hazel Marie, and their little ones, and after them would come a number of others. To my way of thinking, I had my hands full, and I intended to remind the Lord that He'd already piled my plate quite high enough.

"Lillian," I said, walking into the kitchen for a late morning cup of coffee. "Sam says I worry too much, so I'm turning over a new leaf."

"Uh-huh, I b'lieve it when I see it."

I turned to look at her. "Do you think I do?"

She laughed. "Miss Julia, you worry 'bout the sun comin' up."

"Oh, I'm not that bad. But anyway, I'm putting a stop to it. I don't have to take on the problems of everybody I know, so I'm not doing it anymore. You want some coffee?"

"Yessum, I can stop for a minute."

We settled at the table and I watched as Lillian stirred several spoonfuls of sugar into her coffee. I started to caution her again, but stopped before a word slipped out. She knew I worried about her.

Instead, I looked away and said, "I've made up my mind, Lillian. In fact, I've already started to fill my time with something constructive, so I won't have time to worry about things I can't do anything about."

"You stop all that worryin' you do, you better have a whole lot of something else to fill up the time."

"I know, so I'm thinking about having a party, maybe a reception for Mattie, for one thing. That's if she gets well and regains her senses so she knows where she is. And for another, I'm going to be counting my steps around here, as well as learning something about putting flowers in a vase. But I need more than that. I'm also thinking of volunteering at the Literacy Council. Lillian, did you know that there're a lot of people—*adults,* I mean—who can't read?"

"Yessum, I know some what can't."

"You *do?*"

"Yes'm, but they get along all right 'cause most things have pitchers on 'em, an' that's what they read."

"Pictures? Like what?"

"Well, like a can of peaches have a peach painted on it, so you know you won't get beans when you open it up. And signs have pitchers, too. Like arrows pointin' the way or curves curvin' one way or the other. An' I 'spect they learn stop signs and such by heart, so they get along all right."

"But they miss so much by not being able to read. What about books and magazines and, well, things like medical information?"

"They make do, Miss Julia, an' likely as not they got chil'ren what can read."

"Well, that decides it. I'm going to spend some of my time helping someone learn to read. I can't fathom a life without that ability, and we take it so for granted. Why, Lillian, imagine Sam without a book at hand. He'd be a different person entirely." I stopped and tried to imagine what Sam would be like if he couldn't read. Then I discounted that image—he would've learned somewhere along the way, either on his own or with the help of someone who could teach him.

And, of course, that's what people who went to the Literacy Council were doing, and I determined to be one of those someones who offered the help they needed.

I leaned back in my chair, enjoying the sense of well-being that swept over me at the thought of how noble it would be to open up the world to some benighted soul.

Just as I was about to announce to Lillian how I was going to allocate the time I spent worrying to something both constructive and fulfilling, the phone rang.

Lillian was quicker than I, as she usually was. To her, answering the phone was her right and privilege.

"Miz Murdoch's residence," she intoned, then cut her eyes at me. "Yessir, she right here."

She covered the receiver with her hand and held it out to me, whispering, "He say who it is, but I forget. He sound like he mean bus'ness."

I took the phone. "This is Julia Murdoch."

"Ernest Sitton, Mrs. Murdoch. Attorney at law. Forgive the intrusion on your day, but I think it's time to meet so that some urgent decisions can be made. When would be convenient for you?"

"I'm sorry?"

He repeated what he'd said, ending by saying, "I'm sure your time is as limited as mine, so the sooner we get this done, the sooner it can be put to rest."

My first thought was that somebody was suing me, and my heart rate sped up and my breath caught in my throat. I racked my brain to think of what I could've done to incur such a threat.

Clearing my throat, I clasped the phone tighter, and said, "It seems to me, Mr. Sitton, that you might've first contacted my attorney, Binkie Enloe Bates. And while you're rectifying that oversight, I shall be consulting my husband, Sam Murdoch, also an attorney at law, although no longer specifically *at law,* being retired."

"Indeed. I only thought that it would be more to your liking for you to tell me what you have in mind so I could begin the proceedings. But it will certainly be a pleasure to see Sam again, and Ms. Enloe Bates as well, if that is your preference."

That didn't sound like any lawsuit I'd ever heard of. Since when was a person being sued given a preference?

"So," Mr. Sitton went on since I was being less than forthcoming, "perhaps you're still considering the various possibilities, but, having dealt with a number of these cases before, I may be able to help you come to some conclusions. I am simply offering my services, Mrs. Murdoch. Anything I can do to help you, I will be happy to do."

And since when did a suer's attorney offer to help the one being sued? Mr. Ernest Sitton had the reputation of being an outstandingly aggressive lawyer, but surely he wouldn't be offering to represent both sides, would he? I'd never heard of such a thing.

"That's . . . that's very kind of you, I'm sure. I'll talk it over with Sam and Binkie, and let you know."

"That will be fine," he said. "But time does appear to be of the essence. Things continue to go downhill, and it is incumbent on you to stay apace. Legally speaking, that is, since you are responsible to the court for any decisions—or lack of same—that are made. Or not made, as the case may be."

"Ah, Mr. Sitton," I mumbled, then cleared my throat again.

"I'm afraid I'm not following you. *I'm* responsible to the court? What court? And what am I responsible for? If someone is bringing suit against me, then it would seem that all I'm responsible for is defending myself."

There was silence on his end now. Then he did a little throat clearing of his own. "Mrs. Murdoch, I know of no one who is bringing suit against you. The court, of course, may become involved if you are unable to meet your obligations, but I'm sure the court will be understanding if you can present a petition with viable reasons for being unable to serve."

"Oh," I said with great relief, "I see. You're calling about jury duty. I can certainly serve if I don't have a conflict on my calendar. Even though, I think at my age, I would be automatically excused."

"No, no, not jury duty. And I assure you, madam, I would not discuss a lady's age for all the tea in China. Mrs. Murdoch," he said, then paused as if thinking how he should go on, then went on anyway. "Mrs. Murdoch, I am speaking of the power of attorney-in-fact as well as the medical power of attorney that Mrs. Mattie Freeman has granted you, which means that you are in charge not only of directing her medical care but also of making all monetarily related decisions. So I'm urging you to shoulder those responsibilities as quickly as possible. Further delay may prove disastrous. Decisions must be made immediately."

The phone slid out of my hand and dropped into my lap. Lillian grabbed it and spoke into it, "She be back in touch," clicked it off, then took me by my shoulders.

"Miss Julia, you all right? You 'bout to slide outta that chair. Come on now, set up straight an' tell me what he say. Here, drink some of this coffee. It cold, but it don't matter. There you go, you feelin' better now?"

"Lillian," I managed to say after a hard swallow, "I may *never* feel better. You won't believe what the Lord has burdened me with now."

"You set right there," Lillian said firmly. "Look like this a case for Mr. Sam."

Chapter 8

"Julia?" Sam said as he leaned over me, his face drawn with concern. "What's wrong, honey?"

I was still doing exactly what Lillian had told me to do—sitting right where I was.

I bestirred myself and looked up at him. "You won't believe this, Sam. *I* don't believe it. And I'd just made up my mind to turn to something useful instead of frittering away my time worrying about things I can't do anything about. And now this falls in my lap."

Sam drew up a chair and sat beside me. He took my hand and said, "Tell me what's going on, sweetheart."

"Oh, Sam, you and Binkie have got to get me out of this. I can't do it. I don't *want* to do it. It's too much responsibility, because how in the world could I know what she wants? Why, I hardly *know* the woman!"

"It's okay, honey," Sam said in his soothing voice. "Calm down now and tell me what's upset you so."

Lillian said, "Whatever it was, it come over the telephone. I was settin' right here when her face went white as a sheet an' look like she 'bout to slide right outta that chair."

"She's all right now," Sam said. "Julia, honey, tell me what happened."

"Sam," I said, gathering myself with a rush of outrage, "never in my life have I been so put upon. It can't be legal to give power of attorney to someone who didn't know a thing about it and who doesn't want it. Can it? Talk to Mr. Ernest Sitton and get it annulled, voided, vetoed, or whatever you have to do."

"Someone's given you power of attorney? Who?"

"*Mattie Freeman,* can you believe it!" I sprang from my chair, too outraged to sit still. "And who knows how long ago she did it, and never told me—much less *asked* me—a thing about it. And now she's lying up there in a hospital bed, not knowing one day from the next, expecting me to make medical and financial decisions for her! What presumption!"

While I stomped back and forth in a rage, Sam leaned back in his chair and studied the ceiling for a minute. "She never mentioned anything to you?"

"Not a word! Believe me, I would've talked her out of it if she had. And now I can't talk to her at all. She's off somewhere getting ready for a debutante ball."

"Then she certainly needs someone to look after her, and obviously she trusted you to do it. It can be an onerous job, Julia, but it's also an indication of the esteem she has for you."

"Well, I don't know why," I said, stopping with my hands on my hips as I glared at him. "The most I've ever had to do with her was to invite her to parties and ask, 'More tea, Mattie?'"

Sam smiled. "Yes, and asked it very nicely, I'm sure." Then he reached for my hand and went on. "Look, honey, it's possible to petition the court to excuse you from the responsibility, but then the court will appoint some attorney who doesn't know her from Adam. And he'll charge her for every move he makes."

"Why," I said, looking into the future, "somebody like that could deplete her assets before she knew it. And I can't imagine that she has that much to begin with. What would she live on when she gets out of the hospital? Maybe she knew that and took it into account. She'd have known I wouldn't charge her anything."

"That's right, you wouldn't. As a matter of fact, you couldn't. All you could charge would be for the expenses you incur, which is exactly what the attorney would do. But his expenses would include the time he'd ordinarily spend on his own clients." Sam stood, put his arm around my shoulders, and led me back to a chair. "Julia, why don't you talk to Sitton, let him explain what you'd be responsible for, then see how you feel. Most people recover from a hip replacement fairly easily. It may be that all you'd have to do is consult with her doctor, make sure her monthly bills get paid, and arrange for her care until she's on her feet again. That's not much more than you were already doing."

"I guess you're right," I said, sitting again. "I can't just turn my back and pretend she's no concern of mine. Oh, Sam," I went on, suddenly feeling both humble and uplifted, "just think of how much she must think of me! I had no idea that I was held in such high regard. But," I said, springing to my feet again, "if she weren't in such a bad way now, I would most certainly wring her neck!"

Sam accompanied me to Mr. Ernest Sitton's office, which was inconveniently located in Delmont, a small town some ten or so miles from Abbotsville. As we sat around an oval conference table in his office, I realized that the short, paunchy man sitting across from us had been the same short, paunchy one I'd seen coming out of Mattie's room at the hospital. It was comforting to know that he'd been on the job all along.

Mr. Sitton, after greeting us, particularly Sam, warmly, had placed a stack of documents on the table and with little fanfare got down to business. I soon learned the name of Mattie's surgeon, whom I was told to consult, received her checkbook, which was noticeably light on the bottom line, and accepted the keys to her apartment, where bills would be awaiting payment. Mr. Sitton had obviously been busy seeing to Mattie's affairs and, if I wasn't mistaken, was now somewhat relieved to pass along the responsibility to me.

"Now, Mrs. Murdoch, you have been granted a durable power of attorney, which gives you complete authority to make medical and financial decisions for Mrs. Freeman. And that authority continues even though Mrs. Freeman is showing some signs of mental incapacity, which of course we asume will be temporary. Sam, I'm sure, will explain the details to you, but I am always at your service as well."

"How long will I have to do this?" I tried not to whine, but I don't think I succeeded.

"Until it's revoked by the grantor, which will be when she's over this little setback she's had."

I wasn't sure how small a setback a broken hip was, but I intended to see that Mattie got all the therapy and rehabilitation she would need. I wanted her back on her feet as soon as possible so she could take control of her own business, which I hoped would include relieving me of all responsibility and of locating those misplaced kid gloves as well.

"Now, Mrs. Murdoch," Mr. Sitton continued as he pushed a paper toward me, "you'll need to sign this document when my ladies come in to notarize it. Then you should take it to Mrs. Freeman's bank. It gives you the authority to sign her checks."

When that was done, Mr. Sitton assumed he was, too. He stood up and said, "Don't hesitate to call if you need anything. I've represented Mrs. Freeman for years, but I can't claim to have known her well. Still, between the two of us, Mrs. Murdoch, we shall attempt to do our best for her." Then, shaking Sam's hand, he said, "Good to see you again, Sam. Mrs. Murdoch, let me know if I can help."

As Sam and I settled into the car for the drive back to Abbotsville, I sighed and said, "After we go by Mattie's bank, we might as well stop by her apartment and pick up the mail. Maybe get a few gowns and a robe for her, too."

"Good idea. The sooner you get on top of things, the easier you'll find it. In fact, I doubt there'll be much to do for now—just keep up with household bills as they come in." He glanced at me and smiled. "You don't particularly mind writing checks, do you?"

"Oh, you," I said, dredging up a smile, as I thought that I

might as well make the best of the hand I'd been dealt, even though I'd never played a game of poker in my life.

After completing our business at the bank, we found Mattie's mail for the two days she'd been in the hospital still in her mailbox. I took out an electric bill and one from the water department, a small cream-colored envelope that looked like an invitation or a thank-you note, and a handful of leaflets, long official-looking envelopes, and colorful advertisements.

Looking at Sam as we stood in the hall beside her door, I said, "I'm not sure I'm ready to just walk into somebody else's home and start poking around in it. You think I could put it off for a few days, maybe get Mildred to come with me?"

"Won't Mattie need some gowns? Toothbrush, too. And her purse. Every woman wants her purse."

"Oh, of course. Actually, I'm surprised Mr. Sitton didn't have it. Well, I guess there's nothing for it but to go on in. Here, Sam," I said, handing the key to him. "You open it."

As Sam worked the key into the lock, a tall, lean man came out of the apartment down the hall, walked toward us, and stopped. "Nate Wheeler," he said easily. "I don't believe Mrs. Freeman's at home, but can I help you?"

Sam turned and offered his hand. "We're the Murdochs, here to get a few things for Mrs. Freeman. You know she's in the hospital?"

"I heard, and I'm real sorry I wasn't here to help. I try to keep an eye on all the residents, but I've been out of town for a couple of days. How is she doing?"

"Fair, I would say," Sam said, while I looked the man over. He seemed fairly young, but that was from my viewpoint, where everybody under sixty looked young. As I peered closer, though, I recognized an old, tired look around his eyes. He was wearing a chambray shirt with the sleeves rolled up over tanned, sinewy arms and a pair of well-worn jeans over clean, but also well-worn, workman's boots.

"They tell us that the surgery went well so we're hoping for the best," Sam told him, then, turning to me, said, "This is my wife, Julia, who has Mattie's power of attorney. You'll probably be seeing a lot of her as she looks after Mattie's affairs."

Mr. Wheeler gave me a nice, slow smile as he said, "Anything I can help you with, let me know. I'm staying in apartment 4A for a few weeks—right down the hall there—while I do some remodeling. Updating the kitchen and so on."

"Very nice to meet you, Mr. Wheeler," I said. "Do you have your family with you?"

The smile died on his face. "No, ma'am, I'm a widower."

"Oh, I'm so sorry. Forgive me for asking."

That nice smile twitched at his mouth. "Perfectly all right," he said. "It's been awhile. But let me know if I can help with anything. I'll be around."

Well, that was reassuring to know. Depending on Mattie's progress—or lack of same—she would have need of a strong, healthy man with a willingness to help. And so would I.

Chapter 9

As Mr. Wheeler went on out the front door, Sam unlocked Mattie's door and pushed it open for me. "Seemed pleasant, didn't he?"

I agreed and walked into the dim living room, its deep crown moldings almost lost in the shadowy corners of the high ceiling. The blinds were closed and the draperies drawn, so I stopped after a few steps inside to let my eyes adjust. When they did, I saw that the room was a far cry from the party-ready condition it had been in on the occasions I had entered as a guest.

"My goodness," I murmured as Sam closed the door behind us and looked around as I was doing.

Furniture—chairs and side tables—had been pushed aside in a haphazard way. A huge chest-on-chest blocked the French doors to the sunroom with two huge Chippendale chairs pushed up against it. An étagère filled with porcelain figurines and vases stood against the far wall. The dining table had been shoved back against a window in the combination room, and two of its chairs were overturned. A lamp with a crooked shade lay on Mattie's hard-as-a-rock damask-upholstered Duncan Phyfe sofa, and discarded packaging materials were strewn across her faded Oriental.

"The EMTs, honey," Sam explained. "They needed room to work and to get a gurney in to pick her up."

"Oh," I said, but wondered why they hadn't cleaned up after themselves. "Well, let's get what we came for, then just leave. I'll send someone over to straighten things before she comes home. I'm in no mood for housework today."

Sam located a large black pocketbook on the kitchen counter, but before tucking it under his arm, he asked, "Is this yours or Mattie's? They look alike."

"Hardly," I said, glancing at the much-used, chipped, and fraying bag, "Mine's a Prada."

"Oh, well," he said, grinning. "There's the difference."

Just as I was going down the narrow hallway to Mattie's bedroom, I glanced in at a neat, but crowded, guest room on my way. Then I proceeded on to the larger bedroom, made smaller by the high Charleston rice bed, a block-front chest, and, against the wall at the foot of the bed, a nice bureau with a gilt mirror over it. An ancient television sat on top. This room, too, was fairly neat, although there were aspects—like a robe on the foot of the bed, slippers in the middle of the floor, and rumpled pillows—that gave it a lived-in look.

Feeling again like an intruder, I nonetheless determined to do my job in as professional a manner as I could manage. So I opened the top bureau drawer, thinking *underclothes,* and mentally checking off a list—gowns, bathrobe, slippers, what else? Oh, toiletries, or beauty products, as Hazel Marie called them. I headed for the bathroom, where I found shampoo, comb and brush, toothbrush and toothpaste, small cases of Estée Lauder face powder and rouge, and a magnifying mirror.

"Sam?" I called. "Would you look for a suitcase? Or a paper sack? She's going to need more than I thought."

I heard him open a closet in the guest room. "Found one," he called back. "Old as the hills, but it should do."

He put it on Mattie's bed and opened it, so that I could pack what I'd gathered into it. "Julia," he said thoughtfully, "I'm having second thoughts about leaving her pocketbook at the hospital. Why don't you take it home with you for now? When she's alert enough to look after it, we'll get it to her."

"I think you're right, and—even though I hate the thought of rummaging around in somebody else's purse—I guess I should see what's in it. For all we know, she has another bank account with a checkbook that she carries around with her. And considering the large but almost empty checkbook Mr. Sitton gave me, that would be a godsend."

"It has something in it," Sam said, hefting the pocketbook. "It's as heavy as lead."

I put a pile of underclothes and three gowns in the suitcase, then stuffed toiletries around the edges. "I hope I've not forgotten anything," I said.

"You can come back anytime. Remember, you have total access."

"Don't remind me," I said, shuddering a little at the thought of making myself free in this dark, crowded apartment by going in and out as if it were mine.

Carrying the suitcase, Sam followed me back to the living room. He had turned on the overhead light, so I stopped for a minute and looked around again. Every other time I'd been in the room, it had been occupied by a number of women, all of whom had taken my attention with their greetings and subsequent conversation. This was the first time I'd looked carefully at the furniture, mainly because it was all I could see.

"Goodness, Sam, I don't know how Mattie lives all crowded in like this. Look at that highboy. The pediment almost touches the ceiling. And there's a bowfront sideboard—Sheraton, I believe, and she only has a dining area, not a room. And look at those huge wing chairs, plus the sofa, and I don't know how many side tables." I walked over to one and lifted the crocheted cloth that covered it. "Would you look at this! I think it's a handkerchief table, Sam, but it's too crammed in to get it open. Oh, look at that little table in the corner." I leaned over to look closer. "No, it's too deep to be a table. It might be a cellarette."

"What's a cellarette?"

"Oh, you know. It's a . . . well, basically it's a wooden box on legs. See, Sam, it's right behind that Chippendale chair. See how deep the box is? It's to keep wine bottles and, I suppose, other spirits under lock and key in case there're tipplers in the house."

"Tipplers, huh?" Sam said, grinning at my choice of words. Then, turning to scan the room, he went on. "You know, Mattie may have more assets than we've given her credit for. If this furniture is as good as you say, it could see her through some rainy days."

"Well, I'm no expert, but some of these pieces have nice lines. That's not foolproof, though, because reproductions can be quite good. Still, if it comes down to it, she could get an appraiser in here to see what it's worth. Of course, it might not matter. If Mattie hasn't sold it before this, who's to say she would now?"

"Your decision now, honey."

"Yes," I said, sighing, "but how could I sell what she so obviously values?"

Before going home, which I was more than ready to do, we went by the hospital to drop off the suitcase and its contents. After locking Mattie's pocketbook in the trunk of the car, Sam and I went straight to her room, intending to visit for only a few minutes, ask if we'd forgotten anything she wanted, and then leave.

"I just hope," I said to Sam as we rode up in the elevator, "that she's making sense for a change. I don't like promising something that I have no intention of doing—like looking for elbow-length kid gloves—even if it does humor her."

Sam smiled. "I hope so, too. If all goes well, she should soon be able to manage her own affairs, and that'll relieve you."

Something devoutly to wish, I thought, as we walked down the hall toward Mattie's room. Clutching my own fairly heavy pocketbook, I turned into the room, nodded to the roommate, as Sam, carrying the suitcase, followed me to the bed next to the windows.

"My goodness," I said, as I saw potted plants and fresh bouquets on every surface in the room. "Look at all the flowers. I guess I should make a list of who sent them for thank-you notes. I expect writing them is part of my job description, too. Just put the suitcase anywhere you can, Sam." Then, turning to the bed, I said, "Mattie? It's Sam and Julia. We've brought you a few things from home. How're you feeling?"

Not so good, it seemed, for she didn't respond. Her eyes were partially open but I didn't think she was looking at anything in particular. Someone had combed her hair, but it hadn't significantly improved her looks. In fact, she looked about half sick, which didn't seem quite right for a broken hip that had just been expertly mended.

I put my hand on her shoulder, but she didn't stir, so I tiptoed away from the bed and whispered to Sam, "I think she's asleep. Maybe we'd better go."

Sam agreed and off we went, stopping at the nurses' station to inquire about Mattie's progress. As expected, we didn't get a straight answer, so I asked a nurse when she expected Mattie's surgeon to make his rounds, intending to waylay him in the hospital if it wasn't in the middle of the night—surgeons can, on occasion, be somewhat eccentric. Telling the nurse that I'd left a packed suitcase in the room, I asked her to make sure that Mattie knew it was there.

"When she wakes," I said, "she'll be glad to have her own gowns and personal items."

"I'll tell her," the nurse said. "I'm sure she'll appreciate your bringing them."

"Just let her know that I'm doing the job she gave me," I said, with a tinge of sharpness I couldn't suppress, then, as we walked away, mumbled to Sam, "The job she *foisted* on me."

Sam grinned and said, "Let's go home."

Chapter 10

The next morning I woke with a firm determination to do that job with all the cheerfulness I could muster. I reminded myself that Mattie had bestowed a high honor on me by entrusting her physical well-being and all her worldly goods to my care. And, really, how difficult or time consuming could it be? She'd soon be up and around with plenty of help, which I would most certainly see that she had. After that, I would have to make sure only that her bills were paid, and that would be it. There was no reason in the world for my days to be disrupted in any measurable way by having her power of attorney wrapped around my neck.

So, accepting what I could not shirk, I began to feel a renewed excitement about the prospect of working with my fellow man, even, or especially, if he were illiterate. Sam, in particular, had been enthusiastic about my plans to volunteer with the Literacy Council and said that he might volunteer along with me.

That being the case, I thought that it behooved me to get my ducks in a row and be ready to attend some training courses as soon as they started. So I decided to visit Mattie early that morning—sort of get it out of the way. I would offer to run any errands she needed taken care of, maybe take her some magazines, assure her that her affairs were in order, and perhaps catch her surgeon on his rounds. I could then consider my obligations as the holder of her power of attorney and as a longtime acquaintance more than fulfilled. At least, for the day.

Before leaving for the hospital, though, I decided to look through Mattie's pocketbook in case there was anything in it that she might want. Sam had plopped it on the desk in the library the day before, his eyebrows going up at the clank the contents made as he set it down.

"She must have the kitchen sink in there," he'd said.

"Oh, you," I said, laughing. "We never know what we might need. We have to be prepared."

That morning, then, I sat at the desk and opened the clasp at the top of the large black pocketbook and began to unload it. On top, there was a handful of Kleenex—fresh, I hoped—which I consigned to the wastebasket. Then I pulled out a big, round, almost empty compact of pressed face powder, a smaller one of Estée Lauder rouge, and a small tube of Tangee lipstick, which I thought had been unavailable for a generation or more, as well as a wallet with four dollar bills and two credit cards in it, and a change purse holding seventy-six cents. I dutifully wrote down the amounts in case I ever had to account for my guardianship of Mattie's possessions. The next things to come out of her purse were a comb, a lint roller, two Bic pens, a notepad, and, at the bottom, a heavy odd-shaped object that I kept pushing aside to get to the small items under it. Those small items included two sticks of Juicy Fruit gum, four pennies, a nickel, three hairpins, a toothpick, a small tube of breath freshener, and a full key ring. And that reminded me, something would have to be done with Mattie's car. What that would be, I didn't know. I mean, who would want it?

Finally, after having everything spread out on the desk, I extracted with some effort what turned out to be a thin, curved silver container with an elaborately etched monogram that I couldn't decipher.

What in the world? Shaking it, I heard the slosh of liquid, but couldn't believe that Mattie would be the owner of what looked suspiciously like a flask. Not that I was so familiar with what a flask looked like, but I'd read that they were flat and curved—just as this one was—so as to fit in a back pocket. This one fit just as well in the bottom of Mattie's purse.

It was a common sight these days to see people carrying around bottles of water from which they constantly sipped, no matter the circumstances or the surroundings. How they managed to get anything done between subsequent trips to a restroom, I didn't know. So, with every vending machine offering water from all over the world, why would Mattie have a flask in her purse?

With some difficulty—the cap was on crooked—I unscrewed the top, laid it aside, then got a good whiff of the emanating fumes. The top of my head almost blew off. My word, Mattie Freeman was a secret tippler!

Let Sam laugh at my choice of words if he wanted to, but this was serious. No wonder Mattie was so cranky most of the time, and no wonder she couldn't half drive, and no wonder she was lying up there in bed with her mind wandering all over the past century. And, finally, no wonder she had fallen in the first place—tipsy people are prone to accidents.

My first thought was to empty the flask, rinse it out, then put it back where I'd found it. But sooner or later, Mattie would want her pocketbook, as well as what she expected to be in it.

So what was my responsibility in this? Give the flask back to her in the same state in which she'd left it—almost full? Or as empty as the day she'd bought it, seeing that the hospital would frown on their patients taking little nips throughout the day?

I didn't know what to do. So for the time being I put everything back into the pocketbook, including the flask with no change in its contents. I had trouble, though, getting the cap back on as the threads had been partially stripped—I put that down to frequency of access. For fear of leakage, I propped the flask upright against the side of the pocketbook and scotched it with the lint roller and wallet.

I was overcome with embarrassment and shame for Mattie and with guilt on my part for uncovering a secret that not one soul had ever guessed. I even lifted the wad of Kleenex from the wastebasket and stuffed it in on top, hoping that Mattie would never suspect that I had rummaged among her things. Then I closed the pocketbook, deciding that I would take it to Mattie as it was—just as soon as she recovered her senses—and if she asked if I'd gone through it, I'd lie through my teeth.

On my way to the hospital, but still unnerved by my discovery, I swung by the bakery on Main Street and, finding a parking place, ran inside to pick up a dozen petits fours. But the shock of what I'd found in Mattie's pocketbook was still disturbing my mind. It was all I could think of.

One thing was for sure, though. No one would hear about Mattie's weakness from me. I wouldn't tell a soul. Well, maybe I'd tell Sam. How could I keep something so shocking from him? And maybe Mildred and Hazel Marie, too, if I just couldn't keep it to myself.

While waiting for the little cakes to be boxed, I thought of how Mattie loved petits fours. I had often seen her stack three or four on her plate at any party she attended, and if the hostess had been slack with her offerings, Mattie wasn't above making her disappointment known. Maybe a dozen petits fours on her bedside table would cut down on the craving for something else.

Hurrying out to the car, I still felt electrified by learning of Mattie's secret vice—and she a lifelong Presbyterian, too.

I certainly could not let even a hint of my discovery escape my lips to Pastor Ledbetter. If he got wind of such a thing, he'd surely make it a sermon topic. Oh, he wouldn't mention a name, but he'd make sure that the congregation knew he had a particular person in mind, and that would throw the church into a frenzy of guessing who it could be.

After parking at the hospital, I went up to the second floor, hoping that I would find Mattie awake and cheerful and on the mend. Carefully carrying the bakery box so the little cakes would stay intact, I threaded my way along the hall to Mattie's room.

And stopped in the doorway. The dividing curtain was pushed back, both beds were stripped to their mattresses, and a man—an orderly from the fact that he was wielding a mop—was moving a chair so he could clean a corner.

"Oh," I said, taken aback, "what happened to the patients in here? Where've they been moved?"

"Don' know," he said, painfully straightening his back and leaning on the mop. "All they tell me is mop the room 'cause one is gone an' one is passed."

"*Passed?* Passed what?" *Kidney stones?* Then, "Oh, my goodness, she *passed*? Which one?"

"Don' know. They both gone by the time I get here."

"Oh, my goodness," I said again and anxiously turned toward the nurses' station. No longer concerned with the care of little iced cakes, I was holding the box by its string and, in my haste, whacked it against the door frame.

Breathing hard, I reached the station and leaned over the desk. "Excuse me," I said, panting, "but Mrs. Freeman? In that room down there?" I pointed down the hall. "How is she? Where has she been moved?"

The nurse looked up, frowned, and said, "Are you a family member?"

"No, a friend. I mean, her attorney. Acting attorney, I mean. I don't think she has any family. But surely you can tell me where you've moved her."

"I'm sorry, but Mrs. Freeman expired early this morning."

"Expired? You mean, like, she *died*?"

"I'm afraid so."

"But," I said, unable to process what I'd heard, "she wasn't *sick*. I mean, a broken hip won't kill you, will it? And she was fine after her surgery. Well, not *fine* exactly, her mind having regressed a few years, but I just . . . well, I just had no idea she was . . ."

The nurse stood up. "Are you all right? Would you like to sit down?"

"Oh, no. No, I'm all right, just stunned, I guess. We didn't know she was that near the end, but, well . . . would you care for some petits fours?" I held out the box. "Fresh from the bakery, and perhaps a little crumbly, but I'm sure Mrs. Freeman would want you to have them."

Knowing Mattie, I wasn't at all sure of that, but the nurse took the box and thanked me.

Then as I turned away toward the bank of elevators, barely aware of what I was doing, the nurse called me back. "Ma'am? We have Mrs. Freeman's suitcase here behind the desk for safekeeping. Would you like to take it now? I can release it to you since you're one of her attorneys. It'll save you from having to come back."

"Fine. Yes, good idea. I can do that." I was mumbling half to myself, but aware enough to know that I didn't want to have to come back.

Struggling with Mattie's suitcase, my pocketbook, and my wobbly knees, I made my way to an elevator, still trying to get my mind around what had happened.

Mattie had died? Being totally consumed by the shock of her passing, all I could hope was that her dress had arrived and she'd found her gloves, so that once again she'd been able to dance at her debutante ball—even if it'd been only in her mind.

But, then, what of her secret? Should it be safe with me? Or did it now not even matter?

The one thing I did know, however, was that I would never tell LuAnne. Good grief, if she knew, everybody would know, and Mattie would never live it down.

Well, I guess I shouldn't have put it quite like that, now that she was no longer with us. But if LuAnne found out, Mattie would have a besmirched reputation that would last long after the memory of her Meissen tea set had faded away.

Chapter 11

"Is Sam upstairs?" It was out of my mouth as soon as I stepped through the door at home. Setting down Mattie's suitcase, I headed for the hall, barely waiting for Lillian's answer.

She turned from the sink. "Yes'm, he in his office workin' away. I jus' take him some coffee. You want some?"

"No, not yet. Oh, Lillian," I moaned, turning back to her, "I just went to see Mattie Freeman, and can you believe that she died last night? I mean, we just visited her yesterday. It doesn't seem possible."

"Oh, Jesus," Lillian said, snatching up a dish towel to dry her hands. "Miss Mattie Freeman, gone? Well, bless her ole heart, I guess she in a better place now."

"I hope so. At least I hope it's better than what was facing her here." I started toward the stairs. "I'm going up to tell Sam. He'll want to know."

I tapped on the door to what had once been my sunroom, but was now reconfigured as a working office for Sam. He had it filled with machines of one sort or another, some of which beeped and flashed and hummed. How he got any writing or thinking done with all that noise was beyond me.

"Sam?" I pushed open the door as he looked up from the book that was open on his desk. "I'm sorry to interrupt, but, oh, Sam, you won't believe who has gone to her reward."

Sam's eyebrows rose. "I didn't know anybody was up for one."

"Well, I didn't, either. She seemed well enough to me. I mean, considering all she's been through and discounting her mental state. I tell you, Sam, I'm shaken by it."

Sam abruptly stood and started around the desk toward me. "What's happened, honey?"

"Mattie Freeman, Sam," I said, feeling a few tears spring to my eyes. "She's gone. And I didn't even know she was leaving."

Sam took my arm and led me to a side chair. "I'm sorry, sweet heart. I shouldn't have been flippant. It's never easy to lose someone you care about. Sit down and tell me about it."

"Well, see, that's the thing," I said, sinking into the easy chair beside his desk. "I never thought I cared one way or the other about Mattie, and I really didn't—I mean, *personally* cared. So I was really upset with her for giving me so much responsibility when we'd never been close. But now I don't know why her sudden passing has shaken me the way it has."

"I expect you'd have been better prepared if she'd been sick a long time. It's probably the unexpectedness of it that's upsetting you."

"I guess. Except at her age, I don't know what else I should've expected. But, Sam, you and I just saw her yesterday afternoon, and of course she didn't look well, but I never thought . . . well, anyway, I spent an awful lot of time worrying about where she would go and who would take care of her when she got out of the hospital—all of which has turned out to be a total waste of time. I guess it should teach me a lesson. Make no plans for the morrow, for the morrow may never come—or something like that. Which is certainly true for Mattie."

I straightened in my chair, struck by a sudden dread. "What about that power of attorney now, Sam? What am I supposed to do about that?" I just didn't think I was up to making funerary arrangements, regardless of how much Mattie had thought of me. That was an honor I could do without.

"It's all right, sweetheart. The power of attorney expires when the grantor does."

"You mean . . . ?" I brightened considerably, realizing that my obligations were over and done with. "Well, that is welcome news. But, you know, Sam, now that I think about it, it hasn't been so onerous, after all."

After a few reassuring words and some comforting hugs from Sam, it occurred to me that I was most likely the only one among our friends who knew about this disconcerting development. So, after thanking Sam for relieving my mind, I left him to his work and hurried to the library. It was up to me, it seemed, to spread the word of Mattie's demise to our friends and acquaintances. To be the town crier, so to speak, certainly gives one a feeling of importance, and I concerned myself with striking just the right note between accuracy in reporting and personal concern.

"Mildred?" I asked when Ida Lee called her to the phone. "I have sad news."

"Who died?"

"*Mildred!* How did you know? You didn't give me a chance to break it to you gently."

"You mean somebody really did?" she asked. "Oh, my, that'll teach me to play around trying to be funny. But, really, who was it?"

"Miss Mattie. Oh, Mildred, I went to the hospital this morning, even took her a dozen petits fours, hoping to perk her up—you know how she loved those things—and her bed was empty. Stripped, in fact, though I thought she'd just been moved. I declare, I was not prepared for where she'd been moved *to*. It's really quite shaken me up."

"Well, me, too," Mildred said, a great deal more soberly than she'd started out. "I had no idea that she was in danger of *leaving* us. Believe me, if I had, I would've bestirred myself to go visit her with you and LuAnne. I wish now I'd gone with you."

"Don't worry about it. She wouldn't have known if you were there or not. But I expect we'll all have a few regrets in the next several days. Sam says we can't dwell on those, though, since nothing can be done about them now. Still, I wish she'd known that I'd thought enough of her to bring petits fours."

"Yes, that's a pity. She loved those things. But, Julia, have you told LuAnne?"

"Not yet, but I will."

"Well, hang up and do it right now. I want LuAnne to know that she's not always the first to know when something happens."

I had to laugh, for LuAnne would be beside herself at hearing a bit of news about which she had absolutely no idea. And especially to hear it from one who was generally the last to know anything.

"LuAnne?" I said when she answered her phone. "I hate to be the one to bring bad news, but Miss Mattie died sometime last night."

"What?"

I told her again, adding, "I just happened to have gone to see her early this morning, and . . ."

"And you didn't call me to go with you?"

"Well, LuAnne, I had several unforeseen obligations to take care of, and I wanted to speak to her about them."

"What kind of obligations did you have that you didn't want me to know about?"

"It wasn't like that, LuAnne. I don't care if you know that Mattie had given me her power of attorney . . ."

"*What!* Why did she give it to you? I've known her as long as you have—longer, even."

"I don't know, but, believe me, I would've been glad to pass it along to you if I'd had the chance. But really, there was little to do, and now, nothing at all. Any powers I may have had expired when she did."

"Well, I still don't understand why she picked you. Why, Julia, I took her a loaf of banana nut bread every Christmas, and picked her up to take her to I-don't-know-how-many parties, just to keep us all safe from that car. I even offered to drive her to and from church every Sunday, but she turned me down. I did that after she backed into two cars in the church parking lot. One of them was mine."

"I know, LuAnne, you were always very thoughtful where

Mattie was concerned. And the only reason I can think of for not naming you was that she didn't want to burden you." I was doing my best to console LuAnne for having been found lacking in Mattie's eyes, or perhaps for having been merely overlooked. Although, to tell the truth, as much as I cared for LuAnne, she would be the last person to whom I'd entrust my business affairs. And the thought of her being in charge of my medical decisions sent a shudder down my spine.

"LuAnne," I said, inspired by a sudden thought, "I would count it a great favor if you would call everyone, starting with Pastor Ledbetter and Emma Sue, the organist who'll need a heads-up for the service, and all our friends and tell them about Mattie. They all need to be notified, and I am just overwhelmed here. Would you have time to do that?"

There was a noticeable silence. Then she asked, "You haven't already called them?"

"No, I just learned about it myself."

"And called me first?"

I hesitated for a moment of silence. "Yes, except I did tell Sam and Lillian. I mean, of course, they were right here when I walked through the door."

"Well, okay. I can do that, if you're sure."

"I'm sure, and I'd be ever so grateful, and," I added with a laugh, "to prove it, I'll dance at your wedding."

"Ha!" she said, her spirits improving by the minute. "How about at my debutante ball instead?"

We laughed together for a minute, then hung up. Or at least, she did. I merely clicked the phone off, then back on, and punched in Mildred's number before LuAnne could.

"Mildred," I said, thankful that she'd answered so quickly, "LuAnne's going to call you about Mattie. Be surprised, and don't tell her you already know."

Mildred started laughing. "Okay, I'll be properly stunned at the news, but keep in mind, Julia, that I intend to hold this over your head for just about forever."

Chapter 12

With Luanne in charge of spreading the word, I declared myself relieved of all legal and social obligations. I felt as free as a bird. In fact, I felt so free I had to sit down and think up something to do. Although I knew I had a tendency to talk things to death, I wished Sam were with me so we could discuss all that had happened, including the stunning secret stash in Mattie's purse. How in the world had she kept such a secret from all the teetotalers she associated with? Maybe Sam would have some answers, but this was his Rotary Club day, so he was gone for lunch and probably for an hour or two more as he caught up with what was going on in town.

I was left with time on my hands. I could've certainly used a student who wanted to learn to read right about then—what a constructive use of free time that would've been. As it was, though, I was still waiting to be taught how to do it.

So I put that aside and began to think of Mattie. A wave of sadness swept over me, but mixed in with it was a deeply grateful feeling that my responsibility to her was over. Lord, what if I'd had to plan a funeral?

I didn't know who would get that job—Mr. Sitton, perhaps? If Mattie had planned ahead enough to anoint me with her power of attorney, maybe she'd gone a step further and honored someone else with the power of burial.

LuAnne? Sitting there in the library by myself, I had to laugh.

LuAnne would love being in charge. She'd do a good job, but she'd drive everybody crazy while she did it because LuAnne didn't know the meaning of the word *delegate*. Not only would she decide the color of the flowers, determine what the soloist would sing, and designate the eulogists, but she would also tell Pastor Ledbetter the Scripture passages to use. Everybody would be mad at her by the time it was over, but she wouldn't notice. Instead, she would fume for weeks about having been left with everything to do herself. At the same time, it wouldn't surprise me if she didn't come out of it so pleased with herself that she'd think she should start a funeral-planning business.

People would run for the hills, though, if she tried to line them up for her services.

Well, enough of this. Surely, Mattie would've known better than to leave such momentous decisions to LuAnne, in spite of the annual loaves of banana nut bread.

Then, my eye catching the large black pocketbook, safely clasped from prying eyes, still on the desk, I wondered what I should do with it. And its contents. I supposed it should go to Mr. Sitton. He would be the obvious recipient. If anybody was able to keep a secret, it would be a lawyer, and as long as he had been privy to Mattie's most private concerns, he might already know what the pocketbook contained. And if he didn't, it had been my experience that very little could surprise a lawyer of any note.

Springing from my chair—as much as I was able to spring, that is—I realized that I had one more task to do for Mattie. I could take care of the mail that Sam and I had picked up the day before. I'd left it on the desk there in the library, along with Mattie's checkbook, so I sat down and began to open envelopes.

The small, cream-colored envelope held an invitation to a coffee given by a Mrs. William Stanton at her home in Asheville in honor of a Miss Betsy Holden, neither of whom I'd ever heard of. Quickly finding one of my informals, I wrote that Mrs. Freeman regretted that she would be unable to accept the kind invitation to a coffee for Miss Holden due to Mrs. Freeman's sudden demise. Addressing the envelope, I marveled at Mattie's wide acquaintance with party givers.

As I pulled out the Duke Power bill—oh, pardon me all over the place, the Duke *Energy* bill—I stopped to wonder if I still had the authority to sign Mattie's checks. It seemed likely that my check-signing authority had ceased at the moment she had.

So it was strange, I thought, that Mr. Sitton hadn't contacted me with an official release-of-duty order. Maybe he hadn't been notified of Mattie's departure.

I picked up the phone, tapped in his office number, and learned that he was out of the office.

"I'm calling about Mattie Freeman," I told his receptionist. "There're some things I need to discuss with him concerning her. Will you have him call me?"

"I'm sure he intends to contact you, Mrs. Murdoch. But I expect he'll be busy most of the day. Making arrangements, you know."

"That would be," I said, hopefully, "*funeral* arrangements?"

"Final disposition arrangements, yes," she replied.

"Thank you, I just wanted to be sure he knew." I hung up, thinking that one always had to determine the *kind* of arrangements a lawyer was making, since making arrangements of all kinds was a lawyer's stock-in-trade.

Deciding then that I probably could no longer sign Mattie's checks, I simply wrote out one to Duke Energy and one to the Water and Sewer Department, and left the signature lines blank. That much I could do for Mattie and for Mr. Sitton. He could sign them and put them in the mail.

Leaving the envelopes unsealed, I placed them in the checkbook, then looked again at Mattie's bottom line. What she had in the bank would cover both bills, but, I declare, not much else.

Feeling a little like a Peeping Tom, but concerned about the due date of the monthly rent on her apartment, I paged back through the checkbook stubs. Nothing, it seemed, was being deposited but Social Security checks, although here and there, I saw small deposits ranging from ten to twenty-five dollars.

And I also saw that a number of checks had been written to Publishing Clearance House, AmeriVets, Cancer Central of America, St. Bernard's Reservation School, as well as some others with names that were almost, but not quite, well known. At that point, I stopped and began looking through the handful of leaflets and long envelopes that had come in her mail.

Opening one of the envelopes, I found an offer I apparently could not refuse. For only nineteen dollars, I would receive not one but two prepotted, guaranteed-to-thrive aloe vera plants that no home should be without. And by doing so, I would be eligible for the drawing to win the "GRAND PRIZE OF $20,000.00!!"

And in small print at the bottom, I read: "To be notified of the GRAND PRIZE winner's name, send a self-addressed, stamped envelope with your order."

"Ah, me," I said, leaning my head on my hand, saddened by the thought of Mattie sending in small amounts of money in the hope of winning a large amount, and receiving in return piles of magazines, half-dead plants, and who-knew-what-else. If I'd had the heart, I would've added up all the small deposits, then the amount of what she'd sent in to be eligible for more, to see if she'd even broken even.

As it was, I closed the checkbook, put the junk mail in a manila envelope on top, and determined to take it all to Mr. Sitton's office. Then I'd be done with whatever power of attorney I'd had.

When Lillian called me to lunch, I was glad to leave it all behind and think of other, more salubrious things. It didn't quite work out that way.

"Lillian," I said as I sat at the table, my mind still churning with Mattie's finances, "why in the world do people think they can win a jackpot of money by doing nothing?"

"What you talkin' 'bout?"

"I'm talking about all these schemes or scams or whatever they are that're designed to fool gullible people into thinking they can get something for nothing. Remember how James, bless his heart, got involved with the same sort of thing awhile back?"

"Well, lotsa people feel like the onliest way they can make money is to win it. An' lots of 'em spend a good bit of their paychecks on Powerball an' Mega Millions and such like."

"Well, see, that's what I don't understand," I said. "They end up spending more than they win, because they're drawn in by being told that they're almost winners. 'Just send a little more and you'll be in the final drawing.' It seems to me that they should just work harder or get another job if they need more money."

"Not so easy to do these days, Miss Julia. Folks get hard up, an' all they got is they hopes an' dreams."

"Oh, I expect you're right, so I shouldn't judge." I ate a few bites of the fruit salad on my plate. "But I have Miss Mattie on my mind, and, I declare, I don't understand why she was spending her money in such ways—she didn't have that much to start with. And, yes, I know she was too old to find a job, but as far as I know, she'd never had one. I guess the Social Security she was living on came from her husband, who died long before I knew her. But it seems to me that she could've supplemented it in other ways. For instance, Lillian, she made the most delicious party sandwiches you'd ever put in your mouth. With all the parties this town has, she could've had a nice little sandwich-catering business for herself. Instead, though, she spent her time and her money trying for a windfall which she never managed to get."

"Yes'm," Lillian said, looking off in the distance as if something else had come to mind. "An' talkin' 'bout Miss Mattie remind me of Mr. Robert Mobley. You 'member me tellin' you 'bout him?"

"No, I don't. . . . Wait, I do remember. He was always running his wife off, then bringing her back, wasn't he?"

"Yes'm, an' I know you think you got trouble with Miss Mattie's powers, but you don't know trouble till you hear 'bout Mr. Robert."

"Why? What's he done now?"

"He died."

"Oh, I'm sorry to hear that. Well, seems like people are dropping like flies, doesn't it? But maybe his wife will have an easier time of it. Anyway," I said, putting my napkin beside the plate, "what's done is done as far as Mattie is concerned, and who's to know how any of us would manage if it came down to it." Standing up, I made a declaration. "Lillian, it's such a beautiful day, I'm going to see if Mrs. Allen will take a walk with me."

"Take your house keys, then," Lillian said. " 'Cause 'member, I got to go see Latisha's teacher this afternoon, so I'll be lockin' up the house."

"Oh, that's right. Latisha's not having any trouble, is she?"

"No more'n usual, I guess. It's the reg'lar end-of-year conference the teachers have, so we know what the chil'ren doin' in school." Lillian sighed, then she smiled as she shook her head. " 'Course I know what Latisha do in school—she talk. That teacher won't be tellin' me nothin' I don't know already."

Mildred was not interested in a walk.

"I declare, Julia," she said when I rang her doorbell, "I don't know why you have walking on your mind. Come on in here, and let me show you what I'm doing."

I followed Mildred to the sunroom, thinking that I might tell her about Mattie's silver flask and its secret contents. She would be enthralled at the deliciousness of something so unlikely. But when we got to the sunfilled room, I saw that she had a pile of swatches, wallpaper books, and carpet samples strewn around on the wicker chairs and sofa.

"I'm going to redo my bedroom," Mildred said, "but I can't decide what I want. What do you think?"

So my mind was diverted from both secrets and walks, for what could be more entertaining than making plans to redecorate a room?

I unlocked the kitchen door when I got home, noting that Lillian hadn't returned from her conference with Latisha's teacher. As I walked across the room, I saw the blinking light on the telephone.

Punching the PLAY button, I stood by the counter and listened to the message:

"Ernest Sitton here, Mrs. Murdoch. We need to meet at your earliest convenience. I'm sure Sam has told you that Mrs. Freeman's power of attorney is no longer in effect, but she went a step further, and that may or may not be welcome news to you. We need to meet as soon as possible. Call me, but in the meantime, I strongly recommend that you clear your calendar for the next several days." He stopped, cleared his throat, then went on. "For the next several *weeks*, perhaps."

What in the world?

Chapter 13

"There'll be no need to put a creditor's notice in the paper," Mr. Ernest Sitton said, as I watched him tick off an item on his yellow legal pad. "Mrs. Freeman's estate doesn't meet the minimum requirement. There is a money market account with a balance of precisely $23,423.31. And, as you know, there's $782.66 in her checking account, which is enough to keep her apartment for another month. That should give you time to dispose of her furniture and other possessions. Of course the usual bills will come in—electricity, water, and so forth. I have a list here of the utilities you'll need to notify when you want them cut off." He pushed a sheet of paper across the conference table.

I didn't look at it. I didn't even pick it up. I just sat there listening, but not really hearing, as he went down a list of the duties of the executor of Mattie's last will and testament.

I wished I had waited for Sam to get home before rushing to Delmont in response to Mr. Sitton's phone message. But no, fearing that there were more power-of-attorney duties hanging over my head, nothing would do but to hurry and find out. And to find out without waiting for the one who could help me, now that I badly needed help.

"And here's your copy of the will." Another set of papers slid across the table. "You'll notice that there are a number of gifts and bequests to various groups and individuals. It'll be up to you to decide what percentage of each bequest the estate will cover, which is what I suggest you do so as to avoid anyone's contesting of the will.

"Now, Mrs. Murdoch," Mr. Sitton continued, pushing aside his legal pad. "You will also notice that the will requires the payment of funeral expenses and creditors, like the hospital, her doctors, and me, before any bequests are distributed—that's standard practice. The medical bills, however, should be minimal—she was on Medicaid. I will be submitting my bill at the end of the month. But you'll be pleased to know that Mrs. Freeman, at my suggestion, made all her funeral arrangements with the Good Shepherd Funeral Home some time ago and went to great effort to prepay those expenses. So, if I may further suggest, it would behoove you not to make any changes or upgrades from what she has selected and paid for. Now, do you have any questions?"

I straightened up in my chair, and said, "Yes. Can you get somebody else to do this?"

Mr. Sitton's eyebrows went up, but he quickly settled them down. Clearing his throat, he said, "You can certainly delegate certain responsibilities to anyone you want, but the responsibility of executing the will is yours."

"But I don't want it. I don't even want to delegate. I want out from under the whole thing."

Mr. Sitton pushed up his glasses and studied me. He sat there across the table and *studied* me. As if I were some strange being that he'd never come across before.

"I was under the impression," he finally said, "that you and Mrs. Freeman were close friends. She led me to believe that she had no concern about your ability and your willingness to execute her will."

I studied him back, not backing down by even a blink, as I tried to determine if there'd been a hint of accusation, or maybe of disappointment, in his words. I didn't care either way. I wasn't in the business of pleasing an attorney I'd never hired or even known two days before.

"You were laboring under a false impression," I said. "Mattie and I were never close, and, frankly, I counted her as more of an acquaintance than a friend. I don't have an idea in the world why she would do this to me, nor do I have any idea of how to execute a will." I pushed the papers back toward him. "Nor do I want to learn."

"Well," he said, gathering the papers and carefully aligning them. "Well, I can't say I haven't run into situations before where a named executor *couldn't* serve for one reason or another, but never one who just didn't want to. Not that it isn't your prerogative to refuse. In fact, it's better to refuse altogether than to accept and do a poor job of it, although the settling of the Freeman estate should be both simple and straighforward with few demands upon the executor."

Regardless of how simple and straightforward he made it sound, I felt no obligation to Mattie or to anyone else to accept a position I didn't want—*another* position, I might add, that I didn't want. But, as usual, I had to try to make him understand and agree with me that I was not the person to take on such a responsibility.

"I do believe that I must exercise that prerogative, Mr. Sitton. I know it might make your job more arduous, but if you knew all the things I'm already committed to, I think you would understand." I thought of my commitment to the Literacy Council, and to Helen Stroud's flower-arranging class, and to the weight loss and general health of Mildred, even though she wouldn't know if I followed through on that or not. In my view, I didn't have time for anything else. But I summed it up for Mr. Sitton by concluding, "I'm really not equal to the task."

"Hm-m," Mr. Sitton said. "Obviously, Mrs. Freeman thought that you were. Her naming you, her selecting you to carry out her wishes, is an honor that indicates an extremely high regard for your abilities. I'm sure she was at peace knowing that her affairs would be in such safe hands."

Well, there was one question answered—obviously, Mr. Sitton had not known of Mattie's private affliction. For how could he consider it an honor when she had made her selection bolstered by the occasional sip of spirits?

Nonetheless, my spine needed a good deal more stiffening, because Mr. Sitton seemed intent on making me feel selfish and self-centered for foiling the wishes of a woman who could no longer speak for herself.

I thought briefly of Mattie, picturing her in the most comfortable chair in the living room of whichever hostess she was honoring with her presence. I thought of her crouched over the steering wheel of that huge Oldsmobile, looking neither to the right nor to the left as she tooled around town. I thought of her entering the Lila Mae Harding Sunday school class, clomping through the door with that walker, expecting everyone to scatter before her. I thought of Mattie, at some point in her long life, giving serious consideration to the writing of her will and the judicious dispersal of her assets. I thought of her mentally listing all the people she knew, trying to decide to whom she would entrust her final wishes.

And I thought of Mattie making out her will while sustaining herself with constant nips from the silver flask in her purse.

How in the world had she decided on me? She must have considered and rejected one after the other of her acquaintances. How had I ended up as the last woman standing?

I tried to feel honored, but it didn't work. And wouldn't have worked even if I'd thought she'd been operating with a clear, unbefuddled mind. As it was, all I felt was hemmed in and trapped.

But not for long. I stood up. "Mr. Sitton, I appreciate Mattie's high regard for the abilities she assumed I have. But I assure you, I am not the person for this job. I don't want it, I'm unprepared for it, and therefore I formally refuse whatever honor there might be." I couldn't leave it there, of course, for I always had to temper any firm stand I felt compelled to take. "I hope you understand and I hope I've not added to your problems in settling Mattie's estate."

"I do understand," Mr. Sitton said, rising also. "I admit that I thought you would do a competent job, but you know what you can take on and what you can't. However, Mrs. Freeman did name a successor executor in case you were unable to serve."

"She did?" I was stunned. Why hadn't he said so? Here, I'd turned myself inside out to make sure that he would not think the less of me for refusing—although why I should care what a Delmont lawyer thought of me, I didn't know.

"Well," I said, sinking back into my chair, "that certainly relieves my mind. I don't feel so bad about turning it down now. Mattie must've known that I might have my hands full. Thank goodness she made provision for that." I smiled. "Now I don't have to worry about her wishes being carried out."

"Oh, yes. They'll be carried out to the letter. I am the trustee, appointed to see that it's all done legally and in accordance with her wishes. As closely as possible, that is."

"Well, then," I said, getting to my feet again. "I will be on my way and let you get on with it." I started toward the door, but turned back. "May I ask who the successor executor is?"

"Um, let me see," he said, picking up the will and scanning the first page. "I don't believe I know her, but perhaps you do. Mrs. Leonard Conover?"

I stood stock-still and stared at him. *"LuAnne?"*

Then I turned to the table, pulled out a chair, and sat back down. "If you don't mind, Mr. Sitton, let's start over again. From the beginning."

Chapter 14

When I have something to do, I do it. I don't put it off, hoping it'll get easier with time or just go away. No, I get right to it and get it over with.

So, with my usual alacrity, I stopped at Mattie's apartment on my way home. Leaving in the car all the papers—folders, envelopes, and so forth—that Mr. Sitton had loaded into my arms, I walked into the building, went directly to Mattie's door, and inserted the key—no hesitation this time. I had a job to do, and the more I didn't want to do it, the quicker I wanted to get it done.

When I walked inside, I didn't even think of it as invading Mattie's personal space. Uppermost in my mind was where I should start in clearing it out, for clearing it of all furniture, clothing, food, bibelots, papers, and general accumulation of junk that's found in any household was what I had to do. And do it quickly so I could release the apartment before more rent payments came due.

Lord, I didn't know where to start. The apartment was crammed full, especially the living room, which looked like a furniture warehouse with chairs and tables and chests having been pushed aside to make space for the emergency workers. And I hadn't even looked into closets and cabinets. The place had been Mattie's home for years and years, and, from the looks of it, had rarely, if ever, had a great and wonderful housecleaning. I almost turned around and left.

But *food,* I thought, as I headed for the small kitchen, glancing at my watch as I went. There was time before my own dinner to make a start, so I decided that I should tackle the refrigerator first. Opening the door, I found the shelves filled with small, foiled-covered bowls of leftovers. Noting that Mattie did not have a garbage disposal or a dishwasher, I quickly began to empty the bowls into trash bags and stack the bowls in the sink. Holding my breath, I continued to dump out small servings of spaghetti and green beans and beef stew and stewed apples and—well, after that I stopped identifying Mattie's menus. I emptied a milk bottle, an orange juice container, a half-full bottle of zesty Italian salad dressing, and jars one after the other of mayonnaise, mustard, pickles, horseradish, olives, and jelly—blueberry, cherry, and orange marmalade. Three eggs went next and a head of lettuce that was turning brown, a wrinkled tomato, and two potatoes that were growing sprouts.

The small freezer at the top of the refrigerator held a few unidentifiable packages—they went into the trash, as did the frozen peas and half carton of rocky road ice cream, along with a package of frost-bitten ground beef.

When I'd wiped the insides of the freezer and refrigerator, I turned down the inner thermostat, closed the doors, and wondered what to do with the Hefty bag of recyclable jars and plastic containers, as well as the squishy bag of food scraps. It occurred to me that a lot of hungry children in Africa or somewhere would love to have what I had just discarded.

Well, I had no way of getting it to them, and to have left it would mean further deterioration and an unpleasant odor. I lugged the trash bags to the door, wondering where a Dumpster might be. Just as I put the last of the bags outside the door, that nice Mr. Wheeler came loping down the hall.

"Looks like you could use some help," he said.

"I sure could. I've just emptied Mrs. Freeman's refrigerator, but I don't know what to do with what I've emptied it of."

"Well, here, let me take them. The Dumpster's out back." He

gathered all the bags with no effort, while I thanked him profusely. Then I pondered how to tell him he'd just lost a tenant, which, considering how word gets around in Abbotsville, turned out to be totally unnecessary.

He hesitated a moment, then said, "I was sorry to hear about Mrs. Freeman. I didn't know her well, but she must've been a close friend of yours."

Hardly, I thought, but thanked him for his expression of sympathy, misplaced though it was.

"By the way," Mr. Wheeler said, "do you know the funeral plans? I'd like to pay my respects."

"No, nothing's been decided yet. In fact, I guess that's next on my list." And I went on to tell him that I was the executor of Mattie's will, so even though I wasn't yet sure of what that position entailed, he'd most likely be seeing a lot of me going in and out of her apartment.

"Well," Mr. Wheeler said with that nice smile of his, "I'm around if you need help with anything. And please do let me know about the funeral."

Assuring him that I would, I stood for a minute at the door and watched as he walked down the hall, clutching the trash bags as Mattie's empty jars clanked with each step he took.

Then I locked the apartment door and went home.

"You been cleanin' *what*?" Lillian stopped in the middle of the kitchen and stared at me.

"Miss Mattie's refrigerator and freezer," I said, putting my pocketbook and the stack of legal papers on the table.

"They Lord," Lillian said with a roll of her eyes.

"Well, don't act so shocked. I've done cleaning before. Besides, I had to get rid of the food before it turned green."

"Did you clean the insides real good? The drawers an' shelves an' everything? And leave a box of Arm and Hammer inside?"

"I did the best I could in the time I had," I said, just a mite huffily because I'd expected a little appreciation for my efforts. "However," I went on, pulling out a chair, "now that you mention it, I forgot to wash the dishes I emptied. Just left them in the sink where the remains will harden and have to be scrubbed. Well," I said, sitting down with a sigh, "I can't think of everything."

"I think you ought to take me next time you go."

"Thank you, Lillian. I think you're right."

"Sam," I said as we sat around the table after dinner, "I am overwhelmed with the magnitude of executing Mattie's will—mainly because I don't know what I'm supposed to do first and what can wait. I don't even know where to start, except that nice Mr. Wheeler reminded me that I need to set a date and time for a funeral."

"That probably should come first, honey," Sam said, putting his hand on my arm. "You don't have to do everything all at once, you know, and there's no reason you can't ask some of her friends to help. As for the funeral, didn't Sitton say that Mattie had made all the arrangements?"

"Yes, and paid for it all, too. Which is a relief to me, because from the state of her checkbook, we'd have had to bury her in the backyard." I rubbed my forehead at the thought of it. "Of course, she does have a few thousand in a money market fund, which I guess should go to honor the bequests she's made. I just hope there're no unforeseen expenses that come up. That's the problem with this whole thing, Sam," I said, sitting up straight. "I don't know what to expect."

"Make a list, then tackle each item, one at a time. And, again, ask some of the ladies to help. They were all Mattie's friends, and they'll be happy to pitch in."

"Well, I know one who will be—if I present it to her in the right way." I smiled as I thought of LuAnne's hurt feelings that Mattie had not honored her with the power of attorney. "Sam," I said decisively, "I've just made my first executive decision. I'm going to ask LuAnne to oversee the funeral. Of course, I may have to imply that Mattie wanted her—specifically named her—to do it. But I know LuAnne will take charge and do a good job, although she'll end up with everybody, including me, mad at her. The best part of it, though, is that she'll take it off my hands. And," I went on, "since the funeral is preplanned, what damage could she do?"

"All right," Sam said with approval, "that's one thing settled. I do suggest, however, that you call the funeral home yourself and double-check Mattie's plans. Make sure it's all paid for, so you're not hit with an unexpected bill. Now, what else can you delegate?"

"Well, all that furniture," I said, sighing. "I have to get rid of it some way, but I can't see having a yard sale. Who would want it, I ask you. Everybody I know already has all the furniture they need. Oh," I said, having had a sudden inspiration, "I know! Helen! Helen Stroud, that's who I'll ask to help. Remember, Sam, she had to sell most of her beautiful furniture when Richard left her with nothing but bills. She'll know what to do."

"Excellent idea. You've always thought a lot of Helen, and I expect she could use the extra income."

"You think I should pay her?" I hadn't thought of that, although I recalled that she was accepting payment for teaching a flower-arranging class.

"I think *Mattie* should pay her. You can ask Helen if she'd prefer to be paid by the hour or by a percentage of what's made on the furniture. And if she's done it before with her own things, she'll know an appraiser, as well as some dealers who'll buy it." Sam leaned back in his chair, studied the ceiling for a few seconds, then said, "The one thing you'll have to watch for, Julia, is appearing—not actually, because I know you won't, but *appearing*—to benefit in any way by what you do with Mattie's belongings. And that goes for allowing anyone else to benefit. Just approach everything you do on a businesslike basis, and realize that you are accountable to the court for however you handle Mattie's estate."

"Yes. Yes, you're absolutely right, that's exactly what I have to do." I sat up even straighter, accepting the heavy responsibility of pleasing the court—whoever or whatever that was. "So that means that I can't allow any of Mattie's friends, or mine, to go into her apartment and take even a memento to remember her by. Right?"

"Right. And that reminds me. How many gifts and bequests are in her will?"

"I haven't even looked. I was too busy cleaning the refrigerator, then coming home to tell Lillian, and then spending the last hour or so telling you what Mattie left to *me*. I don't know what she's left to anybody else."

"Then," Sam said as he got up from the table to get the coffeepot, "I suggest you study that will until you know it by heart. Figure out how much she's left to each person or charitable group, then see if she has enough money to cover it. If she only has what's in her money market fund, then you may need every cent you get from her household goods to meet the will's requirements."

"Oh, my," I said, "every time I think I'm getting on top of this job, something else comes along to remind me that I'm not. What if there's not enough, Sam, even with selling everything in her apartment? Used furniture won't bring in much at all."

"Well, you can't get blood from a turnip, as they say. So you go with percentages and distribute whatever the total ends up being. Just keep accurate records, whatever you do."

"That means," I said with a moan, "that I'll have to do arithmetic—adding and subtracting and multiplying and dividing by fractions and I don't know what all. I'm not good at that, Sam. You'll help me, won't you?"

"You know I will, sweetheart." Sam smiled, passed me the cream pitcher, and went on. "Don't worry about it. Wills get probated all the time, and you'll do fine."

That was reassuring to hear, but it didn't sink in far enough to do much good.

One thing was for sure, though. All my plans to learn to arrange flowers, teach people to read, and get Mildred on a walking schedule—all in an effort to fill up the time I usually spent worrying—were for naught. As far as I could imagine, there would be no empty time just pleading to be filled in the foreseeable future.

So in order to follow through on at least one of those good intentions, I immediately went to Nick's Sporting Goods, purchased a pedometer, and presented it to Mildred.

"What's this?" she asked, looking at it warily.

"It's a step counter. Try it, Mildred. You'll love it."

"Uh-huh," she said with a laugh. "I just bet I will."

Chapter 15

"Helen?" I said when she answered her phone. I wasn't waiting around—I'd dialed her number as soon as Sam and I had adjourned to the library after supper. "It's Julia. How are you?"

"I'm well, thank you. And you?"

"Oh, except for having more to do than I can handle, I guess I'm all right. A little overwhelmed by the responsibility of executing Mattie's will, but I guess you've heard all about that."

"No, but if that's the case, you've inherited a huge responsibility."

With that, I knew I didn't have to explain further, so I went right to the reason for my call. "Helen, it looks as if I'll have to back out of the flower-arranging class. I hate to do it, but with all I have to do for Mattie, I just can't fit it in right now. You see, besides burying her, I have to do something with her furniture, and I was wondering if you'd have time to help. Apparently it's incumbent on me to get the highest price possible for it, but I don't have a clue as to what it's worth or who would want to buy it. But I know that you're knowledgeable about the value of such things, and," I went on hurriedly, "I'm not asking you to do it out of the goodness of your heart. I've been advised that Mattie's estate will pay for any expert help I need to employ."

There was silence on the line as Helen considered my offer, which didn't surprise me. Helen had always been deliberate and judicious in what she committed herself to do. So while I awaited her response, I thought about what I'd just said because I had no intention of offering to pay LuAnne for handling the funeral. First of all, LuAnne would do it for the love of being in charge, and second of all, she'd probably pay *me* for letting her do it.

"Well," Helen said, "I'm not an expert on much of anything. But furniture has always been an interest of mine, so I could probably weed out the reproductions. But, Julia, if Mattie has any really good pieces, you should call in an accredited appraiser."

"Yes, Sam suggested that, too. Problem is, I don't know any appraisers, accredited or not."

"I can put you in touch with the one who did a good job for me. Diane Somebody—an unusual last name I can't remember. I have it in my address book."

"That would be a great help. But, Helen, you won't believe the amount of stuff in that apartment. I could really use you if you have time to help me with it."

"Well, I have an office job every morning, but I'll be happy to help in the afternoons." Then, in a voice tight with the strain of shame and need, she went on. "And thank you for the opportunity. A small percentage of any proceeds would be appreciated, if that's all right with you."

Indeed, it was, so after making plans to meet at Mattie's apartment the following afternoon, I hung up and turned to Sam with a relieved smile.

"I'm on a roll, Sam. One more call and that'll be it for my first day as an executive."

"LuAnne?" I said when she answered her phone. "Sorry to call so late, but it's my understanding that Mattie would like you to oversee her funeral. So I thought I should let you know the plans she made and make sure that you have the time to take it on."

Another silence on the line. Then she said, "Mattie wanted me to do her funeral?"

"That's what I was advised. I had a conversation with her

attorney, Mr. Ernest Sitton, and he said you were mentioned as she made out her will." That wasn't too far from the truth, although I hoped that LuAnne wouldn't push me for any details. If she learned that she was named successor executor—which gave her absolutely no authority unless I was out of the picture—of the entire will, she would question every move I made. My plan was to turn the funeral over to her, thereby taking it off my hands and, also thereby, keeping her too busy to interfere with anything else.

"Well, I am honored," LuAnne said. "And vindicated for putting up with her all these years. Julia, I tell you, that woman would drive a normal person crazy. Nothing ever pleased her, but, then, I guess we shouldn't speak ill of the deceased. And she did have her good points, although I can't think of any right now."

I almost laughed, but LuAnne was so deadly serious that I restrained myself. "Then I can leave the funeral in your hands?"

"Of course!" she said, as if it had been a foregone conclusion. "If Mattie wanted me to do it, I most certainly will and, believe me, she's going to be pleased this time. Abbotsville will see how a funeral *should* be conducted."

"Now, wait, LuAnne, let's not get carried away. Mattie has already planned her funeral and paid for it and everything. All you have to do is see that the funeral home follows through."

"Well, you just wait a minute, Julia. Are you talking bare bones here?"

"I really don't know. I've not seen her plans, but I can't imagine they'll be elaborate. LuAnne, she was not a wealthy woman—not then and not now. You have to stick to what she selected and not add any additional expense."

Another long silence on the line. "Well, Julia," she finally said, "you do realize that Mattie Freeman was a longtime member of the garden club, don't you? And the book club and the Lila Mae Harding Sunday school class and DAR and, as old as she was, maybe even a founding member of the First Presbyterian Church. And she could be so sweet, just a *good* person. She deserves something more than a bare bones funeral, to my way of thinking."

I knew right then that I would have to put my foot down or LuAnne would present Mattie's estate with a bill that would cut her bank accounts to the bone. "All right, LuAnne, if you think that what she's already paid for isn't enough for a fitting funeral, then you can add whatever *you* want to pay for. But, as executor of her will, I am not beholden to honor any further expense."

"*You're* the executor?" LuAnne's expression of surprise didn't help my feelings of competence. "I thought you just had power of attorney. How did that happen?"

"I don't know, LuAnne, and since Mattie's dead and gone, I can't ask her. Now, why don't you go to the Good Shepherd Funeral Home and see exactly what she chose? It may be that it will prove perfectly satisfactory, and there'll be no question of any added expense."

"All right, I'll do that, but I still don't understand why she chose you."

"Believe me, I don't, either. We can ask her when we all get to heaven."

"Well, be that as it may, I want you to know that I am not going to be held responsible if her funeral ends up being about half tacky. I'll just let everybody know that my hands were tied because you wouldn't let me give Mattie the send-off she deserves."

I rolled my eyes and sighed. "Don't worry, LuAnne, I know I'm the one who's responsible. I doubt it'll be the only thing I'll be blamed for."

Settling back on the sofa, I picked up the stack of papers that Mr. Sitton had saddled me with and began to study Mattie's will.

"Oh, my word, Sam, what in the world was Mattie thinking? You should see this." I held up the pad on which I'd just listed the names of all the people and entities that Mattie had wanted to benefit from her estate. I rubbed my forehead in despair at the impossible feat of having to turn almost nothing into enough to go around.

"What is it, honey?"

"This!" I said, waving the pad. "I'm doing what you told me to do—making a list of the beneficiaries and adding up all the bequests. Mattie runs out of money less than halfway through the list." I stood up and walked across the room, so agitated that I couldn't sit still. "Why did she do this? She must've known how much she had. She *had* to've known that her estate wouldn't cover what she was so blithely handing out. Don't you think? I mean, *what* was she thinking?"

"Well," Sam said, "didn't you say that she was showing signs of dementia in the hospital? Maybe she was suffering from it long before anyone was aware of it."

"She was suffering from *something,* if this is any indication." I grabbed the pad and waved it around again. "But, Sam, we were told it was the aftereffects of the anesthesia because, other than that debutante episode, none of us had noticed any changes in her behavior." I stopped and considered a few scenes with Mattie over the past year or so. "I never saw any signs of her going off the rails before that. Maybe she was a little more tetchy, a little less tolerant, in recent years, but we were used to her ill humor. And of course, we may not've noticed, because—I hate to admit this—but maybe we didn't notice because we just generally ignored her."

"Well, there's another possibility," Sam said, "which I hesitate to suggest, but have you given any thought as to why she named you her executor?"

I shrugged my shoulders. "I guess she trusted me to do it right. After all, she'd seen me follow through on everything I've ever put my hand to in all the clubs and groups we'd both been a part of."

"I'm sure that entered into her thinking," Sam said. Then he cocked an eyebrow and went on. "But could she have assumed that you would see that her bequests were honored whether she had the funds or not? Maybe she wanted to be generous—show her appreciation to her friends—and hoped that you'd fill in the blanks."

"You mean she hoped *I'd* make up the difference between what she had and what she wanted to give away? So *she'd* appear generous and appreciative? And get all the credit?" I sprang to my feet again. "I've never heard of such presumption! No, Sam, no way in the world am I going to fill her bank accounts so everybody'll think well of her."

"And you shouldn't," Sam agreed. "I shouldn't have brought it up, because it's more likely that she wasn't thinking clearly. Didn't you say she was trying to win some kind of contest?"

"*Many* kinds of contests," I corrected through a tight mouth.

"Well, there you are. She may have been counting on a windfall and wanted to share it with her beneficiaries."

"Oh," I said as my anger dissipated, "I think you're right. That does explain it, but, bless her heart, she was certainly counting her chickens before they hatched."

Then, tired of balancing Mattie's wishes with the balances in her accounts, I said, "I can't worry with this anymore. Let's go to bed."

Chapter 16

"Julia?" Sam said, turning over toward me just as I was about to doze off.

"Hm-m?"

"Just thought of something. Jewelry. Did Mattie have any?"

My eyes popped open. "I don't know. I haven't thought about it."

"You should make sure first thing in the morning. The funeral home will put the obituary in the paper, probably tomorrow. Thieves have been known to watch them for places to rob."

I sat straight up in bed. "Oh, my goodness, and I'll be responsible. Should I go over now and look?"

"No, honey," Sam said, pulling me back down. "It's unlikely anybody would try to break in tonight. Besides, Mr. Wheeler's around. I expect he'll be keeping an eye out."

"Well," I said, settling down in my warm place, "I wish you'd waited till morning to bring it up. I may not sleep a wink."

Sam laughed. "I'm sorry. I should've waited, but I just thought of it and had to ask."

"I'm glad you did. I guess." I laughed a little, too. "But that's what frightens me about this job, that I'll forget something as obvious as jewelry. Although," I murmured as my eyes began to close, "Mattie never wore anything anybody'd want to steal." Then, "Nothing memorable, anyway." And a few minutes later, "That I ever saw." And began to fall asleep.

"*Sam!*" I sat straight up in bed again.

"What! What?"

"I forgot to tell you who all Mattie named in her will. You won't believe it."

"In the morning, honey. Now lie back down, and let Mattie rest in peace. Us, too."

So I did and felt the better for it.

"All right, Sam, listen to this." We were in the library right after finishing breakfast. I was so eager to tell him how outlandish Mattie's will was that it had been all I could do to hold my tongue long enough to eat. Actually, I'd wanted to tell him in the kitchen with Lillian listening in as well, but, fearful that I wasn't supposed to tell anybody anything, I'd waited until we were alone.

Then I had a second thought. "Is it all right to tell you who's in the will?"

He smiled. "I won't tell anybody, and you're going to notify the ones involved fairly soon anyway, aren't you?"

"Well, that's the thing, isn't it? If there's not enough to go around, maybe I shouldn't tell anybody. Of course, by the time I sell Mattie's furniture and her jewelry, maybe there will be."

I glanced down the list of the names of the beneficiaries again and sighed. "However, there's not a chance in the world for that. Listen, Sam. She's left five thousand dollars to each of ten people, some of whom I've never heard of. One is just 'Carl at the Shell station for exemplary mechanical work.' Have you ever heard of such a thing? If he's the one who kept that Oldsmobile of hers running, I ought to disinherit him. And another five thousand to a Junior Haverty for carrying her groceries to the car. With just these ten names, she's distributed twice as much as she actually has. But that didn't stop her, because she's left ten thousand dollars to the PEO scholarship fund, ten thousand to the library, and ten thousand more to the Humane Society." I stared at the page. "And I had no idea that she liked cats and dogs.

"How much is that, Sam?"

"Eighty thousand. How much did you say she has?"

"A little over twenty-three thousand in a money market account, and less than a thousand in her checking account." I looked up at Sam in despair. "I'm getting a headache. Because you haven't heard the worst of it yet. In that first ten who're to get five thousand each, she's named LuAnne, Hazel Marie, Callie Armstrong, Sue Hargrove, Helen Stroud, Roberta Smith, and—good grief! Norma Cantrell and Mildred Allen! Sam, Norma is the most officious person I've ever known—I can't imagine she's ever done one gracious thing for Mattie. And Mildred? She needs another five thousand dollars like she needs another five pounds. I'm sorry to say that, but it's the truth."

Sam's quizzical look matched my feelings. "It's an interesting lineup, all right. And she didn't mention you?"

"No, and if I weren't a committed Christian, I'd be highly embittered."

"She probably intended the executor's fee to make up for leaving you out," Sam said, probably to make me feel better. "If, that is," he went on, "you want to go to the trouble of applying to the court for it."

"I have enough trouble already. I don't need to go to court for a percentage of next to nothing." Glaring at Mattie's improbable will, I said, "I've a good mind to turn this back to Mr. Sitton so he can hand it to LuAnne. Let them worry with it because here's almost the final straw. In a separate paragraph, she wants another five thousand dollars to go to the Lila Mae Harding Sunday school class for refreshments every Sunday morning—I'd vote against that right now.

"And, oh, my goodness, Sam. Listen to this. She wants thirty thousand dollars to go to the church to buy pew cushions for the ease and comfort of the congregation and aisle carpeting in the same color as the cushions. *And* she wants paperback hymnals to replace the hardcovers because they're too heavy to hold. Then she wants new robes for the choir—blue being the preferred color to match the carpet and pew cushions. And here's the kicker, Sam. In a codicil, she added another five thousand to go to the Shriners children's hospital, and I didn't know she even *liked* children. But get this," I went on, "the *remainder* of her estate is to go to the church—can you imagine! There'll be no remainder. There's not even enough to begin with, much less having anything left over."

"Maybe," Sam said, frowning, "she has an investment account somewhere—some stocks and bonds, an IRA—funds that she knew would be available."

"No," I said with a deep sigh, "not according to Mr. Sitton. What I've seen is what I have to work with."

I leaned my head back against the sofa, just overcome with who and what Mattie had considered important enough to underwrite with money she didn't have.

"This is unreal, Sam," I said. "Can we make a case to the court that she was of unsound mind so they'll release me from this?"

Sam smiled and patted my hand. "Hard to prove at this point, honey. But I concede that she has some unusual bequests. Still, a will is where a testator can pretty much do as she wants, unless there're relatives who decide to challenge it. No mention by Mattie of any family, though—right?"

"Well," I said, sifting through the pages, "I think there's something here about having no living relatives known to her. Yes, here it is." I handed the page to him.

"Uh-huh," Sam said, scanning the page. "Of course, that doesn't forestall any relatives who were *un*known to her. But let's not worry about that unless somebody pops up somewhere along the line. Your job is to follow the will as closely as possible and let Sitton handle the rest, which will include making the proper notifications."

"I'll try," I said, tired before even starting. "Jewelry is first on my list today. What will you be doing?"

"Oh, I have an appointment to interview old Judge McCormick again, which will probably be as unproductive as the last time. But I have to try to get a straight story out of him, so I can finish a chapter." Sam had been involved with writing a legal history of Abbot County for some years now. I had my doubts that he'd ever finish it, but it gave him something creative to do and he enjoyed the interviews he conducted. The thing about it was, though, he'd get a story from a defense lawyer about a particular case from years ago, then get an entirely different one from the prosecutor—which I guess was par for the course in any case.

"And," Sam went on, "I'm going to stop by the drugstore and get a plentiful supply of sunblock. We'll be off on our fishing trip in about a week."

"Well, thank goodness you won't be leaving until after the funeral. LuAnne is probably expecting you to be a pallbearer."

"Lillian," I said, walking into the kitchen, "do we have any of those little ziplock plastic bags?"

"Yessum, they's a whole box full in the pantry." She quickly found the box and handed it to me. "You want some snacks to put in 'em?"

"No, no snacks today. I'm going to Mattie's apartment to look through her jewelry. I'm going to put each piece in a separate bag so they're not all jumbled together. And that way, I can take the good pieces to a jewelry store for appraisals. See, Lillian, Mattie named me as the executor of her estate, and it looks as if her estate is in a mess."

"Law, Miss Julia, that sound jus' like what Mr. Robert Mobley done to the Reverend Abernathy. Yes, ma'am, look like you both got your hands full."

Lillian nodded to affirm what she'd said, then jerked around toward the door. "*Listen!* You hear that? Law, Miss Julia, somebody yellin' they head off."

I heard it, too, and we both ran for the back door just as Ida Lee, Mildred's composed and highly capable housekeeper, broke through the boundary plantings.

"Miss Julia! Miss Julia! Come quick, hurry!" Then she bounded back through the rhododendron bushes and disappeared toward Mildred's house.

"Oh, my word," I said, dashing out the door and across the yard. "Something's happened. Come on, Lillian, hurry!"

Chapter 17

Just as I reached Mildred's columned porch, gasping for breath as I struggled up the low steps, I heard the wail of sirens coming closer. I had never in all the years I'd known Ida Lee seen her in an agitated state. But there'd been nothing composed or regal about her as she'd bounded back across Mildred's lawn like a deer, Lillian and me struggling along behind her. Even so, the blaring sirens announced that she'd kept her head long enough to call 911.

Lord, what had happened? I hurried inside, Lillian panting right behind me.

"Ida Lee? Where are you?" I called. "What's happened?"

"In here, Mrs. Murdoch." Ida Lee's voice, reverting to its usual professional tone, came from Mildred's wicker-and-chintz sunroom.

I ran across the foyer to the sunroom and found Mildred sprawled on the floor. Her eyes were rolled back in her head, and she was as white as a sheet.

"Oh, Mildred, what happened?" I knelt beside her and felt her forehead. I don't know why, just that it was what people seemed to do.

"She fell," Ida Lee said. "I was in the kitchen and I felt the thump when she hit the floor. I can't get her up, and I'm afraid to try. She might've broken something."

"Mildred? Mildred, do you hurt anywhere?" I patted her face, but she didn't answer. Then, as the blare of the sirens died away, I looked up at Ida Lee. "Run meet them, Ida Lee. Get them in here. She's not responding. No telling where she's hurt."

As professional men and women, loaded down with cases and tanks and I-don't-know-what-all hurried in and set up shop all around Mildred's fallen body, Lillian, Ida Lee, and I moved aside. Even though there were five emergency workers milling around, I wondered how they would get Mildred on a stretcher. She was a large woman, so I knew lifting her would be a problem. I didn't get to see how they managed it, though, because they ran us out to wait in the foyer.

Ida Lee, wringing her hands, stood trembling beside me, her lovely, caramel-colored face drawn with anxiety. "Oh, I hope she's all right. I should've watched her better. I try to, I really do."

"Ida Lee, nobody could do better than you. Mildred's lucky to have you. But let's don't fall apart until we know what's going on." Although in the back of my mind, the memory of another friend who'd so recently suffered a fall kept popping up, and look what had happened to her. I began to tremble a little myself.

Leaving Lillian to close up Mildred's house, I drove Ida Lee to the hospital, where we waited and waited in the waiting room of the emergency room. Finally a doctor who wasn't old enough to shave or to wear a decent pair of shoes came out to talk to Mildred's family. There were only the two of us.

"How is she?" I asked, jumping up from my chair. "Mrs. Allen, how is she?" He kept looking around, apparently for a family member.

"Is she married?" he asked. "I should speak with her husband."

"Obviously," I said, waving my hand at the empty room, "he's not available. Ida Lee, do you know where Mr. Allen is?"

"Yes, ma'am, Mr. Horace is sailing on the Mediterranean. I think you can reach him by ship to shore or maybe shore to ship."

The young doctor looked taken aback—not many people from Abbotsville sailed anywhere, much less on the Mediterranean. "What about children? Does she have any children?"

"Ida Lee?" I asked again. "Do you know how to reach Tonya?"

"Miss Tonya is somewhere in Provence."

"That's in France," I said, in case he'd missed geography in grade school. "Now, look, Doctor, we're all she has at the moment, so you can tell us how she is. Ida Lee here is as close to kinfolk as you're going to get."

His eyebrows went up at that, but he had enough savoir faire not to comment on the relationship.

He cleared his throat. "Well, the X-rays show that nothing's broken, but she had a hard fall. She'll be bruised and sore for a few days. The thing is, though, we don't know why she got dizzy and fell, which is what she says happened. I want to admit her for a few days and do a battery of tests. Someone will have to speak with the admitting office. Does she have insurance?"

Has it come to this? I thought. *What would he do if she didn't? Call Washington and report her?*

"Doctor," I said, "Mrs. Allen underwrote this fancy emergency room you're working in, so you don't need to worry about insurance, be it term or whole life, home owner's, health, or final expenses."

Well, somebody finally recognized Mildred's value to the hospital, for when Ida Lee and I were directed to the third floor, we found Mildred in a private room with not one but two windows. She was lying in bed hooked up to some kind of intravenous apparatus, and, I declare, she looked mountainous under the covers.

"Mildred?" I whispered as I tiptoed to the bed. "How're you feeling? Can I get you anything?"

"You can get me out of here," she said, but with only a smidgen of her usual commanding tone. "What happened?"

"You don't remember?"

"No, I couldn't find the swatch I'd decided on for my new curtains, so I got up to look for it . . . and the next thing I knew some doctor was feeling me up." She managed a weak smile. "Where's Ida Lee?"

"Right here, Mrs. Allen." Ida Lee moved in closer as I stepped back from the bed. "You've given us a real fright. Are you sure you're feeling all right?"

Mildred clasped her hand. "Don't leave me, Ida Lee. I feel better when you're around."

"You don't need to worry about that." Ida Lee began to straighten Mildred's bedcovers and smooth her pillow. "I'm right here."

"Tonight, too? I don't want to be left alone at night." Mildred looked up at her, and I realized how dependent Mildred was on Ida Lee. And also realized that Mildred may've been thinking, as I had, of what had happened to someone else who'd fallen, gotten better, then, alone in the hospital, died in the night.

Glancing at my watch, I saw that I would soon need to leave to meet Helen at Mattie's apartment. Before I could say anything, the door opened and a technician came in to draw some of Mildred's blood—a process I'd just as soon not witness.

"Let's walk out to the hall," I whispered to Ida Lee, then, standing outside Mildred's door, I asked, "Are you planning to stay?"

"Oh, yes, ma'am, I can't leave her. I'll stay until she can go home."

"Not day and night, Ida Lee. That's too much. I have to leave now to meet Mrs. Stroud, but I'll relieve you after supper tonight. That way, you can go home and get some rest."

"Oh, Mrs. Murdoch, you can't do that. I don't mind staying. I can nap in a chair."

"So can I. No, Ida Lee, you're not going to stay around the clock. She's going to need you in good health when she goes home, so you must take care of yourself. I'm going now, but I'll see you later this evening."

On my way to Mattie's apartment, I went from worrying about leaving Mildred to fretting about being late for Helen. And on top of that, I had no time for even a bite of lunch, and, as I'd forgotten my cell phone, I couldn't call Lillian. So as soon as I got inside the apartment, I used Mattie's phone to give her an update on Mildred's condition and also to tell her where I was.

"Let Sam know what happened," I told her. "He should be home anytime now. And tell him where I am, and, Lillian, please help me remember not to ever leave home again without my cell phone."

"Yessum, but you got to 'member to plug it in to keep it workin'. Won't do no good if it die on you."

"I know, and I will. Oh, I think Helen's here." I hurried to the door to let her in. "And, Lillian, you might mention to Sam that I'll be spending the night in Mildred's room tonight."

"Why I got to mention it? Seem like that be 'tween you and him."

"I want to give him time to get used to it." I opened the door, smiled in welcome to Helen, and motioned her in. "I have to go, Lillian. I'll be home before supper.

"How are you, Helen? Come in and look at this mess." I waved my hand at the jumble of furniture in Mattie's living room. "I'm so happy to have you help make sense of it all."

Helen, a small, slim woman who always looked put together from the stylish cut of her hair to the tip of her wedge-heeled shoes, looked around in astonishment. "I had no idea," she said in wonder. "Where did all this furniture come from? I don't remember it being so crowded when we visited her."

"I don't, either. But I think maybe she had some of it in the bedrooms. Why she had it all moved in here, I couldn't tell you. Anyway, I have to go through her dresser drawers and collect her jewelry, so I'll let you wander around and see what you think should be done with it.

"Oh, by the way, Helen," I went on, "we had to take Mildred to the hospital this morning." And after Helen's proper expression of dismay, I went on to tell her what I knew about Mildred's condition. Which wasn't much, but I knew I couldn't avoid reporting on our mutual friend's hospitalization.

Leaving Helen to examine the undersides of the furniture, I went to Mattie's bedroom and began opening drawers. Her jewelry drawer was crammed full of gold chains, pearl necklaces, and silver links of one kind or another. And under all of that were several small boxes whose appearance was pregnant with the promise of a sizable increase in Mattie's estate.

Maybe, I thought as I removed the drawer and sat on the bed with it, *her beneficiaries won't go begging after all.*

Chapter 18

Untangling chains from ropes of pearls and other chains, I began to separate the pieces, laying them in individual piles on the bed. I didn't see anything that made my heart flutter. They looked pretty much like the costume jewelry that Hazel Marie dearly loved, and I doubted they'd be worth the trouble of a trip to Benson's Jewelry on Main. Still, I would take everything and let them have the responsibility of determining their value.

Finally, hoping for something outstanding, I opened the first little box—more pearls, but this strand had what looked like a sapphire on the clasp. Along with the strand was a pair of pearl earrings, each with a small dangling pearl. I put them together in a ziplock bag and set it aside.

The next little box held a brooch. I lifted it out to examine it, but it didn't look any better than when it lay on cotton in the box. It was in the shape of a flower, outlined with gold filigree and studded with a few diamonds. Or maybe gold-*plated* filigree and studded with a few zircons or glass chips—who knew? Into a separate bag it went.

The next box held a ring made of silver, white gold, or platinum—better eyes than mine would have to decide which. The setting was an old-fashioned one with what I hoped was a small diamond surrounded by diamond chips. It looked very much like the engagement ring that had belonged to my mother.

As I studied it, I wondered if Mattie had inherited it or if it had been her own engagement ring, which made me wonder in turn if I'd ever seen her wear a wedding ring. And I hadn't, because, I assumed, of her swollen arthritic knuckles.

Sighing, I slipped the ring into a bag and opened the next box—another brooch. This one, I was fairly sure, was costume jewelry and hardly worth a careful examination. It was one of those that people wear during December—a Christmas tree–shaped pin with colored stones sprinkled on it. Still, I bagged it and went on.

Earrings, or rather studs, were in the next box, and I did remember Mattie wearing them some time ago. If they were real diamonds, then they would be worth something. I looked at them carefully, then smiled because one of them was missing the little piece on the back that held the earring in place.

I declare, I didn't know why earring makers couldn't come up with a better method. I'd simply stopped wearing the studs I had because they required both good eyesight and nimble fingers to put them on. And once you dropped the little back piece, you could never find it again.

A wide gold bracelet was in the last box. At least I hoped it was gold—it was an etched bangle with a few small dents in it, which indicated that it might be gold. But whether ten, fourteen, or eighteen karat, I couldn't see the markings on the underside well enough to determine.

The drawer was slowly emptying, and I'd yet to find anything that would noticeably increase Mattie's wealth. I opened a larger box and found what the French call a parure—a matching set of necklace, bracelet, brooch, and dangling earrings made up, unfortunately, of tiny jet beads. The image of a Roaring Twenties flapper came to mind, but I seriously doubted that a jet set would thrill a jet-setting millennial.

The last box held another parure of what I assumed were garnets, consisting of earrings, brooch, and ring. Pretty, but garnets, I knew, were not at the top of the value list.

Putting those in a bag, I sighed in disappointment at what I'd found—or not found. The entire contents of Mattie's jewelry drawer would be unlikely to bring much more than a couple of hundred dollars.

But, I thought with a lift of my spirits, maybe she had a safe-deposit box at her bank. If so, that's where the valuable pieces would be, if she'd had any. I wrote a note to myself to call Mr. Sitton to see if she'd had a lockbox. At least, there was still a hope—though dim at best—of increasing the amount of money I would be able to distribute.

I spent the next few minutes opening every drawer in the bedroom and running my hand under and through underclothes, bedclothes, sweaters, and so forth hoping to find more jewelry boxes. Then, remembering my own attempts at hiding special pieces, I went to the closet and took down three hard-used pocketbooks. Excepting piles of Kleenex, hairpins, a stick or two of gum, and lint, they were empty. I sighed, conceding that I'd probably found the limit of Mattie's jewelry collection.

"Julia?" Helen, holding a yellow legal pad, appeared in the doorway. "I've made a list of the pieces I've been able to reach and examine, but we're going to need some help with the larger pieces."

"Yes," I said, nodding. "I figured as much. Have you found anything interesting?"

"Maybe. I just can't get to them. But most of it seems to be fairly good reproductions. If we could hire someone to move things around at the same time we have Diane Jankowski here, we might make some headway."

"That's your appraiser?"

"Yes, and she knows her business. Do you want me to call her?"

"Yes, but wouldn't it be nice if we could get those twins in here."

Helen frowned. "What twins?"

"You know. The ones on *Antiques Roadshow*—they could walk in the door and give us an appraisal down to the penny. Of course," I went on, laughing, "we'd have to listen to a thirty-minute dissertation on Queen Anne legs, claw feet, underside patina, and ebony inlay, complete with hand and arm gestures, but they'd be entertaining."

"Julia," Helen said, smiling, "you're off on a tangent. I think Diane will suit us just fine."

"Oh, I know. I'm just a little giddy about the amount of work in front of us. But it's still early, so let's see if you and I can move a few things."

I carefully placed all the jewelry-filled ziplock bags into one of several wadded-up bags that Mattie had assiduously saved, ready to be taken to Benson's Jewelry on Main. Then Helen and I moved, with a lot of to-ing and fro-ing, a large Chippendale chair in bad need of reupholstering so that she could examine the mahogany commode behind it.

Pulling out the top drawer, Helen shook her head. "Very nice, but it's a reproduction. See, Julia, here's the maker's stamp with the year of manufacture—1930."

"It's a pretty piece, though. What do you think it's worth?"

"Maybe seven or eight hundred retail. Half of that if you sell it to a dealer. If you're lucky."

"Oh, my. Well . . ." I stopped at the sound of a knock at the door. "Who can that be?"

Opening the door, my eyes lit up with the prospect of some strong-arm help. "Mr. Wheeler, do come in. Can we help you?"

He smiled, standing there with his shirtsleeves lopped up over his elbows and sawdust sprinkling his forearms and a smattering of it in his dark, though slightly graying, hair. "No, I just stopped by to see if I could help you."

"Well, you're just in time. We'd like to move some furniture around—just a few pieces for now." Turning to Helen, I said, "Helen, this is Mr. Wheeler. He's remodeling one of the units here and has been kind enough to offer a hand. Mr. Wheeler, this is Helen Stroud, a friend of mine and Mattie's. She knows furniture better than I do."

Mr. Wheeler's gray eyes took in Helen, specifically—I thought—her carefully manicured but ringless left hand. She, in spite of having crawled around and under tables for the past hour or so, looked as cool, unruffled, and unimpressed as she always did. He nodded and shook the hand she held out. "Nate," he said. "Nate Wheeler. Happy to help."

So for the next thirty minutes we made use of a man with a strong back and muscular arms, for which I make no apologies for noticing. I myself am partial to a well-turned arm. Helen noticed, too, if I wasn't mistaken, although I doubted that she'd be really interested in a man who worked with his hands. She leaned more toward the professional and/or executive suit-and-tie type, who were rarely called upon to sweat while getting their hands dirty. Still, there was a paucity of such types in Abbotsville to choose from, and at one point, probably at her wit's end, she had almost succumbed to the dubious charms of Thurlow Jones. She'd finally come to her senses, though, and settled back into her unmarried state, seemingly with relief for having escaped an even worse existence with Thurlow.

After that fiasco, I doubted that the sawdust-covered Mr. Wheeler had much of a chance with her, although the amount of eye cutting he was doing toward her revealed his possible interest.

"Oh, look, Julia," Helen called out. "It's a handkerchief table. See how the triangles open out to make a square game table. Oh, this is lovely." She ran her hand over the green felt on the top of the table. "Surely this is worth something."

"I truly hope so," I said, standing back to admire it.

Mr. Wheeler squatted down beside the table. "Look at these casters," he said, rubbing a finger over the tiny wheels. "They've got to be the original ones—eighteenth century, I'd say. With a little careful cleaning, this brass will shine."

"Oh," Helen said, somewhat taken aback, "do you know furniture, Mr. Wheeler?"

"Nate," he said with a smile. "Not really, just enough to recognize good workmanship. I make a few pieces now and then."

Helen gave this handyman type an appraising look that seemed to indicate a shift in her thinking. Still, once burned with the likes of Thurlow Jones, twice shy with anyone else, even if he did know good furniture when he saw it.

"Perhaps," I suggested, "we'd do well to move what we've looked at to the guest room. That way we can get to the pieces in the back. Besides," I went on, "I'd love to get to that cellarette back there, if that's what it is."

So Mr. Wheeler moved the tea table and the handkerchief table to Mattie's guest room, and Helen and I pulled out the lovely little cellarette.

"Mr. Wheeler, Nate," Helen said as he came back into the room. "See what you think of this. Julia's in love with it."

Actually, I was less in love with it than fearful that it might hold a cache of Mattie's bottles. Helen wasn't a gossip, but I'd as soon not share Mattie's secret vice with anyone.

Mr. Wheeler grinned at me, then leaned over and lifted the lid—no bottles, I was relieved to see. "Uh-huh," he said, "it has the dividers and it's deep enough to hold bottles, and—look here! The key's still with it. That's amazing and probably because it's been in the same family since it was made."

Mr. Wheeler squatted beside the small table, running his hand lovingly up and down the slender legs. "Walnut," he said, "with some kind of fruitwood inlay. I'm guessing a Southern provenance, maybe Tidewater Virginia or the Carolinas. There were a lot of itinerant cabinetmakers making the rounds of the coastal plantations. They'd stay at a place for a few weeks or months, make whatever was wanted, then move on to the next place."

Helen, if I wasn't mistaken, was captivated by Mr. Wheeler's knowledge. "Do you have any idea what it might be worth?" she asked.

"Not a clue," Mr. Wheeler said, standing. "I wouldn't even venture a guess. You'll need someone better informed than I am."

"Yes," Helen said, nodding. "Julia, I'll see if Diane can meet us here tomorrow afternoon, if that works for you."

"That'll be fine. Mr. Wheeler, thank you so much for your help. At least we've made a dent in this pile of furniture and have a glimmer of hope that Mattie might have a few things of value."

Chapter 19

By then the hours had edged on toward suppertime, so I put a hold on furniture inspection for the day, although Helen said she could come again the following day and Mr. Wheeler declared himself available anytime we needed him. For myself, I had hoped to get to Benson's before it closed to drop off the contents of Mattie's jewelry drawer, but I didn't make it. So I locked the bags of jewelry in the trunk of my car, then hurried home for supper, after which I would show up at the hospital to keep Mildred company through the night.

Sam wasn't at all thrilled with the prospect of my spending the night at the hospital, noting that Mildred was certainly old enough to stay alone. "Not," he'd added, "that she won't have half a dozen nurses at her beck and call."

"I know, but what happened to Mattie in the same situation has her worried." I stopped, thought about it for a minute, then went on. "Although why she thinks I'd be of use if the Grim Reaper showed up, I don't know."

Then Lillian chimed in. "You keep on burnin' candles at both ends, you be piled up in bed your own self."

"I know, I know. But there's a nice recliner in the room, and I intend to get a good night's sleep on it."

So Sam drove me to the hospital and waited in the lobby for me to send Ida Lee down so he could drive her home. She was reluctant to leave, but I insisted, mainly because I wanted her rested and in good health to look after Mildred. I'd already decided that one night on the recliner was going to be my limit.

After Ida Lee left and the hospital quieted down for the night, Mildred and I chatted for a while. I asked if she wanted me to try to reach Horace and Tonya.

"Lord, no," she said. "I don't want either one hovering around, wringing their hands, and worrying about my estate."

"Oh, Mildred, they wouldn't do that."

"Huh," she said darkly, "you just wait. You're just starting on Mattie's estate, which probably doesn't amount to a hill of beans, and already you're having trouble. Think what mine will be like."

"Well, promise you won't make me your executor," I said, as lightly as I could manage with such a serious subject.

"Don't worry. I wouldn't do that to you. Anyway, I'll call them both when I get home, when I feel more like dealing with them."

"All right, let me know if you change your mind." Then, to change the subject, I asked her what the doctors were saying about the reason for her fall.

"They don't know," she said with a wave of her hand, then went on to tell me of the various tests she'd had during the day and moaned a few times about how hard it was to lose weight, which was what she'd been told a dozen times she needed to do.

"How many walks do you think we'll have to take for me to lose fifty pounds?" she asked at one point.

"Goodness, Mildred, I don't know. Maybe you should think about hiring a personal trainer."

"Well, not if I have to wear a leotard." We both laughed.

Finally, about eleven o'clock a nurse came in with Mildred's medication for sleep. At the same time, she found a blanket and a pillow for me, which I was glad to have. I was about on my last legs after the long, busy day I'd had and figured I'd have no trouble falling asleep and staying that way.

Turning off all the lights except a night light, I wished Mildred pleasant dreams and settled in on the recliner, which I quickly learned did not recline in exactly the same places that I did.

Nonetheless, I had just about drifted off when Mildred said, "Julia? You asleep?"

"Almost. What do you need?"

"Oh, nothing. Just wanted to be sure you were here."

"I'm not going anywhere until daylight, Mildred, so you can rest easy. Nobody's going to come in here and snatch you away."

"Well," she murmured, turning ponderously over in bed, "don't forget that Mattie got snatched away in the middle of the night."

"I'm watching out for you," I assured her, but I'm not sure she heard me. She murmured off and on as the sleep medication began to take effect, and before long, she was deep in the arms of Morpheus, although from the chest-rattling sounds of her breathing, it's a wonder he didn't dump her out. I no longer wondered why Horace was sailing on the Mediterranean.

Ida Lee was back in the room by seven the next morning, just as the breakfast trolleys began to roll down the hall, infuriating Mildred, who couldn't have anything to eat until after a few more tests. I wished her a good day and took myself off to call Sam to come get me.

"Never again, Sam," I said as I slid into the car when he pulled up in front of the hospital. "Some things are beyond the boundaries of friendship, although of course it wasn't that bad. It was just that between the recliner that wouldn't fully recline and Mildred's snoring, I feel as if I've been running all night."

"Why don't you take a nap this morning?" he said. "Lillian has made blueberry muffins for you, so get a good breakfast and then lie down."

"I may just do that."

But we'd barely walked through the kitchen door before the phone rang, letting me know that LuAnne Conover had taken the bit between her teeth and was about to run wild.

"Julia," she announced, "I'm reporting in. Almost everything is arranged. The visitation will be tomorrow night at the Good Shepherd Funeral Home, and don't tell me that's too soon because it's already in today's paper. And the service will be at the church at two o'clock Friday, with the interment immediately afterward. Now, you haven't seen fit to let me look through Mattie's clothes, and she needs something to wear for the viewing. I'm going to need to get into her closet, although I'll tell you here and now that if she doesn't have anything better to wear than what she usually wore, I'll have to go shopping."

"There's no money for shopping, LuAnne. Besides, there's no need to buy something new—nobody would recognize her. Let's just use what she ordinarily wore. I can meet you at the apartment anytime you say and you can pick out something."

"That's just not going to do," LuAnne said. "All she ever wore was black or gray, neither of which is suitable for a funeral. I mean, they are if you're *attending* a funeral, but not if you're the main attraction. She needs to wear something white—it's her funeral, after all, and I want her to look nice."

"Well, LuAnne," I said, "I'm not even sure we should have an open casket, and if we don't, it won't matter what she has on."

"No open casket? Why, why else do people come if not to see how she looks? And it all reflects on *me*, Julia. People will talk if we have a closed casket. They'll wonder what happened to her, like, maybe her face is bruised or something. We have to let people look, which reminds me that I'm going to ask Velma to go to the funeral home and fix her hair. I hope there's money enough for that."

My eyes rolled back in my head, but I took a deep breath and tried to calm her down. "LuAnne, I've just spent the night in the hospital listening to Mildred snore, and I have a blue million other things to do today. I don't have time for this. The funeral is entirely in your hands—you can do whatever you want to do, but there's no money for anything extra."

"*Well!*" she huffed. "I'll bet Mattie wishes now that she'd put somebody else in charge, because the visitation will be her last great party, and I know she'll want to look her best."

"It's up to you, LuAnne," I said, tiredly. "Just don't send the estate any bills—they won't get paid. The bequests that Mattie made have to come before anything else, and if it helps to know this, you are on her list."

There was dead silence on the line. Then, in almost a whisper, LuAnne asked, "She named me as a beneficiary?"

"Yes, along with a number of other women we know and the church as well."

"Well, why didn't you say so? We certainly do not want to deplete her resources with unneeded outlays, do we? If you can meet me at her apartment right after lunch, I'm sure I can find something in her closet that'll be entirely suitable."

After Lillian's very nice breakfast, I decided to take Sam's advice and lie down for a while. But not before calling Mr. Sitton to ask if Mattie had a safe-deposit box at one of the banks.

"Yes," he assured me, "there's a key to one at the First National. It's in one of the envelopes I gave you. You'll need to take a copy of the will so they'll let you access the box." He stopped, then said, "I hope you haven't misplaced the key. If so, we'll have to have the box drilled."

"Oh," I said, feeling backward and totally unprofessional, "I'm sure it's right where you put it. I should've looked more carefully. Frankly, I've hardly had time to go through everything."

But I immediately made time as soon as I hung up, and found the key in an envelope among several other envelopes with various papers in them. I needed to go over every page to be sure I wasn't overlooking anything else, but, I declare, I was so tired I simply couldn't face another piece of paper.

"Lillian," I said, teetering on my feet, "I've got to take a nap. If anybody calls or comes by, tell them you don't know where I am or when I'll be back."

She grinned. "That'll teach you not to spend the night with anybody 'sides Mr. Sam."

"Don't worry. I've learned my lesson. Mildred will have to watch out for the Grim Reaper by herself from now on."

Chapter 20

I crawled out of bed about lunchtime, feeling worse than when I'd gotten in it. Sleeping in the middle of the day had never been a habit of mine, and I didn't intend to start it at this late date. Still, after the night I'd had, I'd needed the rest.

"Miss Norma at the church call you," Lillian said as soon as I entered the kitchen. "She say she need to talk to you, an' for you to call her soon as you come in."

"She can wait," I said and headed for the coffeepot. "I'm in no mood to deal with her."

"Uh-huh, you get up on the wrong side of the bed, didn't you? Set down and eat something. Maybe you feel better."

"Maybe," I mumbled, but I sat at the table and tried to eat the bacon, lettuce, and tomato sandwich that Lillian put before me. Glancing at my watch to see how much time I had before meeting Helen, Helen's appraiser, and LuAnne at Mattie's apartment, I could've put my head on the table and gone back to sleep.

I finally began to feel more like facing the day, as late as the day was at that point. "Well, Lillian," I said, standing up. "Did Norma say what she wanted?"

"No'm, just it real important."

"I can't imagine, but I need to check in with Mildred first."

So I went to the library, called Mildred's room at the hospital, and was relieved to hear Ida Lee answer. She told me that Mildred was feeling much better, convinced now that her fall had been an aberration, and that she'd had her fill of tests, especially the ones that required nothing by mouth after midnight.

"She's in X-ray now," Ida Lee told me, "but she says she's going home this afternoon. She says she'll not spend another night here because she didn't sleep at all."

"Oh, for goodness' sake. *I* was the one who didn't sleep, because she snored all night long. What do her doctors say?"

"Well, you know how they are. They don't say much, but I know they've not discharged her."

"All right, but you tell her that I'm coming up there right after I go through Mrs. Freeman's closet, and she'd better still be in that bed. If I have to stay another night to keep her there, I will."

Goodness, I thought as I hung up, *what I'm willing to do to care for my friends.* I just hoped that Mildred would come to her senses before I lost mine.

Then I called Norma, gritting my teeth as I did so. The woman got under my skin worse than anybody I knew.

"It's Julia Murdoch, Norma," I said when she answered, and that's all I needed to say.

"Hold just a sec, Miss Julia," she said in her most professionally clipped manner. "Pastor Ledbetter wishes to speak with you."

Oh, Lord, what now? I held for more than a second and almost hung up. I had too much to do that afternoon to be kept on hold for somebody else's convenience.

But finally Pastor Ledbetter picked up, and at the false heartiness of his voice, I knew that trouble lay ahead. "Miss Julia! How *are* you? It's been a while since we've had a good sit-down together, and I thought this afternoon would be the perfect time for it. Why don't you walk over so we can catch up with each other?"

The only times he'd ever asked me to walk across the street to the church were when he had something he wanted from me or for me to do. This would be no exception, because the pastor wasn't in the habit of merely keeping in touch with his parishioners. He always had an agenda.

"Well, I'm sorry, Pastor," I said, "but my afternoon is completely taken up. I'm meeting a furniture appraiser at Mattie's apartment in just a few minutes, and then LuAnne's coming by to select Mattie's funeral ensemble, and I have to be there for both. After that, I'll need to go to the hospital to check on Mildred Allen. She's having a few tests done."

"Oh, yes, I intend to look in on her, too. She's an Episcopalian, but"—he stopped and chuckled—"I don't let that stop me. What about early tomorrow? I want to go over the funeral program with you."

"LuAnne is in charge of that. Maybe she can meet with you, but I assure you that whatever you and she decide will be fine."

"I'll tell you what," he said, not at all put off by my unwillingness to hop to and get across the street. "I have a fairly busy day coming up, so why don't we have a few words at the visitation tomorrow evening? I'll be there early and stay until it's over—the least I can do for such a faithful member as Miss Mattie. We're going to miss her, aren't we?"

Maybe so, I thought, *but so far I've been too busy looking after her affairs to feel any kind of loss.* Not wanting to hear a minisermon on my lack of compassion, though, I agreed to see the pastor at the funeral home the next evening, hung up, and went to Mattie's apartment, ready to once again tackle the job she'd left in my hands.

Helen and Diane Jankowski pulled into the gravel lot beside Mattie's apartment building about the same time I did. Helen introduced us as we walked to the entrance, and I must say that I approved of Ms. Jankowski right away. For one thing, she was just the right age, whatever it was—young enough to be able to bend and stoop and get around easily and old enough to know her business. And for another thing, she had come dressed ready to work, from which I assumed that Helen had told her not to expect a neatly arranged assortment of furniture.

She was wearing khaki pants that were full and loose for ease of movement and a pink polo shirt that matched her pink tennis shoes. She was carrying a large Lily Pulitzer tote bag—which I identified by the pink and green paisley design—filled with note-books and reference books.

Not only was she ready to work, she was quite professional in her greeting and in her immediate attention to business matters.

"Before we begin, Mrs. Murdoch," she said as we approached Mattie's door, "let me just say that I can charge by the hour if you just want a walk-through to get a general idea of value. But if you want a thorough inspection and evaluation of certain pieces, along with help putting them up for auction or contacting deal-ers, then I get ten percent of whatever the furniture brings. Is that agreeable with you?"

In any other situation, I might have thought her abrupt and too interested in what was in it for her. But at the moment, I was relieved to place the furniture problem in her capable hands, and even more pleased to know what she expected to get from it. To me, that indicated that she knew her own worth. She wasn't let-ting me go blindly into something that would turn around and bite me, or rather, bite Mattie's estate.

"Perfectly agreeable, and while we're on the subject, Helen, why don't we say that you will get five percent of whatever it brings?"

"Oh, Julia," Helen said, "that may be too much."

"I doubt it," I said, inserting and turning the key in Mattie's door. "For all we know, the furniture is worth next to nothing. I may end up paying somebody to haul it away. Here we go." I pushed the door open and motioned them in. "Diane, give it a quick glance and see if any of it is worth a closer inspection. There are some pieces in the bedrooms, too."

"Oh, my," Diane said, her eyes lighting up. "I see why you needed help. I can tell you right now that if that's a butler's desk in the corner, you need to think of contacting an auction house, maybe one in Atlanta. And look at the carving on that sofa! It's early Victorian and will bring a pretty penny if we can get it to New Orleans. Oh, my," she went on as she upturned a large or-nate vase to see the marking, "French porcelain of the Aesthetic movement, I believe. Very nice."

Helen said, "Wait till you see the handkerchief table and the cellarette." Then, turning to me, she went on, "Oh, Julia, this is exciting. Who knew that Mattie had such treasures?"

"Well, hold on," Diane said, smiling as she pulled out a notebook. "I'm not promising anything yet, but it's certainly worth a closer look."

Feeling considerably lighter of heart at Diane's reaction to her first glimpse of the furniture, I said, "I'll have to leave it to the two of you. I thought I'd go ahead and empty Mattie's closets. LuAnne is coming by in a few minutes to select something to take to the funeral home. When she's done, I'll take everything else to Goodwill, and that will be one more job completed. Call me if you need help, or, Helen, you might want to see if Mr. Wheeler is around."

Helen gave me a quick glance, then looked away. I didn't know what that signified, if anything, but I figured she could call on him or not, whatever she was inclined to do.

I walked back to Mattie's bedroom, opened the closet door, clasped an armful of hanging clothes, and laid them on the bed. Then I took out several shoe boxes, opened them, and sighed. Mattie had had trouble with her feet, her knees, or her hips, or maybe all three, for so long that I doubted she had bought a new pair of shoes in years. Each pair I examined had run-over heels, scuff marks, and Dr. Scholl's gel inserts.

Well, I thought, *even if LuAnne insists on an open casket, at least her shoes won't show.* We could just let her wear the rubber-soled moccasins that she usually wore.

I could occasionally hear Helen and Diane talking to each other, but I was too intent on emptying dresser drawers to pay much attention. It wasn't until the doorbell rang and LuAnne bounced in full of the importance of dressing the dead that I started toward the living room.

By the time I got there, she and Diane had recalled an earlier meeting at a book fair, and Helen had walked down the hall to call in Mr. Wheeler.

"I'm all ready for you, LuAnne," I said. "Just a few more drawers to empty and everything will be out for you to look through." Turning to Diane, I asked, "How's it going? Have you found anything interesting?"

"Oh, yes, several things. I'm making a list and tagging each piece that should go to auction. I'm also making an estimate of what I think each one might bring. But please don't hold me to it, because you never know how an auction will go. It all depends on who's there and what they're looking for."

"So you think we should auction it, rather than selling to a dealer?"

"At this point, maybe both," Diane said, smiling. "I'm making two lists."

I smiled back at her. "Good. I need all the help I can get. LuAnne, let's decide what Mattie's going to wear."

Just then, Helen and Mr. Wheeler came in, so he had to be introduced to LuAnne, and of course she had to stand around and ask him a dozen questions—how long he'd lived in Abbotsville (not long), where he was buying new appliances (Lowe's), what church he attended (none at the moment), which brought on an invitation to the First Presbyterian. LuAnne took every opportunity she had to learn whatever she could.

Finally, as she and I walked down the hall to the bedroom, she whispered, "*Where* did that good-looking man come from?"

"I have no idea," I said, too anxious to get done what had to be done so I could go to the next thing. "Now, LuAnne, everything Mattie has is here on the bed. See what you think might do, while I check the closet in the guest room."

She wrinkled her nose at the pile of what could possibly be called vintage dresses if you wanted to be kind. Actually, they were merely old and well worn, and each one looked pretty much like all the others. LuAnne began snatching them up, one after the other, holding each one out to study it, then throwing it back on the bed.

"By the way," LuAnne said, stopping me on my way out of the

room, "I have five pallbearers lined up—Leonard, Sam, Mattie's lawyer, Dr. Hargrove, and Jim Armstrong, but I need one more. You have any ideas?"

"Why don't you ask one of the elders."

"*Because,* Julia, they're all so decrepit, they'd have a heart attack halfway down the aisle."

"In that case," I responded, "ask a deacon. They're generally younger. Besides, I don't think they actually carry a casket. They bring it in on wheels now."

"Oh. Well, I'll ask Thurlow Jones then, even though lightning might strike him if he enters a church."

I laughed and went to the guest room for an armload of clothes and almost gave up. They were crammed in so tightly that I could barely lift even a few of the hangers off the rod. I wondered if Mattie had ever thrown anything out. Unhappily, none of them would offer more choices for LuAnne. Mattie had kept her winter things separately, and I doubted that any of the guest room woolens would be suitable for a June funeral. I decided to leave them for another day and returned to see how LuAnne was doing.

"Julia," LuAnne said as she plopped on the bed next to the pile of clothes, "I could just cry. I didn't know that Mattie was so hard up, but there's not a decent thing here. What are we going to do?"

"We're going to find something," I said firmly. "Look, LuAnne, she'll only be seen from the waist up, so we don't have to worry about a skirt, whether it's too long or the hem is out or there's a stain on it. Just think from the waist up."

"Well, we can't do that," LuAnne said, somewhat accusingly. "You don't understand that the funeral home told me to bring everything. And I mean dress, slip, panties, and bra, along with shoes and stockings—*everything* that she ordinarily wore."

"Really?" Wondering what possible use all of that would be to Mattie, I stared at LuAnne. "Why?"

"Well, I'm sure *I* don't know," LuAnne said, getting a little testy. "But how would you like to be on public display with no underclothes on?"

"I guess I wouldn't like it," I conceded, then pointed to a pile of underclothes. "Start there, then. I saw what looked like a fairly new Spanx girdle under those brassieres. She probably saved it for special occasions, but I think her funeral qualifies, don't you?"

"Oh, yes, I do. You know, Julia, a lot of times you can sound so hard-hearted, but underneath I know you're just as thoughtful and tender-hearted as I am."

"Thank you, LuAnne, that's very sweet." But my eyes rolled just a little.

"And, anyway," she went on, "after thinking about it, I'm sure that it would be better to have a closed casket for the church service. Otherwise, we'd have a constant stream of people going up and down the aisles to look, and then trying to find a pew. I'd rather they come in and sit down, so we can start and finish on time. Besides," she said with a sideways glance at me, "I've ordered the Cherished Memories full casket cover of pink roses, and we wouldn't want to be taking that on and off. Just think what a beautiful focal point it will make throughout the service. That's all right with you, isn't it? I mean, I ordered it from you and me since we're sorta in charge."

"Oh, how thoughtful. I'm glad you did, because I didn't even think of flowers. Let me know what I owe you."

"Half of five twenty-nine," LuAnne murmured as she busied herself with Mattie's dresses.

My eyebrows went straight up. "Half of five hundred twenty-nine *dollars*? My word, LuAnne, maybe an open casket wouldn't have been so bad. It would've certainly been cheaper."

Chapter 21

On my way to the kitchen for more plastic bags for Mattie's underclothes, sweaters, and so forth, I spoke to Mr. Wheeler, who was busy pushing aside furniture so Diane could get to the highboy against the back wall of the room.

"Oh, phoo," Diane said as she slid behind the sofa to study the large piece up close. "I was afraid of this. It's new. Well, not *new*," she corrected herself, "but certainly not old. I thought it might be tiger maple, which would be a find, but the grain has been painted on."

That was a disappointment, but I left them to it and met Lu-Anne at the hall doorway with a scowl on her face and a dress over her arm.

"I want another opinion," she said, holding up a navy blue dress. "Look, everybody, what do you think of this for Mattie? I'll tell you right now, it's the best of the lot and if you don't like it, I don't know what I'll do. Julia won't let me buy her anything."

"LuAnne!" I said, just so put out that she was blaming me for the state of Mattie's wardrobe. "It's not my money to throw around. And I think that dress is perfectly fine."

Helen said, "I think Mattie wore it at the last book club meeting at my house. She looked very nice in it."

I nodded my thanks to Helen, while Diane, who hadn't ever seen Mattie in anything, agreed that the navy blue frock was suitable attire for a viewing. Mr. Wheeler just smiled and offered no opinion.

"Some pearls would look nice with it," Helen said, which gave LuAnne another opportunity to disparage me.

"Well," she said, "Julia's already packed up all of Mattie's jewelry and gotten rid of it."

"No, LuAnne, no," I said tiredly. "It's locked in the trunk of my car, waiting to be taken to Benson's. We can walk out together and you can look through it. There're several strands of pearls to choose from."

"Well, okay," she said, "but you better not let them get buried with her."

"They won't. The funeral home people will give them to you when the visitation is over. You can get them back to me so they can be appraised."

"Well, what about the service on Friday?" LuAnne demanded. "Don't you want her to look nice at church?"

"LuAnne, please. I thought you'd agreed not to have an open casket at the church. In fact, I'd as soon not have the casket there at all."

"I've never heard of anybody being absent for their own funeral," LuAnne said. "I think Pastor Ledbetter is expecting her to be there."

"Fine," I said. "Whatever you two decide will be fine. Now let's go find some pearls so we can get her dressed."

The rest of the afternoon was mostly taken up with getting Mattie's wardrobe off the bed and out to the Goodwill store on the boulevard. By the time I straightened the clothes that LuAnne had picked through—leaving a jumble on the bed—I decided to leave the winter clothes in the guest room for another time. What I had was enough to fill the backseat and the trunk of my car, anyway.

Mr. Wheeler had been kind enough to help me load up the car, although I had been careful to gather up Mattie's underclothes myself. I didn't want to embarrass the man by saddling him with her huge pink brassieres.

After getting a tax form from Goodwill, which from the state of Mattie's clothing I didn't think was worth filling out, I found a parking spot in front of Benson's. Running in with a sack full of jewelry, I told the appraiser, "Just do the best you can. It's vintage, if that helps."

Then I went to the First National Bank to open Mattie's safe-deposit box.

Upon presentation of my papers of authority, I was ushered to a small cubicle and left alone with her lockbox. Hoping against hope for some wonderful source of funds, I found several things of interest, but none of value. There was a birth certificate for Mattie Iona Cobb, born in 1931 in Versailles, Kentucky, as well as a few outdated and canceled documents—old stock certificates and the like—made out to Mattie Cobb Freeman and one Thomas Edgar Freeman. And right at the bottom, I found a death certificate along with a wrinkled photograph wrapped in tissue paper. It showed a piercingly young man in an army uniform with the name *Tommy* written in pencil on the back. Glancing at the date of death on the certificate, I saw that Mattie had been a widow much longer than she'd been a wife.

Sighing, I looked through everything again to be sure that I'd not overlooked anything. And a good thing I did, because there was a small ziplock bag stuck in the folds of a canceled deed. In it was half of a torn index card with a string of indecipherable—at least, by me—letters and numbers written in ink by a shaky hand. Under my breath, I read what I could make out

$$l7Rl0l2^3Rl0$$

"El seven—the European way, or maybe seventeen—RIO, el two, superscript three, and RIO again."

Vaguely wondering why Mattie had not only saved, but also locked away, a meaningless scribble, I put it back in its ziplock bag and stuck it in my purse. Perhaps, I thought, it had been Tommy's army identification number when his body had been shipped home. That which seems of no account to one person could be precious to someone else.

I carefully stacked everything together to eventually take to Mr. Sitton. Then I told the teller that Mrs. Freeman no longer needed her lockbox and asked about a refund on the rental.

Tired and hungry by that time, I had to swing back by the apartment to lock up behind Helen and Diane, both of whom said they'd be back the following afternoon. Afternoons were the only times that either of them could give to Mattie's furniture—both had part-time jobs that took up the mornings. I didn't like it, but had to take what I could get.

Diane had made a cursory examination of the contents of the living room, but she still needed to examine the Charleston rice bed and the highboy in the bedroom, which had a tantalizingly eighteenth-century-looking patina, as well as the Oriental rugs throughout the apartment. Then there were several old portraits on the walls, which she said would have to be looked at by an art expert. "But," she'd said with a wry smile, "I don't have much hope for them unless somebody at auction is looking for ancestors—*any*body's ancestors."

I didn't have much hope along those lines, either, for all I'd seen had been faded photographic portraits of fierce, bearded men and thin-lipped women with high collars.

Hurrying home to have dinner with Sam, I knew I'd have to listen to Lillian tell me that everything didn't have to be done in one week. But I wanted it *done,* and done as quickly as possible. Mattie's estate had already taken over my life and I was tired of it.

Nonetheless, Lillian started in as soon as I came through the door. "You gonna make yourself sick, runnin' 'round tryin' to do it all at one time. What's the hurry? Miss Mattie don't care when it get done."

"I know, Lillian, but there's not enough money for me to fiddle around paying unnecessary rent on her apartment."

"Huh," Lillian said, almost, but not quite, under her breath. "You don't have to tell me 'bout payin' no rent. Pore ole Reverend

Abernathy don't know what to do, 'cept ev'rybody in the church tellin' him what he *ought* to do."

"Oh, yes," I said, taking my place at the table and smiling at Sam. "You started tellin' me about that. What's going on with the reverend and who was it? Mr. Mobley?"

"Mr. Robert Mobley, yes, ma'am. That's who got it started, all right. But I got to get this gravy stirred 'fore it's too lumpy to eat."

So as we ate, Sam and I chatted about our day, catching up with each other. Sam confirmed that he'd agreed to serve as a pallbearer, and I gave him a blow-by-blow account of LuAnne's search for the proper funeral attire, along with an update of Diane's discoveries.

"She thinks it's worth having somebody from a big auction house in Atlanta come up and get it all. She says even the reproductions will have a better chance there than trying to contact individual dealers around here."

"That sounds encouraging," Sam said. "With all the furniture gone, you can have the apartment cleaned, then give up the lease. That'll be a huge step forward for you."

"Well, I was a little concerned about letting a stranger from Atlanta just come in and carry everything off. Who knows how honest he'd be when things were auctioned? But Diane is taking pictures of each piece, and she's going to be there when the lot comes up for auction. So that's one big worry off my mind. I think Helen might go with her.

"Oh, Sam," I said, leaning my head on my hand—an elbow on the table was fine under the circumstances. "I hope I'm doing things right, but it seems just one thing after another."

"You are, honey. Nobody could do it better. But Lillian is right. You don't need to push yourself."

"I know, but if I can get through the visitation and the funeral, and get Mildred home and started on a fitness routine, I'll rest easier."

We both turned from the table as the telephone rang. "Suppertime," I said wearily. "Who calls at suppertime except fund-raisers or bad news?"

I wished it had been a fund-raiser. When Lillian answered the phone and told the caller that I was having dinner, she listened for a minute, then said, "Yes, sir, I b'lieve she can."

Frowning, she handed the phone to me. "When a lawyer call, it worth interruptin' your supper."

"Mrs. Murdoch," Mr. Ernest Sitton said when I answered, "I have unexpected news, and I recommend that we both tread carefully until I've had the opportunity to look further into it."

What in the world? I looked worriedly at Sam while responding carefully to Mr. Sitton. "It doesn't sound exactly like good news, Mr. Sitton. What is it?"

"An apparent distant relative of Mattie Freeman came to my office late this afternoon. Seemed personable enough, but of course we need to confirm his relation to her, if indeed there is any."

I glanced at Sam, wishing he could hear what I was hearing, which I thought was more than a tinge of caution in Mr. Sitton's words.

"Did he say what he wanted?" I asked, as if I couldn't guess.

"Well, that's the thing," Mr. Sitton said. "He immediately announced that he'd never known Mrs. Freeman, and he doubted that she knew he even existed. Referring, it seemed, now and then to some huge family breakup. But he'd heard of her through family stories and had always planned to visit and get to know her. He seemed to truly regret his late arrival. But he said he's been on the road, traveling and living from hand to mouth for a long time. He assured me that he had no intention of contesting, or even questioning, any estate plan she'd made. He said, 'I don't expect anything and I don't want anything.' Then he went on to tell me what he did want."

"Oh, me," I said, foreseeing lawsuits and disappointments and wranglings over reproductions and paste jewelry and the minimal amounts of money in Mattie's accounts. "What was it?"

"Family memorabilia. He wants to look through Ms. Freeman's apartment for scrapbooks, letters, and pictures because he has plans to write a family history. And, interestingly enough, he also asked for a sample of Ms. Freeman's needlework as a memento. He said that he grew up hearing about the expertise of Cobb women in handiwork of one kind or another—a family tradition, so to speak, with *Aunt Mattie,* according to family lore, being the most artistic and proficient. Anyway, I put him off until I could speak with you. What do you think?"

"Lord, Mr. Sitton, I don't know." I looked at Sam again, longing to talk with him. "Well, I do know, too. I say we don't let him have access to anything until you confirm that he is who he says he is. And, as far as Mattie's skill in needlework, be it embroidery or needlepoint or cross-stitch, is concerned, I have never seen her with so much as a thimble on a finger. Nor have I seen even a sewing basket in her apartment. But, then," I said, pausing to consider, "her eyesight hasn't been good for years. Maybe she had to give it up."

Then, suddenly making a startling, though delayed, connection, I said, "Wait! Did you say the man's name is Cobb? Mr. Sitton, that was Mattie's maiden name."

Sam's eyebrows went straight up.

Mr. Sitton said, "Yes, I'm aware of that. Nonetheless, red flags went up when he asked if he could stay in his great-aunt's house—that's what he called her, his great-aunt. I had to explain that she'd lived in a rented apartment and had never owned a house. Didn't want to tantalize him, don't you know."

"Oh, you're right. He can't stay in her apartment. We'll be moving the furniture out in the next week or so. Besides, we haven't gone through everything yet, and I don't want a strange man scrounging around in there before we do."

"Absolutely. He has a place to stay, anyway. He's living in what he called an Airstream Sport trailer, by which I know to mean an aluminum two-wheeled trailer hitched to the back of his car. He apparently has it unhooked now and parked out at Walmart.

"So my feeling is that if it's been good enough for him so far, he can continue to stay in it. I just wanted to warn you that he might show up at the apartment while you're there. And, Mrs. Murdoch, to warn you that he can be quite engaging, and we must also keep in mind that he might indeed be who he says he is."

When we finally hung up, I turned to Sam and said, "Well, wouldn't you know it? An even bigger problem has just reared its ugly head."

Chapter 22

"You mean," Lillian said, enrapt with what I'd just recounted of Mr. Sitton's phone call, "somebody jus' pop up outta the blue an' say he kinfolk an' say he want to stay in Miss Mattie's apartment so he can look around all he want to? But he don't want nothin'? I don't think I b'lieve that."

"Me, either, Lillian," I agreed. "What do you think, Sam?"

"I'm wondering," he said in a musing way, "if Mattie had something of value that nobody knows about. Something whose value wouldn't be immediately recognized and could be easily hidden. Why else would he want to move in unless he wants to look around when nobody else is there?"

"But what in the world could it be? He told Mr. Sitton that he only wants to look through her letters, scrapbooks, and family pictures." I stopped and studied the possibilities. "Maybe Mattie has a letter from somebody important whose signature would be valuable. Or maybe there's a picture that shows somebody in a compromising situation. Or maybe there're some old deeds that have suddenly become valuable. Or maybe—well, I can't think of anything else."

"Anything's possible," Sam said. Then, somewhat wryly, he went on. "I certainly understand what it takes to research a non-fiction book, though, and if he's really writing a family history he's doing exactly what it takes."

"Well, I'll tell you one thing—he's not staying in Mattie's

apartment. The idea! Wanting to move in and have the freedom to rummage through her things so I'd never know what he found or what he took away. And I'm the one who's responsible for what happens to everything that Mattie owned. Right, Sam?"

"Absolutely. You're within your rights to refuse him any access at all. Now, if Sitton confirms the man's relationship to her, that might be a different matter. You could allow him access, but under your supervision. But even with that, he couldn't take anything without your permission."

"Well, Lord," I said, wiping my face with my hand. "How can I determine the value of an old letter or of a picture of people I've never seen? Or," I said, jumping up from the table to get the ziplock bag, "a scrap of paper? Look at this, Sam, as an example of what I have to put up with."

Sam put on his glasses, studied the string of letters and numbers, and said, "Hm-m, looks like seventeen, RIO—or KIO— twelve to the third power, and RIO again. What do you think it is?"

"I was hoping you could tell me, but you certainly see it differently than I do. I found it in Mattie's safe-deposit box at the bank, so it must've meant something to her."

Lillian said, "It sound Mexican to me. You know, like Rio Grande or something."

"I don't know, Lillian," I said. "It could be anything, but how can I know if it's something valuable?"

"You can't," Sam said soothingly. "But there are people who can. Ask your appraiser. Maybe all of Mattie's papers and scrapbooks should go to the auction house—they'll have historians and other experts who can determine the value of anything. But," Sam went on, "back to this man who's shown up. If he decides to contest the will, then you have a problem. Or rather, Sitton does."

"Well, if that happens, I hope to goodness Mr. Sitton is up to the job."

"Don't worry," Sam said with a reassuring smile. "He is."

Lillian, who was leaning on the counter listening to us, asked, "What that man's name so I know him if he come here?"

Shocked at my lapse in the gathering of all necessary information, I stared at her. "Well, Cobb was all he told me. And that was Mattie's maiden name, which doesn't bode well. But I didn't get the full name. What in the world was I thinking?"

"You'll learn it sooner or later," Sam said, motioning me back down as I started to go to the phone. "I expect Sitton is already working the phones, finding out who the man is. All you have to do is refuse admittance to the apartment to anybody who comes by."

"Yes," I agreed, "and I hope I have the only key. I just hope that Mattie didn't spread any around. But, Sam, the owner or manager or somebody at the building would have a master key, wouldn't they? What if this man goes around me and gets in that way?"

"First thing in the morning," Sam said, "call a locksmith and change the lock. Get at least two keys—one for you and one for Sitton. Then you'll know who gets in and who doesn't. Of course that means you'll have to be there to let *any*body in."

"I'm calling one now. That way, he can meet me as early as possible." I quickly found a locksmith in the Yellow Pages and, after a small discussion about rearranging his schedule, he agreed to meet me at seven the following morning.

"Well, that's done," I said. "Now the next thing is to call on Mildred in the hospital. I know she's still there because her house is dark."

Sam wasn't too happy about my making a hospital visit that late in the day, and Lillian kept murmuring about candles burning down to stubs. I promised that I had no intention of spending another night on a recliner, but I felt I had to at least visit Mildred. There she was, lying up there in a hospital bed, all alone except for Ida Lee, with no family within half a world away. A quick visit was the least I could do. Besides, one did not abandon one's friends in their time of need, regardless of the million other things one had to do.

When I arrived in Mildred's room, I found her in bed, as I expected, but the bed had been raised to a semisitting position. Ida Lee had been busy, for Mildred was wearing makeup and her hair was beautifully arranged, except for the flat area at the back of her head.

Ida Lee jumped up from the recliner as I entered, but I insisted that she stay where she was. "I'm here for just a minute. Mildred, you look wonderful. How're you feeling?"

"Terrible. I've been poked and prodded and looked into by every kind of machine you can imagine. But I'm going home in the morning, I don't care what they say. Julia, you won't believe what they want me to do."

"What?" I asked, holding her hand as I stood beside the bed. I had read that grown people take on childish ways and attitudes when they're sick, and I thought I was seeing that in Mildred. I do believe she was sulking.

"They say I have to lose weight, and I've tried. You know I've tried."

I knew no such thing. What I did know was that she'd *talked* about losing weight, but I'd seen no evidence of her actually doing it. Still, I nodded in agreement.

"You can do it, Mildred," I said. "Ida Lee and I will help you. What about trying Weight Watchers? Marie Osmond swears by it."

"I think she's with Nutrisystem," Ida Lee said, smiling. "But either one could help."

"Oh, for goodness' sake," Mildred said. "Anybody could lose fifty pounds if they ate cardboard every day. I have to lose more than that, and I can't live on prepackaged microwaved meals that pretend to be what they're not." Mildred shuddered.

Ida Lee moved up to the other side of the bed. "Oh, Ms. Allen, it won't be that bad. And you can do it, I know you can. And if it proves too hard, remember that they gave you another option."

"That's right, and I'm ready to do it. I think." Mildred clutched my hand. "Julia, would you let them staple your stomach?"

"Ah, well," I said, stammering because I knew I wouldn't let a staple gun anywhere near my stomach. "I guess if it was a matter of life and death, I would."

"Why, that's exactly what they said!" Mildred cried. "Life or death, they told me. One way or another, I have to lose weight. So that's why I'm going home—to make a decision. I mean, who could make a decision in this place where they never leave you alone? Julia, somebody's in here every few minutes. I don't have a minute to myself."

"I think you're wise to give it serious consideration," I said in as soothing a tone as I could manage. "And that's best done in the comfort and quiet of your own home."

We talked about the proposed surgery for a few more minutes until Mildred got teary-eyed at the prospect. So I changed the subject and told her about the sudden appearance of an apparent relative—and possible heir—of Mattie's.

"You don't mean it!" Mildred exclaimed, quickly diverted from her own concerns by such an event. "Julia, you better be on guard, and I know what I'm talking about. I don't care if he is kin to her, you have to do what she wanted. You can't let some Johnny-come-lately just walk in and take over."

"I have no intention of doing that," I assured her. "And neither does Mr. Ernest Sitton, and Sam says he's a good man to have on your side." I patted Mildred's hand, preparing to leave. "I'm having the lock changed first thing in the morning, so, Ida Lee, I'm sorry, but I can't stay the night. I still have a number of things to do tonight. Mildred, I declare, this executing a will is not what it's cracked up to be. I hardly know if I'm coming or going."

"That's why my will is tighter than Dick's hatband," Mildred said, somewhat complacently. "I've made provisions for every possible contingency. But, I'll tell you this, I have no intention of dying anytime soon. So," she said, looking from me to Ida Lee, "maybe I've made my decision about that stapling operation."

"That's good, real good," Ida Lee said. "But let's get you home first. You might want to try losing some weight on your own for a few weeks, and keep the operation on hold till you see how you do."

"That's excellent advice, Mildred," I said. "Save the operation for a last-ditch effort." I stopped and reconsidered. "Well, I wouldn't exactly call it last-ditch—a lot of people have it done and get along fine. But you don't want to jump into anything that drastic until you're sure about it. Well," I added, looking at my watch, "I must run. Mildred, I don't know if you'll feel like going, but Mattie's visitation is at six o'clock tomorrow evening. You can go with Sam and me if you'd like."

"We'll see," she said. "I may have to save myself for the funeral. Besides, they gave me a pile of information about the operation, and I want to study it. But come by tomorrow, Julia—anytime. I want to know more about that strange man."

After a few more good-byes, I left and hurried toward the elevators. *So much to do and so little time.* Then, *Staples? Like I put in a stack of papers and can never remove without ripping the pages?*

Such thoughts were running through my mind as I got on the elevator. As it began to descend, I crossed my arms over my stomach.

Chapter 23

By seven-thirty the next morning, Mattie's apartment had a new lock, and I felt as safe and secure as her belongings now were. I had tossed and turned half the night, worried about that so called relative sneaking his way in somehow. A picture of him frantically searching through Mattie's things in the dark of the night kept running through my dreams.

After paying the locksmith and making a note of my expenditures, I carefully labeled four keys—one went into my purse, one would go to Mr. Sitton, another to Helen, and the last one to Diane. Then I drove to Delmont to Mr. Sitton's office. His receptionist, or rather gatekeeper, did not want me to see him.

"You can leave the key with me," she said. "I'll see that he gets it. He can't be disturbed now."

"No," I said. "This key is going into his hand only, and I will sit here and stare at you until I can give it to him. Please tell him I'm here."

It took her a few minutes, but finally she let him know I was there. I think being stared at made her nervous.

Mr. Sitton came immediately to the door and invited me in. He seemed both surprised and pleased by my taking the initiative to change the lock. But I had only one thing on my mind.

"Have you found out anything?" I asked. "And what is the man's full name, so I'll know him when he shows up?"

"A little, to the first question, but I'm still on it." Mr. Sitton motioned me to a chair in front of his desk, which I took—but only the edge of it. "And to your other question, his name is Andrew—not Andy—Cobb."

"And we just take his word for it?"

"Hardly." Mr. Sitton leaned back in his chair and gave the ceiling a thin smile. "I explained to him that as Mrs. Freeman's attorney of record and as an officer of the court, I would have to verify his identity. And that until that was done to my satisfaction, he would not be permitted access to the Freeman property."

"Very good, Mr. Sitton. And how did he take that?"

"He seemed taken aback at first, but quickly became quite agreeable. Said he not only understood, he expected to be able to prove his identity. Then he handed over his driver's license to be copied and apologized for having no other form of identification. That's when he told me he'd been a traveling man for most of his life—working here and there, then moving on. Apparently he has no permanent home, no living family, no passport, no credit cards, nothing but his driver's license. Curiously, though," Mr. Sitton went on, looking at me over his glasses, "it was either a new issue or it was just renewed. The date on it was three months ago."

"Oh, my goodness, that sounds suspicious to me."

"Well, the license was issued in Kentucky, and it listed a post office box number in Versailles as his address—that's pronounced *Ver-sales* in Kentucky. He was born there, according to him, so he keeps it as a legal address."

"According to Mattie's birth certificate, that was her birthplace, too," I said. "I guess that makes another connection."

"His license is only a start, but I can search vital statistics and other forms of identity with that information."

I studied on what he might or might not find, then said, "Depending on what you find or don't find, it could come down to whether we believe him or not. So, what did you think, Mr. Sitton? Is he telling the truth?"

"Hard to say. He seemed straightforward enough, said right up front that he'd never met *Great-Aunt* Mattie and had no interest in claiming anything that belonged to her." Mr. Sitton tapped his pen against the desk, then said, "However, we shall see."

"Then let me get this straight. As long as he makes no legal claim or contests the will in any way, I should ignore him and go ahead and follow Mattie's wishes?"

"That is correct. Now, as far as letting him look through her papers and things, we will put him off until you've had time to go through them. You shouldn't release anything to him, not even an old postcard, until you're sure it has no value. It's incumbent on you to evaluate everything that belonged to Mrs. Freeman, turn it into cash, and distribute it exactly as she set out in her will. And keep doing that until further notice."

"Good," I said, nodding my head. "I just wanted to be sure, but I'll tell you, Mr. Sitton, I wish this Andrew Cobb had never shown up. And I think it's bordering on unbelievable that he doesn't want anything. It seems to me that this is a most convenient time for him to appear—right after Mattie's passing, when she can't identify him, and right before her estate is settled, when we can't."

"So it seems to me, too, Mrs. Murdoch, thus we must be vigilant. I will let you know if I turn up any more information."

I thanked him then and turned to go. Mr. Sitton stood up and walked around his desk.

"One interesting and perhaps disturbing detail. His driver's license gives his name as Andrew *F.* Cobb, which, along with some vague references he made to problems in the family, made me take notice."

I was so intent on leaving that I got to the door before it sank in. I stopped and turned back. "Oh, my goodness. Could it be Andrew *Freeman* Cobb?"

"He smiled when I asked him and said that his mother had told him it could be anything he wanted—Franklin, for his father, or Frederick, for an uncle. or Freeman, for the convict in the family. Then he said he hadn't decided yet."

"My word!" I said, scandalized at the thought of a convict in Mattie's family, but shocked to the core at the possibility that Andrew F. Cobb was kin to both sides of her family. It was no wonder that she'd taken to drink. I opened the door and stepped out. "Keep me posted, Mr. Sitton, I've heard all I can take at one sitting."

While driving to Mattie's apartment, I turned over in my mind all—or rather, the little—that Mr. Sitton had learned about our visitor who had turned up with such an unerring sense of timing.

My stomach rumbled as I reached Abbotsville, reminding me that it was time for lunch. It also reminded me of Mildred's possible appointment with a staple gun, but I quickly put that thought aside, thinking instead of Etta Mae's penchant for Mc-Donald's hamburgers. A glance at the clock on the dashboard made me drive right on past the golden arches. Helen and Diane would soon be at Mattie's apartment, but, with the new lock, unable to get inside.

Briefly wondering about the wisdom of distributing keys, I put that aside as well. If Helen and Diane were unworthy of trust, then everyone was, and it was a settled fact that I could not personally guard admission against unauthorized visitors to the apartment at all times, day and night. I had to trust someone.

The two women were, in fact, waiting for me by Mattie's door when I rushed into the hall, apologizing as I approached them.

"I've had the locks changed," I said as I unlocked the door. "And I have keys for you both, but I must warn you about an un-expected development." I went on to tell them about Andrew Cobb and the possibility that he might come by. "So whatever you do," I said, "do not let him in. Mr. Sitton is not sure that he really is kin to Mattie, and until we know who he is, he is not to have access—not even just to look around."

"Oh, my goodness," Diane said, patting her bosom. "You think he'll cause trouble?"

"I don't know what to think. All I know is that the sooner we clear this apartment, the less we'll have to worry about."

"I'm going to need a few more afternoons here," Diane said, giving the door a worried glance. "I've brought my camera to take pictures of each piece of furniture, and that'll take some time. I'll give you a set, I'll keep one, and one will go to the auction house."

"Excellent," I said, thinking how fortunate I'd been to have engaged such a meticulous appraiser. "That way there'll be no question about what belonged to Mattie when it goes to Atlanta."

Helen, who had been looking more and more troubled, said, "What if somebody comes to the door when you aren't here? Do we answer it or what? It could be Nate. I mean, Mr. Wheeler."

"Maybe you should walk down the hall while I'm still here with Diane. Tell him what's going on and tell him he has to give the password before you'll let him in."

Helen, who wasn't the most lighthearted of women, frowned. "I didn't know we had a password. What is it?"

"I'm just teasing," I said with a smile. "But you could make up one and tell it only to him. If you want to."

"Oh," she said, her face clearing. "That would work, wouldn't it? That way, we could let him in, but nobody else."

"That's right," I agreed, but with a lift of my eyebrows. "Anyway, I'm going to empty Mattie's desk while I'm here. I'll take everything home with me so I can go through it—something I should've done before this. No telling what's in it, but whatever it is, I want to see it before Andrew Cobb does." I went to Mattie's kitchen and gathered more of the plastic grocery bags to fill with whatever I found in her desk.

On my way back I stopped, rummaged in my purse, and handed a new key to Diane and one to Helen. "Guard those keys with your lives. Be sure to lock the door if you leave before I get back, and call me if anyone comes by." I had my cell phone with me, because now I didn't leave home without it.

"We won't be leaving anytime soon," Diane said. "In fact, it's going to take longer than I thought to get all the pictures made.

We haven't even looked in the sunroom yet, though from what I can see around that chest-on-chest in front of the French doors, it's mostly wicker furniture.

"So, Helen," Diane went on with a smile, "think of a good password because we're going to need Mr. Wheeler to help move some of this stuff around."

As I turned to go back to Mattie's desk, Diane opened a drawer in the lovely Federal sideboard. "Oh, my," she said. "Look at this silver." She began clattering through the pieces stacked in the divided drawer. "Strasbourg by Gorham. There must be, yes, twelve place settings. *Complete* place settings, too, with iced tea spoons, butter knives, salad forks, and soup spoons, to say nothing of a dozen serving pieces. But, my goodness, look at the teaspoons. There must be thirty or more—some are coin silver, monogrammed and very old. Now, why in the world would she have so many teaspoons?"

I smiled. "That means that she got her silver in another era, just as I did. Those spoons are for occasions like a reception, when you're not having a seated meal. You don't need place settings for a coffee or a tea, but you do need lots of teaspoons for stirring."

"Well, it's beautiful," Diane said, "but unfortunately it won't bring the retail price. Young women today don't seem to want silver like they once did."

"That's the truth," I said somewhat mournfully. "It used to be commonly said that if you didn't get all your silver for your wedding, you'd never get it. But brides nowadays don't seem to care. Instead of registering sterling silver and fine china patterns, they list stainless steel and pottery mugs. Well," I said, heading back to the desk, "it's their loss."

Relieved to leave the evaluation in the capable hands of Diane and Helen, I quickly emptied Mattie's small desk of pencils, pens, opened envelopes, address book, and pads covered with notes, stuffing it all into the bags. In a banker's box beside the desk, I found two years of tax returns and check registers, which would all go into the trunk of my car for later perusal. In the side drawers of the desk, there were instruction booklets, warranties, old Christmas and birthday cards, as well as a number of files. After filling two more bags and making three trips to the car, I left Diane and Helen to it and went home to sift through piles of papers, both those that Mr. Sitton had given me earlier and those that I had just collected. And to eat lunch.

Chapter 24

I would've sat on the floor if I'd thought I could get to my feet again without the help of Lillian or a crane. The floor would've been the ideal place to spread out the papers I had to go through and sort, but I didn't want to chance having to call for help when I finished.

So I cleared the top of the large desk in the library and began sifting through piles of papers, pages torn from magazines, envelopes, sheets of notes and scribbles, recipes, and folders with more papers. It's a caution what we tend to hold on to and cram into drawers, thinking that we might someday need that very thing. And we never do. So somebody ends up having to go through the accumulation and separate the valuable from the trash.

I determined right then that as soon as I was through with Mattie's things, I would go through my own accumulation so that somebody else—who? Sam? Hazel Marie?—wouldn't be saddled with the job.

Just as I found an insurance policy that I couldn't make head nor tail of, the phone rang. I answered before Lillian could get it in the kitchen and was pleased to hear Etta Mae's voice.

"I'm sorry to disturb you, Miss Julia," she said, and before she continued, I quickly assured her that she wasn't.

"It's good to hear from you, Etta Mae, and I'm glad to have a break. You're not disturbing me at all."

"Well," she went on, as I detected a hint of hesitancy in her words, "I didn't know who else to call, 'cause, see, I think I have a problem and I was hoping you could maybe help."

"I can certainly try, but I'm sorry you're having a problem. What is it?"

"I'm not sure," she said. "It's a little hard to explain on the phone. I kinda have to tell what led up to it, so I was wondering if you'd have time for me to come by for a few minutes? Maybe tomorrow? Or I could take you out for lunch if you have time."

"I'd love to go to lunch with you, Etta Mae, but we might be pushed for time. I have a funeral to go to at two, and to be sure it doesn't turn into a carnival sideshow, I should be there by one. Why don't you drop by in the morning? I'll be here doing just what I'm doing now—sorting and clearing out."

We decided that around ten would suit us both, and I returned to going through Mattie's papers. Finding an insurance policy had given me a lift—maybe it meant money would be coming in, which I could disburse without having to scrounge for nickels and dimes to meet Mattie's inflated ideas of what she was leaving behind. I set the policy aside to take to Mr. Sitton, checked the time on my watch, and saw that I'd soon have to stop to check on Helen and Diane—not that I didn't trust them to lock the door when they left, but I wanted to make sure. Then I'd have to get ready for the visitation, have some supper somewhere in between, and in general be pushed to get everything done.

When the doorbell rang, I listened as Lillian answered it, then heard LuAnne's voice in the hall coming toward the library. I stood up and started toward the door just as she sailed in, dabbing at her eyes with a Kleenex.

"Oh, Julia," she said, collapsing on the sofa. "I am simply a mess, and I had to come talk to you. I know we have to get ready to go to the visitation—I set the time too early, but they told me it was the usual time, so I went with six o'clock. But, anyway, I just needed to talk to you."

Lillian stood in the doorway, looking troubled. "Y'all want some tea? Or something?"

"I don't think so, Lillian," I said, then walked over to her. "If you're planning to go to the visitation, just leave everything, and Sam and I will fix our plates. As for Mrs. Conover, she won't be long."

"No'm," Lillian whispered. "I got Latisha to see to this evenin', so I won't be goin'. And the onliest time Miss Mattie talk to me was when she tole me my chicken salat be better with Duke's 'stead of Hellman's. She won't care if I don't go, 'cause I'm still using Hellman's."

"I'm glad you are. Your chicken salad is the best in town, and everybody knows it. But you run on home now, and I'll see you in the morning."

Turning back to LuAnne, who was wiping her face, I sat down beside her. "What's wrong, LuAnne?"

"Oh, Julia," she said, then had to stop for a sob or two. "It's just hit me all at once. I've been so busy arranging everything. . . ." She stopped and looked at me through weeping eyes. "Did you know you have to *pay* to have your obituary in the paper? I didn't, but thank goodness the funeral home had included it on their bill, so Mattie had already paid it. But when I thought of Mattie paying for her *own* death notice—who knows how long ago—it just got to me so bad. And I thought of how often I'd *resented* her—having to pick her up every time I turned around, and having to manhandle that walker of hers into the car. And, Julia, she was always so cranky, like she was entitled or something, but now, now the poor old thing is gone, and I'm, well, I'm *grieving*."

"Oh, LuAnne," I said, moved in spite of myself, "I think we all feel that way. She wasn't the easiest person to be around, and that's the truth."

"Well, still," she said, blotting away the tears, "I wish I'd been kinder, more understanding, or something. And, Julia, I apologize to you, too, for giving you such a hard time about the funeral. I think I've been grieving ever since she passed and just didn't realize it. Instead of crying, I've just gotten harder and harder to get along with." She managed a strangled laugh. "If I'm not careful, I'll turn out just like Mattie herself."

We both looked at each other, the same thought blooming in our minds. "You think. . . ?" I started.

"I do!" LuAnne said, her tears instantly drying up. "Oh, my goodness, Mattie must've had some great and awful grief in her life, and it finally turned her into a plain, ole, ill-tempered crab. That's it, Julia! I'll bet that's it."

"Could be," I said, thinking of a young soldier moldering in his grave, as well as that convict somewhere in Mattie's past, to say nothing of a sloshing flask in her pocketbook. I didn't dare mention a thing to LuAnne—right at that moment, anyway. Furthermore, I'd have to think hard before revealing any of it to her at any time.

But at the same moment, I began to look forward to meeting Andrew F. Cobb and learning more about Mattie Freeman. I hate to admit this, but Mattie had become much more interesting now that she was gone than when she'd been with us.

But having designated LuAnne the funeral director, I had to tell her about Mattie's self-proclaimed, recently arrived relative. "Mr. Sitton told him about the visitation, so we should be on the lookout for him. He'll probably be the only person none of us knows." Except, I mentally added, the mechanic who kept Mattie's car on the road.

"Why," LuAnne said brightly, "it's almost like a romance novel. A strange man shows up just as his dearly beloved aunt or whatever has passed on, and now he'll have to prove who he is. Although," she said, frowning, "it's usually a beautiful young woman who gets there just a little too late. Anyway, what're you going to do about him?"

"Not one thing. Mr. Sitton is in the process of checking him out, then we'll go from there. But, LuAnne, I do want to thank you for handling the visitation and the funeral and for dealing with the funeral home. I know it hasn't been easy for you, but it's been a tremendous help to me."

"Oh, that's all right. I haven't minded. Besides, now I'll know what to do when I have to do it again. Leonard is a good bit older than I am, you know. But, listen," she said, getting to her feet, "it's getting late and we have to be there before anybody else. You and I will be the receiving line, so make sure you're there early."

We walked toward the door, and just as we reached it, Lu-Anne turned to me. "Oh, I almost forgot. I had the church put in the service bulletin that a reception would be held here at your house right after the interment. You don't mind, do you? I mean, your house is more central than anybody else's, and I've asked several people to bring food over in the morning, so it shouldn't be too much of a problem. And I'll be helping, of course."

Well, what could I say? She had it all arranged and announced except for one minor thing—informing the hostess. I just nodded my agreement and, after seeing LuAnne on her way, went to the kitchen to warn Lillian that we would be receiving mourners after the funeral.

Then I went back to the library but was in no frame of mind to continue sorting through the piles of papers. LuAnne's belated sadness had gotten to me, and I realized that I, too, had barely given a passing thought to Mattie's passing, other than to moan about what she'd passed along for me to do. So I took a few moments to regret that I had not cultivated her friendship, had not taken the time to really know her. For one thing, if I had, I might've learned something about her family. Namely, if she had any.

Sam and I quickly ate the supper that Lillian had left, got dressed, ran by Mattie's apartment to check the door—it was locked—then hurried to the Good Shepherd Funeral Home. It was going to be an interesting two hours—not only did I have to be a gracious greeter in the receiving line, I had to watch for a strange man purporting to be an heir who wanted no part of Mattie's estate—which I didn't believe for an instant—but also be available to Pastor Ledbetter, who was expecting to have a word or two with me before the visitation was over. And on top of all of that,

LuAnne had gotten her way about an open casket, so I'd have to look at least once.

"Sam," I said, taking his arm as we walked from the parking lot to the funeral home, "I'm telling you right now, I do not want an open casket when my time comes."

He smiled and pressed my arm to his side. "That's a long time off, sweetheart, and I hope I'm not around to make that decision."

After thinking about it for a few minutes, I decided that his response didn't make me feel one bit better.

Chapter 25

The visitors who attended the visitation held for Mattie—who, unfortunately was open to all who wanted to view her—made a skimpy but steady line for an hour and a half. Several small groups continued to linger in the viewing room, taking advantage of the sofas and chairs placed around the walls and talking in quiet tones. Flower arrangements, ordered by Mattie's acquaintances and delivered by florists, were on all the tables and a few had been set on the floor beside the casket.

By the time the line was beginning to thin out, my feet and back were killing me. Standing for that long was not as easy as it once was, but LuAnne and I had shaken hands with each visitor and received condolences as if we were Mattie's survivors.

Almost all the members of the Lila Mae Harding Sunday school class had presented themselves, as they did for every member who predeceased the rest of us. And so did Pastor Ledbetter and his wife, Emma Sue, who was dripping with tears. Emma Sue was a sensitive soul and she cried at the least little thing. The funeral of someone she'd known for years made her a veritable fountain.

As Pastor Ledbetter shook my hand, he whispered, "As soon as you can take a break, we'll talk."

I nodded and reached for the next hand, mentioning as I did that the visitors' book should be signed. Who it would go to, I didn't know, as Mattie had no family to treasure it. Unless you counted the unconfirmed upstart who'd recently paid a call to her attorney.

Several members of the garden club and most of the book club members signed the visitors' book, then came through the line, quickly shook our hands, glanced into the casket—though some averted their eyes as they passed—and moved on out.

It struck me more than once that our group of friends was a mannerly and respectful one—they did what was properly called for in spite of their personal feelings. And it also struck me as painfully sad that Mattie seemed to have had no one who truly grieved for her—other than LuAnne, who had apparently gotten it out of her system and was now enjoying the social hour. But, as it's said, we reap what we sow, and I determined to be a better friend to those for whom I cared. I mean, I wanted to be *mourned* when I passed, which I had no intention of doing anytime soon, but you never know.

"Miz Murdoch?" A soft, slow drawl drew my attention from Pierce Adams, the church organist, who was passing from my hand to LuAnne's on his way to the casket.

"Yes, how do you do?" I turned and immediately knew that I was face-to-face with the stranger who'd been in Mr. Sitton's office claiming a far-fetched kinship to Mattie. Thinking that he shared no apparent physical genes with Mattie, I took him in from head to foot. He was a short, slight man with hardly any heft to him and blond from the thinning hair on the top of his head to the full mustache above his lip—his only obvious similarity to Mattie, only hers had been black. The man was sunburned from his scalp and peeling nose to the calloused hand that shook mine. He had a shy smile full of large teeth and the corners of both eyes revealed white crow's-feet deep enough to account for at least forty—maybe fifty—years out in the sun.

In a room half filled with men in suits or dark sports jackets, he stood out. He was wearing some sort of long-sleeved brown-and-white-checked shirt with a brown knit tie, for which the best I could say was that at least it was a tie. Khaki pants that were not permanent press and scuffed shoes finished his funeral attire. I could picture him getting ready in what Mr. Sitton had described as the two-wheeled trailer in which he'd been living for some time. Maybe he'd done the best that could be done, so I tried not to be critical until he turned his head and I saw the curl of a ponytail clasped by an Indian-looking beaded band.

"Fine, doin' fine," he said, responding to my conventional greeting. Then he ducked his head, gave me an ingratiating smile in a shy way, and said, "You prob'bly don't know me, but I'm Andrew Cobb, Aunt Mattie's great-nephew. I sure am sorry I didn't get here in time to get to know her. But from the looks of the crowd here, she had lots of friends."

Actually, the crowd was sparse, but perhaps he'd not been to many visitations.

"Yes, Mattie was well loved," I lied, as one does under the circumstances. "I'm glad to meet you, Mr. Cobb. Mr. Sitton told me that you were in town."

"Yes, ma'am. Fine man, real fine. He mentioned you, so I guess we'll be seeing a lot of each other pretty soon."

That didn't sound good.

"I started to stop by this morning," he went on in his soft drawl, "but figgered you'd be busy. Just ridin' around, don't you know, an' wanted to see where Aunt Mattie lived—real nice place. Real nice."

"Oh? Mr. Sitton gave you the address?"

He smiled a lazy smile. "She was in the phone book."

"Yes, of course. LuAnne," I said, disconcerted enough to pass him along, "this is Mr. Cobb. And, Mr. Cobb, this is Mrs. Conover, a dear friend of Mattie's." Then I turned to the next in line. But the presence of Mr. Cobb had put me off my stride, and I continued to think of him even as I kept up my end of the receiving line.

The man made me uncomfortable—I wasn't sure why, other than the fact that he'd made it his business to find out where Mattie had lived, and he smiled more than necessary. But he didn't look intimidating; just the opposite, in fact. He put me in mind of a country boy—even though he was far from boyhood and that beaded band said *hippie*—because, perhaps, he was so rawboned and weather-beaten. And seemingly ill at ease in the soft-toned, middle-class attempt at a comforting milieu for grieving families.

And maybe also he made me uncomfortable because I was Mattie's gatekeeper, so to speak, and it was my job to keep what little she had safe, especially from strangers with unknown bloodlines.

I didn't want him asking questions of me. Questions like, when would it be convenient to look through Mattie's apartment? Or, may I have a copy of her will? Or, what about copies of the death certificate? Death certificates were important, I'd learned, as they gave access to bank accounts, insurance policies, and a number of other things that I wanted to keep to myself until we knew exactly who he was.

So I decided, as I shook another hand, that I'd defer all questions that he posed to Mr. Sitton and keep everything entrusted to me to myself alone—until otherwise notified and in spite of his pleasant enough manner.

Just as there was a gap in the line and I looked for the nearest unoccupied chair, Pastor Ledbetter slid up beside me.

"Let's walk out in the hall," he said in a low voice. Then to LuAnne, "Hold the fort for a few minutes, will you? Church business. We'll be right back."

He took my arm and walked me out into the hall of the funeral home and back to the end of it, as far from the entrance to the viewing room as he could get without risking an intrusion into someone else's visitation.

"Miss Julia," the pastor said, his large frame looming over me as I took a step back. "I understand that Miss Mattie remembered the church in her will, and I want to tell you that it is an answer to prayer. I just praised the Lord when I heard about it."

Yes, and I knew from whom he'd heard it. LuAnne was the only one I'd even hinted to about what was in Mattie's will. I should've known better.

"Well, Pastor," I began, taking a deep breath to explain the dilemma of trying to follow Mattie's wishes with nothing to follow them with. He cut me off.

"You just don't know," he went on, his face glowing with anticipation, "what a serendipitous occasion this is. Why, the deacons had just given us the bad news that the air-conditioning unit in the church had about seen its last days. To replace it, we'd have to raise funds from the congregation or go into debt, which I am loath to do. So to learn that Miss Mattie is coming to the rescue, so to speak, well, it's lifted a load from my mind." He paused, but before I could even begin to deflate his expectations, he went on again.

"Now here we are at the beginning of summer when the heat is already putting a tremendous strain on the old unit. It's going to quit on us any day now. Think what it's going to be like in the middle of August if we're without any cooling at all. So, I'm wondering how long it will take for the will to go through probate. See," he said, lowering his voice to take me into his confidence, "if we know the money's coming in, oh, say, in the next few weeks, we can go ahead and contract for a new unit. Maybe even arrange to make a small down payment which the church can handle, then to pay it off in full as soon as you hand us a check. I'm sure Mattie was generous enough to foresee the problem—she complained about the church being too hot the last Sunday she was with us."

I was so taken aback that when I opened my mouth I wasn't sure what was going to come out. He didn't give me a chance to find out.

"Well," he said with a little laugh, "of course, I may be counting too heavily on Miss Mattie. I expect we should determine if her gift is enough to cover an air-conditioning unit. They're quite expensive—thousands of dollars—you know. Have to have a lot of BTUs to cool an area the size of our church. But she loved the church, and I feel sure that she would not be niggardly."

"Well, Pastor," I began again, knowing full well that he wanted to know the exact amount that would be coming to the church. "It's like this: Mattie certainly showed her love of the church by leaving what one would hope to be a sizable amount to it. The problem, however, is twofold: she specifically designated how it was to be spent, and secondly, she . . ."

"Oh, I'm sure we can get around that," he said, not in the least unsettled by Mattie's desires. "If she had known the emergency situation we're now in, I'm sure she would've wanted to help."

I took a step to the side to get out of the corner he'd backed me into and said, "I will have to consult her attorney about that. I'm not at all sure that funds designated for one thing can be transferred at will to something else. I'll keep you informed, but now I have to get back to the receiving line."

And I slipped past him and headed for the visitation room, where a discussion of Mattie's bequests couldn't be held.

I was wrong. The very next person who walked up to the receiving line was Callie Armstrong, a good-natured soul with a house full of children. She took my hand and, with a mischievous look, whispered, "I hear we're all in line for a windfall. And thank goodness for it, because all five of my crew need new shoes."

As soon as she walked on, I leaned over and did some whispering of my own. "LuAnne," I said, "I am never going to tell you another thing for as long as I live."

Chapter 26

"Why? What did I do?" LuAnne said, a look of innocent surprise spreading across her face.

"You told the pastor about Mattie's bequest to the church, that's what, and now he's already spending it."

"I did not!" She was indignant at the idea. Then she reconsidered. "I might've *mentioned* it, but I didn't actually *tell* him."

We had to stop then, because a straggler had just finished signing the visitors' book and was holding out a hand to be shaken. I took it, spoke through a mouth so tight with anger that I could barely get out a word of greeting, much less of consolation, and passed him on to LuAnne.

When he walked on over to the casket, I spun back to her. "There won't be many more visitors, so I'm leaving. You can handle it from now on." And I turned to go.

"But, Julia, you can't leave. We have fifteen more minutes to go, and what am I going to do with all these flowers?"

"The funeral home will take them to the church. Or," I said, unable to restrain myself, "you can get the pastor to help you since the two of you are so close."

And I walked off to look for Sam and get myself home before I said something I'd regret. I was feeling hemmed in and hounded, because every time I turned around, some new problem cropped up. Now the pastor would be breathing down my neck, to say nothing of the board of deacons, with air-conditioning on their minds, as well as Mr. Andrew F-for-whatever Cobb.

And on top of that, as Sam and I walked out of the Good Shepherd Funeral Home, we saw that very same Andrew F. Cobb drive out of the parking area in an ancient, low-riding, mud-splattered Cadillac.

"That's . . ." I started to say.

"Yes, I met him," Sam said. "Probably needs that big car to pull his trailer. He told me—quite proudly, I thought—that it's a sixteen-foot, one-axle Airstream Sport aluminum trailer with all the comforts of home."

"Huh," I said, "I'd rather take my comforts of home *at* home. Remember that, Sam, if you ever decide to go RVing."

He laughed. "His little trailer hardly qualifies as an RV. But, you know, we might think about renting a large, roomy one some-time and taking a cross-country trip. You'd enjoy that, wouldn't you?"

"Maybe so, if you'd drop me off at a four-star hotel every night."

Sam laughed again, his good humor making me sorry for being in such a bad mood. But after dealing with LuAnne, Pastor Led-better, Mr. Cobb, and standing on my feet for two hours, I was in no mood to think of anything but how ill used I'd been. I took his arm and pressed it close.

Poor Sam. He had to listen to my moaning and groaning—which occasionally passed over into ranting and raving—all the way home. I didn't stop as we prepared for bed or when we got into bed. In fact, my complaining kept him awake for so long that I was up, dressed, and in the kitchen before he rolled out the next morning.

You might've thought that I would be the one needing sleep, but I was still so on edge that it was all I could do to sit still, much less sleep late. So I was up long before Lillian arrived, had made a breakfast of toast and coffee, and had gone to the library to start again on Mattie's papers. That insurance policy that I'd come across the day before had stuck in my mind so I searched it out, hoping it would prove the answer to the pressing question of *Where would the money come from?*

It wasn't, however, the answer to anything. I had put the policy in the stack that was to go to Mr. Sitton as something that he should handle, but I needn't have bothered. How I'd missed the large red stamped letters across the front of it, I didn't know. But I understood what CANCELED meant.

I leaned my head back against the chair, breathing out in disbelief. Why would anyone hold on to a canceled insurance policy? I put it back into Mr. Sitton's stack—if Mattie had been unable to throw it away, then I couldn't, either.

Which reminded me that I'd intended to ask Mr. Sitton if that strange scribbling I'd found was important enough to keep. But when he'd given me the news of a possible Cobb relative in town, I'd not given it another thought. I'd stuck it, still in its ziplock bag, into my purse so I'd have it with me the next time I saw him.

Hearing Sam come into the kitchen, I went back to going through the unsorted papers, but I could hear him talking to Lillian. Having left the library door open, I could hear their words wafting easily from the kitchen, across the hall, and into the quiet room where I was working.

"Julia already eaten?" Sam asked.

"Yessir, she eat 'fore I get here, an' now she in there doin' something with all that stuff of Miss Mattie's."

"I'll take her a fresh cup of coffee. Probably needs one right about now."

Lillian lowered her voice, but I could still hear her. "Yessir, but I'd be tippy-toed about it if I was you. She on the warpath this mornin'."

Sam laughed, and I had to smile. That was it, I decided. I was not going to have everybody on edge and tippy-toeing around because of my own ill humor. If Mattie didn't have enough funds to go around, it had nothing to do with me. I would do the best I could with what she had, but I would not keep distressing any-body else about it.

Then I perked up again when Lillian said, "Mr. Sam? I hate botherin' you 'bout this, but the Reverend Abernathy, he might could use a little bit of help. He havin' a real hard time with Mr. Robert Mobley."

"Mobley?" Sam asked. "I thought he died awhile back."

"Yessir, he did, but, bad as he was when he livin', he worse now he dead."

Sam and Lillian moved over to the kitchen table, and I could no longer make out what they were saying. But I made a mental note to sit down with Lillian and listen to what seemed to be an ongoing problem for her and for the reverend.

"Julia?" Sam said as he came into the library bearing a cup of coffee. He set it on a coaster for me, then said, "Honey, you don't need to do all this right away. Take your time, and don't let it get to you."

"I'm not. I've just decided that it took Mattie fifty years to ac-cumulate all this, so I can't be expected to sort it out in a few days. But, Sam, I meant to ask you last night—have you given any more thought to those letters and numbers I showed you? I'd like to start throwing some of this stuff away, but here I am holding on to mere scraps of paper."

"I don't know, honey. It could be a formula of some kind."

"You mean, like a chemical formula? I can't imagine why Mat-tie would have something like that."

"Well, you could show it to a pharmacist, or maybe to a hair-dresser. Don't they mix different shades to get the right color when they dye somebody's hair?"

"I wouldn't know about that," I said, and changed the subject. "Have you had any more thoughts about Mattie's long-lost nephew or whatever he is?"

Sam drew up a chair beside me. "Not many. He was pleasant

enough, but not particularly forthcoming. All he had to say for himself was that he'd been on the road a number of years—seeing the country, he said. We talked a little about writing nonfiction and the research it required. He said he gets a lot of ideas from following the picking season."

"Picking what? Apples? Beans?"

"That, too. But mostly guitar."

"Oh, my," I said with a lift of my eyebrows. "He's a drifter, isn't he?"

"Pretty much," Sam agreed. "Other than that, I didn't learn much more than what you'd already told me."

That was disappointing, for if anyone could elicit information, it was Sam. He was so friendly, so open, and so interested in people that he was usually told more than he wanted to know.

After a little more speculation about Andrew Cobb, Sam left me to my sorting. So I was still going through envelopes and sorting old receipts and warranties when the doorbell rang a few minutes before ten. *That will be Etta Mae*, I thought, just as I picked up an envelope stamped on the front with the words YOU ARE A WINNER!! Wouldn't that be nice, I said to myself, but gave little credence to it. Still, with a little thump of hope, I put it aside to look at later and stood to welcome Etta Mae.

She came in with a big smile, but there was a little less bounce than usual in the blond curls on her head, so I assumed the advice she was seeking was of some import. I welcomed her and motioned to the sofa in front of the fireplace, which held a summer arrangement of magnolia leaves instead of a fire.

"How are you, Etta Mae?" I said, as Lillian waited at the door to see if we wanted refreshments. "Would you like a cold drink? Coffee?"

"No, ma'am, I'm fine. Well, not fine, but thank you anyway." Etta Mae Wiggins was a pretty young woman, and small except in the places that seemed to count with a certain segment of the population. She also had a somewhat checkered background, bless her heart, that included divorcing two husbands and burying a third. You'd be hard pressed to count the third one, though, since he went to his eternal reward on the same night that he was expecting his marital reward. None of that bothered me. She was my close friend.

Needless to say, however, Etta Mae's reputation around the county had suffered some slings and arrows, but no one dared say a word against her in my presence. I will admit, however, that I, too, had at one time disapproved of her, but that had been before circumstances had thrown us together time after time. I simply didn't know what I would have done without her when I chased jewel thieves down through Florida, or the time I was forced to climb the town's courthouse dome to rescue the statue of Lady Justice, or when Mr. J. D. Pickens, PI, had to be bodily removed from a hospital in the wilds of West Virginia. She had proven to be a trusted and willing—though not always an eager—companion when called upon.

She now sat on the edge of the leather sofa, her hands clasped in her lap, looking about half miserable. Her nurse's outfit, consisting of a blue pullover tunic and baggy pants over thick-soled running shoes, revealed that she was on duty and between patients. Etta Mae was a licensed practical nurse who worked for the Handy Home Helpers, a for-profit semimedical business that made home visits to the elderly, the shut-ins, and the invalid.

"Etta Mae," I said, leaning toward her, "what's wrong, honey? You look worried about something."

"Yes'm, I am, and I hope you can tell me what I ought to do. See, Miss Julia, I've got this patient—Irene Cassidy?" Etta Mae glanced up to see if I recognized the name—I didn't.

"Anyway, she was a Webber before she married, but he's been dead a long time. You probably know some Webbers, there's a lot of 'em out in the county. So anyway, I've been looking after Miss Irene every week for, oh, I guess a couple of years now. She's the sweetest thing in the world, and I just love her, but she told me the other day that she's leaving me something in her will."

"Why, Etta Mae, that's wonderful. Obviously she thinks a lot of you."

"Yes'm, I guess, but it's keeping me awake at night, worrying about it. I've tried to talk her out of it, told her that I appreciate it, but that I wish she wouldn't."

"I don't understand," I said. "Most people would be thrilled to be remembered in somebody's will." I could think of any number of them just panting over Mattie's will.

"But, Miss Julia," Etta Mae said in a plaintive way, "you know what people will say. They'll say I took advantage of a poor, old, sick woman, playing on her loneliness, and wheedling things from her, even though I'd never do that. I don't even want whatever it is because of all the talk I'd have to put up with afterward. I could lose my job if it got around that I was taking advantage of old and sick people."

"I can see that it could be a concern, but I was always taught that when somebody wants to give you something, you should say thank you and take it. Because they wouldn't give it if they didn't want you to have it." I watched as she took her lower lip in her teeth and considered the advice. It didn't seem to have helped, so I went on. "And I'll tell you something else, Etta Mae. A lot of people are bad to make promises that they don't keep—they may mean to, but they never get around to doing it. So you may have nothing to worry about."

"That's true," she said, nodding, "and that's what I thought when she first mentioned it. But this week, she had her lawyer come to her house, and she told me again after he left. I'm afraid she means it."

"She could change her mind. You know, after she thinks about it for a while, and after she gets well from whatever is wrong with her. The world will look different then."

Etta Mae shook her head. "She won't get well. She's a fragile diabetic and . . ."

"Fragile?"

"Her blood sugar is hard to stabilize—it just fluctuates all over the place and she's in and out of the hospital all the time. And you know that diabetics have to be real careful about their feet— that's why I go, sometimes on my days off, to give her a pedicure. She's just so appreciative, and I'm glad to do it."

"That's very good of you, especially doing it on your own time." That didn't surprise me, though. It was exactly the kind of thoughtful thing that Etta Mae would do.

She shrugged as if it were of little account. "It doesn't take long. I mean, one leg has already been amputated so it only takes half the time."

"Oh, my," I said, realizing that Etta Mae's promised inheritance might be more imminent than I'd thought. "Is she, this patient of yours, a well-to-do woman? What about her family? Will they resent her leaving something to you?"

"No'm, I don't think she has a whole lot, but she's not a Medicaid patient, so I guess she has something. And the only family she has is a sister who takes care of her, and she was there when the lawyer came, so whatever Miss Irene did, her sister already knows about. And she's still just as nice to me as she ever was."

"Well, I think that tells you something. It's unlikely that your patient would cut her sister out in favor of someone unrelated. I'll tell you what I think, Etta Mae. I think that your patient wants to show you how much she appreciates your care of her, and she's left you a token remembrance. It could be a small piece of jewelry or some favorite books or a few hundred dollars—there's no telling. But whatever it is, she's pleased about being able to give it to you, or she wouldn't have told you about it. And remember, nobody else has to know anything, so I wouldn't worry about people talking. It's not as if it'll be in the newspaper." *And*, I thought, *it was not as if she had a friend like LuAnne Conover who would spread it from one end of the county to the other*.

"Well," she said, straightening herself, "that's true. She really doesn't have much as far as I can tell, so she wouldn't have much to give, would she? That makes me feel a little better—if she left me something nobody else wants, they couldn't accuse me of taking advantage, could they?"

"They certainly couldn't. And, listen, if it turns out to be more, take it and be thankful. And enjoy it."

"Oh," she said, frowning again as she stood, "I hope it's not. I hope it's some little trinket or something like that."

"Etta Mae," I said, standing to see her out, "you are the only person I know—perhaps the only person on earth—who'd be happier to get a little rather than a lot."

And even though I am not a hugging kind of person, I put my arm around her, resisting the urge to tell her that whatever she missed getting from her patient's will, my own would make up for it.

Chapter 27

My word, I thought as I returned to the library. It seemed that last will and testaments were to be my portion in life for some time to come. Etta Mae's problem was easy enough to solve, but mine was still hanging over my head. I sighed at the stacks on the desk and wondered if I'd ever get through them.

And, I thought, *I haven't even gotten to the stacks of scrapbooks, photograph albums, and various boxes waiting on the shelf and in the back corner of Mattie's guest room closet—the very things that Mr. Cobb was apparently so eager to see.*

"Miss Julia?" Lillian stood in the door, a dishrag in her hand. "You an' Mr. Sam got to be at that funeral in a little while, an' you need to eat something 'fore you go."

"Yes, and I have to get there early enough to see that it doesn't descend into chaos." I looked at her, noting that she was in a housedress that was nothing like her usual funeral attire, which would certainly have included a large hat. "I thought you were planning to go."

"No'm, 'cause when it come down to it, I'm jus' not up to it. And ladies be startin' to bring trays an' casseroles an' so on for the reception. I need to be here to get things ready."

"I'm sorry LuAnne sprang that reception on us—I didn't know a thing about it. But we'll have plenty of help. So if you want to go to the funeral, you can walk over with me or with Sam when he goes a little later. I'm sure Miss Mattie would appreciate it." If she knew about it.

"No'm, I got to thinkin' I jus' didn't know her all that good, an' she didn't know me, so I'd jus' ruther stay here. 'Sides, I about had my fill of funerals, what with the trouble that come from Mr. Robert's."

"Oh, yes, I want to hear about that. What did he do?"

"Well, he died, like I tole you, so he didn't do nothin' 'cept leave a will. An' that's the trouble."

"Don't tell me!" I cried, simply as an expression, because as Lillian had had her fill of funerals, I'd about had mine of wills.

"I can't right now, anyway," Lillian said, turning toward the kitchen. "I got lunch 'bout ready, an' I got to get the silver an' china out 'fore them ladies start comin' in. And you need to get dressed for Miss Mattie's funeral. It gettin' late."

"Yes, I'll do that right now." With a lingering glance at the envelope that promised a win for Mattie, I went upstairs to prepare to lay her to rest.

I'd had a vague intention of wearing a lightweight navy blue dress with long sleeves against the chill of the air-conditioned church. I had to rethink that. For one, Pastor Ledbetter seemed to think that the air-conditioning unit would be giving up the ghost any minute, and I didn't want to suffer in the heat. And for another, Mattie was wearing navy blue, and even though she wouldn't be seen at the church, she had been at the visitation. So, just as guests should avoid wearing white to a wedding, I figured that since Mattie was the star of her funeral—as a bride is at her wedding—she should be the only one in navy blue.

That being determined, I put on a dove-gray summer-weight suit with a jacket over an ivory blouse. I'd just slipped into gray Ferragamos with a manageable heel when Sam came in, surprised that I was ready so early.

"I can't afford to fiddle around," I told him. "We have to have lunch, then I'm going on over to the church. You can come later if you want—whenever the pallbearers have to be there—but I've got to check on LuAnne's plans. For all I know, she's run amok."

Sam's eyebrows went up as he grinned. "Amok?"

"She's been known to before, as you well know. She already has the entire choir up in arms because she asked Tina Doland to sing a solo. And Tina's a Baptist."

"Oh, horrors!" Sam said, laughing.

"Yes, but it makes sense in a way. Mattie did like to hear Tina sing—she always went to the First Baptist's rendition of Handel's *Messiah* every Christmas. But our choir feels slighted because they have a few good soloists, too. And did I tell you," I went on, "that LuAnne ordered a full casket cover of roses, for which I'll be billed for half?"

"I believe you did—sometime between midnight and one o'clock last night."

"Oh, you," I said, smiling at his good humor. Then I went downstairs to wait for lunch.

While I waited, I went into the library to see what was inside that winning envelope. I looked again at the bold announcement on the outside—YOU ARE A WINNER!!—and hoped against hope that Mattie was. Tearing it open, a few slips of paper fell out, each advertising something to be ordered: a miraculous cleaning product, an easy-to-use grout applicator, and a never-fail wrinkle cream. And a check for ten dollars. But with just one more order, Mattie would be in the semifinal drawing for ten thousand dollars.

Oh, me. Another scam, just as I'd feared. How many of them had Mattie fallen for? Only a thorough audit of her checkbook register would reveal how gullible she'd been. And I didn't have the heart to do it. I thought of how years ago, when my first husband was alive and each day had seemed like the one before, I'd looked forward to hearing the postman put something in the mailbox. Not that I'd been expecting anything, it was just that the thump of the newspaper landing on the porch in the morning and the rattle of the mailbox in the afternoon were the high points of my day—each holding the potential for something new and different.

Maybe Mattie had felt the same way. And maybe she made sure that the postman would have something to put in her mailbox, something she could look forward to, as well as the possibility that whatever it was would change the sameness of her days.

By that time I was feeling so sorry for Mattie that I knew I'd have no trouble being appropriately grieved at her funeral.

Which reminded me that I had an even closer friend to be concerned about, and I picked up the phone.

"Ida Lee?" I asked when she answered, as one does even though the voice is recognized. "Did Mildred come home this morning?"

"Yes, ma'am, we've been home about an hour, and she's trying to decide whether or not she feels like going to Mrs. Freeman's funeral."

"Well, that's why I'm calling. Would she be able to walk over to the church with me? I'll be going in about an hour."

"No, ma'am, I don't think so. She mentioned something about my driving her around to the front of the church and letting her out at the door—if she goes, but I don't think she will. She's lying down now—feeling a little low, she said. Would you like to speak to her?"

"No, that's all right. Just tell her I called, but tell her that if she feels up to it, we're having a reception here after the funeral. She may want to come to that."

We hung up, and I stood there for a minute, feeling torn between attending the funeral of an acquaintance and attending to a much closer friend. Mildred was facing an uphill battle with her weight, and I didn't doubt that the prospect of being stapled was enough to make social obligations a matter of little concern.

I decided that if I wasn't feeling more than a little low myself by the time the funeral and interment and reception were over, I would visit her that evening. In the meantime, I hurried to put away the papers and folders that I'd been going through, straightening the library for the influx of mourners after the funeral. I didn't want anything belonging to Mattie setting out in full view of curious eyes. Not that I'd found anything of significance, but still.

Entering through the back door of the basement level of the church, I almost walked right past the choir room. The lack of a hubbub of voices stopped me, and I cracked the door to look in. Not a soul was inside, the choir robes were neatly hung, and sheet music was carefully stacked on shelves in the bookcase.

I sighed and backed out. Either every choir member was running late or they weren't coming. Maybe they were on strike because LuAnne had preferred a Baptist soloist to a Presbyterian one. The grass always seems greener, you know.

Refusing to add the choir to my list of concerns, I walked up the stairs to the area behind the apse, where I found plenty going on. One of the large Sunday school rooms had been designated the family waiting room, and in it LuAnne was busily giving last-minute instructions to the organist, the soloist, and Pastor Ledbetter.

"Julia!" she cried and broke away from the group around her. "I'm sorry, I'm so sorry. I didn't even think of it, because not every funeral has them. It just didn't occur to me, or you know I would've gotten somebody." She clasped my arm. "Will you do it?"

I stepped back warily. "Do what?"

"Give the eulogy. You knew Mattie as well as any of us, and obviously she knew you well enough to trust you with her estate. I think you'd be the perfect eulogist."

"No, LuAnne, no. How could you ask me to do that, here at the last minute?" Although I wouldn't have done it if I'd had a month's notice.

"Well, that means I've just totally messed up Mattie's funeral. I can't believe I forgot something so important."

I thought she was about to cry, so I took her arm and walked her over to a corner. "Listen, LuAnne, the pastor will love having the pulpit to himself. Just ask him to mention Mattie's faithfulness to the church and maybe her love of getting together with friends. Especially if petits fours were served. He'll do a good job, because he's used to speaking in public. People will be glad not to have to listen to some rambling, stumbling attempt to eulogize Mattie by somebody who barely knew her."

"You think?" LuAnne carefully blotted her eyes.

"I know they will. Just pretend you planned it this way, and they'll think you're brilliant. Now, go tell the pastor what he should say."

"Well, okay, but I've already told him a lot."

I didn't doubt that, but Pastor Ledbetter had officiated at an untold number of funerals, so I knew that he'd do this one exactly as he wanted, regardless of what he'd been told.

Chapter 28

If you've seen one funeral service, you've pretty much seen them all, unless one is held under a tree in a cow pasture, as I'd been shocked to hear about not long before. The only discordant note at Mattie's was when LuAnne insisted that she and I, along with Leonard and Sam, should sit in the front pew as representatives of Mattie's family.

"I'm not going to do it, LuAnne," I'd said. "We're not family, and we shouldn't pretend to be."

"But, Julia, somebody has to. That pew will be empty if we don't sit there."

"It's empty every Sunday, too," I reminded her. "Nobody ever sits there." And, assuming I'd taken care of that, I went off to find my usual pew about five rows back on the side and wait for the service to begin. Sam, of course, sat with the other pallbearers, none of whom bore anything. Instead, they wheeled the rose-laden casket down the aisle to a spot beneath the pulpit, then took their seats.

About the same time, Hazel Marie and Lloyd slipped in beside me. Pleased to see them, I patted Lloyd's knee as he squirmed in between us. Wearing khaki pants, a white shirt under a navy blazer, and a tie, Lloyd looked every scanty inch the well-groomed young gentleman that he was.

"You all packed for your trip?" I whispered.

He nodded and smiled with anticipation. "Don't forget," I

went on, "to use a lot of sunblock. I don't want you burned to a crisp out on the water."

"No'm, me, either. But Mama's already told me." Then he grinned. "'Bout a dozen times."

Hazel Marie leaned over his head and whispered to me, "Guess who's babysitting."

I smiled, picturing J. D. Pickens, PI, running after two laughing, screaming, into-everything toddlers for an hour or so. He had certainly calmed down since marrying Hazel Marie and becoming a father of twins, as well as a stepfather to Lloyd, for which I will be eternally grateful. Who would've thought that a man who had cut such a swath among the ladies could be domesticated by the likes of Hazel Marie?

But Hazel Marie was as sweet and caring a woman as you'll ever meet. And I should know, for if anyone had reason to disparage her, I was that person. Instead, though, of despising her for bearing a child by Wesley Lloyd Springer, my first, now deceased but unlamented, husband, I valued her for what she had brought into my life.

Such thoughts were running through my mind as they always did when I attended a funeral service, being reminded, you see, of Wesley Lloyd's funeral—the one that freed me from a dull, gray existence to one in which I took charge and kept it.

After struggling through a congregational hymn, my thoughts returned to the present as I concentrated on respectful attention to the service. Mattie deserved no less.

As we settled back into our pews, Tina Doland rose beside the organ to sing "There Is a Balm in Gilead," a lovely selection that I would've enjoyed under other circumstances, even though she did get a little screechy a couple of times. Then Pastor Ledbetter took over. I didn't hear a word he said.

As the mourners, some more quickly than others, had taken their seats after the hymn, I had glimpsed a familiar ponytail tied with a beaded Indian band. I couldn't believe it, and I stretched and craned to assure myself that it wasn't so.

But it was. LuAnne had seated Andrew F. Cobb in the front pew, and there he sat as a publicly recognized member of Mattie's family. And, for all anyone knew, he was no more akin to her than I was.

As soon as the service was over and the pallbearers had rolled Mattie out to the waiting hearse for the trip to the cemetery, Hazel Marie, Lloyd, and I slipped through the crush to hurry to my house. A crowd would soon be pushing through my door, intent on deconstructing the pastor's sermon, exchanging favorite stories about Mattie, and partaking of the food on my dining table.

But I was still fuming over LuAnne's high-handed conduct. She'd had no business elevating Andrew F. Cobb to familial status, especially since Mr. Sitton had not confirmed his identity. For all I knew, she'd undercut all of Mr. Sitton's legal attempts to establish who the man was, and I intended to let her know it as soon as I could get her off alone somewhere.

By the time we crossed the street to my house, Lillian had already put out the spread of food on the table in the dining room, so Hazel Marie mixed the punch and I lit the sterno beneath the coffee urn. For a hastily put together repast, it was plentiful and attractive, even though Callie had brought a huge tray of cold cuts and so had Sue Hargrove. Lillian had had to run to the store to pick up enough bread for sandwiches.

When cars began to file into the church parking lot across the street, I knew the interment was over and we'd soon be inundated. An early arrival rang the doorbell, and I hurried to answer it.

"Mildred!" I cried. "Come in. I'm so glad to see you, but you didn't have to come to the front door." Whenever she bestirred herself to visit, she generally came across our yards and entered through the kitchen door, as the rest of us did.

"Ida Lee dropped me off here at the front," she explained as she entered. I had to laugh, for no one but Mildred would have herself driven from next door.

"You look wonderful," I said. "How're you feeling?"

"I'm fine, but I don't want to talk about it. What can I do to help?"

"You can sit at the head of the table and ladle the punch," I said, directing her to the dining room. "The coffee urn is on the sideboard, so if anyone wants coffee in this heat, they can pour their own."

"Listen," Mildred said as she took her place at the table, "I said I didn't want to talk about my dilemma, but I do want to join you on your walks—if you don't mind starting with short ones and maybe gradually building up. I have to do something so I won't need that operation."

"Of course we can do that. I need the exercise, too. We can lengthen the walks as we get used to them and keep up with how much we do with that pedometer I gave you."

"That's the most discouraging thing I've ever seen," Mildred said as she rearranged the cut-glass cups on the tray. "Although I thank you for the gift. But did you know we're supposed to start with two thousand steps and work up to ten thousand—a *day*? Impossible, because I'm starting with barely five hundred. I'm so far behind, I'll never catch up."

"We'll work at it, Mildred. Don't give up before we've even started." Hearing footsteps on the porch, I said, "Uh-oh, they're beginning to come in. Well," I went on, sighing, "it's Mattie's last party. It's a pity she's not here to enjoy it."

The living room, dining room, and library were fairly crowded for the first thirty minutes or so with people talking, laughing, and eating, but soon after that, the crowd started to thin out. There were, of course, no true mourners to make anyone uncomfortable by their tears or to put a damper on the socializing by their grief.

Delayed by his pastoral duties, Pastor Ledbetter and Emma Sue came in late. As soon as I saw them, I busied myself with hostess obligations to avoid further questioning about the settling of Mattie's estate. Asking Emma Sue to relieve Mildred at the punch bowl, I guided Mildred to a wing chair in the living room.

"I hope pouring didn't tire you too much," I said to her. "Rest for a while, and I'll bring you a plate."

"I'm perfectly all right, Julia," she said, "but I could eat a bite."

I carefully selected a few broccoli florets, carrot sticks, radishes, and grape tomatoes, sprinkling them all with a spoonful of dip. Then I piled fruit—pineapple chunks, green grapes, and strawberries—on the side. As a special treat, I added one cracker spread with cheese.

Picking up a fork and a napkin, I took the plate to Mildred. She looked at it, then up at me with such a pitiful expression that I almost went back for three cold-cut sandwiches and several petits fours, which had been brought by Helen in honor of Mattie. Instead, I steeled myself against Mildred's wan look and went to the door to see a group of mourners out.

A while later, after Sam came in and only a few mourners were left, we sat around the living room, recalling fond memories of Mattie.

"You know," Sue said, "I think we're going to miss her. I mean, she'd long ago given up actually doing anything, but she was always there."

"That's true," I agreed. "I'm not even sure that she read the assigned books for the book club. She never offered a comment on anything we read."

"I know she didn't read them," LuAnne said. "I'd pick her up for book club, and she'd complain about every book we were reading—too long, too involved, too modern for her taste. I don't know why she bothered to go."

"Well . . ." Callie Armstrong said, and we all laughed because we knew why Mattie bothered to go. She didn't want to be left out of anything.

Then Mildred said, "Do y'all remember the time that Mattie drove Claire Mcdonald and Evie Addison to Greenville to see some art show at the museum?"

Most of us did, and laughed about it, but Mildred told it again anyway.

"All three of them are gone now," she went on, "so this was about ten years ago when they decided to make a day of it. Mattie agreed to drive—her car was the largest—and they planned the day down to the last detail. For a full week beforehand, they were on the phone every day, making sure they had tickets, discussing what they'd wear, how long it would take to get there, and which tea room they'd go to for lunch. Mattie had her car serviced and washed, made sure she had a map in the glove compartment, and told the other two the exact time she'd pick them up. An army general couldn't have planned a battle more carefully than those ladies planned that day.

"Well, the morning finally came, and Mattie drove around to their houses and picked them up. Claire brought some finger sandwiches and cookies, while Evie brought a thermos of coffee and some cups, in case anybody got peckish. Now, you realize that Greenville's only about forty miles down the mountain, but they were prepared for a *trip*. So there they were, three powdered and rouged dowager ladies, each wearing a huge hat, white gloves, and dressed to the nines for their cultural outing in the big city. Somebody who saw them leaving said they looked like three pouter pigeons tooling out of town."

"So what happened?" Callie, who'd apparently not heard the story, asked.

"They got a mile past the city limits and ran out of gas."

After the laughter died down, LuAnne looked at Sue and said, "I don't know if you know about this, but Mattie told me about it one day when I'd picked her up for some meeting. She said she'd been to see your husband on a Friday for a complete physical exam, and the very next Sunday, she of course went to church. 'I started in the door,' she said, 'and the first person I saw was Dr.

Hargrove, who was ushering that morning, and I just turned right back around and went home.' When I asked her why, she said, 'I wasn't about to walk into church with a man who'd seen me upside down only two days before. I *knew* what he'd be thinking.'"

Sue laughed as much as the rest of us.

Chapter 29

As we closed the door behind the last guest, I turned to Sam and said, "That went fairly well, don't you think?"

He nodded, put his arm around my shoulders, and turned me toward the library. "As always, honey. Mattie had a good turnout."

"She certainly did, but that's mainly because there's a high level of socially correct behavior in this town. We do as we ought to do."

"Or," Sam said, as we sat on the leather sofa in the library, "a good many of them expect to profit from her will. I hate to tell you, but the word has gotten around—both Leonard and Ledbetter asked me when you'll have the will probated." He grinned. "And that was before we'd even gotten to the cemetery."

"Oh, for goodness' sake. Well, they'll have to hold their horses. I'm nowhere near making any distributions. For one thing, we have to wait until Mattie's so-called great-nephew, or whatever he is, makes a legal declaration that he has no claim on her estate." I leaned my head against the back of the sofa. "I just wish that Mr. Sitton would get that little matter of his identity cleared up. I mean, either find out he's not actually kin to her or, if he is, get him out of the running completely by making him sign a quit-claim or something to her estate."

"He'll get it done, but . . ."

"But, Sam," I interrupted, "part of me wishes he'd prove to be a direct relative and that he'd petition the court to be declared the legitimate heir to her entire estate. Just think what a relief it would be to me. No more appraising furniture and sending it to Atlanta, no more going through recipes and twenty-year-old postcards, and no more worrying about where the money's coming from to carry out Mattie's instructions."

"I'm not sure it would be that easy," Sam said, "but you just may get your wish. Andrew Cobb didn't come to the reception, did he?"

"Why, no," I said, sitting up as I realized the oversight. "I don't recall seeing him. And, as a matter of fact, I don't think Mr. Sitton came, either."

"I saw them leave the cemetery together and assumed they were on their way here."

Still disturbed by my seeming lapse, I said, "Surely they didn't expect a personal invitation. It was printed in the service bulletin, so they should've known.

"Oh, Sam," I cried, turning to him. "Even though I'd love to be free of the problems, what if those two are cooking up some way to bypass Mattie's will?"

"No, not Sitton," Sam said, pulling me back. "Don't worry about that. He's a stickler for the law. If anything, I'd say that he's getting close to Cobb so he can figure him out. Believe me, the only one Sitton is working for is Mattie Freeman—you can count on that."

"Well, that's reassuring," I said. "I guess. But I hope he works a little for me while he's at it."

Sam was quiet for a moment, then he said, "Did anyone tell you what happened at the cemetery?"

"No, what?"

"Well, Cobb was pretty much treated as the chief mourner by the funeral home. He was directed to a place by the graveside and LuAnne and Leonard stood beside him. Everything went smoothly—Ledbetter said a few words and had a prayer, and that was about it. Until Cobb started crying."

"Crying! Why, he didn't even know Mattie."

"I know, but he held this huge handkerchief over his face and his shoulders starting shaking, and of course everybody was trying to console him."

"You, too?"

Sam smiled. "No, I was watching for actual tears. I didn't see any, but I heard a lot of moans and groans." Sam pushed his hair from his forehead. "I don't know, Julia, it could've been an act, or he could be one of those tender-hearted souls who tear up at any funeral. After they got him to sit down—you know, in one of those wobbly folding chairs—he tried to explain. Said it just hit him that all his family was now gone, and he was the only one left. And he regretted not getting here sooner so Mattie wouldn't have thought that she was the last one." Sam shook his head and said, "I can't figure him out. He could've been sincere, but it was a little over the top—a real meltdown, as Lloyd would say."

"Oh, my," I said. "I'm glad I wasn't there to see it, but, Sam, it had to've been an act. Who makes a public spectacle of themselves over the burial of a perfect stranger?"

Sam smiled. "Well, that seemed to be the general opinion. Most turned away and left. Even Ledbetter could barely offer a sympathetic word."

"No one believes he's Mattie's kin—that's the reason. Or, at least, they *hope* he isn't. He could surely play havoc with their expectations if he is."

We sat for a few minutes, both lost in thought of the dire consequences that might be in the offing—all dependent upon the decisions of a stranger in a two-wheeled trailer.

Sam broke the silence. "Did you get a chance to talk to Helen?"

"No, why? I mean, we spoke, but she came when everybody was crowded around the table, so that was about it."

"She was leaving as I got here, so we stood on the porch and talked a bit. A little unusual, I thought, because she's always friendly, but rarely stops long enough for a conversation. At least, with me. I think, though," Sam said, smiling at me, "I figured out the reason. Nate Wheeler came out the door, and Helen lit up like a Christmas tree."

"Really!"

"Yep, and he looked equally glad to see her still there. They talked a few minutes about Mattie's furniture, then they left together."

"How interesting."

"Well, don't read too much into it. They came in separate cars."

"Even so," I said, musing over a possible mismatch with romantic overtones. "Mr. Wheeler does clean up quite nicely. I saw him inside and almost didn't recognize him without all the sawdust sprinkles."

"He does, indeed," Sam said, then turned to another subject—one that he'd apparently been thinking about since this wasn't the first time he'd brought it up. "Listen, Julia, we'll be leaving Monday as soon as Lloyd picks up his report card. And I'd feel better if you had someone in the house with you. Why don't you ask Lillian and Latisha to stay over while I'm gone?"

"Well," I temporized, "I'll see if they can, but with Lloyd gone, Latisha may not want to. There're no children around here for her to play with. And with school out, she'll be underfoot and bored all day long."

"Then how about you staying with Hazel Marie? She'll be alone, too."

"Sam, she's the least alone woman in town. She has James living over the garage, and Granny Wiggins is in and out, to say nothing of running after toddling twins all day long. Believe me, she doesn't need a houseguest. And, to be honest, I'm not sure I could put up with all the turmoil for an entire week. Don't worry about it," I went on, "I'll be fine right here by myself. Did you pack your sunblock?"

"Two tubes. My lovely complexion will be well taken care of."

"Oh, you," I said as we laughed together.

"Actually," I went on after a few minutes, "it's the three of you floating around on the ocean that I'm concerned about. I want you to have a good time, but, Sam, do keep an eye on Lloyd. I don't want him falling off the boat."

"He's not going to fall off. Besides, we'll have on life jackets or vests or whatever they are. If anybody goes overboard, it'll be me because I plan to catch the biggest fish in the gulf, have it mounted, then hang it right here in our fancy library. Don't you think it'll fit right in with the decor?"

"I don't believe I'll tell you what I think. Oh," I said, sitting up with a sudden, perfect thought, "I know what I can do. I'll ask Etta Mae to stay the week with me."

Sam smiled. "That's a good idea, which I think I suggested some while back."

"You did, but now that we're down to the wire, it'll be a comfort to have her here at night. So I'll ask her, and that'll put your mind at rest."

"Well, I don't know about that. There's no telling what you and Ms. Wiggins will get up to."

From previous experience, I had to agree with him, but not out loud. Besides, I was too busy with Mattie's affairs to go looking for any more trouble.

The following morning, Saturday, found me torn between doing what I should do and what I wanted to do. What I wanted to do was to go to Mattie's apartment, which would be empty for the weekend, and get started on the albums and scrapbooks stacked up in the back of her guest room closet. I wanted to sit down all by myself and go through them without any distractions. It had come to me during the night that there just might be some hint of Andrew F. Cobb's existence in the things she had saved. Wouldn't it be interesting to find a baby picture with the name *Andrew* penciled on the back?

But, no, I did what I should have done because Sam hadn't. His idea of packing was not mine, so I spent most of the day folding clothes, packing them, and listening to him tell me he wouldn't need them.

"Just some shorts," he said. "That's all I'll need." And he started unpacking what I'd just packed. "Honey, it'll be in the nineties down there. I won't need a jacket."

"Well, I thought you might go to a nice place to eat, one that requires a jacket."

Sam laughed. "Think about who I'm going with. You think Pickens and Lloyd will want to dress for dinner?"

"You're probably right," I conceded. "Just put everything you want to take on the bed, and I'll pack them. Don't forget your hat and . . ."

"And the sunblock," Sam finished. "I gotcha. Now, why don't we go out for dinner and put a lid on Mattie, Andrew Cobb, and getting sunburned."

So we did, putting aside all the troublesome matters, and enjoyed each other's company. My word, I was going to miss him. The week stretching out ahead seemed an eternity.

Chapter 30

Monday came, and by midmorning Lloyd had called to say that he was back from school with his almost perfect report card. So Sam stowed his one small suitcase in the trunk of his car, kissed me good-bye, and drove off to pick up Lloyd and Mr. Pickens. They had a long road ahead of them to the bottom of Mississippi, which would've been worse if they'd gone in Mr. Pickens's cramped sports car as he'd first suggested. Both Lloyd and Sam vetoed that in favor of Sam's roomier Lincoln.

They'd also discussed flying to Biloxi, but that would've involved changing planes in Atlanta, and there wasn't an easy connection. "Besides," Mr. Pickens had said, "I like road trips, and with two good drivers, we'll be fine."

I stood on the front porch after Sam had driven off to pick up the other two, and waited. Sure enough, in a little while his car nosed onto Polk Street, slowed as it neared the house, while all three of them, grinning, waved until they were out of sight.

It's close to heart wrenching when people you love go off from home. You're happy for them, but you also fear for them. I wished the week were over already and that they were driving in rather than out.

Sighing, I went inside, determined to stay so busy during the days with Mattie's affairs and so entertained in the evenings with Etta Mae's company that the week would fly by. She had accepted with enthusiasm my invitation to spend a week in Lloyd's room along with all meals included.

"It'll be like a vacation," she'd said. "I haven't had a real vacation since I don't know when, and this will be like room and board in a fancy hotel. I'd love to, Miss Julia."

Recalling that conversation, I got as far as the living room and sat down to process all that had happened between packing for Sam on Saturday and seeing him off on Monday. Sunday had been close to a lost day, as Sam had wavered about leaving at all. Concerned that the entire church, it seemed, was now expecting me to come to the rescue, he felt he should stay home to fend them off. I had insisted that he go—the fishing trip had been planned for months—telling him that I would unplug the phones, refuse to answer the door, and stay out of sight for the duration.

"Let them clamor, Sam," I'd told him. "There's nothing I can do about it."

It had happened like this: we'd gone to church as we usually did on Sunday morning and had just settled in our pew, preparing to focus on Pastor Ledbetter's sermon. The congregation waited in respectful silence for him to begin. But just as he clasped the pulpit and opened his mouth, a far-off clanking sound issued from the bowels of the church, followed by a low groan that filled the sanctuary.

We all sat up, looked around, then to the pastor for guidance. What in the world was it? Then a woman—it might've been LuAnne—on the far side of the church stood up and screamed, "*Smoke!* The church is on fire!"

And sure enough, a wisp of smoke emanated from the vent high up on the wall beside the apse. There was a great stirring of the congregation as people got up to leave, while the pastor called for calm and orderliness. We Presbyterians do like things done decently and in order, you know.

"Slow down, people, it's all right!" Pastor Ledbetter shouted. "Don't panic. No fire, no fire! It's just the air-conditioning." The explanation didn't help, for his lapel microphone amplified his voice to an unbearable decibel level, making the scramble to get outside even more frantic.

Sam kept his hands on my shoulders as we joined the surge for the doors, but by that time the smoke had dissipated and the groaning and clanking had died away.

Well, of course that hadn't been the end of it, although it had ended the service. We'd barely gotten home when two trucks from Nichol's Heating and Air-Conditioning pulled into the parking lot of the church. Thank goodness for workmen who answer emergency calls on the weekends.

Sam and I had sat on the front porch after a light lunch and watched the goings and comings across the street. Pastor Ledbetter, sweating in the sun, followed the men from truck to church and back again over and over. One truck left, apparently to retrieve some parts for the unit, and a group of deacons gathered under the porte cochere, probably to discuss what was to be done and how to pay for it.

"Think I should take some sandwiches over?" I asked, but made no move to do so.

Sam smiled. "Oh, I wouldn't bother. They ought to go on home and let the repairmen do their job."

"My thought exactly," I said, and continued to sit, lazily waving a fan in the heat. "Sam, let's go in the house. There's no need to swelter out here just because they are. Our air-conditioning is working."

"Good idea," he said, rising from his rocking chair.

We spent the afternoon reading the Sunday papers and occasionally checking on the activity at the church through the front windows. Finally, around five o'clock the repairmen left, and so did the pastor and the deacons. I hoped that was a sign that all was well.

It wasn't. About five-thirty, the phone started ringing and it didn't stop until we turned it off and went to bed. The pastor was first in line, with every one of the twelve deacons taking his turn to appeal to my loyalty to the church.

"We *need* air-conditioning, Miss Julia," the pastor had said. "The old unit can't be repaired. We can't even limp by on it, and there're too many windows to be opening and closing them every day and every night, and, besides, most of them are painted shut. I just don't know what we'll do if you're unwilling to distribute Miss Mattie's assets in a timely manner."

"It's not that I'm unwilling," I said, trying to patiently explain my position. "It's that I'm unable to distribute what doesn't exist." And I went on to recount the many snags that were holding up Mattie's assets—mainly that she had so few.

"But surely," he pled, "she has a little something somewhere. You could perhaps manage a partial payment of the bequest she made to the church. Just so we can get a new unit and keep the church cool. You know, Miss Julia, that some of our elderly members and small children will truly suffer in the heat."

"Pastor, all I can tell you is that I will check with Mattie's attorney to see if I can legally do that. But I'll tell you right now that I don't think I can. In fact, Mr. Sitton has said that most wills take six months or more to be probated."

"Six months! Why, that'll be the dead of winter, and we won't need air-conditioning."

By that time, I had had enough. It wasn't my fault, or Mattie's, that the deacons hadn't planned for expected expenditures or for obsolescent air-conditioning units. Taking care of the church property was their job, after all. Besides, not every church had to be air-conditioned—Lillian's, for instance, wasn't. They had overhead fans and handheld ones, too. Spoiled, that's what we were.

Fed up, I said, "My advice, Pastor, is for the church to go into debt and keep the congregation cool. I know you don't want to do it, and I appreciate that, but my hands are tied. Besides," I went on, "you can have a campaign to raise funds to pay for it, and I'll be the first to contribute."

He was not happy with me. One of the things that I could admire about him was that he was disinclined to incur debt—unlike another minister I knew who had once gone into a frenzy of bank-financed church construction, then answered a call to another church before the roof was on.

I had barely gotten off the phone with the pastor when one of the deacons called. And after that, one after the other was either pleading with or nagging at me, as if a hot church were entirely my fault.

To whom, I wondered, would they have turned if Mattie hadn't died?

"Come sit with me," I said as I walked into the kitchen after Lillian had called me to lunch. I had been mentally picturing Sam's Lincoln going farther and farther down the mountain, and I needed a distraction. "I have got to think of something besides those three on the road dodging crazy drivers, while I'm here trying to dodge overheated deacons. Tell me about the Reverend Abernathy. He was having some kind of problem, wasn't he?"

"Yes'm, he sure was and still is." Lillian hung a washcloth over the faucet and came over to the table with my plate. "See, Mr. Robert Mobley, he died, like I tole you. An' ever'body was happy for Miss Bessie, 'cause he treat her so bad. We all figgered she was set for life in that little house he have an' doin' jus' for herself without wonderin' what he gonna do next. Well . . ."

"Knock, knock, yoo-hoo, Julia!" Mildred rapped on the back door.

"Why, Miz Allen!" Lillian greeted her as she opened the door. "Come in, come in. You lookin' mighty fine for a lady right outta the hospital."

"I'm feeling fine, too. So fine that I'm thinking of taking a walk. Julia," she said, turning to me, "if you've finished lunch, let's walk a while."

"Wonderful!" I jumped up, anxious to strike while the iron was hot or before she changed her mind. "But come in for a minute. I want to show you something."

I hurried to retrieve Mattie's scribble from my pocketbook, as Mildred sank into a chair at the kitchen table, saying, "Whew, I'm out of breath from walking across the yard."

"Look at this," I said, handing the scrap of paper to her. "I found it in Mattie's safe-deposit box, but I can't make head nor tails out of it. And neither can Sam or Lillian."

Mildred frowned as she studied the numbers and figures. "Well, I've seen some of Mattie's writing, and it looks kind of wobbly like this does, Julia," she said, as she carefully placed the scrap on the table and pushed it away. "You ought to get rid of it. It may be a spell of some kind, like if you wanted to put a hex on somebody."

A pan clattered in the sink, as Lillian spun around. *"What you say?"*

"Oh, no," I said, laughing. "Our Miss Mattie? Surely not. Mrs. Allen's just teasing, Lillian."

"Mattie had her ways," Mildred said, but she was laughing. "And she was strange, you have to admit."

"You won't believe how strange. I'll tell you as we walk." I opened the door and urged her up and out. "And, Lillian," I said, turning back, "Christians don't have to worry about hexes. We'll talk when I get back. This won't take long."

And it didn't. Mildred's idea of a walk was a leisurely stroll to the far end of the block and back again.

"That should do it for the first time," she said as we returned to her driveway. "I forgot the pedometer, but how many steps do you think that was? I lost count when you were telling me about finding a flask in Mattie's pocketbook."

I was tempted to say about fifty, but was afraid of discouraging her. "I wasn't counting, but I think we should aim to go all the way around the block the next time."

"Well, I don't know," Mildred said, blotting her face with a Kleenex. "It's awfully hot to be outside that long."

"We don't need to push it, but maybe walking later in the day would be better. We got a good start today, though, and I'm proud of you, Mildred. Every step you take and every calorie you turn down pushes that operation further away."

"That's why I'm doing it, but, boy, am I tired!"

Chapter 31

Mildred urged me to come in for a restorative lemonade break, which I was happy to do. We sat on her side porch and discussed the disposition of Mattie's furniture.

"Well, I'll tell you, Mildred," I said, folding a napkin around my frosted glass, "I couldn't be more pleased with Diane Jankowski. She's so knowledgeable and competent. I feel sure that she'll get the best price possible for everything. And, believe me, I am going to need every penny to carry out Mattie's wishes."

"I know you can't do anything about it now," Mildred said, "but I'd be interested in that little cellarette you told me about—if it's as good as your appraiser says." She took a sip of her lemonade. "Let me know when the auction will be. I may have business in Atlanta about the same time."

After a little more discussion of antiques in general, I sighed and mentioned the telephone campaign that Pastor Ledbetter and the deacons were on.

"I hate to go home," I said. "They just keep calling and not a one listens when I say I can't release what I don't have. It's as if the air conditioner died the same time as Mattie, so the timing makes it a sign of some kind." I managed a weak laugh, but I was really tired of fending off church leaders bent on getting what they wanted.

"Julia," Mildred said, "why don't you leave that church? You've threatened to long enough, and St. Mark's would love to have you."

"I've thought about it, but the First Presbyterian is Sam's church. And Hazel Marie's and Lloyd's. I can't leave them."

"Well, I was in the same boat, as you remember. I joined the First Pres because it was Horace's church, so Tony grew up in it. Then he moved to New York and you know the change that came over him. Well, her now. By that time Horace had stopped going at all, and there I was all by myself. So I decided I'd go where I belonged which was St. Mark's. I was a cradle Episcopalian, you know."

"I do know, and I know you're happy there. And I've been tempted to move my letter, believe me, I have. I guess, though," I mused aloud, "I'm holding St. Mark's in reserve. It's my out if things get too bad across the street."

Kind of like she was holding that stapling operation in reserve as a last option if nothing else worked. But I didn't say that out loud because being compared with a line of staples in one's stomach was hardly a compliment to St. Mark's Episcopal Church.

Then, after a brief discussion of Mattie's funeral and Lu-Anne's management of it, I slipped across our yards and went home.

"'Bout time you got back," Lillian said when I walked in. "That phone been ringin' off the hook. I write all the names down on that piece of paper. They want you to call 'em back."

I glanced down the list—the names of four deacons and one elder—then wadded up the paper and threw it in the trash. "I know what they want, Lillian," I said, turning to her. "If they call back, you haven't seen me. I'm going to Mattie's to help Helen and Diane, and I plan to stay until they're ready to leave. I'll get some work done and be away from the phone at the same time. Don't tell anybody where I am."

"Miss Etta Mae be here for supper, so you better be on back here by six."

"Oh, I'll be back before then. Is Lloyd's room ready for her? I have time to change the sheets."

"Already done, an' I put out towels an' things, too. Bed turned down an' flowers in a vase. An' I'm fixin' fried chicken, creamed corn, and fried okra for her supper."

"Well, I hope you're including me for that supper," I said, laughing. Lillian thought that Etta Mae needed some mothering and fattening up. She was looking forward to having her around. "Actually, I'd better not tell Sam what we're having when he calls. They might all turn around and come back home."

Just as I put the final labels—either MR. SITTON or THROW AWAY—on the bags of sorted papers and odds and ends from Mattie's apartment, I heard the phone ring. I ignored it, but Lillian didn't.

"Miss Julia?" she called as she came across the hall. "You better take this. It's Miss Helen, an' she real upset."

What now? I thought, but wondering, *Andrew F. Cobb,* as I picked up the phone in the library. "Helen? What's going on?"

"Julia," Helen said, her voice tight with concern, "I hate to ask you, but, well, did you take it? Or move it somewhere?"

"Move what?"

"The cellarette. We can't find it. I mean, it was here Friday afternoon. We'd moved it into the guest room, because Diane had already taken pictures of it. But it's not there now."

"Have you . . ." I started, knowing full well that they had, "looked everywhere?"

"Everywhere," she affirmed. "Even asked Nate to help us move things around. It's just not here, Julia. I'm so upset, I don't know what to do."

Neither did I. Feeling that the floor had dropped from under me, I asked, "The door, was it locked when you got there? Any signs of tampering?"

"No, and we checked for that. The door was locked. In fact, I had trouble opening it with the new key. Oh, Julia, I feel responsible, and I'm so sorry."

"It's not your fault, Helen. But surely it's there somewhere—it couldn't have just walked off. Keep looking, I'm on my way."

I didn't take time to say good-bye, just clicked off the phone and headed out.

"Lillian," I called, grabbing my pocketbook, "there's trouble at Mattie's place. I'll be back as soon as I can." And off I went, my nerves snapping like a tangle of hot wires.

I pushed open Mattie's door and almost knocked Mr. Wheeler over. "Oh, sorry. Have you found it?" I cried, knowing that I looked as wild-eyed and frantic as I felt.

Helen and Diane just stood there, Helen near tears and Diane frowning over her camera.

Mr. Wheeler was the only one who seemed able to answer. "It's not here," he said. "I've moved everything and looked everywhere. But . . ."

"But how could it just disappear?" I asked, throwing out my hands.

"Come over here and I'll show you." Mr. Wheeler walked over to the large chest-on-chest that had been in front of the French doors to the sunroom. "See here," he said, squatting down and pointing to a wide, deep scratch on the floor, "this chest has been moved—shoved back. And the French doors weren't locked. I was able to slip behind this thing and get into the sunroom. There's a back window that wasn't locked—it is now, though. Whoever it was got in that way."

"Oh, my word! What else is missing? What else?" I couldn't believe I'd been so focused on getting a new lock for the front door that I'd completely overlooked checking the windows. But who would've thought of three walls of small windows, high off the ground, in a room that we couldn't even get into? "Who could've done this?" I demanded.

"Someone," Mr. Wheeler calmly answered, "who knew enough to choose a small, easily handled piece, and who knew the value of it. The real question is, who would know where to sell it?"

"That's a good question," Diane said, suddenly looking up. "I have pictures of it and I know the local antiques dealers and some regional ones. I'll make copies and send them out. In fact,

I'll call everybody I know in the business and ask them to watch for it."

"Do that," Mr. Wheeler said, then turned to me. "But the first thing we need to do is report the theft. You'll need a police report to prove ownership when it turns up. Or to make a claim on a homeowner's insurance policy. If Mrs. Freeman had one."

"I'll have to look," I said, but I was thinking that finding it would be a job for Mr. Sitton. "I haven't seen one so far. All right, I'll call the sheriff's department."

We spent the next two and a half hours watching three deputies examine the crime scene, including dusting the offending windowsill for fingerprints. When they'd first walked in, one of them looked around at the furniture-filled room, and mumbled, "Somebody *live* here?"

"Not any longer," I said, then went on to explain what we were doing and what had occurred. I also had to explain what a cellarette was and why anyone would want one. I'm not sure the deputies were convinced, for they kept asking if anything else was missing.

"We got some prints," the detective—who wasn't Sergeant Coleman Bates, I'm sorry to say—told me. "But they're probably the owner's—same ones everywhere else. The rest is mostly smudges. Prob'bly from wearing gloves."

He was thorough, though, taking prints from a few things that we knew only Mattie had touched—like her Bible in a drawer by her bed—as well as from Mr. Wheeler, who had recently closed and locked the window, for comparison.

At one point, the detective checked a few things in his notebook, then looked up. "You have an estimate as to the value of what was taken?"

"Maybe a thousand or so, I guess," I ventured, then turned to Diane. "But here's the expert."

"More like eight or ten thousand," she said. "It's museum quality."

My mouth fell open as I thought of the dent that money could've made in the lists of bequests.

The detective's eyebrows went straight up. "Really? For a little . . . whatever it was?"

"It's not something you'd pick up on eBay," Diane said drily. "Or at IKEA, either."

As the deputies prepared to leave, the detective took me aside. "Mrs. Murdoch, it looks to me like this was a professional job—not just a kid lookin' for some quick cash. Whoever did this knew what he wanted, got it, then left. Didn't bother anything else. Chances are, if y'all hadn't been checkin' everything Mrs. Freeman had, you wouldn't even have missed it. I hate to tell you, but I wouldn't be surprised if that little box thing was settin' right now in an antiques store in Charleston or Richmond."

With a sinking heart, I knew he was right. We didn't even know when the break-in had happened—it could've been at any time over the weekend when none of us had been there. That gave the thief plenty of time to whisk the cellarette to far-flung reaches of the country, and, furthermore, plenty of time to get back to Abbotsville and appear innocent.

But there was one question that narrowed the field of possible suspects, which was: who even knew that the cellarette existed? I began to list them in my mind, my eyes flicking over the obvious ones standing there in the room—Helen, Diane, Mr. Wheeler—and quickly discounted them.

Then there was Mildred, whom I'd told about the cellarette, but she had no reason to steal it. She wanted to buy it. And Lillian had heard me tell Sam about it, but to suspect either of them was beyond comprehension. I couldn't remember if I'd mentioned it to LuAnne, though she wouldn't have done it. She could've told any number of other people, though, and if so, I'd never track them all down. Mr. Sitton? No, impossible.

Who was left? It came down to the fact that whoever had stolen the cellarette knew what he or she was doing. So I swung back to considering Helen, Diane, and Mr. Wheeler, and hated myself for doing it. But who else was there?

Well, Andrew F. Cobb, for one. But he'd never been in Mattie's apartment, although he knew where it was. He'd told me as much at Mattie's visitation. But did he know furniture? How could he have known that a valuable cellarette was in Mattie's collection? Did he even know what one was?

The fact was, we didn't know enough about him to consider him a suspect. But I knew the others—except for Mr. Wheeler and Diane—well enough to know they couldn't possibly have done it. But I could not bring myself to seriously think either Diane or Mr. Wheeler could be the guilty one. As for Diane, she was an accredited appraiser and her career would be over if there was ever a hint of dishonesty on her part. Besides, she was already sketching out a mock-up for the flyers to be sent out to dealers so they'd know what to look for if anyone tried to sell or pawn the cellarette.

And Mr. Wheeler? Well, if he was the one, I'd never again be able to trust my judgment about anybody I met. I'd turn into a beady-eyed, suspicious old woman distrusting everyone around me. I was skeptical enough about people already. I didn't want to get any worse.

After further discussion among us about how awful it was and how we all regretted that it had happened, I suggested we lock up and go home. No one, least of all myself, felt like doing more work in the apartment, so after following Mr. Wheeler around, squeezing behind the chest-on-chest to double-check the sunroom windows, he made the obvious but overlooked suggestion of taking out the drawers so we could move the chest out of the way. And, of course, found all seven drawers full of more stuff for me to go through. But with just the frame of the chest, Mr. Wheeler, Diane, and Helen were able to move it enough to allow us to go freely in and out of the sunroom.

With that done, I shooed them all out, locked the door myself, then headed for home. Actually, I didn't want to linger and look around too much for fear of discovering that something else was missing. I mean, who would know? There were still boxes in the guest room closet that I'd not even looked into, and who knew what was under the beds.

I had to go home, report the theft to Mr. Sitton, and try to come to terms with the fact that I had failed to safeguard Mattie's possessions.

Chapter 32

"After thinking about it," I said to Etta Mae as we were finishing supper that evening, "which is what I've done all afternoon, I've come to one clear conclusion: it was not a random theft."

"Uh-huh," Etta Mae said thoughtfully as she buttered another of Lillian's yeast rolls. "It sure sounds like somebody knew what he wanted, where it was, and where he could sell it. And how to get in, too."

"That's the thing that gets to me," I said. "I hate to admit it but I never thought of checking the windows in the sunroom. I mean, we couldn't even get to them. That huge chest-on-chest was right up against the French doors. Why, Etta Mae, the thing is so tall that the pediment almost touches the ceiling. We couldn't move it today until we'd taken the drawers out, and even then it wasn't easy. Whoever came in gouged a huge scratch in Mattie's floor just by pushing on it from behind. It's a wonder it didn't topple over."

I shivered at the thought of the damage that would've been done if the chest had fallen over—it would've stretched more than halfway across the room, smashing everything in its path. On the other hand, though, the noise would've awakened other tenants, and Mr. Wheeler would have come running.

I sighed. What could've happened didn't happen, so you deal with what did.

Etta Mae bit into the buttered roll, a look of bliss sweeping across her face. "Think he'll come back? The thief, I mean."

"I don't see how in the world he could get in, if he does. Everything is locked up tight—he'd have to smash in a window if he tried to get in. And all the tenants know about it, so they'll be listening out. No, I'm hoping that if he sells the cellarette for even a fraction of its worth, he'll be satisfied." I stopped, then got up from the table. "Hold on a minute, Etta Mae. I want you to look at something."

Returning to the table, I held out the scrap of paper with the puzzling scribble on it. "See what you make of this."

She studied it for several minutes, then said, "Hm-m, eleven numbers and figures. Could I have something to write with? And a phone book and a phone with a dial."

When I handed them to her, she began jotting down figures. "Okay, look at this. See, this first one here could be a one. I'll add some dashes, then the next one is a seven, then an *R*, which on the dial is also a seven—you know, where *PQRS* is. And if we take these two little squiggles as ones, too, and this two to the third power as plain old twenty-three, we come up with 1-771-012-3710. Looks like a phone number to me."

"Etta Mae, you're a genius!"

"Not hardly," she said, but she grinned, pleased with herself. "Now let's look up that area code code and see where the number goes to."

But the area code pages in the phone book brought us to a screeching halt—there was no 771 area code, either nationally or internationally.

"I'm trying it anyway," I said, punching in the numbers on my flip-top cell phone. All I got was a high-pitched screech on the line and a voice telling me that my call couldn't be completed. "No use, Etta Mae. It's not a long-distance number."

"Sure looks like one," she said, not at all discouraged. "But let me think about it for a while. It may be in code—you know, where one thing stands for something else. If it is, we'd have to have the key that was used. It could take forever to break the code without it. We could try, though."

"Goodness, Etta Mae, how do you know so much about codes?"

"Oh," she said, smiling, "I used to fiddle around with secret codes and messages when I was a little girl. I remember a few we could try, but I'd like to think about it first."

I wanted her to think about it, as well as think about everything else, so I sat down at the table and opened up. I told her about the problems I was having with Mattie's will, the difficulty of turning furniture into cash, the church expecting a handout, the sudden but questionable appearance of a possible heir to Mattie's estate, who, "didn't want anything," and the theft of a valuable antique from a supposedly locked room. Then I had to explain what a cellarette was.

"Lord, Etta Mae," I concluded, "with the proceeds from that one little item I could've started on the bequests in the will. Or, if I were so inclined—which I'm not—I could've made it possible for the church to put a down payment on a new air-conditioning unit. And now here we are with a coded message that's driving me crazy. The whole mess is giving me a headache."

"You need to stop worrying about it," Etta Mae said, sounding like Lillian, as she put her napkin on the table. "I bet the sheriff will track that thief down and you'll get that little liquor chest back. And I'll bet that code's a simple one, and we'll figure it out. So put it all on the back burner for now, and let's go watch *Antiques Roadshow*."

The show that night didn't capture my full attention—too many Civil War rifles, old violins, Art Deco bracelets, garishly colored posters, and only one piece of furniture, which was an elaborately carved Victorian coatrack that I wouldn't have had on a silver platter.

Etta Mae, however, was entranced, sitting forward in her chair to watch intently. It was, she told me, one of her educational programs through which she learned things she didn't know. "History stuff, you know," she said.

So I sat back and thought about the phone conversation I'd had with Mr. Sitton as soon as I'd gotten home that afternoon. Deeply dreading to admit I'd failed in my executor's job by allowing a theft, I'd told him what had happened. Surprisingly, he'd taken it in stride, consoling me by saying that he should've been more concerned about obituary readers.

"They keep up with obituaries the same way they keep up with wedding announcements—knowing that houses will be empty during a ceremony. It's a shame, but it is what it is.

"Now, Mrs. Murdoch," he went on, "I've spoken with the sheriff in the county where this Andrew F. Cobb grew up—in Kentucky, as you'll recall—and he put me in touch with his own father, who'd been the sheriff for many years before him. The old man remembered Andrew well, apparently a troubled boy—nothing truly egregious, but he spent a few years in and out of jail for breaking and entering and joyriding when he was a young man. And, I'm sorry to say, a short prison term when a judge had had enough of him."

Aha! I thought, then murmured, "Breaking and entering means he knows how it's done."

"Well, I wouldn't jump to any conclusions. As far as both sheriffs know, Cobb's been on the up-and-up ever since. Learned his lesson, so to speak. And I've been unable to find him having had any other run-ins with the law, and, believe me, I've looked.

"Now, Mrs. Murdoch, the following consists of pure gossip from an old man, but it does throw some light on Mrs. Freeman's relationship with her family, and may, therefore, help us evaluate Mr. Cobb." Mr. Sitton took a deep breath and proceeded to give me a summary of the old sheriff's memories. "It seems that there was a wealthy family of Cobbs years ago—came from Virginia after the Civil War and bought up a lot of land. Did real well for a good while, but by the time we're talking about, the Cobbs were down to one son and one daughter who inherited the family estate. It was divided between them. But there were problems because each of them felt that the other had gotten the best and the most of what had been left. So there was a fairly deep rift between brother and sister early on, and, consequently, between their families. The sister, along the way, married a Freeman, who was, from all accounts, a decent enough sort who tried to heal the rift, or at least calm the waters. He didn't succeed.

"Bear with me now, because it gets complicated. The sister, now Mrs. Freeman, had a son, Thomas Freeman. And over the years, the brother, name of Cobb, who was a hard, implacable man, had a couple of sons and, late in life, one daughter. That, as it seems, would've been our Mattie. Well, when she was still a young girl, she ran off with Thomas Freeman, her aunt's son, and married him."

"Oh, my," I said, as I recalled the photograph of a soldier named Tommy that I had seen among Mattie's papers. "She married her cousin?"

"Her *first* cousin, which in Kentucky is a criminal offense. Well, the Cobbs were outraged. They went after their daughter and brought her home, started annulment proceedings, and pressed charges against the Freeman boy, which sent him to prison."

"That's horrible," I said, although I didn't know how I would've handled such a misalliance.

"Others thought so, too. The Freeman boy was given early release on the condition that he join the army. He was killed in either Korea or Vietnam—the sheriff wasn't sure which, and I've not had time to pin it down. After that, the rift was even deeper, and to make matters worse, both families were in financial difficulties—land sold off to pay taxes, crop failures, some fatal accidents, long illnesses, and a lot of bad decisions had taken their toll. The Freeman house burned down, and the Cobbs died out. The sheriff said it was like both families were snakebit. They went from the top of the heap down to next to nothing—all in a couple of generations or so. And now here we have Andrew F. Cobb, who it seems would be the son or maybe the grandson of one of Mattie's brothers."

"And therefore," I concluded, "Mattie's legitimate heir. I will gladly turn everything over to him. When do you want to do it?"

"Not so fast, Mrs. Murdoch. Andrew F. Cobb will have to

formally challenge the will, and he continues to tell me that he does not intend to do that. He says he likes the freedom of the road and doesn't want to be tied down with material goods." From Mr. Sitton's tone, I could tell that he had little understanding of such a disinterested attitude toward material goods.

Neither had I. Material goods had eased my life considerably, and, like Mr. Sitton, I had no desire to live without them. Especially on the road in a trailer while wearing a hippie headband.

"Man, that's hard to believe." Etta Mae broke into my reverie as she peered closely at the television set. "I can't believe that a *poster,* of all things, with an airplane on it would be worth that much. I mean, who would want it?"

"Well, some people collect them, I suppose. But I agree, I wouldn't want it. It wouldn't go with my decor."

"Mine, either," Etta Mae said. "It would be too big to hang in my single-wide, for one thing. I'd sell it and buy something prettier than that thing. Or pay some bills."

We laughed together, then I said, "Etta Mae, you must do as you please while you're here—go to bed and get up when you want and whatever. I want you to make yourself at home. I'm just so happy to have you here. And so is Sam. When I talked to him earlier, he said again that he was glad you were here to keep me out of trouble."

Etta Mae cut her dark eyes at me, an impish look on her face. "I have a feeling . . ." The ringing of the phone interrupted her and I got up to answer it.

"Mrs. Murdoch?" an unfamiliar feminine voice asked. "It's Isabelle Wickham, and I'm calling for the church. Reverend Ledbetter has given several of us lists of members to call, and you're on mine."

"Oh?" I said, vaguely placing the woman as a new member—one of those who'd hit the ground running. She volunteered for everything.

"Yes, the pastor wants to spread the word that Sunday services are being changed from the regular eleven o'clock hour to eight o'clock."

"In the *morning*?"

"Well, it's cooler then," she informed me. "And as you may know, the church is without air-conditioning. It's been suggested that we put folding chairs on the basketball court in the Family Life Center because it has its own unit. But, of course, we'd have to refinish that floor when we move back to the sanctuary, and the pastor looks on that as a needless expenditure."

"Thank you for calling," I said, slightly amused, "although I've been in church at eleven o'clock every Sunday for so long that I may show up then anyway."

She was not amused. "That would be too bad. I don't know much about it, but it seems that for some strange reason, one of our members is preventing us from buying a new unit."

I gasped. It was all I could do because I was rendered speechless. Stammering my thanks for the information, I hung up and stood by the phone until I was able to return to my chair.

Chapter 33

"Church business," I told Etta Mae, apologizing for the interruption, but she was still entranced with *Antiques Roadshow*. Maybe that was a good thing. I might've spewed out my outrage at having had the onus of a broken air conditioner laid on my shoulders. And I knew who had put it there—don't think I didn't.

But I put a clamp on the fiery words that wanted to boil out, restrained by knowing that it was bad form to speak ill of one's church to a nonmember. Although I had been occasionally guilty of doing just that when I'd been pushed to my limit.

"I just love this room," Etta Mae said, sitting up and looking around as the program ended. "It's so elegant and everything. You have real good taste."

"Thank you, but I can't take all the credit. I had some help from a designer, although I had to put my foot down when she wanted to paint the walls navy blue."

"Really? It was your idea to paint the walls white and the trim this pretty green? Usually it's the other way around."

"The color on the trim is Raleigh Tavern Green, and it wasn't my idea at all. It's the way they painted rooms in Colonial times and still do in Williamsburg." I looked around as she was doing, feeling again the sense of history that the room evoked for me. "I like to think that if Mr. Jefferson came to call, he would feel right at home."

"I don't think I know him."

I almost laughed out loud, but I wouldn't have hurt her feelings for the world. So as deftly as I could I explained that I was speaking metaphorically of our third president, and she laughed at herself. Then we had an interesting talk about the country's early years, and she proved a rapt, but short-lived, pupil. As her interest waned, she began to go over her schedule of patients for the following day, and I decided to go upstairs to bed. But the whole episode reminded me of my intention to work with the Literacy Council, which of course I had been unable to do, my time having been wholly taken up with Mattie's affairs.

Maybe one of these days, I thought, as I trudged up the stairs after a long day of dealing with Sam and Lloyd leaving for a week, the theft of something valuable that was under my guardianship, welcoming a houseguest with a change of clothes in a plastic grocery sack, and learning that I was to blame for a lack of air-conditioning—any one of which was enough for one day alone. I was tired.

But did I sleep? No, I did not. Well, off and on, but mostly off, for images of someone sneaking into Mattie's apartment and emptying it out while I lay in bed worrying about it kept running through my head.

At one point, I sat straight up in bed, thinking I'd heard a noise downstairs. *Etta Mae,* I thought. *Maybe she's getting a midnight snack.* If so, she was quiet about eating it, for I heard nothing more.

I was glad that she was in the house—I would've slept even less imagining somebody breaking in. I mean, a thief was *out there* somewhere. Any house could've been the next target.

Lying down again, my mind was racing so fast that I couldn't get back to sleep. Who had burgled Mattie's apartment? I went over again all the prime suspects—all those who had knowledge of and access to what was in her apartment. And could come to no other feasible person of interest than Andrew F. Cobb. But was that because I didn't want it to have been someone I knew and trusted? Was he a likely candidate only because he was a stranger to us?

Lord, I didn't know. If, however, I could find out where he'd been over the weekend, that might answer some questions. Why, he could've been out of town, which would take him out of the running entirely. He could've taken his little two-wheeled trailer up to a campsite in the Smoky Mountains and spent the weekend hiking on the trails, cooking over a campfire, and sleeping in a bedroll.

On the other hand, I thought, as the other possibility popped up in my mind, even though he'd said that he didn't want to be tied down by material goods, those goods could be turned into cash, which had never tied anybody down. And actually that was exactly what I was in the process of doing.

Maybe that was it! Maybe he was waiting for me to do the hard work of evaluating, sorting, culling, transporting, and selling all of Mattie's material goods, then he'd step in with a court order and an extended hand for the cash.

But here was the question: if Andrew F. Cobb was the thief—why had he bothered? If he was Mattie's great-nephew, everything she had could have been his. Oh, he would've had to prove his kinship, then go through some legal rigmarole to contest her will, but I couldn't imagine that any of the beneficiaries would go to the trouble of challenging his rights to her estate.

Well, I had to rethink that. The church might, but surely Pastor Ledbetter and the elders had more class than to attempt to override a legal heir. Besides St. Paul having had a few words to say on the subject of lawsuits, it was also quite tasteless for a church to involve itself in one. But, then again, the session might figure it was worth it. After all, the church was Mattie's major beneficiary, and the sanctuary was in dire need of cool air. Maybe when it came to a choice between taking the high road or fighting for their rights, the elders would rather be thought tasteless than to swelter all summer.

I had just drifted off to sleep when the phone rang beside the bed. Scared to death, my first thought was that something had happened to Lloyd or Sam.

"Hello?" I quavered, then cleared my throat.

"Mrs. Murdoch? It's Nate Wheeler. Sorry to wake you, but we've had an incident here, and I thought I'd better let you know."

I sat straight up in bed, wide awake. "What kind of incident? Another break-in?"

"No, I think we nipped that in the bud. But somebody was sneaking around the building. Nothing happened because Mrs. Henderson up on the third floor saw something or somebody moving down below. She was sleeping in her sunroom and got up to go to the . . . Ah, well, anyway, she was awake and looked out the window and saw a shadow creeping around below near Mrs. Freeman's sunroom. So she thought . . ."

"The thief! He was coming back for something else."

"That's what she thought, so she called the sheriff, then me. Deputies are looking around outside now, but they haven't found anything."

"Oh, my," I moaned. "Mr. Wheeler, are you sure that nobody got in?"

"Yes, I'm sure. I went all around outside Mrs. Freeman's sunroom with a deputy and we checked every window. There's no breach anywhere, and I guess we have Mrs. Henderson to thank for that."

And her call of nature, I thought, but didn't say.

"Well, that settles it," I said. "If you hear noises in the hall in about fifteen minutes, it'll be me. Mr. Wheeler, I am moving in for the duration, and I just dare that thief to come back."

Mr. Wheeler began to say that he didn't think my coming over was necessary, but I cut him off. Mattie's things were my responsibility, and I intended to take care of them.

Throwing back the covers—my air-conditioning was working just fine—I pulled on a robe and hurried across the hall.

"Etta Mae?" I whispered. "Are you awake?"

"Yes, ma'am. Is everything all right? I heard the phone."

I told her that I was leaving to spend the night elsewhere because of a possible impending crime and that she should go back to sleep. "Lillian will be here to give you breakfast, so you can tell her where I am."

"No way," she said, swinging her feet out of bed. "I'm not staying here by myself. I'm going with you."

To tell the truth, I was glad to hear it. She put on a cotton robe and pink, fluffy bedroomers that looked like a pair of rabbits on her feet, grabbed her grocery sack, and followed me down the stairs, both of us still in our night clothes. I grabbed my pocketbook, wrote a quick note to Lillian, left it on the kitchen counter, and off we went.

The deputies were gone by the time we drove the five blocks, but Mr. Wheeler was waiting for us in the building's vestibule. Thinking that I should've taken time to dress, I clutched my robe closer. I needn't have bothered. It was Etta Mae for whom he had eyes—an uncommonly inappropriate reaction at midnight after an attempted criminal entry.

I didn't linger in the hall, just quickly unlocked Mattie's door, shoved Etta Mae through it, and thanked Mr. Wheeler for his rapid response to the emergency.

Well, of course, the apartment was unprepared for overnight guests, so the first thing we had to do was to put sheets on the guest room bed for Etta Mae. Mattie had kept it with just a spread over the mattress pad. Her bed, on the other hand, had been frequently used and the sheets looked it. As tired as I was by that time, there was no way I was going to crawl in between Mattie's, or anybody else's, slept-in sheets. But there was something else that needed doing first.

"One more thing, Etta Mae," I said as we finished with her bed. "Then we can sleep in peace. Let's block those French doors, so if anybody gets in the sunroom he can't get in here."

"I'd rather he not get in *any*where," Etta Mae mumbled, but she followed me into the living room and began shoving a chair in front of the doors.

I placed a brass lamp on the chair seat, then stepped back. "That's not going to stop anybody. Anything heavy enough to keep somebody out is too heavy for us to move. I tell you what, let's get these boxes off the sofa and I'll sleep on it."

"Oh, no. Let me sleep in here, and you sleep in the guest room. I was just thinking about doing that, anyway."

I looked at the hard-as-a-rock Victorian monstrosity, thought of what the state of my back would be in the morning, and said, "Etta Mae, you're my guest, and I hate to put you up on a sofa. But, I declare, those sofa arms are so large I wouldn't be able to stretch out."

"Well, see, I'm short enough to fit, and I've slept on sofas before—pallets, too, which are a lot worse. And I'm a light sleeper. I'll hear anything that moves."

I hated taking her bed, but was glad not to have to sleep in Mattie's, clean sheets or not. It just wouldn't have felt right. So I agreed to the arrangement, helped Etta Mae find a blanket and a pillow, then crawled into the bed in the guest room, thankful for the comfort, though feeling guilty for ill using my guest.

And, by the way, Etta Mae wasn't such a light sleeper. She was prone to snoring, but at least that was proof that the sofa was conducive to sleep.

Etta Mae and I, hunched over, scurried from the car to my kitchen door before any early risers could catch sight of us creeping in after a night out somewhere—especially dressed, or undressed, as we were.

Lillian slewed around from the sink, her eyes wide, staring at us in alarm. "What you doin', comin' in here like that? Where you been? You s'posed to be in bed!"

"Oh, Lillian, you wouldn't believe." I collapsed in a chair at the table, as Etta Mae waved at Lillian and went straight through the kitchen on her way to get dressed for work.

"Well," Lillian said, her hands on her hips, "I jus' wanta know what you two been doin', runnin' 'round without hardly no clothes on. Folks gonna be talkin' all over town."

"Nobody saw us," I said, "but if they did, I don't much care." And I went on to tell her of our night and why we'd been running around in our bedclothes. "I left you a note—it's here on the table. And you know I had to look after Miss Mattie's property, Lillian, as I am legally constrained to do."

"Look like to me you coulda done it with some clothes on, but sound like you couldn't much help it. What you want for breakfast?"

"Anything. Whatever you fix for Etta Mae—she'll need a big one before she goes to work." I stood up and pushed my chair back. "So to make you feel better, I'm going up and get dressed."

"It don't make no never mind to me," she said, setting a skillet on the stove. "'Cept I gotta have something to tell everybody what asks, an' they'll be askin', you know they will. 'Cause you can't do nothin' in this town without somebody knowin' about it."

"We were fully clothed, Lillian, from head to toe. And I don't care who saw us." I stopped and considered for a minute. "Although I don't think anybody did—it's too early and we scrooched down in the car."

Lillian's shoulders started shaking, and, trying to hold back a laugh, she said, "I wisht I'd seen you out runnin' 'round, 'speci'lly Miss Etta Mae in them big, ole, fluffy rabbity-lookin' shoes of hers."

Then we both started laughing and I had to sit back down to get my breath. Besides, why hurry to dress by that time?

Chapter 34

After Etta Mae left for work, I decided to make good use of the morning to go through the closet in Mattie's guest room—at least to clear it out and to transfer any valuable papers to my house, where they would be safe. And, I determined, I would urge Diane and Helen to finish their appraisals so we could get the furniture out of there as well. When that was done, there would be no need to spend another night in somebody else's lumpy bed. I had absolutely no desire to actually move into Mattie's apartment for an unlimited span of time. One night was enough for me.

Telling Lillian where I was going, and being told in turn to take my cell phone, I checked my checklist and said, "One of these days it'll become a habit and I won't need to be reminded. But it better be quick because Mattie's phone will be cut off tomorrow, which means one less bill to pay."

I met Mr. Wheeler in the building's vestibule as I was going in and he was coming out.

He smiled, wished me a good morning, and said, "I hope you and your friend rested well last night."

"As well as could be expected under the circumstances, thank you," I replied. "But I'd as soon not do it too many times. I intend to light a fire under Diane and Helen so we can get this place empty and off my hands."

"I don't blame you," he said with an easy smile. "But you have somebody new helping you now, don't you?"

"Oh, you mean Etta Mae? No, she's my houseguest and insisted on keeping me company last night. I couldn't ask her to help. She has her hands full with her own job."

"Well," he said, as I moved on toward Mattie's door, "maybe I'll see you both tonight. That is, if you're planning to stay over again."

"I am. I mean, we are, and I guess it'll be for the duration."

"Good," he said on his way out. "Call me if I can help. I'll be around."

Hm-m, I thought, as I closed and locked Mattie's door behind me. If I wasn't mistaken, Mr. Wheeler was exhibiting interest in a certain young woman, when all the while I'd thought it was Helen who had taken his eye.

I stopped in the middle of Mattie's crowded living room and thought, *Hm-m*, again. Maybe that nice Mr. Wheeler had eyes for the ladies—*any* ladies, that is. Whoever happened to cross his path, which made me wonder about the accuracy of my earlier assessment of him.

"Well, you never know about people," I mumbled aloud with a little thump of disappointment.

Then I headed for the guest room closet, where I found my work cut out for me—it was still crammed full of coats and jackets and wool skirts and dresses—all of which meant another trip to Goodwill. The top shelf was stacked high with boxes, and as I lifted armloads of clothes off the rod, I saw that the back corner of the closet was also stacked high with more boxes, albums, and who-knew-what-else.

After emptying the rod of hanging clothes, I reached up and took down a stack of boxes to put on the bed—one good thing, I would have to get this task done before nightfall so I would have room to crawl in. Another good thing, the boxes weren't heavy. One held a collection of gloves, some with mates, some without. Another held woolen scarves, and another was full of pages torn from magazines—for the recipes, I supposed.

I started a Goodwill stack on one side of the bed, opened a trash bag at my feet for the magazine pages, and placed a few grocery store boxes nearby for anything valuable that should go to my house for safekeeping.

Then the problem cropped up—what was valuable and what was not? Mr. Sitton had said that I should use my own discretion in determining value, but after possibly misjudging Mr. Wheeler, how could I trust my own discretion?

I could just hear Lillian: "Jus' do the best you can, that's all anybody can do."

Then my cell phone rang, startling me because it rarely did so. When I hesitantly answered it, Etta Mae said, "Miss Julia, I know what it is. I was standing here ready to give a bed bath, and it just came to me. You have a pencil and paper?"

"Yes," I said, scrounging in my purse until I found a pen and a receipt from the bookstore. "I'm ready."

"Okay, it's the combination for a safe."

"What safe?"

"There has to be one somewhere. Write this down: left seven, right ten, left twenty-three, and right ten again. I'm taking every little scribble at face value, but I'll bet you anything it'll open a safe somewhere."

Where in the world would Mattie have kept a safe? Excited by the thought of finding one, I hurried through the apartment, looking under beds, peeking behind portraits for a wall safe, and opening cabinets for hidden dials. All of that was just to reassure myself because I knew where a safe had to be. If, indeed, there was one—that deep, dark guest room closet that I had yet to explore. So I went back to it, reminding myself that there was more to look for than an imaginary safe. I was responsible for sorting through everything before Andrew F. Cobb got his hands on it. Removing the last of the clothes hangers, lifting down boxes from the shelf, and going through each one of them, I learned little more than that Mattie had pretty much saved everything she'd ever come across.

But then, blowing dust off an old shoe box that had once held a pair of Thom McAn oxfords, size 10D, I hit pay dirt—of a sort. Fewer than a dozen letters, some held together with faded pink ribbons, and a few in the distinctive red-and-blue-bordered flimsy envelopes, stamped AIRMAIL, that I knew at once were from Tommy. How had she received them with an irate father watching her every move? There was no telling, but get them she had, for here they were in a shoe box.

I opened one at random from each pack to confirm the sender, and a quick scan identified one as a missive from prison and the other from a war zone.

I sat for a moment, there on the side of the bed, holding a box of sad memories on my lap, and thought of Andrew F. Cobb. If he was who he said he was, these things belonged to him, whether or not he was writing a family history. And if he was writing one, the letters would be a treasure trove for him.

I carefully set the box aside—it would go to my house until it could be legitimately claimed. And if it never was, perhaps a library somewhere in Kentucky would archive them for future historians.

With the shelves now empty, I felt around in the dark corner at the back of the closet and brought out several dusty photograph albums from a stack of books, ledgers, and boxes that was almost shoulder high. Flipping through albums, I saw that they contained pictures that looked as old as the hills—some had come loose from the little corner tabs, others had faded to a sickly yellow, and some were so old that they could've been tintypes. Whatever tintypes were. Most were of what I assumed were family members— perhaps grandparents, both tall, broad shouldered, and of wide girth, standing stiff and unsmiling on the porch of a stately two-story farmhouse. There were several pictures of two little boys in knee britches and a few of a little girl in a pinafore who looked as unhappy as Mattie often had when I had known her.

Looking through another album in the stack, I came across the wedding picture of Mattie and Tommy. I knew what it was because of the studio background with handpainted wedding bells in each corner. So young, I thought as I studied the happy faces, it was heartbreaking. Especially since I knew what the future held for them. Mattie was wearing a white dress down to her ankles, but it wasn't an evening gown. With black buttons down the front and a black belt at her waist, it looked more like a house-dress. She wore dark shoes with a small heel and—my word—white socks.

And Tommy? He was in shirtsleeves without a tie and pleated trousers that looked a size or two too large for him, but the smile on his face as he held his bride close would move the heart of a person of stone. Unless it was his bride's father, whose heart was apparently never moved.

Lord, I thought as I closed the album, it's a good thing that none of us knows the future. If those two had known theirs, they wouldn't have had even that one happy day.

I sighed and consigned the albums to my take-home-with-me pile, thinking that they might be archived along with the letters. If, that is, no legal heir appeared—or wanted them, if one did.

Chapter 35

I made short shrift of the remaining boxes and their contents, finding some lovely, though undoubtedly old, cutwork table linens, embroidered handkerchiefs and pillowcases, as well as a multitude of crocheted doilies and place mats, all carefully stored in tissue paper.

Having never seen Mattie do needlework of any kind, I assumed that what I was holding had been done in her salad days growing up in her old Kentucky home. Perhaps she had kept them as mementos of her family's once prosperous holdings, along with some of the fine furniture with which Diane was more and more impressed. But crocheted doilies? If that was the kind of memento that Andrew Cobb wanted, as far as I was concerned, he could have them.

Then, with a deep and hopeful breath, I got down to it. I confess that I'd been putting it off for fear of a great disappointment. But it was time, so I did it.

Putting aside the albums and boxes, I rose to my feet and marched back to the almost empty closet—no light, of course. I'd already searched diligently for a hanging cord to no avail. I leaned over so I wouldn't crack my head on the shelf above and crept to the far corner, feeling my way as I went. And there it was, a small—about the size of a one-drawer file cabinet—unassuming safe covered by a tapestry. Feeling around in the dark, I found the dial on the front.

Etta Mae, I thought, *you smart girl, you.*

Delighted with the find and eager to try the combination she'd given me, I tried to slide the safe out of the closet. It wouldn't budge. There was nothing for it but to get on my knees so I could see the dial.

That didn't work, either, because I almost couldn't get off my knees. Finally backing out of the closet, I tore through the apartment, hoping to find a flashlight. I could've run down the hall and borrowed one from Mr. Wheeler, but I didn't want him coming back with me, insisting on helping. Whatever Mattie had valued enough to place in a safe that she hid the combination to in a bank was going to be my find and my secret. Whatever was in the safe could possibly justify the many bequests she'd made, as well as purchase a huge air-conditioning unit.

I jerked open kitchen drawers, frantically searching for a flashlight, all the time wondering what could be in the safe. Stock certificates? Jewelry? Deeds to the family farm? Cash from illicit deals? My imagination was running away with me.

Finally I found a flashlight—a small one with a weak battery—which I turned off to save what power was left. Then I scrambled through my pocketbook for the scratch paper on which I'd jotted down the combination that Etta Mae had phoned in to me.

With shaking hands and great trepidation of further disappointment, I crawled back into the closet, hunched down, and began to turn the dial, first left to seven, then right to ten, then left to twenty-three, then right to ten again. Then I pulled down on the handle—and it opened.

I sat back on my heels and stared at the open door, hardly daring to look inside.

Well, for goodness' sake, I thought, *what's holding you back now?*

With the flashlight on its last legs, I felt around inside, surprised at how little space was in such a heavy safe. But a little space was all that was needed, for there was only a shirt box on the one shelf.

Holding the box carefully, I backed out of the closet, sat on the bed, and looked at what I had. The once white box was tied with twine, and a logo from Rich's in Atlanta was on the front. When, I wondered, had Mattie shopped at Rich's? But I couldn't answer because there was a lot about Mattie that I hadn't known. A long-ago trip to Atlanta was only a tiny part of a long life.

Holding the box from Rich's on my lap, I brushed away the dust around the edges, and picked open the knot in the twine. Then I lifted the lid and found a layer of cotton, which I carefully removed. Under the cotton I found what felt like a framed picture wrapped in a swath of fine, soft flannel and lying on another layer of cotton. I lifted it out—it was about eight inches by twelve inches, perhaps a little larger—but I was reluctant to remove the flannel. I sat there holding it, sure of what I'd find and, knowing what I knew of the future, I could hardly bring myself to look at it. I pictured that young Tommy in his army uniform, a cap set jauntily on his head, with an encouraging smile for his bride who was so many miles away, both actually and otherwise. For it would've been taken, I assumed, after he'd spent months in prison and after Mattie was back in her father's home and before he headed overseas. How she had come to have it, I didn't know. Maybe his family had taken pity on her grief and had slipped it to her after his death.

Teary eyed with the thought of it, I almost put the picture, unwrapped and undisturbed, back in its box and turned to something else. I'm glad I didn't.

Steeling myself against the compassion that welled up for what could have been but hadn't, I unwound the flannel wrapping to discover . . . The breath caught in my throat. It was not a photograph, browned by age, of an army private, or even an enlarged wedding picture to set on a mantel—it was the most remarkable thing I'd ever seen.

I'd never seen anything like it. Well, yes, I had viewed some of the same kind at a museum display, but none of the same quality. I sat and studied the framed sampler for the longest time, for the longer I looked at it, the more I saw in it. Even though a glass pane covered it in its simple frame, I could tell upon close inspection that the background was silk and the embroidery done in silk floss—that was high quality right there. Silk on silk, I thought, and was amazed that such delicate materials were in such good condition. There was no fraying or pulled stitches or faded colors. Everyone who had owned it, including Mattie, must've known the care it needed. A framer's sticker on the back, placed there years before, assured me that the sampler was mounted as it should have been on an acid-free mat and covered by a special type of glass.

But the sampler itself! My word, it was a wonder. There were two borders done in a variety of difficult stitches—I knew because I'd done some embroidery years before and had always ended up with a soiled tea towel full of dropped stitches and crooked letters. I recognized the blanket, cable, feathered chain, padded satin, and herringbone stitches, plus some French knots, but there were many that were so intricate, I couldn't put names to them.

In the center, a large rectangular monument had been stitched—a tombstone on which the words *Sacred to Memory* had been inscribed. The figure of a man in a black frock coat and a high stock at the throat stood in profile beside the tomb. He held a large white handkerchief in one hand. Two small children—the girl in a full dress with pantaloons and the boy dressed similarly to the man, even to the black coat—played nearby. I leaned over to see the figures up close and, yes, just as I thought. The flesh color of the faces and hands had not been stitched in. They had been painted onto the silk with gentle strokes of a brush, the features carefully delineated.

Two weeping willow trees framed the scene—typical, I knew, of funerary art of the period. Shrubs and bushes surrounded the scene, and as I studied the variety of stitches and shades of green that made the greenery so realistic, I was amazed to see figures of small animals—a rabbit, a squirrel, and maybe a fox—emerge from under the leaves.

In the middle of the sampler, below the tombstone and above the two rows of the alphabet, I read the name of the creator of this example of extraordinary stitchery:

> *Wrought by Henrietta Cobb*
> *In the sixteenth year of her life*
> *1787*

And under that in running stitches were the following words:

> *Comes the sun after the rain,*
> *After the night, the morning.*

As I turned the framed piece just the tiniest bit, the greenery shimmered and moved as if a small breeze had brushed past, and in one corner I discovered a single blooming flower—a peony, perhaps. And, perhaps, a symbol of Henrietta's hope.

I don't know how long I sat there holding what I recognized as a sampler of uncommon age and of the highest quality of needle-work art. How had it come into Mattie's possession—she, who had been in discord with her family and who had defied not only her father but the law? She, who had been brought home in shame to await the return of her husband in a casket? I didn't know, and likely never would.

But there was this one thing that I did know: the value of Mattie's estate had just gone up. Way, way up.

Chapter 36

I wanted to tell somebody. I was so excited that I wanted to call everybody I knew and tell them. And I wanted to show it to Sam, but where was he? Why, out on the bounding main angling for fish and nowhere near or even interested in being near a phone.

Whom could I tell? Who could be trusted to keep such a secret? I knew already. With one theft behind us, the answer was clear—hardly anybody. So I calmed myself down, knowing that I could not broadcast this amazing find.

I carefully rewrapped the sampler and placed it back between the cotton layers in its box. This would be my secret, except, of course, Etta Mae deserved to know. Without her, I would've had to hire a safecracker—a legal one, of course—and who knows who all he would've told.

That brought up another problem—should I leave the sampler in the safe where it had been safe for years? Or should I keep it in my personal care? I sat and pondered the problem and decided it would be safer with me.

Besides, I'd have to show it to Diane and do it in total privacy. She was the only one who would know what to do with it and where to market it. For market it, I had to do. The bequests in Mattie's last will and testament demanded it.

If the sampler had been my own, I would have taken my burdensome tax situation into account and donated it to an Early American museum—the Abby Aldrich Rockefeller Folk Art Museum in Williamsburg, for one. But there were others that might be eager for it. And all to the good as far as I, Mattie's executor, was concerned—let them all vie for the privilege of purchasing it for their collections.

Then I stopped short, my mind sorting through a jumble of questions. First of all, did Andrew Cobb know about this? Was it part of the family lore he'd grown up with? If so, I'd be hard-pressed to refuse him a memento of such high sentimental value. On the other hand, if he did know of it, he would also know its pecuniary value and was probably hoping that we didn't.

But maybe I was overvaluing what might be only one of many examples of many a young girl's needlework. Merely because I'd never seen another sampler like it didn't mean there weren't any. I couldn't let myself be carried away by some fantastic notion of its rarity or its value. Better to calm down than to risk bitter dis-appointment.

So, after leaving an urgent note to Diane to call me as soon as she got there that afternoon, I carried the box of photograph albums, the shoe box of letters, and the box containing the sampler to my car. By that time, I was about wiped out. I kept hoping that Mr. Wheeler would show up to help me, but his pickup was gone from the parking lot—out picking up supplies from Home Depot, I supposed.

I locked the car doors—the sampler was on the seat beside me—and sat in the hot car while I called Etta Mae.

"Etta Mae?" I said when she answered. "You are the smartest person I know. I not only found a safe, I opened it, thanks to you."

"Really?" She sounded as if she couldn't believe she'd been right.

"Yes, and you'll be amazed at what I found. Hurry home and I'll show you."

She wanted to know right then, but I told her I wanted it to be a surprise. I mean, who knew who might be listening?

Driving home, I kept trying to tamp down my elation. Over and over I speculated about its worth and how many bequests it would cover. Would it bring five thousand dollars? Ten? I had no idea, but put together with what the handkerchief table, the chest-on-chest, and maybe a few other things might bring, Mattie's estate was slowly mounting up.

Anger flew all over me, though, as I thought of the stolen cellarette. That would've helped considerably, but whatever price it had brought was most likely now resting comfortably in somebody's pocket—or being freely spent. I hoped the thief enjoyed it, because if I ever found out who it was, he wouldn't enjoy anything else for a good long while.

I couldn't stand it. I had to show Lillian. So after she helped me bring the boxes into the house, I asked her to come up to the bedroom, where I made her promise that she wouldn't breathe a word of what she was about to see.

"What you done now?" she demanded, frowning as she eyed me closely.

"Not one thing, except clean out Mattie's closet. Why would you think I had?"

"'Cause you us'lly doin' something you ought not be doin'."

"Lillian," I said, just undone at being so misunderstood. "For goodness' sake. This is something that belonged to Mattie and I think it's a jewel of its kind. I simply want to show it to you without being accused of something underhanded. I don't do that sort of thing anyway." I took the lid off the box. "Look at this and tell me what you think."

"Why, jus' look at that pretty thing," she said as the flannel came off and I held it up for her to see. "But it kinda sad lookin', too. Who done all them little-bitty stitches?"

"Henrietta Cobb, Mattie's ancestor, years and years ago. Have you ever seen anything like it?"

"No'm, 'specially since it showin' a graveyard and people mournin' somebody dead—that's jus' real pitiful. My granny used to do some crochetin', but nothin' like that. What you gonna do with it?"

"Hide it and keep it safe for now," I said as I put it back in the box. "Of course I'll show it to Diane Jankowski. She's the expert and will know who'll want to buy it—some museum with a huge endowment, I hope. Don't tell a soul, Lillian."

"My lips is zipped, but where you gonna hide it?"

That stopped me for a minute. "That's a good question. I'll have to think about it. Somewhere that nobody would think to look, I guess."

"Nobody be lookin' a-tall, if you don't say you got it."

"Well, there is that. But don't worry, it'll just be me, you, Diane, and Sam, when he gets home, who'll know about it. Oh, and Etta Mae. Why, Lillian, she was the one who figured out what that scribbling was."

"You mean what Miz Allen say could th'ow a spell on you?"

"She was teasing, Lillian. It was the combination to a safe all along." I sighed, looked again at the sampler, and said, "I just hope that it's as good as I think it is. I mean, there may be dozens like this stacked up on storage shelves in museums all over the country."

"Maybe so," Lillian said, sounding a doleful note. "'Cause they's death an' dyin' an' grievin' people ever'where you look these days. Take Miss Bessie, she still grievin' like nobody's business."

"Hold on a minute while I put this away." I walked into my closet and stuck the precious box under a stack of flannel gowns that wouldn't be disturbed until winter came. If it had been safe in Mattie's closet, it should be in mine as well. Until I could think of a better place, preferably one with an unreadable combination to it.

"Now, Lillian, let's go have some coffee or something. I'm ready to turn my mind to something besides responsibilities. I want to hear all about Miss Bessie."

Deciding to forgo coffee due to the increasing heat of the day, Lillian brought two tall glasses of iced tea—heavily sugared and lemoned—to the table and set each one on a napkin.

"Sit down, Lillian, and tell me about Miss Bessie. I thought she'd be getting along quite well by now. I mean, it's been several months since Mr. Robert died, hasn't it? And I expect she hasn't had a beating since."

"Yes'm, but they's all kinds a beatin's. An' that mean, sneaky ole man still a-beatin' on her from the grave. You won't b'lieve what he done to her."

"I can't imagine what else he could do."

"Well, see, I tole you how he come to find Jesus—the Reverend Abernathy showed him the way, but I 'spect now the reverend wisht he'd left well enough alone." Lillian stopped and sighed. "I guess I don't really mean that 'cause the Lord, He take every crooked soul what want to come, but, Miss Julia, I declare, it makes me wonder if He wouldn't be better off without Mr. Robert Mobley. We all was sure Miss Bessie would be better off without him, but, see, the last year or two after Mr. Robert got saved, he didn't do nothin' but think about and do for the church. Why, he was over there all the time—it right across the road from his ole house, you know—and he was all the time workin', an' fixin' up, an' sweepin', an' hammerin', an' doin' for that church day in an' day out. An' we 'preciated it, don't think we didn't. It was good to see that ole sinner workin' hard as he was for the Lord. An' he was doin' real good till the day he drop dead shovelin' up that last snow we had."

"Oh, I thought he'd been sick," I said.

"No'm, jus' sick in his crazy, ole head. You know what he done, Miss Julia?"

I shook my head, caught up by the indignation in Lillian's voice.

"He write a will, got a lawyer an' all to do it for him so he could leave ever'thing he had, which wasn't nothin' but that ole house Miss Bessie livin' in, *to the church*. Can you b'lieve that? The church only been puttin' up with him for a year or two, an' she been doin' it for twenty years or more, an' he jus' jerk that house right out from under her feet, an' leave her nothin'."

Oh, my goodness, I thought. *Wills and thoughtless bequests again. I couldn't get away from the trouble they caused.*

But then, struck by the memory of something similar that had happened to me, I sat up straight and said, "Well, wait, Lillian. I don't think he can do that."

"I know," Lillian said with a judicious nod of her head. "An' the reverend, he tell Miss Bessie that, but at the time he don't know all there is to know. An' he get in hot water with the deacons 'cause they want that house to sell an' bring some money in to build us a add-on buildin' with a kitchen and extra Sunday school rooms. Which would be a blessin' 'cause we need 'em, but what would pore ole Miss Bessie do while we enjoyin' a new buildin' settin' right across the road from where she ought to be?"

So, I thought, *now it was not only wills but deacons, too.*

"Well, Lillian," I said, hoping to reassure her. "It probably won't come to that. I doubt Mr. Robert's house would bring enough to even lay the foundation of a new building."

"Yes'm, I thought the same thing, but that was 'fore a Red Dot grocery store come wantin' to buy the house. It got a real big lot, you know. An' we sure could use a grocery store without havin' to drive way across town to get to one. So lotsa people standin' with the deacons an' not the reverend."

"That certainly changes . . ." The telephone interrupted me just as I'd begun to get a glimmer of the moral predicament in which the Reverend Abernathy found himself.

Lillian handed the phone to me—she always insisted on answering it first.

"Miss Julia? It's Diane Jankowski. I got your note. You wanted me to call?"

"Yes, Diane. I'm wondering if you would mind coming over to my house to look at, well, an object I found at Mattie's this morning. I brought it home with me for safekeeping, and I'd like your opinion on what it might be worth."

"Well, yes, I can, but you could bring it with you the next time you come by. If it's not too heavy, that is."

"It's not heavy at all. The thing is, Diane, I think the fewer people who know about it, the better. Not that I distrust anybody, but it could be mentioned to any number of other people. I think you'll understand when you see it. I'd as soon keep it between the two of us for the time being. Has Helen gotten there yet?"

"Yes," Diane said, her voice noticeably lowered. "She rounded up Nate Wheeler to come move some things around for her. I offered to help, but she thought he'd want to do it." Diane summed up the situation with an indulgent laugh, as I thought, *Well, well.*

"Can you make an excuse to run out for a while?" I asked. "I mean, without saying why? I'm probably being overly cautious, but I'd rather have your appraisal before anybody knows about it."

There was a brief silence on her end, as I heard a muffled conversation in the background. Then, slightly raising her voice, Diane said, "Mr. Wheeler is helping Helen get the drawers out of that block-front chest in the guest room, and I'm just waiting for them to finish. So if Mrs. Freeman's lawyer is that anxious to get a set of the furniture pictures, I can run them right over to you."

I was impressed by Diane's ability to light upon a plausible reason to leave—just in case anyone wondered. A good woman to do business with. "I'll be here," I said, smiling.

"Sorry, Lillian," I apologized as I hung up. "Mrs. Jankowski is on her way, but we have a few minutes before she gets here."

I picked up my glass and wiped the condensation from the outside. "So back to Miss Bessie and the church," I said. "There is a way they can work things out to the benefit of both. In this state, a husband can't leave his wife destitute, regardless of what he puts in his will. So Miss Bessie will get half of Robert's estate— whatever the house brings—and the church will get the other half."

"Yes'm, we all know that. It don't do no good, though, 'cause Miss Bessie not Mr. Robert's wife an' Mr. Robert not Miss Bessie's husband. They never went and tied the knot."

Chapter 37

Well, that put a whole different light on the matter. I leaned back in my chair and blew out my breath. "So she doesn't have a legal leg to stand on, does she?"

"No'm, but she got something better'n a legal leg. She got the Reverend Abernathy, an' he standin' for her. Though he right surprised when he hear how they been livin'. But he don't let that stop him, 'cause he say the church oughta take that house like the will say, then give it right back to Miss Bessie—free an' clear. He say that the Christian thing to do, 'cause nothin' good come from takin' a widder woman's house out from under her."

I couldn't help but recall the desolation I'd felt when I learned that Wesley Lloyd Springer's will made no provision for me, even after forty-some-odd years of legal cohabitation. Of course, the state of North Carolina came to my rescue, but what a comfort it would've been to have had the Reverend Abernathy by my side at that time.

I nodded to encourage Lillian to go on with the rest of it.

She crossed her arms on the table and leaned over. "See, Miss Julia, the reverend, he say it don't matter if she not a real widder woman. She be jus' as good as. An' the reverend, he get that happy look on his face an' say maybe she write her own will an' leave the house to the church when she pass. So ever'body come out doin' good an' not hurtin' nobody."

"The Reverend Abernathy is a good man," I said, "and I hope

the deacons . . . Oh," I said, looking up at the sound of the door-bell, "that's Diane. Come go up with us, Lillian."

After greeting Diane at the front door, thanking her for coming, and introducing her to Lillian, I led the way down the hall and up the stairs for the unveiling. Along the way, I noticed Diane's head turning from side to side, scanning the furniture in each room as we passed, evaluating and appraising as she went. I expect she couldn't help it. It probably came naturally for her to pass judgment on any piece of furniture she saw, and I was quite proud of the quality of my home furnishings. They would stand up to anybody's speculative eye.

"Here we are," I said after retrieving the sampler box from under my winter gowns. Lillian, crossing her arms under her bosom, and Diane, setting down her large bag, gathered beside my bed as I unboxed and unwrapped the sampler. Then I placed it against a pillow so that Diane could get a good view of it. "What do you think?"

Diane leaned over, reached out so that her hand hovered over the glass, then she straightened up, her face flushed with excitement.

Then with both hands flapping as if she were fanning her face, Diane looked at me and cried, "Oh, oh! Oh! It's . . . oh, it's exquisite! A marvel! Where *was* this? How did you find it? Surely I didn't overlook it."

"Well, the way it happened was like this: I opened Mattie's safe-deposit box at the bank and found absolutely nothing of value, except . . ."

But she wasn't listening. "Oh, Julia, may I hold it? May I just hold it up close?"

"Of course, I want you to. Look at the details, Diane—you'll see more every time you look. And the stitches, there're some I've never seen before. And notice the skin tones on the figures—they're painted in, not sewn. Mixed media, I think it's called."

Diane picked up the sampler, holding it as gingerly as she would a newborn baby. She brought it close to her face, her eyes running over every inch.

"I'd love to look at this under a microscope and a brighter light, but not sunlight. The colors haven't faded at all—even after so many years—and I don't want to ruin them now. Oh, Julia, this is unmatched! Absolutely unmatched. A marvelous example of funerary art!"

Funerary art, I thought, *come to light only because of Mattie's passing. Coincidentally? Or had Mattie counted on it being disinterred in the nick of time?*

Diane whirled around to me. "You must keep it covered and *safe.* I understand your insistence on secrecy now, and you were right. I wouldn't make any kind of announcement if I were you, to anybody. We need to get it to a textile expert who'll take it out of the frame under the proper conditions and examine it for authenticity as to age and so on." Then she flapped her free hand again and said, "I think I'm about to hyperventilate."

Lillian turned toward the door. "I go get a paper bag."

"It's all right, Lillian," I said, smiling. "She's just excited. But, Diane, how and where will we find a textile expert? The closest thing to an expert around here just makes draperies."

"Don't worry. I have a list—they mostly work for museums. But I'll start making some calls today. Oh, I can't wait to tell them what I've found."

Well, *I* was the one who had found it, but I let that pass.

I didn't let the big question pass, though. "So, Diane, what do you think it's worth?"

"Wait just a minute," she said as she propped the sampler against the pillow again, then rummaged in her bag for a pencil and a notebook. And her camera. "I want to take some pictures. Then I'll write down everything on it so they'll know just what we have."

So I waited as she took pictures of the sampler—some from a distance and others from up close to capture the details. Then she sketched the scene and drew arrows to the names of some of the stitches that she apparently recognized. She drew in the tomb, the man's figure and those of the children, copied the inscriptions and the alphabet, and indicated where little animals peeked out from under the leaves. It seemed to take forever. I fidgeted, anxious to hear how far along on Mattie's list of bequests the sampler might get me.

Certainly I appreciated the beauty, the age, and the uniqueness of the sampler, but when you get right down to it, it was its *value* that interested me the most. That's what happens to one's appreciation of art when a long list of bequests is made one's responsibility.

"Okay, that's it," Diane said, stuffing her notebook and camera into her bag. "Oh, I can't wait to get on the phone and tell somebody about this."

I knew the feeling. "Diane, let me caution you now. Nobody, and I mean nobody—not Helen, not Mr. Wheeler, not your husband or your best friend, can know about this. The word would get around this town like wildfire, and I do not want to have to hire off-duty deputies to protect my home." Especially from hot-under-the-collar-and-everywhere-else deacons who wanted an air-conditioning unit.

"No worries on that score," Diane said, smiling at me. "The last thing we want is for word to get around. Then we'd begin to have speculations about its value, and who knows where that would lead. No, Julia, no one but out-of-town experts will hear a word from me."

"Well, speaking of speculations about the value . . ." I said.

"I couldn't begin to tell you. It will depend on its being authenticated, first of all, but I have no worries about that. Of course I don't have much experience with textiles, but this has to be unique—because of its pristine condition, if nothing else. Then the next thing it will depend on is how many similar samplers Early American museums already have. I do think, however, that this has to be among the oldest—textiles don't age well." Diane paused and tapped her pencil against her cheek as she studied the sampler again. "And if it goes to auction, it will depend on who and how many museums and private collectors want it. If everything goes well, I'd venture it'll bring at least forty thousand."

"Forty . . . ? Good land above!" I stumbled back, stunned and lightheaded. "Lillian, I may need that paper bag."

"It could go higher, depending," Diane said, her excitement tempered now as she resumed a professional tone. "My job will be to find the right hands to put it in. He—or she—will know how to handle the rest of it. Oh, and Julia," she went on, "I was going to tell you until I got sidetracked by this, but the auction house can send a truck Monday morning if that suits you. After I talked with them and sent pictures of Mrs. Freeman's furniture, they'll take everything. The better pieces will go on their prime auction list, and the reproductions will go on a lesser list. They'll take care of it all."

"What a relief!" I said. "When will I get a check?"

"It could be a few weeks. They'll want to be sure the pieces are correctly listed and advertised for auction. And, anyway, they'll send a check to me. I'll subtract my commission, then get a check to you. Everything," she said as she noted my look of dismay, "will be properly noted down and confirmed. You need have no concerns about that—we're dealing with the top of the line in auction houses."

"I'm only concerned about the beneficiaries," I murmured. "They're getting a bit restless."

"Well, Lillian," I said, after seeing Diane out and making another trip upstairs to hide the sampler under a stack of towels in the linen closet of my bathroom. No need, I thought, to keep it in the same place all the time.

"Well what?" she asked. "You ready for lunch?"

"Oh, anytime is fine with me. I'm just overwhelmed with what that sampler might be worth. But the thought of sending it off to a stranger in New York or somewhere is worrisome. I may have to go with it and you know how I love to fly."

Lillian laughed. "You got to trust somebody sometime, Miss Julia, so you jus' give that pretty little thing to the FedEx man an' he fly it for you. You don't have to go with it."

"That's right, and I won't. Actually, Diane might want to hand carry it, which might be the best way. And I'll stay here and try to figure out who'll get what."

Chapter 38

I worried half the afternoon about taking my every-other-day walk with Mildred. I didn't know how I could chat and visit with her while we strolled along and, all the while, keep silent about the sampler. But we had a shower with a few rumbles of thunder about three o'clock, and I knew we wouldn't be walking at all. That was a relief, for I would've been sorely tempted to tell her what I'd found in Mattie's closet. Of all the people I knew, Mildred was the most knowledgeable about art in general, and I would've loved to have shown the sampler to her.

But I knew for a fact that Mildred told Ida Lee everything, so that would be two more who'd know the secret. Ida Lee was, from all I'd seen, absolutely trustworthy, but the further from the source a secret gets, the less the urgency of keeping it secret.

I knew how it worked. A friend will swear to keep something to herself, but she'll tell her husband and not think for a minute that she's breaking a vow of silence. And where it goes from there, well, you'll find out when somebody you barely know calls to tell you the same secret.

When I walked into the kitchen later in the afternoon with a small overnight bag, Lillian stopped what she was doing and demanded, "What you doin' with that? You spendin' the night at Miss Mattie's again?"

"Yes, I am. Lillian, I have to. That furniture is setting over there unprotected at night, and I don't want anything else stolen. It'll just be until Monday, when everything will be on the way to Atlanta."

"But didn't you get it all locked up better'n it used to be?"

"Well, I hope so. But you never can tell what a determined thief is able to do. I need to be there."

"Yes'm, and what if that thief come creepin' in while you sleepin'? What you gonna do then?"

"Etta Mae will be with me."

"Law! You countin' on a lot from that little woman. She s'posed to be on a vacation, an' here you are puttin' her to work lookin' out for you."

"I fully intend to make it up to her. Besides, she wants to go with me."

"Uh-huh, and who gonna watch out for what you got upstairs while you both gone?"

I smiled and patted the overnight bag. "It's going with me. In fact, I just might sleep with it."

"You do that, you break the glass when you roll over."

"I'll be careful," I said, getting out silverware from the drawer to set the table. "You'll eat with us, Lillian?"

"No'm, I got to pick up Latisha in a little while, so y'all can help your plates from the stove. 'Less you want me to dish it up in bowls."

"No, don't do that—too much to wash. But take enough for supper for you and Latisha. How is she, anyway?"

Lillian laughed. "She mad at me right now 'cause I won't let her stay home all day by herself. She go to the day-care center where she have a real good time, but she play like she don't like it." Lillian laughed again. "She tell me that place be for after school, an' she never heard of after school bein' all day long."

"Lillian," I said, laughing with her, "that little girl is as smart as a whip."

"Yes'm, she pretty smart, but she get downright sassy more times than suit me."

"Just don't break her spirit. She and Lloyd both will need every bit of gumption they have, the way the world is today. Oh," I said, glancing up from the table, "I think I hear Etta Mae's car. It's nice, isn't it, having someone come home from work at the end of the day?"

"Yes'm, an' I 'spect she think so, too."

"Lock the door, Etta Mae," I said as soon as she stepped into the kitchen. "I don't want anybody barging in and seeing this." I put my overnight bag on the counter, opened it, and took out the Rich's box. Carefully opening it, I held out the sampler for her to see. "This is what that bright mind of yours uncovered for us."

She stood there in her visiting nurse's outfit—light blue tunic and pants—frowning as she studied the sampler. "Cross-stitch?" she asked, skeptically.

"Hardly. Just look at it. It's a remarkable example of needlework, and it's quite old."

"Well, it's cute, I guess, but I wouldn't want it hanging on my wall. Too depressing. Shoo, Miss Julia, I thought it might be jewelry or stock or stacks of cash—something like that. I'm sorry this thing is all you found."

"Then let me unsorry you," I said, smiling. "This *thing* is worth many, many thousands of dollars."

"Well, good," Etta Mae said, looking up with a laugh. "It's looking better and better all the time."

Etta Mae and I lingered at the table when we finished dinner—both too sated to move. Lillian had left us a plentiful and tasty meal—roast beef, rice and gravy, an asparagus casserole, and, along with her yeast rolls, a peach pie. We would have roast beef sandwiches for lunch the next day and roast beef hash the following evening—all of which suited me just fine.

"Etta Mae," I said, "I hope you don't mind spending another night at Miss Mattie's. Of course," I hurriedly added, "you don't have to, if you'd rather stay here. The auction house will be moving the furniture out on Monday, so I have to watch out for it till then. There's too much at stake and it's too close to the end to risk any more thefts."

"Oh, I'll go with you," she said, agreeably enough. "Besides, I don't want to stay in this big house by myself." She grinned. "I'm used to little places."

"That's good, then. I'll sleep better with you around. See, Etta Mae . . ." Then I stopped, not wanting to frighten her.

"Ma'am?"

"Oh," I said, drawing back, "I just worry about another break-in, especially now that we've found the sampler." A growing worry had been occupying my thoughts. It seemed more and more likely to me that the man calling himself Andrew F. Cobb had known of Mattie's treasure all along.

"Anyway," I went on, "we should take our nightclothes and get ready for bed over there. No need to keep shocking people by traipsing around in our bathrobes."

"Sure, we can do that. I thought that man—the one we met in the hall last night? I thought his eyes were going to bug out of his head."

"That was Mr. Wheeler. He's remodeling an empty apartment for whoever owns the building. Although, come to think of it, Sam mentioned that Mr. Wheeler himself might be the owner. He's very nice. And nice looking, as well." I cut my eyes at her. "He'd be quite a catch, especially if he is the owner. Don't you think?"

"Don't ask me. I'm off men these days. Had my fill of 'em, and then some." She glanced up and asked, "You think Miss Lillian would mind if I had another piece of that pie?"

"She'd be thrilled. Go ahead, but tell me, why're you off men?" Actually, I'd thought she *liked* them.

"Too much trouble. They're either hanging around all the time, or they're making themselves scarce. There's no in between, and I'm tired of arranging my life around somebody else's schedule. Besides," she added, putting a slender slice of pie on her plate, "it's a lot more peaceful when you don't have to worry if he's going to call or not."

Hm-m, I thought, *this is a major change in attitude. And just when a decent, hardworking man has come along with a spark of interest in his eyes.*

Well, maybe being decent and hardworking was the problem. There are some women, you know, who like only the bad ones. They can pick them out of a crowd, although, I will admit, some bad boys can eventually be housebroken—just look at Mr. Pickens.

The car crunched and listed over the gravel when I turned into the dimly lit parking area at Mattie's building. The lot was almost full of parked cars—everybody home from work, I supposed. I had to park in a far corner next to, I suddenly realized, Mattie's old Oldsmobile, reminding me that I should get rid of it. Advertise it? Maybe so. It would make a good second car, though I wouldn't take it far from a gas station. Or perhaps it would suit a new driver—a teenager who needed the extra protection it would provide in the inevitable accidents.

Lloyd? My goodness, in a few years he'd be learning to drive, and that Oldsmobile was like an armored tank—just the sort of thing I'd want him in. So I decided to buy it from Mattie's estate, garage it, and present it to Lloyd on his sixteenth birthday. I was well aware that such a vehicle was unlikely to be what he would want, but if it was either that or nothing, he'd be happy enough with it.

Something to talk to Sam about, I thought, recalling as I did so our phone conversation that afternoon. The fishermen were apparently having a good time, except that Mr. Pickens had taken to smoking a cigar every time he caught a fish. Lloyd, Sam had assured me, was being faithful about applying sunblock, and he himself was enjoying his companions and the seafood. Carefully avoiding any mention of spending another night at Mattie's, I told him that as much as I liked having Etta Mae around, I much preferred him. I had also remained silent about finding the sampler for fear of some unauthorized collection of phone data—whatever that was. You never know who's listening in.

But I put thoughts of Sam aside for a while as Etta Mae and I got our bags from the backseat and headed for our overnight stay. Even though it was not quite fully dark by that time, I was glad that we were presentable and not running from one shadow to another in our bathrobes. Still, I determined to mention to Mr. Wheeler that the parking area needed better lighting. There was a safety light at the back corner of the building and another one at the front corner, but neither reached the full expanse of the parking area. With the poor lighting and the gravel underfoot, it was a hazardous undertaking to walk across it in the dark. I stumbled twice and almost twisted my ankle—a lawsuit in the making for those so inclined, and Mr. Wheeler needed to be made aware of the liability.

When we got inside, I unlocked Mattie's door, put my overnight bag inside, and said, "I'm going to run down the hall and tell Mr. Wheeler that we're here. I don't want him calling the police if he hears us."

"Okay," Etta Mae said, brushing her hand against the wall to flip the switch of the overhead light, which couldn't have produced more than forty watts' worth of illumination. "Don't stay too long. It's kinda creepy in here."

There were more shadows in the room than outside and just as many hazards from the displaced furniture. "It sure is. Find some more lights, if you can. I'll be right back."

At the last apartment on the other side of the hall, I tapped on the door. Expecting to see Mr. Wheeler in his work clothes with the usual amount of sawdust and paint splatters, I was somewhat taken aback when he opened the door. He looked as if he were going to another visitation. I quickly took in the nice gray suit, white shirt, traditional striped tie, fresh haircut, and an aroma that wasn't Old Spice but almost as tantalizing.

"Oh, I hope I'm not interrupting anything," I said. "I just wanted to tell you that my houseguest and I are spending the night in Mrs. Freeman's apartment. In case, you know, you heard us and thought somebody was breaking in."

"Thanks, I appreciate that," Mr. Wheeler said, treating me again to his nice smile. "But with the furniture all scrambled around, are you going to be comfortable in there? We spent the day sorting it out—all the chairs together, all the chests, and so on—but I can move some things for you, if you want."

"That's kind of you, but as long as we can get to the beds, we'll be all right. We'll be up and gone early in the morning. Etta Mae has to be at work."

"Is that her name? Etta Mae? That was my aunt's name, so I've always liked it." He reached over and switched off a lamp, then said, "I was just leaving. I'll walk down the hall with you. You'll probably hear me come back in. Helen has asked me to dinner, so I won't be late."

Well, well, I thought as we said good night at Mattie's door and he left the building. Helen Stroud, so serene and composed, had a dinner date with a carpenter who might be more than a handyman. And from the sound of it, *she* had asked him, not the other way around. It was possible, of course, that more had been going on than I was aware of, so her dinner invitation did not necessarily mean that she had been the initiator of closer contact with Mr. Wheeler.

Still, Mr. Wheeler seemed more than a little interested in Etta Mae, so he wasn't exactly committed to Helen. Unless, as I had speculated earlier, he was a man of varied tastes. In which case, even given his seemingly desirable qualities, I'd as soon that he stayed away from Etta Mae.

Chapter 39

"Etta Mae," I called as I stepped into Mattie's dark, shadowy apartment and locked the door behind me.

"Ma'am?" she whispered right beside me.

I jumped, then patted my chest. "Oh, goodness, I thought you were in the bedroom."

"No'm, I was waiting for you."

"Well," I said, with a laugh to dispel the fright she'd given me, "let's go together and find some lamps."

"I think they're all packed up. I found three in a box over there." Etta Mae pointed to a corner of the room, where I could make out the harps of a number of shadeless lamps.

So we felt our way to the hall, swiping our hands against the walls in search of light switches. There was another dim bulb in the high ceiling of the hall, one in the ceiling of the guest room, and another in Mattie's room. One of the two sconces beside the bathroom mirror wasn't working.

"Law, Etta Mae," I said, scanning Mattie's bedroom from the door. "I never realized how beneficial bedside lamps are. I want both of us in beds tonight, but we could maim ourselves trying to get into them with the switches across the rooms."

"Um, that's the truth, 'specially with all the boxes on the floor. Let me move some around." She began to push a few boxes aside to clear a trail. "I'll keep my light on till you get in bed."

"Let's just keep the bathroom light on in case either of us has to get up. I'll probably have to."

She giggled and said, "Me, too."

Using the trail between the boxes, I laid my overnight bag on the bed, then hesitated before opening it. The box with the sampler in it would be right on top, and I didn't want to explain my reluctance to have it out of my keeping. Foolish, probably, but I felt better having it with me.

But Etta Mae was lingering beside Mattie's bed, hesitant, I thought, to go to the guest room alone. Why was that, I wondered, and wondered why I, too, felt ill at ease in the apartment. We'd had no such qualms when we'd dashed over in the middle of the night less than twenty-four hours before.

We should've felt safer after foiling an attempt to steal something else. The sunroom windows had been locked, checked, and rechecked. Deputies with dogs had walked the premises, and every tenant in the building was on the alert.

So why were we so on edge this night?

"Etta Mae," I said, straightening up, "I'll tell you what. I think we'll sleep better if we do something about that sunroom."

"Okay," she agreed. "What?"

"Let's go see. Mr. Wheeler moved the chest-on-chest so he could lock the windows in the sunroom—and he didn't move it back. So if anybody gets into the sunroom, he can walk right through those French doors into the apartment."

Etta Mae shivered. "I know," she said, nodding. Then, frowning, she said, "I don't think we can move the chest back by ourselves. That thing is huge."

"No, I'm thinking of moving something else—several somethings else, if need be—to block the doors. All we really need is something that'll make a lot of noise if it's moved."

Etta Mae's mouth twisted as she thought of somebody besides us being in the apartment. "You think somebody'll try to get in? Tonight? While we're here?"

"No, not really. I think we're safe—I just want to *feel* safe. Come on, let's go see what we can do."

Sure enough, not only was there no furniture blocking the French doors to the sunroom, the doors themselves weren't locked.

I walked out into the sunroom, partially lit by the light on the front corner of the building, and looked around. The wicker sofa was still there, now with two wicker chairs upended on it. Two Chippendale chairs that had been in the living room took up most of the center of the room, and a rolled-up Oriental on the floor nearly upended me. There were several taped boxes stacked up around the perimeter of the room, but, still and all, if someone broke a windowpane and unlocked a window, there'd be enough space and light for free access to anything in the apartment.

Maybe I was giving too much credit to the athleticism and determination of a potential thief, but to my mind it was the executor's job to think ahead and plan accordingly. Mattie's apartment was on the ground floor, so even I could've reached the sunroom windows from outside. For me to be able to climb through one of them was another matter, but I doubted that anyone bent on larceny would have to contend with physical limitations like creaky limbs and a stiff back.

Returning to the living room, I shut the French doors behind me. "All right, Etta Mae, let's look around and see what we can put in front of these doors. Not anything real heavy, but a lot of small things that'll tumble over and make enough noise to wake us up."

"Uh-huh, okay, but what do we do if we hear a noise? I mean, just waking up won't do us much good."

"Well, we scream and call the police." I stopped, recalling that I had had Mattie's phone disconnected. "You have your cell phone, and I have mine—I think. Anyway, keep yours close, and at the least little thing, call for help."

I looked around, trying to make sense of the way that Helen and Diane had sorted the furniture for the moving van. "Here's an idea, Etta Mae," I said. "I don't know why Diane hasn't already packed these things up, but let's clear off this étagère and move it in front of the French doors."

"Clear off what?"

"Étagère—it's just a whatnot."

"Oh, well," Etta Mae said, "I know what a whatnot is."

We began removing the decorative vases, the Lladró porcelain figurines, and the chubby Hummel child figurines from the crowded shelves. As we moved the ornamental odds and ends of Mattie's collection, I decided that none of the pieces was of great value. Which was probably why Diane had left them for last. The same statuette of a woman in a large hat and a flowing blue gown, for instance, I had seen in several Abbotsville homes.

Etta Mae, on the other hand, seemed entranced with each decorative piece, turning them around in her hands and looking for the makers' marks on the bottom.

"Do you collect anything, Miss Julia?" she asked.

"Ha!" I said, laughing. "Only the odd child or two. But, no, I've never been a collector. On second thought, though, I do have several Limoges boxes—the little, tiny ones, you know, in different shapes. What about you? Do you collect anything?"

"Barbies," she said. "I collect Barbie dolls. I only have a few because I like the ones that're in fancy dress, like a special evening gown or something. I have the Midnight Tuxedo Barbie, and she's beautiful. And I love the ones with outfits for a special outing, like the Resort Barbie or the Bowling Barbie." She studied a brightly colored Hummel figure, wrinkled her nose at it as she put it aside, and said, "They're awfully expensive, though, because they're to look at, not to play with."

I nodded and stored that information away. I'd told Lillian that I'd make it up to Etta Mae for helping me keep Mattie's apartment safe, and now I knew how to do it.

When we'd removed all the knickknacks from the shelves of the étagère, I said, "Okay, let's move it where the chest-on-chest was—right in front of the French doors to the sunroom."

"Miss Julia," Etta Mae said, as she helped me slide the étagère over. "This thing is as light as it can be. I mean, it's tall and awkward, but if that big chest couldn't keep anybody out, how can this?"

"We're going to put all the china things back on it. If a thief tries to push through the door, he'll create an almighty crash that'll wake up everybody in the building. Especially us."

I had a moment of hesitation about putting Mattie's collectibles in harm's way, but I did it anyway. Better a few gewgaws get broken than a thief get in.

I felt so comfortable with what we'd rigged up that I urged Etta Mae to forgo the sofa and sleep in the guest room. That meant that I would sleep in Mattie's bed—with clean sheets, of course—but I closed my mind to what had happened to the last occupant and crawled in. In fact, it didn't bother me at all. I fell asleep right away, safe and secure with Mr. Wheeler at one end of the hall, Etta Mae in the next room, and our homemade alarm system guarding the only means of access.

The next morning as we hurriedly dressed, taking turns brushing our teeth at the bathroom sink, a few second thoughts slowed me down. What was I doing carrying around a highly valuable object everywhere I went? And what was I doing leaving it under a pile of winter gowns or bathroom towels when I had to go out? Lillian couldn't guard it all day every day for me, especially since she had the weekend off.

There was only one thing to do, though I hated doing it. "Etta Mae," I said, "if we open that safe, then close it, we'd be able to open it again, wouldn't we? I mean, the combination isn't just good for one time, is it?"

She looked at me for a minute, seeming to understand my concern. "Let's try it and see."

And that's what we did. First, without putting anything in the safe, we closed the door and spun the dial. Then, looking at the scrap of paper I'd kept in my pocketbook, Etta Mae opened it right back up again. "It'll work, Miss Julia," she said.

So, with great trepidation, I slid the Rich's box into the safe, closed the door, and respun the dial.

"Lord," I said in as prayerful a tone as I could manage, "I hope I've done the right thing. But it's back where it's been safe for years and years. I really shouldn't have been carrying it around or trying to hide it in half a dozen different places. Why," I said, laughing, "I might've forgotten where I'd put it."

"Yes, ma'am," Etta Mae agreed, "or spilled coffee on it, or dropped it and broken the glass, or had it snatched on the street. It's safer right where it is."

I hoped she was right.

Chapter 40

"Good morning, Mrs. Murdoch," a strong, confident voice greeted me that morning as I answered the phone right after seeing Etta Mae off to work. "Ernest Sitton here. A few matters have recently come to my attention that might interest you. Would it be possible to meet with me here in about an hour? I'd prefer not to discuss it over the phone." Which I certainly understood, having had that same preference.

My first thought was that I had done, or was doing, something wrong. My second thought was that if so, I'd gladly relinquish all benefits and duties to anyone who was willing to sleep in Mattie's bed. My back was killing me. That mattress had been so old and so soft that Mattie had left a furrow down the right-hand side, and I'd kept rolling into and out of it all night long.

After agreeing to meet with Mr. Sitton, I called Helen and asked her to delay packing up the items on the shelves of the étagère until there was no longer a need to have a guard on duty.

"They're our alarm system," I told her.

She was silent for a few seconds, then said, "You mean they'll get broken if somebody breaks in? Is that a good idea?"

"As good as I could come up with and be able to get any sleep. Helen, as far as I can tell, none of the items is worth anything. And if you're worried about them, ask Diane to put a price on them, and I'll pay for any breakage. If," I went on, "it saves something a great deal more valuable from being stolen, it'll be worth the expense. And if, at the same time, it also saves me from bodily harm and mayhem, it most certainly will."

"Oh, yes, I see. Don't worry about it, Julia. Diane and I will be there early this morning—there's still so much to do before the moving van comes. But we'll leave whatever's on the étagère until Monday morning. I'm so sorry that you feel the need to stay overnight to protect everything. It's all been a real burden for you, I know."

After saying our good-byes, I hung up feeling somewhat compensated for all my efforts. At least Helen understood and appreciated the heavy load I was under.

Greeting Mr. Sitton, who had come forth from his inner sanctum upon my arrival, I entered his office, hoping to hear confirmation of Andrew F. Cobb's kinship to Mattie. What a relief it would be to let Mr. Cobb deal with her inflated idea of her estate's worth, and at the same time be able to dump on his shoulders the pleas of the pastor and the board of deacons of the First Presbyterian Church of Abbotsville.

But while driving to Delmont, I'd had a sinking feeling about relinquishing control of the sampler, which was still in the safety of Mattie's closet. Even though very few knew of its existence, there was really no telling what Mr. Cobb knew. For all I knew, his knowledge of the sampler could've been the reason he'd shown up in Abbotsville in the first place.

I had not told Mr. Sitton of my discovery, and wondered as I took a seat at his conference table if I should maintain my silence. He could be trusted to keep it to himself, but could his secretary? She, by her chilly demeanor, had not inspired in me a whole lot of confidence in her trustworthiness. But, then, not a whole lot of people did.

"Mrs. Murdoch," Mr. Sitton began. I nodded as he sat across from me and folded his hands on the table. "I have disturbing news. Although as yet unconfirmed, I felt I should share it with you."

I nodded again, feeling my entire body tighten up as I waited to hear what he had to say. I didn't need any more such news from him. Being named Mattie's executor had been disturbing enough.

"You will recall my telling you the Freeman/Cobb family history as related to me by the retired sheriff in Kentucky. From further research, I am inclined to accept all that he told me as a true account—excepting one thing. The man who has presented himself as Andrew F. Cobb is quite likely not Andrew F. Cobb."

"Really? You think he's an impostor?" My hands tightened on my pocketbook at the ramifications of this news. "But how could that be? How would he know so much about Mattie and her family?"

"Actually, he doesn't. He himself told me very little other than his name and that Mrs. Freeman was either his aunt or his great-aunt. There was some discrepancy about the specific relationship, which he put down to his being so long away from home and family."

"So what does this mean for us? I mean, for me? What am I to do?"

"You should continue what you're doing. As long as Mr. Cobb, or whoever he is, makes no move to qualify as Mrs. Freeman's relative and beneficiary, her will stands as the only legal document pertaining to her estate."

"Well," I said, able finally to begin thinking of what Mr. Cobb's lack of legal moves might entail. "Maybe the reason that he's made no move to qualify as her relative is because he isn't. It has always struck me as passing strange that he would deny any interest in her estate other than pictures and letters and so forth. I can understand that a roving man would not want the encumbrance of an apartment full of furniture and an old car on its last legs, but I can't understand why he's so indifferent to the cash those things would generate. Nobody, to my way of thinking, would want to be footloose and fancy-free without a penny to his name."

"Very true." Mr. Sitton nodded sagely. "I'm in full agreement.

Now, perhaps you'd like to tell me how you're coming along with generating cash from Mrs. Freeman's possessions."

But I was barely paying attention, for something had rung a bell in my mind. Where had I found that remarkable sampler? Why, stored away among Mattie's photograph albums and boxes of letters, that's where. Certainly it had been in a safe, but would the nameless man who called himself Andrew F. Cobb have known that? Or had he known it? Could there be something else of value among the letters and pictures crammed into the boxes that were stacked on the floor of my library?

"I'm sorry? Oh, her possessions." I was brought back to his question by the twiddling of his thumbs. "A moving van from the auction house will be here on Monday to take everything. After cleaning the apartment, I'll give up the lease. As far as I know, all I have to do after that is wait for the checks to come in. Disbursement of whatever amount I recieve will immediately follow. But, Mr. Sitton, if there's not enough to cover all the bequests, I will need your help in deciding who gets what.

"But I'll tell you one thing," I went on. "I don't know how your church would respond under similar circumstances, but mine—and Mattie's—is, well, let us say, eager to get its share. We've lost our air-conditioning, and you'd think the world was coming to an end in a ball of fire, beginning in our sanctuary."

"Although," I continued, somewhat contritely, "I don't believe in discussing the difficulties in my church with a member of another church. So I am depending, Mr. Sitton, upon the constraints of client confidence and upon your discretion."

"I'm quite familiar with difficulties within a church," he said, with a twist of his mouth. "Have no fear of anything said in this room going any further."

"That is certainly reassuring," I said—and it was, especially since I'd revealed the unwillingness of a certain number of local Presbyterians to suffer a little discomfort. "But what are we to do about Mr. Cobb? Or whoever he is?"

"Yes," Mr. Sitton said, returning to the main subject, as he straightened himself in his chair. He had a tendency to slump during long conversations. "What are we to do? I am, of course, continuing to follow every lead to enable us to make a determination of his authenticity. At the moment, I am awaiting word—and, hopefully, pictures—from the state prison in Kentucky where Andrew F. Cobb was incarcerated for a few years sometime ago—I told you about that. It's taking longer than I'd hoped because the sheriff who told me Cobb had been in prison couldn't remember the exact years. He's also checking the local records, even as the state is checking theirs."

"Wait, wait," I said, doing some straightening up of my own. "Let me be sure I understand. I know that Mattie's husband had been in prison, but her nephew—or whatever—was also incarcerated?"

"Yes, as a young man and only for a year or so. I thought I'd told you that."

"You may have. But between the Cobbs and the Freemans and the mess they made of their lives, I keep getting the generations mixed up. Well," I said, sighing, "it's no wonder Mattie moved to North Carolina. With a background like that, I would've, too."

In a musing way, as I studied the ceiling and the problem, I said, "If the man who's presented himself as Andrew F. Cobb is not Andrew F. Cobb, then he has to have known or known *of* the real Andrew F. Cobb. How else would he have known about Mattie, where she lived, or anything else about her?"

"True. But according to the sheriff I talked with, when the real Cobb was a young man, he followed the picking seasons. Migrant workers make up a whole subculture, and he would've met and talked—perhaps shared confidences—with any number of people of various stripes. The big question is this: if this man isn't Cobb, where is the real one?"

"Oh, my," I said, a whole new can of worms beginning to open up. "Do you think . . . ? Could this man have done away with the real one? I mean, if he's not the real one?"

"Not necessarily," Mr. Sitton hastened to assure me. "It could be that he learned that the real Cobb is deceased, and that gave him the incentive he needed to impersonate him, especially if he'd previously learned something of the Cobb and Freeman families."

"But it sounds as if this all happened years ago when both would've been young men."

"Mrs. Murdoch," Mr. Sitton said with a sigh, "you are apparently uninformed about sociopaths. They store away information like squirrels store acorns, then wait for an opportunity to use it. Mrs. Freeman's death would present just such an opportunity."

"*Socio*path? Oh, my, that is truly disturbing. Do you really think that's what he is?"

"If he's not Cobb himself, it's a distinct possibility. But, I caution you, Mrs. Murdoch, what *I* say in this office must also be kept in confidence. We should know more when and if I get pictures—mug shots—of Andrew F. Cobb from either the sheriff or the warden of the prison he was in. Preferably both."

"Well, have mercy," I said, sprawling back in my chair. "I don't want to have anything to do with a crazy person. I have enough to deal with already."

It was a settled fact that dealing with Mattie's estate and her kinfolks was getting messier and messier.

Chapter 41

"'Bout time you got back," Lillian said as I walked in. She wrung out a dishcloth, draped it over the faucet, and turned to me. "Miss Helen been callin' an' callin'. She need you real bad over at Miss Mattie's place."

"Why? What's going on?" I waited halfway in the doorway, noticing my cell phone still in the charger on the counter and not in my pocketbook.

"She say that man, kin of Miss Mattie's, is over there lookin' 'round, an' not havin' much in mind 'bout leavin'."

"Oh, my word! I'm on my way." I spun around and headed back out.

All the way to Mattie's apartment, I pictured what I might find when I got there. An angry kinsman? A greedy impostor? A sociopathic thief already filling his pockets with whatever he could pick up?

But, I reassured myself, Helen and Diane had already packed up a good many of the small odds and ends—there wouldn't be too much he'd be able to fit into a pocket. He could, however, get an overall idea of what Mattie had owned, as well as a clear impression of just where her valuable pieces were located in the apartment.

Ready to do battle if need be, I parked the car in the lot next to the building, noting as I did so Andrew F. Cobb's long and much-used Cadillac, minus its trailer, parked nearby. Hurrying into the building, I rushed through Mattie's front door, only to find Diane, Helen, and Mr. Cobb sitting around in variously placed chairs and stools drinking coffee from paper cups and eating Krispy Kreme doughnuts.

"Julia!" Helen said, standing up. "We're so glad you're here. Andrew has brought us a snack and your coffee is getting cold. Come have a doughnut."

I stopped short and glanced around, making note of the broom and long-handled dustpan, ready but, from the state of the floor, not yet used, leaning against the chest-on-chest.

Quickly adjusting my demeanor to one of bustling authority, I said, "Well, how nice. Thank you, Mr. Cobb, that's very thoughtful of you. But we do need to finish our work here, else we'll be at it all weekend. Is there anything I can help you with?"

"No'm," he said softly as he shook his head. "Just wanted to see where Aunt Mattie lived. You know," he went on with that ingratiating smile of his, "so I could picture her in her home."

At the word *picture*, all my senses perked up. What did he know about pictures, specifically one framed and ready to be hung in an art museum?

I glanced at Diane, but she was avoiding my eyes as she gathered up paper cups and napkins. I wondered how much looking around Mr. Cobb had been able to do, but I dared not put him on the defensive by asking. Better to keep things on a friendly basis, accept his visit at face value, and get him out of there as quickly as I could. Who knew what would set a sociopath off on a rampage?

Yet he was so calm and easygoing, friendly and seemingly anxious to please, that I couldn't imagine such a complete change of personality. Even so, that constant smile on his face when there was no reason in the world for it kept my guard up. Nobody was that accommodating. Actually, though, I would've been more easily taken in if his teeth hadn't been so large.

"Okay, ladies," I said, bustling around. "We have a lot to do, so we'd better get at it. Mr. Cobb, thank you for the snack, but we have to finish this up. Oh, and, by the way, I spoke with Mr. Sitton this morning, and I think he's trying to get in touch with you. You might want to call him, or, better still, see him at his office." In other words, it's time to leave, so get going—which, of course, I didn't say, but he got the message.

"Yes, ma'am, I'll do that right away," he said, just so humble it made my own teeth ache. Then, including Diane and Helen, he said, "If I can ever help in any way, just let me know." And turning back to me, he went on, "I'm ready to pick up the family papers whenever you want me to. I don't know how Aunt Mattie ended up with all that stuff, but my dad said she was the onliest one interested in it. He always kinda laughed about how he couldn't figure out why she'd want it 'cause she about ruint both sides of the family. I'm glad she did, though, 'cause it'll make a good book that I can sell on my travels."

"Oh?" I said, eyebrows raised. Maybe he was more legitimate than I'd thought. "You already have a publisher?"

"Anybody can get a publisher these days," he assured me, as I thought, *Uh-huh, if you pay for it yourself. And maybe a certain cellarette would make the payments*. "Anyway," he went on as he turned to leave, "I just wisht I'd got here in time to get to know Aunt Mattie and interview her. But I really 'preciate what y'all are doing for her, and I know she does, too."

Well, *I* didn't know it. If all had gone well with Mattie, she was too busy growing wings to be watching us sort her furniture and ransack her drawers, or listen to us wonder how she'd lived in such a mess.

As soon as Mr. Cobb was out the door, I went into the sunroom and watched as he crossed the parking lot to his car. When he drove out, I turned to Diane.

"How much looking around did he do?"

"Not much. Really. He walked down the hall and looked in each room, then came back to the living room. We followed him every step of the way. I'm sorry, Julia, we thought he was Nate when he knocked, and after we'd opened the door and saw him standing there holding coffee and doughnuts, there was nothing to do but let him in. At least, it felt that way at the time, but I promise you, he was never out of our sight."

"It's all right, Diane. I would've done the same, I'm sure. I just hope he doesn't come back, but all the more reason to get this packing done and all this stuff out of here."

"Um, Julia," Diane continued, "he did specifically ask about photograph albums and old letters, as well as deeds and such that might be in a safe-deposit box, because of that family history he's writing. I just told him that as far as I knew the lockbox had been empty, and that we'd not gotten to everything here yet. I didn't want to tell him that you'd taken it all home with you. Was that all right?"

"It was perfect, and I'm glad that's all you told him. If he knew that I have them, he might show up at my house. And I'll tell you this, Diane, I'm skeptical of his reason for being interested in them—most people who talk about writing a book never get around to actually doing it."

Then, realizing that we'd walked into the sunroom through the wide-open French doors, my heart gave a thump and I said, "Where's the étagère?"

"In the kitchen, behind the counter," Helen said, pointing. "We moved it as soon as we got here so we could get to the sunroom."

"What about the things on it?"

"It's all on the counter. We'll move it back before we leave this afternoon. Why? Should we have left it?"

"No, I'm glad you didn't. I'd as soon that nobody but you and Helen know about my alarm system. Let's leave it where it is in case we have any more visitors. I'll set it back up when I come over tonight."

I left them to it then, returning to my house to delve into the boxes of papers, letters, photograph albums, and who-knew-what-else that were waiting in my library. But I'd been shaken by the thought that Andrew Cobb might have seen the étagère, loaded with every possible means of creating a sleep-shattering noise, standing in the way of an easy entry. A sociopath or even your common, run-of-the-mill type of burglar would've made note of that and quickly made plans to avert such a disaster.

After a couple of hours of looking through Mattie's albums and reading the letters she'd saved—some of the handwriting was like hen scratching—I was getting a headache. I had found nothing that I thought would attract the interest of a legitimate historian, much less an amateur one, so more and more I feared that Andrew was after the sampler.

When the phone rang and Lillian told me Mrs. Allen was on the line, I was happy to stop and talk with her.

"Mildred," I said into the phone, "you have rescued me from a pile of papers that have crossed my eyes. How are you?"

"Starving, but what's new? Listen, Julia, I have to get out of this house and away from the kitchen. You have time to walk around the block?"

"I sure do. I'll be over in a few minutes."

She was leaning against a column on the porch, waiting for me. I hurried across the yard, waving as I went.

"I don't know how far I'll get," Mildred greeted me. "I'm so weak from hunger, I may collapse any minute." But she pushed off from the column and joined me in the yard.

Then we started down the sidewalk on one of Mildred's typical outings—that is, we didn't take a walk, we took a stroll.

"I hope you've noticed, Julia," Mildred said. "I've lost two pounds."

"Why, that's wonderful! And, of course, I did notice. You're looking quite trim." Every woman alive knows when it's best to avoid the truth in the nicest way possible.

"Well, it's been hard, but I just don't want to have that operation. So the sacrifices I'm making are worth it—I think. But tell me how settling Mattie's estate is going. What's the status with her furniture?"

So I told her of the upcoming auction and how the auction house would be taking care of everything. Then I told her a little about the continuing saga of Andrew F. Cobb and his unverified identity without, however, mentioning any possible psychopathic tendencies. She was intrigued, as I would've been as well if I hadn't been personally involved. She speculated about any number of possibilities involving Mr. Cobb, unaware of my discomfort at the thought of more snarls and tangles for me to manage.

One good thing, though, the more Mildred entertained herself with Mattie's estate, the farther we walked. It was only when we crossed the second street that she abruptly turned and said, "Let's go back. It's about dinnertime, anyway."

So we turned back, and I took the opportunity to get her onto another subject, telling her about Etta Mae spending the week with me.

"Oh, she's just the one I need to talk to," Mildred said. "She'll know all the ins and outs of stapling. Why don't you both come over for lunch tomorrow? Sam won't be back, will he?"

"No, he won't be back till late Monday, so we'd love to come for lunch. But, Mildred, I wouldn't count on Etta Mae knowing much about that operation. She's not a hospital nurse, you know, or even an office nurse. She may not know enough to help you."

"That's all right. I like her, and I've been wanting to have some people in, but I've been hesitant about entertaining. See, Julia, I'm on a really strict diet, and you and your houseguest—with your knowledge of the problem and her nursing background—won't mind my having something different on my plate. You can be sure, though, that I wouldn't insult my guests by serving a local lunch just because that's what I have to eat. I'll ask Ida Lee to prepare something especially tasty for you and Etta Mae."

"No, please don't do that. We'll have just what you're having and be delighted with it."

"Really?"

"Of course. I wouldn't dream of anything different."

"Well," Mildred said mournfully, "you don't know what you're in for, and I'll feel like a terrible hostess. It's just so hard to resist a decent meal, but it'll be easier if I don't have to watch somebody else have one. If Ida Lee were to serve you some gorgeous, calorie-laden plate, then put a bowl of leaves in front of me, I might grab both your plates and gorge myself."

"Oh, Mildred," I said, laughing. "We'll happily eat leaves along with you." And hurry home afterward for a thick roast beef sandwich with a side of chips. Neither of which I mentioned.

Chapter 42

After spending an additional uneventful two nights on Mattie's ancient mattress, I could hardly straighten up. I moaned so much about my aching back that Etta Mae offered to give me a massage. It was tempting, but I declined. By the time on Saturday morning that we'd returned to my house and gotten dressed, we were ready for lunch with Mildred. Why go through the process of undressing and redressing again? I took an aspirin or two and made the best of it.

When it came right down to it, though, I would've much preferred to bypass Mildred's lunch, not only because I knew that we'd be discussing bypass surgery but also because I had had an epiphany during the night. I had come awake with a clear path stretching in front of me, and I didn't know why I hadn't thought of it before then. All I had to do to either get rid of Andrew F. Cobb or make him declare himself was to finish going through the family letters, pictures, and so forth. As soon as I determined there was nothing of value among them, I could turn them all over to him. They were the extent of what he'd claimed he wanted, so once he had them, he would surely be on his way. If, that is, they were indeed all that he wanted.

On the other hand, if he was really after the sampler, then he'd stick around and try to find it. That thought almost made me reconsider giving him anything. He would fairly quickly realize, as he sorted through Mattie's family documents, that the sampler was missing, and I would be the obvious one to have it. No telling what he would try if he felt he'd been tricked.

But the apartment would be emptied Monday morning, so Etta Mae and I wouldn't need to spend any more nights there. In addition, Sam would be home Monday night, and his presence would be a burglar deterrent at home. I had nothing to fear from Mr. Cobb.

So I was anxious to start again on the boxes in my library, make sure there were no more samplers or other valuable items in them, then make arrangements with Mr. Sitton to pass it all to Mr. Cobb. Instead, I was committed to a luncheon that would not only be on the light side but also would be heavily laden with conversation about stomach surgeries.

But one does not insult a hostess by backing out at the last minute, even when one has significant work to do.

"Now, Etta Mae," I said, "I hope you won't think the less of me for accepting an invitation without consulting you. If you have something else you'd rather do today, just tell me and I'll make your regrets to Mildred. She will completely understand."

"Oh, no, I want to go," Etta Mae said. She looked lovely in a sleeveless print dress, although the fabric was just a tiny bit on the clingy side. "I just love her house. I hope she'll let us look around a little."

"She'll be delighted for you to see it. Her decor is mostly French inspired, and she has some very nice pieces. Oh, and, Etta Mae, I should warn you. I told Mildred that you and I would have exactly what she'll be having on that strict diet of hers. I have no idea what it'll be, but let's just smile and pretend we like it."

"Suck it up and eat, right?"

"Well, yes, whatever that means. Anyway, you'll enjoy seeing her furniture and the huge collection of Boehm porcelain birds she has."

And she did, but not nearly as much as Mildred enjoyed showing them to her.

When Mildred pointed out a Louis-the-something-or-other

chest that she called a commode, Etta Mae asked, "You mean they had a special place for bedpans that long ago?"

Mildred exploded with laughter, which I thought would hurt Etta Mae's feelings, but it didn't. When Mildred explained that *commode* was a fancy name for a plain old chest of drawers, Etta Mae laughed and said, "Well, you can tell where my mind is."

Our plates, when Ida Lee served them, held a beautifully arranged salade Niçoise on each, although I detected no potatoes among the green beans, radishes, and tomatoes. Each was topped with a small serving of water-packed tuna and the greens glistened with a vinaigrette dressing. At least mine and Etta Mae's glistened. Mildred's didn't.

No bread or crackers were offered, but unsweetened tea was. When Mildred lifted her fork, Etta Mae reached for her glass. As soon as she swallowed, her eyes widened and her mouth puckered.

"Please pass the . . . uh—" She stopped, swallowed again, and said, "The salt. No, pepper, I mean the pepper. I love pepper." Then she bravely lifted her glass again, suppressing a shudder as she took another sip. "Delicious," she said.

Ida Lee, looking somewhat abashed at the lean pickings served to guests, came from the kitchen to refill our glasses. I complimented her on the beautiful arrangement of greens on our plates, and ate as if I enjoyed every bite. Dessert was a baked pear half with raspberry sauce, barely sweetened. No wonder Mildred complained about her diet.

"Etta Mae," Mildred said as we finished dessert, "tell me everything you know about stomach stapling. I'm in need of some straight talk."

"Well," Etta Mae began, propping her elbow on the table, then quickly retracting it. "Well, I don't know much, but I did help a lady a couple of years ago who had had her stomach done. She got along real well, but it was hard at first. She couldn't have anything but broth and clear juice for the first few days—even though she didn't have staples. They put a band around her stomach instead, which worked the same way. Anyway, she gradually added stuff like pudding, hot cereal, and pureed food. After about a month of that, the doctor let her have a little solid food."

"A *month*!" Mildred cried. "A month of not having anything to *chew*? All of a sudden, a plate of green leaves sounds a lot more appetizing.

"Julia," she went on, "I'll tell you what's a fact. I am not going under the knife and end up eating baby food for the rest of my life. I'm going to lose this weight if I have to starve myself to death. Which," she said, raising her voice, "Ida Lee, you are about to do for me."

"Maybe," I said, "you need something to take your mind off of it. Think about taking the instruction class with me—if they ever call me about it—so you can teach in the literacy program. You'd enjoy it, Mildred, and it would give you something uplifting to think about."

"I'll think about it," she mumbled. "I need something uplifting."

"I'll tell you something uplifting," Etta Mae chimed in. "I don't think you're a good candidate for stomach stapling. You wouldn't weigh anywhere near what the lady I worked for did. Compared to her, you're just a little on the plump side. I'd get a second opinion if I were you."

I cringed at Etta Mae's bluntness, but Mildred, staring at her in wonder, said, "You're absolutely right. That's exactly what I'm going to do." Then she raised her voice and called, "Ida Lee, bring some rolls."

As soon as we returned home, Etta Mae and I both headed for the refrigerator for a piece of cold fried chicken to tide us over until suppertime. Lillian was off for the weekend, but she had left us well stocked with food, even though I had told her of my intention to take Etta Mae to the country club for dinner that evening.

Soon afterward, Etta Mae left to check on her single-wide, pick up her mail, and run a few errands. I headed to the library, eager to finish going through Mattie's family records and turn them over to whoever—Mr. Cobb or Mr. Sitton—wanted them. Or, I thought, a real writer from the Kentucky county where she'd grown up and had had that disastrous marriage might also be interested in them. Something to think about, anyway.

Plopping my pocketbook on the desk, I was brought up short by something else that needed doing. There, also on the desk, was Mattie's pocketbook, its contents still undisturbed, awaiting some determination of what to do with it. And what to do with what was in it. But, unwilling to face more decisions, I put it off for another day and started on the pile of papers.

After several hours of sorting through photographs, hard-to-read letters, canceled deeds, newspaper clippings, and certain documents—including Mattie's marriage license and Tommy's death certificate—as well as any number of papers, like the original lease on the apartment and twenty-year-old canceled checks, that I could see no value in at all, I was exhausted. Why in the world had Mattie kept such things?

Finally, just as I heard Etta Mae coming in, I decided that I had done my duty diligently enough. I didn't want to see another album, letter, or piece of paper ever again. I would take everything to Mr. Sitton as soon as the moving van from the auction house left on Monday and dump it all on him. If Andrew F. Cobb—be he Andrew F. Cobb or be he not—could find anything of value in the pile, he was welcome to it. Good-bye and good riddance, as far as I was concerned.

Chapter 43

Etta Mae had no trouble convincing me that the fried chicken and potato salad that Lillian had left in the refrigerator would be much better than what the clubhouse dining room would serve. We steamed some broccoli, sliced a tomato, and warmed up the yeast rolls, then sat at the kitchen table, congratulating ourselves on the decision to eat at home.

"This is going to work real well," Etta Mae said, reaching for another paper napkin. "We'll be through by the time the news is off. That's when they'll start the marathon again."

"Marathon? Who's running?"

"*Sex and the City*. They've been running it all day, so we've missed the oldest ones. Did you watch it when it first came on?"

"Etta Mae," I said, "I don't have an idea in the world what you're talking about, but it doesn't sound very edifying."

"It's not as bad as it sounds. Just a serial TV show about some women who live in New York. I just love it, so I hope you don't mind if I watch it again."

"Of course not. I don't believe I've seen it, so I'll enjoy watching it with you."

So, since Mattie's television set was so small and there were no comfortable places to sit in her apartment, we delayed our nightly trek until the marathon ended around eleven that evening.

Etta Mae, in shorts and her pink bunny bedroomers, curled up in one of the leather chairs by the fireplace in the library, while

I stretched out on the sofa. We were both thoroughly engaged in the antics on the screen.

During the last thirty minutes of a fairly explicit episode, I cleared my throat and said, "My word, Etta Mae. Do young women of today really carry on like that?"

"Um-m, I'm not sure," she mumbled. "Maybe in New York they do."

"Yes, that probably explains it. Or else the writer just wishes they would."

When the phone rang at an embarrassingly delicate point in the last episode, I was relieved to excuse myself even though a call at that time of night usually meant trouble of some kind. This one was no exception.

"Julia?" Helen said when I answered. "Sorry to call so late, but did you by chance pick up my key to Mattie's apartment yesterday?"

It took me a minute to process the concern in Helen's voice as well as the question. "Why, no, I didn't. Don't you have it?"

"Oh, Julia, I am beyond distressed. I didn't realize it was gone until just a few minutes ago. Diane locked up behind us when we left yesterday afternoon, and I've been gone all day today— Nate and I went to Charlotte for the *Southern Living* home show—so I've just realized it's not here."

A chill went down my back as I recalled the visit that Mr. Cobb, bearing coffee and Krispy Kremes, had made the day before. Without bringing that up, I asked, "When was the last time you remember having it?"

"Yesterday at the apartment. I got there before Diane, so I went on in. Julia, I *always* put that key—it's on a chain by itself—in my purse after I use it. I mean, I don't ever leave it lying around. But I've dumped everything out twice, and it's just not here." She stopped, then went on. "You know it's not like me to be careless, and. . . Oh, Julia, I am so sorry. I so hoped that you had it."

No, I didn't have it, but I had a fairly good idea of who did.

All I could do at that point was to assure Helen that all would be well, and that she shouldn't concern herself about spilled milk or lost keys. After hanging up, I decided not to frighten Etta Mae by mentioning the likelihood of a creeping night visitor who could now avoid our alarm system. It was simply up to me to stay awake all night long.

It was after eleven by the time we got ourselves together to go to the apartment. I packed my overnight bag while Etta Mae filled her grocery sack, and we turned off lights behind us as we went downstairs.

"Etta Mae," I said, "would you get the lights in the library while I turn off the living room lamps? Oh, and bring my pocketbook, please. It's on the desk."

Both of us were silent on the short drive to the apartment. But after several hours of watching the questionable exploits of young women in the big city, what was there to say? And after Helen's call, I had more pressing problems on my mind than Mr. Big's vacillations.

"Good grief, Etta Mae," I said as the tires crunched on the gravel of the parking lot at Mattie's building. "The safety light at the back corner is out, and worse than that, the lot looks full."

She sat up to look through the windshield. "It sure is. Somebody must have company."

"Well," I said with some sharpness, "guests shouldn't be permitted to take the parking places of people who live here."

"Uh, Miss Julia," Etta Mae said, "we don't live here."

I had to laugh, although having no place to park frustrates me no end. And even more so when, as it happened, I reached the end of the double row of parked cars and had no room in which to turn around. There was nothing for it but to crank my head around and back out—always a hazardous procedure.

"We'll have to park on the street," I said as I finished the reverse manuever. "Help me look for a space."

I drove slowly down the street, passing one car after the other parallel-parked all along it. I turned at the corner, where we saw a house with all its lights on, music blaring from the open doors and windows, and people moving around on the porch and in the yard.

"That explains it," Etta Mae said. "They're having a party."

"But it doesn't excuse the rudeness of parking in personal spaces," I fumed. "We'll have to walk a country mile to get to the apartment."

"That's all right," Etta Mae said, as amenable as always, "but I should've worn better shoes." She laughed as she lifted a bunny fur–clad foot to show me. "Anyway, we could use the exercise."

"I guess. Too bad Mildred's not with us."

After turning another corner, we found a parking space on the far side of the block that Mattie's building was on. After getting my overnight bag from the backseat and slinging my pocketbook on my shoulder while Etta Mae got her sack, I made sure the car doors were locked and we set off along the sidewalk. I didn't like it—for one thing, I was tired and what I was carrying seemed heavier than usual, putting a strain on my shoulder. And even though the streetlights were a help, we still walked through places where overhanging branches from shrubs and bushes kept the sidewalk in full shadow. Some people do not prune their shrubbery as they should.

Anxious to get inside now that Helen's key was in the wind, I stepped out right smartly. Silently castigating myself for not putting the sampler in the absolutely safest place for it, I thought of the immovable, unbreakable-into, and directly-wired-to-the-sheriff's-department safe in Mr. Sitton's office. That's where it should've been kept while Diane contacted a textile expert. But had I turned it over to Mr. Sitton? No, I had not. For one thing, I was loath to relinquish the guardianship of it. And for another, Mr. Sitton's office was closed over the weekend. So with Lillian off for the weekend and unable to guard it when I wasn't home, I was glad that I'd returned the sampler to its safe haven in Mattie's guest room closet. I was banking on the fact that since no one had ever known about her hiding place, the sampler would remain undisturbed until I took it out again.

Etta Mae and I stumbled along on the broken pavement and protruding tree roots of the sidewalk, giving each other a hand when needed. We could hear and almost feel the thump of the music from the party we'd passed, but everything else was quiet. The houses along the street were dark—decent people asleep in their beds—and the street was empty of cars except for a few parked along the side.

"Hold on, Etta Mae," I whispered, coming to a stop in the shadow of a spreading oak tree. I pointed across the street where a tall privet hedge bordered the parking area of a podiatrist's office.

"What is it?" she whispered back.

"You see that over there?"

"I don't think so. What is it?"

I grabbed her arm and started across the street. "Come on, let's get a closer look."

We scurried across the street and stopped on the opposite sidewalk.

"What're we doing?" Etta Mae whispered.

"See that grille sticking out from the hedge? Don't you think that's a Cadillac?"

"Law, Miss Julia, I couldn't tell a Cadillac from a Camry in this light."

"Well, me, either, if it weren't for that trailer hooked to the back. Don't you think it's an aluminum, one-axle, sort of bullet-shaped Airstream travel trailer with a door on the other side and a drop-down door for ease of loading at the back?"

"Well, not really," Etta Mae said in a normal tone. "Why? You thinking of buying one?"

I stared at her, although I could barely see her in the dark. "Etta Mae, can you picture me driving around town with something like that hitched to the back of my car? Of *course* I'm not thinking of buying one. I'm just telling you that that outfit, rig, whatever it is, parked half hidden in the dark behind that hedge, is exactly like what Andrew F. Cobb has, which means . . ."

"Which means," she said, dropping her voice down to an urgent whisper, "that Andrew F. Cobb himself is somewhere around here."

"Exactly," I whispered back. "And there're only two reasons for him to be within half a block of Mattie's apartment in the middle of the night—he's either planning to go in or he's already in."

Etta Mae moaned.

"Come on," I urged, taking her arm.

"Where're we going?"

"We're going to catch that sneaky little ponytailed thief redhanded in the very act."

Chapter 44

"Come on, let's go!" I grabbed Etta Mae's arm again and we dashed back across the street. "Cut through this yard, Etta Mae. We'll come out in Mattie's parking lot."

"Wait, wait! Where're we going?"

I stopped because I'd almost run into a swing set. Dodging that, I headed for the hemlock-planted property line next to the parking lot—and stepped into a plastic baby pool. Water splashed, and I nearly did, too. Those things are slick on the bottom.

"Are you all right?" Etta Mae steadied me, then said, "Listen, we've got to slow down. We could run right into him, or kill ourselves, one."

"But he could already be in the apartment. *Ransacking* it!"

"No, he can't get in. We burglar-proofed it, remember?"

"Etta Mae," I said, breaking the news to her, "I hate to tell you, but I'm afraid he has a key."

That stopped her for a minute. "But he'll have to come back to his car." Etta Mae, never eager to jump into the fray, took the news in stride. "So let's just wait right here and watch. I'll call the sheriff."

"Good idea," I said, puffing from the run. "Let's watch for him from under these hemlocks." I bent down and crawled under the low hanging limbs, pulling Etta Mae along with me. "But I tell you, if he comes out with that safe, I'm going after him. Call the sheriff, Etta Mae."

She rummaged in the grocery sack for her phone, while I put my overnight bag well back under the drooping hemlock limbs, freeing myself for whatever might happen.

"Finally," Etta Mae said, pulling her phone, along with something edged with lace, from the bottom of the sack.

Just then, as I peered through a curtain of hemlock branches, a shadow darker than the lot itself came wobbling out from between two parked cars, and headed diagonally, but laboriously, across the lot toward us and the Cadillac. I strained to see through hemlock needles, trying to figure out what I was seeing. It looked like two shadowy blobs—one pulling something and the other pushing something. Whatever they were doing, the gravel was giving them a hard time—the one in front either listing to the side or getting bogged down, while the second one struggled along behind with a lot of pushing and grunting. As the shadow neared, the blob separated momentarily as the back figure stopped and mopped his face. Then I knew what I was seeing.

"Look at that, Etta Mae! It's *him* and he's got a dolly! He's pushing a dolly."

"A what?"

"Just look! He's moving furniture!"

Then, as the dark figure of Andrew F. Cobb resumed his toil, he reached the sidewalk and bumped the dolly off onto the street. Cobb, wrestling with the heavy load and pushing hard, picked up his pace on the smooth pavement. And so did I, for in the light from a streetlamp, I could see not only Andrew F. Cobb as plain as day—who could miss that ponytail—I could also see Mattie's safe on the dolly.

"Oh, no, you don't!" I hissed, slinging aside my pocketbook. Ignoring Etta Mae's muffled screech, I backed out from under the hemlocks in a scramble to get to my feet and started across the yard toward the street.

"Wait!" Etta Mae said in a loud whisper. "What're we doing?"

"Executing Mattie's will," I said, fighting that blasted swing set again. One wooden seat whacked my shin, and I almost folded up right there. "Come on, Etta Mae, we've got to stop him. He's got most of Mattie's estate on that dolly!"

"What about our things? Your pocketbook?"

"Leave 'em," I said, making a jog around the baby pool. "Leave everything and come on."

She did, and we scampered across the street—me in my low-heeled, but not flat, Ferragamos and Etta Mae in her pink bunny bedroomers—rounded the end of the privet hedge, and dashed along the side of the car to the trunk, where the Airstream was attached.

I stopped then and held out my arm to slow Etta Mae. "Listen," I said, crouching down in the space between the car and the trailer. Whatever Cobb was doing, he was doing it at the back of the trailer—something was bumping against it, making it teeter back and forth on its single axle. Right next to where we crouched, we heard the creak and groan of the bolts that held the trailer to the car.

"Etta Mae," I whispered, "if we unhook this trailer, he'd be up a creek."

She felt around the coupling with both hands. Then, leaning up close, she whispered, "I don't know, Miss Julia. Even if we got the bolts out, we might need a winch to lift it."

"A *wench*?" Shocked, I dropped that idea.

Peeking around the end of the trailer, I could see the edge of the back gate ramped down and Mr. Cobb struggling to push the dolly inside. The night was hot and humid, and I could feel perspiration trickling down my back. Andrew F. Cobb was feeling the heat, too. I could hear him panting and gasping for breath—and smell him, too.

"What's he doing?" Etta Mae whispered as she scrunched up against me.

"*Stealing!*" I whispered back. "When's the sheriff coming?"

I sneaked a quick peek around the trailer again and saw Cobb pull the dolly a few feet back from the ramp. Then, hunching over, he took a firm grasp on the handles and ran toward the trailer, pushing hard, and, with a mighty groan, wrestled it over the hump and into the trailer. We could feel and picture and hear every step of the process, for almost, but not quite, under his breath, Cobb was panting and groaning and cursing gravel parking lots, unwieldy dollies, heavy loads, and cramped trailers for all he was worth.

After a minute of silence, as he regained his breath, the trailer began to bounce from one side to the other.

"What's he doing?" Etta Mae whispered.

"I don't know. Maybe trying to unload the safe. It weighs a ton."

I turned, grasped her, and sank down beside the trailer tire. Whispering right against her ear, I said, "Call the sheriff again."

"Uh, I can't. You said leave everything, and I did."

"But *did* you call?"

"I started to. I got to nine-one, and then got hit with something. Then you said leave it and come on, so I did."

"Oh, my word," I moaned, just done in that no help was on the way. "What're we going to do?"

"I'll go back and find my phone," Etta Mae said, "or wake somebody up or something. Five minutes, and I'll have a cop car here. Just don't let him leave, Miss Julia." And with that, she turned, crawled a few feet, then sped away without a sound.

I stayed plastered beside the tire, but knowing I'd soon have to move. The early warning of a cramp began to knot up in one leg, so I eased upright before it took hold.

An eerie silence surrounded the trailer and, without Etta Mae breathing down my neck, the night itself. What was Cobb doing in there?

Then I heard the pop and fizz of a bottle being opened—he was taking a break. Which meant a break for us, too—giving the sheriff time to get there. *Hurry, Etta Mae, hurry!*

What would I do if Cobb suddenly decided to leave? He already had the centerpiece of Mattie's estate, but how had he known about it? Not everybody kept a safe in their guest room closet. Well, I figured out the answer to that—while Etta Mae and I had been entranced with young women romping around in New York, Cobb had had a good three hours of darkness to plunder around in the apartment. No telling what else he'd already pilfered and had stacked up in the trailer.

Actually, I was hoping he'd take that dolly and go back for more. I'd even sit back and watch him bring the handkerchief table if that would buy a few more minutes for the sheriff to get there.

Then I felt the trailer shudder as Cobb walked from the front to the back, tromped down the ramp, turned, and leaned down to pick it up. He was closing up shop!

"*Stop!*" I screamed, and ran at him. I couldn't stop myself, but I had to stop him.

He was so surprised that he dropped the ramp, and I hopped up on it. Facing him, I said, "You're not stealing another thing, you thief, you! What do you mean, coming here and claiming you don't want anything, and mooning around like a grieving nephew, when all the time you were waiting your chance! You might as well give it up now. A dozen deputies're on the way." I stood at the top of the ramp, folded my arms, and stared him down, fully confident that my accusation would stop him in his tracks. And confident, too, in the ability of the Abbot County sheriff's department to deploy in a matter of minutes.

He glared at me, the surprise gone as malice took its place.

"The heck you say!" he said, which wasn't exactly what he said.

With a flicker of rage and a hunch of his shoulders, he barreled up the ramp full force, shoving me backward until we both rammed into the dolly, with the safe still on it, in the middle of the cramped interior. I remember the amazement I felt as images of a tiny sink, a hot plate, a table, and a cot flashed past as we fell across the dolly to the floor. Why, I remember thinking, it does have all the comforts of home.

I didn't think much of anything after that, for I was stunned by his gall and breathless from hitting the floor. The trailer and my head rocked from the impact. He rolled off, kicked at the safe—which still didn't budge—then he was gone.

Crawling toward the door, hoping nothing was broken, I started after him. I intended to point him out to the deputies and say, "There he is. There's the thief," but before I could drag myself to my feet, he picked up the ramp and slammed it home. I heard a bolt being thrown, and he heard me throw myself against the door as I hammered and banged on it, screaming for help.

A car door slammed, the motor turned over, and a door slammed again. With a lurch that rocked the trailer, the Cadillac pulled out of the lot and bounced onto the street—giving the trailer a double bounce that almost bumped my head against the ceiling. I clung to the counter to stay on my feet.

Oh, my Lord, I thought, *he's driving away and I'm locked in here and Etta Mae won't know where I am and the deputies will give chase and no telling what'll happen then and Sam's going to be so upset with me—to say nothing of what the beneficiaries and the First Presbyterian Church will say for letting Andrew F. Cobb confiscate Mattie's most valuable asset.*

The trailer swayed, then tilted, as the car took a curve. I held on to the dolly for dear life and eased myself down to the floor. I kept thinking that there was no need for panic or for heroics. I would just ride it out, protect myself as well as I could, and await the rescue that was surely on its way—because, disregarding all evidence to the contrary and despite whatever Andrew F. Cobb assumed, right at that moment and for as far as I could see, Mattie's safe with the sampler inside was now in my possession, which was where I intended it to stay.

Chapter 45

Not for long, though, because I didn't think I'd live long enough. Cobb hadn't had the time nor the strength to wrest the safe off its current site on the ledge of the dolly, so there it sat. Even worse, it was looking more and more doubtful that I'd be around to get it back to Mattie's apartment, my house, or Mr. Sitton's office. We were going awfully fast, tires screeching on the turns, and the trailer rocking perilously from side to side and, occasionally, sickeningly from front to back.

Clinging desperately to the dolly with one hand and bracing myself against the wall with the other, I began to panic. Was Cobb evading the deputies? Were the deputies even after us? Where was Etta Mae? Had Cobb had an accomplice who'd gotten her? Was the trailer going to turn over? Was I going to throw up?

Then the sirens started, and red and blue lights began flashing through the windows, lighting up the interior of the trailer like a psychedelic light show. It was enough to make one dizzy and cause a headache, too, so I closed my eyes and clung to the dolly. And a good thing I did, for the car and the trailer went crazy, speeding up, slowing down, then skidding back and forth across whatever street we were on, bouncing against one curb and caroming off the other. The trailer tilted, swerved, and swayed. I really thought I would throw up.

Without warning—though, come to think of it, I'd had plenty

of warning—there was an almighty crash and banging and screeching of metal as the car came to a sudden stop. The trailer kept going as debris thudded against the roof. Then it shuddered from the impact, scraped over pavement, and flipped over onto its side. I flipped over as well, and ended up on my back under the fold-down table bolted to the side of the trailer. The dolly, minus the safe, landed on top of me. Kicking it aside, I scrambled up and found myself squatting on a side window, looking around for the safe. The flickering light bars of I-didn't-know-how-many, but a lot of, cop cars lit the interior sporadically, and I was finally able to locate the safe. It had been flung against the tiny under-the-counter refrigerator, and was now safely embedded in a crumpled dent in the door.

Cars screeched to a halt, doors slammed, and loud voices began yelling. Feet pounded on the pavement, somebody smacked a hand against the back of the trailer, and a fire truck rolled to a stop, its ear-splitting siren also dying to a stop. I could see the gear on it from the opposite side window above my head, but mostly all I could see were the tops of trees and a few stars way off in the sky.

I gingerly felt my way to the back door, wondering if I'd suffered an injury that would maim me for life. So far, so good, but I recalled reading that adrenaline takes over in such circumstances, and a victim may not even know she's injured. I was well aware, however, that my shin had been whacked by the wooden seat of that blasted swing set. Throbs of pain were shooting up to my knee.

Dragging my leg along, I reached the ramp door of the trailer, recalling the slam of bolts as Cobb had locked me in.

Banging against the door, I screamed for help. For all I knew, the deputies had no idea that I was imprisoned in the crumpled wreck. What if they couldn't hear me? What if they towed the trailer and left it—and me—to be pancaked into scrap metal? Then I heard a sweet and most welcome voice from the other side of the door.

"Miss Julia! Miss Julia!" Etta Mae yelled at the top of her voice, as she pounded against the back door. "Are you all right? Help, somebody! Somebody, help!"

"Etta Mae," I yelled right back. "Get me out of here!"

Then there was the comforting voice of Sergeant Coleman Bates. "Miss Julia! Are you injured? What's your status in there?"

"Coleman, my status is upside down and highly uncertain. Get me out of here!"

"Hold on, we're coming!" he yelled. "The door's jammed. Got to use the Jaws of Life. We'll get you out, don't worry."

Well, I did worry—needing the Jaws of Life was no minor concern. I sank down on the floor—I mean, the wall—next to the final remains of the refrigerator and put my arms around Mattie's safe. As I waited, I pictured those hydraulic jaws opening the aluminum trailer like a can opener cutting into a tin can.

With the hydraulic pump pumping and the metal shrieking and groaning, the door finally popped open. Coleman stuck his head in, then looked around for a second, getting his bearings. Believe me, a deputy's uniform never looked so good. Etta Mae crawled in beside him, and they nearly got stuck in the opening.

"I got you, Miss Julia," Coleman said, leaning over to put his arms around me. "Are you hurt? The EMTs are here. They'll take a look at you."

Behind him, Etta Mae stood on the wall of the trailer, which was now the floor, wringing her hands. She was as white as a sheet and moaning under her breath.

"I thought I'd killed her," she mumbled in a singsongy way, her hands twisting at her waist. "Is she all right? I really thought I'd killed her, I just knew I had. I didn't know what else to do. I just had to stop him."

"Etta Mae, honey," I said, standing up with Coleman's help, "get a grip. I'm perfectly all right. A few bruises, I expect, and some hair-raising dreams ahead, but other than that I am remarkably fit. Get me out of here, Coleman, but get the safe out first."

It didn't quite work that way, because Coleman lifted me out of the trailer and into the care of two EMTs, bless their hearts. Then he put his hands on Etta Mae's shoulders, turned her around, and marched her to the EMTs' truck.

"Sit down," he ordered, "and let them look you over. You got thrown around a bit when he hit the wall."

I processed that for a minute and realized that Etta Mae must've been in the car with Cobb. How had she managed that? Or had *he* managed it the same way he'd managed me? I'd thought she was across the street getting her cell phone.

Oh, well, I thought, too rattled to think clearly, especially since the EMTs were engaged in an all-over examination of my person. Then they put me on a stretcher and wrapped a blanket around me for the shock, and it being a ninety-degree night. I kept throwing it off and sitting up, and they kept pushing me down and wrapping me up.

"Etta Mae," I called, "where are you?"

"Right here," she said, looking upside down at me from above my head. "Can I get you anything? Drink of water? Your pocket-book? I brought it back for you, but he was already cranking the car. So I had to use it a little bit."

"Listen, Etta Mae," I said, reaching for her hand. "Forget my pocketbook—just don't let that safe out of your sight. Tell Cole-man that it's in my legal possession and, for goodness' sake, don't let them leave it in the trailer. It'll get mashed to a pulp."

Fearing that Coleman or some other deputy would override her, I sat up, flung off the blanket, and got off the stretcher.

"Hey. Hey, now," one of the EMTs said. "Lie back down. We're going to transport you to the hospital. Just hold tight."

"I don't need to go to the hospital," I said firmly. "I have more important matters to tend to, and if you push me down one more time, I will smack you good."

He laughed and called Coleman over.

While waiting, I became aware of the activity around the Ca-dillac. The car had jumped the curb and was halfway off the street, its front end buried in a brick wall that I knew had cost a fortune to build. Firemen and EMTs were tripping over the scattered bricks, and as I watched, they lifted Andrew F. Cobb from the front seat and placed him on a stretcher. EMTs, crouching beside him, blocked my view as they worked on him.

Coleman walked over and said, "Miss Julia, you have to do what they tell you. You've just been through a really bad accident, and you need to be looked at. Why don't you just lie down and let them take care of you?"

"I will, Coleman, I promise. But listen, there's a little safe in there stuck in the door of the refrigerator. It's very heavy and you may need the Jaws of Life to get it out, but I *need* it. I need it to go with me. It belongs to Miss Mattie Freeman, and I'm responsible for it."

"Is it stolen property?"

"Well, certainly not by me. Actually, though, it *was*, but I'd gotten it back."

"Ordinarily," Coleman said, "recovered property goes into the evidence and property room and stays there until after the trial of whoever stole it. Especially if the item is of some value. If it's not, we can probably let you retain possession."

Good grief, I thought, *some trials don't even go to trial for years. The deacons of the First Presbyterian Church would be up in arms, and I might really have to move my letter to the Episcopal church.*

"Miss Julia?" Coleman asked, a frown of concern on his face. "Are you all right?"

I nodded and continued processing.

Running through my mind was not only the thought of the extended length of time that it would take to probate Mattie's will if the safe were to be confiscated but also the possibility that someone would pilfer the evidence from the evidence room. I'd heard of such things happening, although how anyone could walk out of the sheriff's department with that heavy safe under his arm, I didn't know.

"Now, Coleman, here's the truth of the matter. The safe itself is of no value—who would want it? And I will tell you that at this point in time, no one has any definite idea of the value of what is in it. It could be one of a kind, or it could be one of a thousand. All I know is that according to Mr. Ernest Sitton, Esquire, I am responsible to the court for its proper dispensation. Coleman," I said, grabbing his hand, "I *need* that safe."

Just then, the bustling around the car increased as the stretcher bearing Cobb was lifted and carried to the waiting ambulance.

"How bad is he?" I asked, pointing in the general direction.

"Nothing obviously major, but they put him in a neck brace. He's conscious, but not clicking too well—shock, maybe, or could be internal injuries."

"Probably not wearing a seat belt," I said, with a touch of self-righteousness.

"Got that right," Coleman said. "He's pretty beat up, though. Especially around the face and head."

"That's too bad," I said, making the automatic response of a well-bred individual. "However, one does reap what one sows."

He grinned. "I'll go see about your safe. No reason, I guess, for us to keep it. We'll know where it is."

As he turned away and the ambulance bearing Andrew F. Cobb headed for the hospital, Etta Mae, still white around the mouth, sidled up to me. "Miss Julia? You think he'll be all right? That man, I mean."

"Cobb? Coleman didn't seem too concerned and, to tell the truth, neither am I. He inveigled his way into town, playing the grieving relative and making people feel sorry for him, and all along he was planning to steal from poor old Miss Mattie. I never wish ill on anybody, Etta Mae, but it seems to me that he got pretty much what he deserved."

"Oh, I hope he'll be all right," Etta Mae said. "I was afraid I'd killed him."

"How, honey? How could you have killed him?"

"With your pocketbook. See, I got back from getting my phone and your pocketbook just as he jumped in the car. And I didn't know where you were until I heard you screaming bloody murder, so when he started cranking the car, I didn't think. I just grabbed a door handle and flung myself in the backseat. I didn't even have time to close the door, because he stepped on the gas and we flew out of the lot with the trailer bumping and jolting along behind us. I kept yelling for him to stop, but he wouldn't, and I didn't have any way to make him, so I just started hitting him over the head with your pocketbook. It was all I had."

"Well, you certainly did the right thing. If it hadn't been for you, I'd still be locked in that trailer heading for who-knows-where. Kentucky, maybe."

"Well, but I'm real sorry, Miss Julia. I hit him so hard that something broke or came loose or something inside your pocketbook. But, really, you don't have to worry. I won't tell anybody."

Chapter 46

What was she talking about? This wreck on a city street would be front-page news in the morning paper—everybody would know.

"Miss Wiggins?" A deputy walked over holding at arm's length my large black pocketbook. "Found this in the car. Is it yours? It come open and strewed things all over the place. You might want to check it, be sure we got everything."

I wasn't seeing too well in the still-flashing lights, but something was wrong with the pocketbook that I'd paid an arm and a leg for and that Etta Mae had run across the street to retrieve. Water, or something, dripped from the seams and a heady aroma emanated from it.

"Oh, thank you." Etta Mae spoke up right smartly as she reached for the wet, squishy bag that I now recognized as faux leather. "It's mine, and everything in it's mine, too."

"Why, Etta Mae," I said, "that's not yours. It's . . ."

"No, ma'am," she broke in, "it's mine, it really is." Then she leaned over and whispered, "Don't claim it, Miss Julia, and nobody'll know."

"Listen, ladies," the deputy said, setting the pocketbook on an errant brick. "Y'all can decide whose it is. I got to get back to work." And he walked away.

"Etta Mae," I said, "why are you claiming that thing? It's soaked through and it reeks to high heaven. There's only four dollars and eighty-five cents in it, so just take that out and throw everything else away. What happened to it, anyway?"

"It's what I hit that man with. And I mean, when it connected, it *connected*. I think I knocked him goofy, because that's when he hit the brick wall. And I'll tell you, Miss Julia, it's a good thing you had that flask in it."

"What?" I said and started laughing, even though the fumes from the pocketbook were burning my sinuses. "For goodness' sake, Etta Mae, that's not mine. Honey, you picked up the wrong pocketbook. That one is Mattie Freeman's and so is what's in it, but don't tell anybody. It would just ruin her reputation." I stopped laughing as I realized what Etta Mae had not only done—freed me from captivity—but also what she'd tried to do—protect *my* reputation.

I could've hugged her, even though I rarely feel the urge to hug anybody.

We watched as Coleman and another deputy dislodged the safe from the refrigerator door and wrestled it back onto the dolly. Then they had to bend over and back out the ramp door, which, of course, was lying sideways because the trailer was also lying sideways. Etta Mae and I picked up some interesting and highly colorful mutterings from both men as they manhandled the dolly to the back of Coleman's squad car. Then, after a few futile attempts to lift the safe, they called two more deputies over and the four of them picked up the dolly and dumped the safe into the trunk of Coleman's car. The car bounced on its heavy-duty shocks as the safe rolled over and came to rest.

"Miss Julia," Coleman said, mopping his face as he walked over to us. "Your safe is safe in my trunk, and that's where it's going to stay. It'll take a winch to get it out again. I'll see if J.D. has one when he gets back."

Wench, *again*! What were Etta Mae and now Coleman thinking? And Mr. Pickens just better not have one.

———

Nothing would do but that I had to go to the hospital. Coleman insisted, and so did Etta Mae, both of whom I could've overruled. But when the EMTs told me they could lose their jobs if Etta Mae and I weren't seen by a doctor, I went docilely enough.

And it took forever. Believe me, emergency does not mean fast. I waited on a stretcher, then waited on an examining table, then waited to be x-rayed, then waited for the ER doctor to decide that no bones were broken, which he took his own sweet time doing. Then I had to wait for them to give Etta Mae a clean bill. And on top of that, we both had to give statements of the night's events so the deputies could fill out their forms.

Coleman gave us a ride to where my car was parked, strongly suggesting that Etta Mae drive, then assured me again that the safe was safe. "Nobody's going to move it," he said. "You can bank on that." Then he followed us home and saw us inside.

"Etta Mae," I said, as she and I walked into my house close to five o'clock that morning. "All I want to do is go to bed. And I know you do, too. But I need to show up at church at eight o'clock—can you believe that? Presbyterian church services have been at eleven for so long, I thought it was one of the Ten Commandments."

She laughed. "Well, if you don't mind, I think I'll pass on either time. I'm beat."

After she went upstairs to Lloyd's bed, I perked a pot of coffee and warmed up one of Lillian's cinnamon rolls. I didn't want to go to church, but with the adrenaline still churning around, I thought I might as well find a use for it. Of course, I had good reason for absenting myself—my goodness, I had been abducted and thrown around in an accident. But if Pastor Ledbetter and the deacons looked over the congregation and saw an empty place in the pew where I normally sat, they'd jump to the conclusion that I'd folded my tent and was ready to give in. They'd think they had me on the run, and they'd ramp up their campaign to get me to make good on Mattie's bequests.

I just couldn't seem to get through to them that I was not

sitting on Mattie's estate, deliberately stalling just to inconvenience them. It might've taken some heat off me if I'd told them about the sampler and its potential, but I had to resist. If word got out that a highly valuable item had been discovered in the back of a closet, thieves would come out of the woodwork, and just one of that crew, namely, Andrew F. Cobb, had been enough to last me a lifetime.

So I drank half a pot of coffee, took a shower, dressed, and marched into church at ten of eight, ready to show them all that I was standing my ground.

I admit that the unair-conditioned church was a bit stuffy and close. Every one of the deacons and a few of the less conservative elders were in shirtsleeves, which I thought was carrying the need for comfort a little too far. But, along with everybody else, I used the bulletin as a fan and prayed for the hour and fifteen minutes to end before I melted.

When the deacons came down the aisle to receive the offering plates, I bestirred myself to dig my envelope out of my pocketbook. Roger Holmes, the owner of Holmes Insurance Company, was the deacon on my side of the aisle. When he passed the plate to the row in front, he stood right next to me to await its round trip. Quite ostentatiously, he stood there in his short sleeves, took a handkerchief from his pocket, folded it, and blotted his face. Then he carefully refolded the handkerchief and began patting the perspiration from his neck—all the time giving me what Lillian would call the evil eye.

When the plate reached me, I deposited my envelope and passed the plate to him. But instead of releasing it, I held it for a minute so he'd have to lean over. "Roger," I whispered, "you keep that up, and I'm moving my business to Geico."

He jerked upright, took the plate, and continued collecting the offerings before taking a seat on the far side of the church.

As tired as I was, I managed to get through the congregational hymns, the Scripture reading, the morning prayer, and the choir's rendition, but the adrenaline ran out about the time the pastor began his sermon. With the deacons in a state of undress, I wondered what he had on—or didn't have on—under his black robe. It didn't much matter, though, because I slept through the sermon.

Before continuing my nap in my own bed, I checked on Etta Mae when I got home. She was out like a light, so I wrote a note telling her to make herself at home while I slept. Then I called Coleman at home and had to leave a message. He was on night duty, so he, too, was sleeping through the day. The message I left was essentially this: "Whatever you do, Coleman, do not be driving around all night picking up criminals and investigating break-ins and car wrecks and whatever else you do with that safe in your trunk. Bring it to my house late this afternoon. I will remove its contents and you can keep the safe. I'll be waiting for you."

Then I went to bed.

When I arose late that afternoon, feeling logy from sleep disruption and achy from having been upended in a tin trailer, I found Etta Mae reading the Sunday paper in the library.

She immediately unfolded her tanned legs—the length of which was revealed by the shorts she wore—and jumped up. "Oh, Miss Julia, how're you feeling?"

"Much better," I said. "But, Etta Mae, I am so sorry that your visit hasn't been quite the vacation I envisioned. Here, I've slept the day away and left you to your own devices. Did you have lunch?"

"I've been fine. In fact, it's been a real nice afternoon. Miss Mildred walked over to tell you that she's lost two more pounds, so I invited her in and we had some iced tea. Then she wanted to take a walk, so we did that, then I came back here and read the paper."

"My goodness, that was nice of you. How far did you walk?"

"About three blocks. Maybe three and a half."

"You did better than I've been able to do." I sat down to rest my aching shin, wishing again that I had a closet full of ladies' pants—the bruise looked awful. "We should think about supper, I guess, but Coleman's coming by so I can take possession of the sampler. I hope you can open that safe again."

She grinned. "No problem, if you still have the combination."

"It's in my pocketbook right over there." I pointed to the Prada bag on the desk. "It's a good thing you got the wrong one last night. If you'd banged the daylights out of Andrew Cobb with mine, no telling where that scrap of paper would've ended up."

"Boy, that's the truth," Etta Mae said as we both laughed. Then she sobered a little and said, "Wonder how he's doing. I hope I didn't do any permanent damage."

"He's probably just glad to be in a hospital instead of a jail cell." I had little sympathy for scofflaws and evildoers. "Let's go see what Lillian left us for supper. I'm starving."

Chapter 47

When Coleman's patrol car rolled to a stop in my driveway, Etta Mae and I hurried out to meet him. Etta Mae was ready with the combination in hand, while I was getting more anxious by the minute. What if she couldn't open the safe? What if Cobb had taken the sampler out before he'd moved the safe? And hidden it where we'd never find it?

But, no, not even he would've been that foolish. He wouldn't have struggled to get the safe from closet to trailer, across a gravel parking lot and up a ramp, if it had been empty. It had to be in the safe.

Still, I couldn't wait to get my hands on that shirt box again. So we watched as Coleman swung out of his car, walked to the trunk, opened it, and stood back.

"There you are, ladies," he said with a flourish of his hand. "Safe and secure, just as we left it."

I leaned in to look, and, yes, there was the safe, but there was also a lot of police gear, including a shotgun, a first-aid kit, a shovel, an extra pair of socks, a rain poncho, a bag of Doritos, and who-knows-what-else. The safe was sitting right where it had been dumped from the dolly, but it had landed upside down with the dial facing the back of the trunk.

"Oh, my," I said, "it'll be hard to get to, but, Coleman, I don't want you trying to move it. It's too heavy, and you could ruin your back. Etta Mae," I went on, turning to her, "you think you can get to the dial with it facing that way?"

"Sure." And with Coleman's help, she hopped up into the trunk, squatted next to the safe, and went to work. And misdialed the first time. "Phooey," she said, "I'm doing this upside down, but hold on. I'll get it."

And she did. She opened the safe, pulled out the Rich's box, and handed it to me. Then Coleman helped her jump out of the trunk.

Coleman looked from me to Etta Mae to the Rich's box, then said, "Is that it? What is it?"

"It's a box," I said. "A shirt box."

"Well," he said, eyebrows raised and a grin on his face, "you went to a lot of trouble for a shirt. I hope there's more to it than that."

"There is, Coleman. It's just about the sum total of Mattie Freeman's estate, bless her heart, and I thank you for taking care of it. And, by the way, you can have the safe. Tell the sheriff that I'm donating it to the department. Oh, and, Coleman, I was about to forget. How is Andrew Cobb? Etta Mae's concerned about him."

Coleman grinned. "Last I heard, he's claiming amnesia. Says he doesn't remember anything that happened last night."

Etta Mae, thinking she'd caused brain damage, moaned.

"He's not going to get away with that, is he?" I was incensed that he'd claim a loss of memory. A lot of us might want to forget what we've done, but it's not that easy—too many other people have good memories.

"Nope," Coleman said. "In fact, they're drawing up charges against him now—breaking and entering, larceny, abduction— that would be of you, Miss Julia—reckless driving, exceeding a twenty-five-mile-an-hour speed limit, property damage, failure to stop, driving on a sidewalk, public endangerment, and a defective taillight. Oh, and driving under the influence—the fumes in that car would knock your socks off."

Just as Etta Mae started to speak, I frowned and slightly shook my head at her to keep her quiet—no need to respond to something that wasn't a direct question.

Coleman didn't notice. He went on with what he was saying. "Cobb's got a lot to answer for, amnesia or no amnesia. But he remembers enough to get a lawyer. They said the first thing he asked for this morning was Mr. Ernest Sitton."

"What!" I cried, stunned. "Mr. Sitton is representing him? Why, he can't do that. He's Mattie's lawyer. Wouldn't that be a conflict of interest?"

Coleman shrugged. "I don't know, maybe not. The court'll straighten it out."

"Well, that just beats all I've ever heard," I said, just done in by Andrew Cobb's audacity and Mr. Sitton's lack of professional sense.

"Etta Mae," I went on, "let's go in. I'm calling Mr. Sitton right now, and"—I stopped and clutched the box to my bosom—"I need to check this out. We may have to lay a few more charges on Mr. Andrew Cobb."

With a wave to Coleman as he backed out of the driveway, we went inside to make sure that we had what we wanted. Holding my breath for fear that something else would go wrong, I untied the twine, lifted the lid off the box, and unwrapped the sampler—just enough to peek at it. Reassured, I rewrapped it, put the lid back on the box, and thanked the Lord for travel mercies—it had been through so much.

Then I put it back among my flannel gowns.

"Mr. Sitton," I said when he answered his phone, and before he could say more than "Sitton here," I demanded, "What do you mean by representing a thief and a scoundrel? Do you know what he did last night? Do you know he endangered my life? And stole from another client of yours—you know, the one who's dead and can't take up for herself? But I can. I mean, I can take up for her, and I want to know just what you're doing by representing both sides of a criminal case."

"I presume this is Mrs. Murdoch."

"You presume correctly, and I want some answers."

He took a mighty breath as if he were not accustomed to being called to account. "Mrs. Murdoch, Andrew Cobb called me because I was the only lawyer he knew. I have since recommended a few to him, and I assume he's followed up on at least one of them. I assure you that I am not representing him. Under the circumstances, it would be highly questionable if I did."

"Well," I said, quickly losing steam, "I should think so."

"And," Mr. Sitton went on, "we may have more congress with Mr. Cobb than we want as far as Mrs. Freeman's estate is concerned. I've been notified that prison records and pictures will be in my office sometime tomorrow. We should know by then just who Mr. Cobb is."

"I can tell you who he is," I said, suddenly sure of what had to be true. "He is *not* Andrew F. Cobb, unless there're two of them. Why would he have gone to the trouble—and it *was* trouble—to steal her most valuable asset if all he had to do was petition the court as Mattie's nephew and he would've had it all? We're dealing with an impostor, Mr. Sitton."

"I expect you're right, but we'll know for sure by tomorrow."

"I'm not going to believe it even if your picture is a dead ringer for that man. I was eager to pass along this entire mess to him at first, but now I will fight him tooth and nail for every penny of Mattie's estate." Even, I thought, if most of it had to go toward an air-conditioning unit.

"Julia?" Diane Jankowski said, an underlay of excitement in her voice when I answered the phone at seven that Monday morning. "The truck's already left Atlanta. It should be here around eleven. Helen and I are going to meet at the apartment at ten to do a last-minute check."

"That's wonderful, Diane. I'll be there, too, with Lillian. We'll have that place cleaned out by suppertime. And, Diane, I can't thank you enough for all you've done."

"Well, hold off on the thanks," Diane said, laughing. "You haven't heard it all yet. I've had a pile of e-mails over the weekend, and three phone calls, too. Everybody I contacted is excited about the sampler, but, of course, they want to authenticate it. Most of them want to do it themselves, but I don't want it to be passed around and fiddled with that much. If you agree, I'd like to take it to the Smithsonian, let them examine it, then put it up for auction. How does that sound?"

"Like I was fortunate to have turned to you in the first place," I told her, feeling a great sense of relief—there was beginning to be a light in the tunnel. "Go ahead and make your plans, Diane, and Mattie will send you to Washington."

Having not lost a thing in the nation's capital, I thought as we hung up, *Better her than me*. Still, I hated the thought of depleting Mattie's meager bank account for plane tickets and a hotel room, but, as they say, you have to spend money to make money. And the best bet to make money for Mattie—or rather, for Mattie's beneficiaries—was that sampler.

Later in the morning, Lillian, loaded down with mop, bucket, brushes, rags, and several spray bottles of cleaning solutions, followed me into Mattie's building, where we had to stand aside as men were already bringing in furniture padding. Helen and Diane were doing their last-minute check, making sure that the real antiques were properly covered and protected for the trip to Atlanta.

It was amazing to watch the men—only one of whom spoke English, such as it was—as they expertly wrapped and tied padding around each piece of furniture, preparing their valuable cargo for the return trip.

Strangely, with all the activity in and out of Mattie's apartment, Mr. Wheeler was making himself scarce. It wasn't at all like him to ignore what was going on—none of the tenants could've helped knowing that Mattie's apartment was going through its last roundup. And Mr. Wheeler had always seemed not only willing but eager to help, yet here we were, working away, and he was nowhere to be seen.

"Helen," I said when I found her labeling boxes in the sunroom. "I thought Mr. Wheeler would be around. Is he out of town?"

"I'm sure I don't know."

Uh-oh, I thought, then said, "He's been so helpful in the past, I thought he'd be here."

Helen straightened up after drawing a heavy line under the last label. She sighed, and said, "Julia, I asked him not to come by. It would be awkward having him around."

"Oh, Helen, I'm sorry. I thought . . . Well, it doesn't matter what I thought, but I hope you're all right with whatever happened."

"I'm fine." Short and sweet. Then she drew herself up, composed her face, and explained, "He wants children."

It took me a minute to understand. "Oh, I see. Well, Helen, life can be full without children, and I should know. But it's too bad that you didn't meet when you both were younger."

Helen gave me a look that could've peeled an onion. "I assure you that age—*my* age—doesn't enter into it. I simply do not wish to have children."

"Oh, well. Well, good for you, Helen. I admire you for knowing what you want and what you don't." Then, turning away, I said, "I better go help Lillian."

I had never really understood Helen, but I appreciated her, and never more than in the past few days when she'd been so much help in sorting Mattie's furniture. But as far as her personal life was concerned, I'd learned my lesson—I was staying out of it. But don't tell me that her age didn't enter into it.

Other than that, I had too much else on my mind to tend to

somebody else's business. Getting Mattie's apartment closed would be a huge step toward ending my executive duties. Sometime during the day, Mr. Sitton would be able to establish Andrew F. Cobb's true identity, and, above all, Sam would be home by nightfall.

He had called the evening before from somewhere in Alabama where they'd stopped for an overnight stay. He'd laughed as he told me that they were in a Sleep Inn right off the interstate.

"Lloyd was disappointed," Sam said. "He wanted to look for a Motel 6, because they were leaving a light on for us. Oh, and, Julia, you better tell Lillian and Hazel Marie to be prepared. We're bringing home two coolers full of fish."

"Just so you bring yourself home," I said. "And Lloyd. Well, and Mr. Pickens, too." Fish I could do without.

Chapter 48

As soon as Mattie's bedroom was emptied, I began sweeping the floor while Lillian wiped cobwebs from the walls. Helen and Diane stood by the door to the hall, checking off each piece of furniture as it was moved to the truck.

When the last chest, the last chair, the last everything was gone, including the last faded oil painting and photograph from the walls, I wandered through the apartment, my footsteps echoing in the empty rooms. I glanced at the trash piles on the floor, the dusty windows, the empty hangers in the closet, and the stained wallpaper, thinking to myself, *"Bare ruined choirs, where late the sweet birds sang."*

Well, I didn't know that any sweet birds had ever sung in Mattie's apartment, but the bare, ruined rooms gave me such a desolate feeling that I was moved to dredge up the little bit of poetry that had stuck in my mind. Poor Mattie, I thought, almost overcome by the sadness of her life. But, I thought, as I mentally shook myself, if everything that I'd set in motion went well, she would create some happiness for others—like the ten friends she'd remembered in her will, plus a lot of children, many litters of dogs and cats, twelve overheated deacons, and one hotheaded minister.

As Lillian rounded up her cleaning supplies, Diane and I discussed for a few minutes her pending trip to the Smithsonian, then I thanked her and Helen again. While they took one last look around the rooms, I walked back to Mr. Wheeler's apartment.

I could hear the sound of a power saw from within, so I knew he'd kept working while we emptied Mattie's apartment without him. Under the circumstances as I now knew them, that had probably been a wise course.

"Good afternoon," I said when he opened the door. "I think we're all finished, but I need to turn in our keys and officially end Mrs. Freeman's lease. Do you know who the owner is?"

"I sure do," he said with that nice smile. "I am."

"Well, good. I knew the building had changed hands recently, but I didn't know from whose to whose. So I'll tell you, Mr. Wheeler, Mattie's apartment could use some rehabilitation before you rent it again."

"It's the next one on my list." He accepted the new keys I'd had made, and as I started to turn away, he said, "Uh, Mrs. Murdoch, is your houseguest still with you?"

"Etta Mae? No, Sam will be home tonight, so she's back at her place in Delmont." It flashed through my mind that Etta Mae was young enough, if childbearing age was really Mr. Wheeler's criterion, for his consideration. But somehow I felt that there'd been more to Helen's breakup with him than either her ability or his desire to have children. "Why?" I asked.

"Well, I thought I might give her a call. Unless," he quickly added, "she's seeing someone."

Knowing that Etta Mae had seen many someones, I said, "I'm not sure, but I think she's in between right now. But I caution you, Mr. Wheeler, she's as fine a young woman as you'll find, but she has a mind of her own. I wouldn't toy with her if I were you."

He grinned. "I wouldn't dream of it."

I nodded, thanked him again for his help, and left, thinking as I went that he'd answer to me if he did.

———————

My cell phone rang as I followed Lillian through the front door of Mattie's building on our way to the car. It took several seconds of rummaging in my pocketbook to find the thing—it rang so seldom that it was rarely to hand.

"Mrs. Murdoch?" Mr. Ernest Sitton said. "Glad I caught you. Your housekeeper once told me that you might not answer. But, be that as it may, I have news for you. Cobb, or the man we know as Cobb, was discharged from the hospital this morning, still claiming amnesia for the events of Saturday night. Of course, he was still under arrest and appeared before the magistrate for arraignment a little while ago. Bond of twenty thousand dollars was set, and he bonded out."

"He's *out*? After all he's done?"

"He was given notice to appear before the district judge in a day or so because of the felony charges, and a court date will be set then. In the meantime, yes, he's out."

"Why, Mr. Sitton, what's he going to do? His trailer's wrecked, so he has no place to live. And his car's in worse shape, so he can't get around. Is he just on the street?" I looked around to be sure he wasn't hiding in the bushes by the front door.

"The fact that he has no transportation is probably the reason he was given bond," Mr. Sitton said, somewhat drily. "His lawyer's found him a bed at the mission."

"Well, what I want to know," I said, still hot about the whole situation, "is how did he pay a twenty-thousand-dollar bond? He certainly doesn't appear to have that kind of money, and we know he has no property to speak of, especially since it's all wrecked."

"A bondsman, Mrs. Murdoch, who, I expect, is now regretting the deal. Cobb is apparently missing. His lawyer dropped him off at the mission, but he never registered with them. Now," Mr. Sitton continued, "it may well be that he's sitting in a restaurant somewhere or walking down Main Street or a dozen other places. I've been trying to contact him, but nobody's seen him."

"He could still turn up," I said, although I doubted it, and didn't much care if he didn't. "Maybe one of those long-haired bounty hunters will go after him."

"Yes, well, maybe so. But a warrant will be issued if he fails to appear on his court date, and the sheriff as well as the bondsman will be after him. They'll get him, especially since we now know who he is."

"We do?"

"I have the pictures and identification that we've been waiting for. I think you'll find them interesting. How soon can you get here, Mrs. Murdoch?"

As quickly as it took me to drive to Delmont, which wasn't very long. I had, however, delayed long enough to take Lillian home and tell her to lock all the doors and not to answer if anyone knocked. If Cobb was on the loose, there was no telling where he'd turn up. He obviously knew that something valuable was—or had been—in Mattie's safe, but whether he'd known what it was, was another matter. He might've been sorely disappointed if he'd opened the safe expecting to find gold coins or bundles of cash and had found, instead, a piece of needlework.

As soon as I walked into Mr. Sitton's office, my eyes locked on a fuzzy black-and-white picture in the center of his conference table.

"Is that him?"

Mr. Sitton nodded. "Andrew F. Cobb, yes. Taken fifteen years ago when he was arrested for larceny and sentenced to six years' incarceration. Released after thirty-six months for good behavior, no further contact with law enforcement."

"Until Saturday night," I reminded him. I approached the table slowly, being of two minds as to what I wanted to see.

Leaning over, I scanned the faxed picture, then snatched it up for a closer look. "Who is this?"

"Andrew F. Cobb, deceased April 26, 2009. Highway accident—here's the police report." He laid an official form on the table for me to see. "Note also his physical description sent by the warden of the prison." Another form slid beside the first one.

"My word," I said as I read it. "He was a big man—over six feet, weighing two hundred ten pounds, and I know these faxed things don't give a true picture of coloring, but it looks to me as if he had black hair and eyebrows. In other words," I went on, in a musing way, "not anything at all like the man presenting himself as Cobb. But, Mr. Sitton, this description of the real Cobb comes closer to the way Mattie looked than that short, blond, sunburned idiot who almost took us in. She was a large-boned woman, tall, though almost hunchbacked, and dark even with some graying, as you may recall. I see, I think, a family resemblance, especially in the heavy eyebrows. And I hate to say this, but in the mustache as well."

He nodded. "I'd say it's confirmed that we've been dealing with an impostor."

"But how did he know about Mattie? How did he know what she had—that she'd be worth robbing? How did he even know she'd died?"

"Remember what I told you about sociopaths. Now look at this." He handed me another faxed picture.

"Why, it's him!"

"Yes, it's William Lee Smith, or, at least, that's one of the names he's known as. We can be grateful to the warden where they were both incarcerated. When I explained our concerns about the man presenting himself as Cobb, he looked more closely through his files. Smith was Cobb's cellmate for almost Cobb's entire period of incarceration. You may not know this, but it's quite common for cellmates to share personal information to pass the time."

"But, Mr. Sitton, that was years ago, when Andrew Cobb, according to you and that sheriff you talked to, was a fairly young man. How would Cobb-Smith-whoever-he-is know about Mattie? And also know that the real Cobb was dead and wouldn't be appearing as the next of kin?"

"Sociopathic behavior, Mrs. Murdoch," Mr. Sitton said, as if such behavior were nothing new to him. "It doesn't surprise me that he tucked away information that could be of use later on. I have no doubt that the real Cobb revealed the entire history of his family, perhaps even that his aunt Mattie was the caretaker of valuable family items."

"Including the contents of a *safe*?" I could hardly believe it.

"A safe?" Mr. Sitton asked, eyebrows raised.

"I'll explain later," I said with a wave of my hand. I needed to first understand sociopathic behavior. "I'm finding it hard to fathom that this Smith could get so much intimate information out of another prisoner, then keep it to himself for years and years. *And* keep an eye out for both Cobb's and Mattie's death notices."

"Perhaps Cobb's fairly low intelligence quotient speaks to your first concern. And we don't know if Smith actually knew they were both deceased. He may have figured he could get by as Mattie's nephew just long enough to steal something from her, then he'd move on."

"The cellarette," I murmured, realizing that if Cobb-Smith or Smith-Cobb was on the run, he had money in his pocket to finance a flight from justice. "No wonder, then," I went on, "that he had no interest in contesting her will. He didn't want to draw too much attention to himself." I shivered as I recalled how willing—even eager—I'd been to turn over Mattie's estate to anybody who would take it—including a bald-faced liar unconscionable enough to sit as big as you please in the first pew at Mattie's funeral service.

"Well," I said, turning away from the paper-strewn table, "if you want to know the truth, I'm glad he's gone and I hope he stays that way. I still have too much to do to spend time testifying in a courtroom, revealing, thereby, all of Mattie's secrets. Some of which, Mr. Sitton, you may be interested in."

Then I told him about finding the unreadable combination that Etta Mae had been able to decipher, the safe and its remarkable contents, and finally I told him of Diane Jankowski's upcoming mission to the Smithsonian.

"Well," he said, a hint of admiration in his words, "you've certainly been busy."

"More than you know, Mr. Sitton," I said, sighing as I thought of a wild Saturday night ride. "More than you know."

Chapter 49

"You didn't use enough sunblock," I said as Sam, sunburned and peeling over a nice tan, stepped out of his car late that afternoon. "But, oh, I am so glad you're home. Did you have a good time? Wait till I tell you what happened here. Oh, Sam, how's Lloyd? Did he enjoy the trip? Did he catch any fish? What about Mr. Pickens? Did he behave himself? Well, come on in. I want to hear all about it."

Laughing, Sam hugged me, and it felt so good to have him close. "Give me a chance, woman," he said. "Let me catch my breath, and I'll give you a blow-by-blow account."

Lillian came running out, greeting Sam with a barrage of questions along the same lines as mine. The three of us quickly unloaded the car, a task that included lugging in a heavy cooler.

"Look like we gonna be havin' lots of fish suppers," Lillian said, brightening considerably upon finding the fish scaled, boned, and filleted.

"I'll take some to Mildred and Ida Lee," I said. "Fish doesn't have many calories, does it?"

"Not 'less you deep-fry 'em in batter like I do," Lillian said, laughing.

Much later that evening, after supper and Lillian's departure, Sam and I sat together on the sofa in the library. His arm was around me and, for a change, all was well with the world. Throughout supper, Lillian and I had peppered Sam with questions about his trip. We wanted every detail of the drive there and back, where they'd stayed, how often they'd gone out on the gulf, how their weather was, whether Lloyd had had a good time, and, finally, who had caught the biggest fish.

Now it was my turn to catch Sam up with the events of my week, and my mind was busily editing the account before speaking. Not that I recommend keeping important happenings from one's husband—not at all. I would say that it was more of an effort to protect him from worry and concern.

So I told him of Etta Mae's stay, her genius in deciphering the safe's combination, and our spending the nights in Mattie's apartment after the cellarette had gone missing.

"Good grief, Julia," Sam said. "You didn't have to *sleep* over there."

"Well, I did, too, because nothing else was stolen after that. One other attempt was made, but we foiled it."

"Foiled, huh?" Sam gave me a skeptical look, then smiled and shook his head.

"But listen to this, Sam," I said, eagerly moving along, "you won't believe what we found in Mattie's safe. I want you to see it before Diane takes it to Washington. We may never get it back after the folks up there get their hands on it." And I described the sampler in great detail. Sam was appropriately impressed with the potential value of such an object, as he was when I told him about moving Mattie's furniture to an Atlanta auction house.

"You've really gotten a lot done," Sam said. "But what about Mattie's nephew? What was he doing during all this?"

I was tempted to say, *Breaking and entering, larceny, and fraud,* but I refrained for fear that Sam would become so exercised that he'd never take another trip. So I told him of our suspicions of the man calling himself Andrew F. Cobb and of Mr. Sitton's confirmation that very day of his true identity.

"He's apparently missing now, and as far as anyone knows,

he's gone for good. Mr. Sitton says that a warrant will be issued if he fails to appear on his court date, but that's several days away and he could be anywhere by then."

"It's confirmed, then, that he was not Mattie's relative?" Sam asked, giving it some thought. "But he wouldn't have been arrested for that, especially since he didn't try to get anything of Mattie's." Sam looked sharply at me. "What else happened? Why would he suddenly disappear?"

So I told him an amended version of what had happened on Saturday night—that Smith-Cobb had stolen Mattie's safe, that he'd tried to outrun the law, that somehow Etta Mae had ended up in the backseat of his car, and that she had brought him into compliance by way of Mattie's loaded pocketbook.

I carefully deleted any mention of my tumultuous ride in that tin can of a trailer.

"So now all that's left," I concluded, "is to wait and see what the furniture and the sampler will bring to Mattie's estate. Then I can distribute it to the beneficiaries, which I hope will bring gratitude and cool air to all the hopeful ones."

Sam, smiling, just shook his head. "Every time I leave on a trip, I wonder what you'll be up to while I'm gone. I'm beginning to think that the most excitement and the best sightseeing is right here at home where you are."

"Oh, you," I said and leaned my head against his shoulder. It was so good to have him home.

It took several months of anticipation, delayed planning, and a full measure of frustration before I was able to complete my duties as executor of Mattie's will. I had carefully added up—a number of times—the bequests so that I would know the exact amount to hope for and—if you want to know the truth—to pray for, if for no other reason than to forestall any lingering animosity over my handling of the disbursements.

I would need $140,000 to meet the demands of the will. I had begun with $23,000 in Mattie's money market account, but that had been decreased to cover Diane's trip to Washington as well as her extended stay there while the sampler was authenticated—which, thank goodness, it was. In addition, Mattie's money market account paid for both Diane and Helen to spend a couple of days in Atlanta when the furniture was offered at auction. All told, that account was down to about $18,000, leaving me to pray for pennies from heaven to the tune of $122,000.

Mattie's checking account had been quickly depleted by the final bills from the water department, phone company, Duke Energy, Shell oil company, and the local Rite Aid drugstore. In fact, I'd had to tap into the money market account to cover them all, and I still had to pay Diane and Helen for their week's work in the apartment.

I quickly adjusted my prayers by rounding off the numbers—if the sampler and the furniture brought in a total of $125,000, I would be able to meet all the debts and all the bequests. I got short of breath every time I thought of how unlikely that would be, and got out pencil and paper to try to figure out how best to determine what percentage each beneficiary would receive. That made me gasp for breath.

But I began to breathe a little easier when Diane called from Atlanta to tell me that the furniture had been auctioned for an amount that would net the estate a total of $70,000, which was hard for me to believe. I looked at my own with an appraising eye, wondering how much it was worth. I was brought back to earth, though, when Diane reminded me of the percentage owed to her and Helen. Still, the furniture put me in a much better frame of mind than I had been in.

The topper came when the sampler was offered for sale by Sotheby's in New York. Just as I'd hoped, several museums wanted it, so the bidding started at $35,000 and went up from there. Diane had flown to New York for the auction and called me as soon as it was over.

"Julia," she said, breathless with what she had to say, "you should've been there. You won't believe what happened! Three museums were bidding and they took it up to forty-five and almost stopped. The auctioneer was about to bang his gavel when a bid came in over the phone offering fifty-two. Immediately one of the museums went to fifty-five, and the phone bidder jumped to fifty-eight. The museum came right back with sixty-two, and that's when the phone bidder stopped. So the Smithsonian got it for sixty-two thousand dollars—can you believe that!" Diane was giddy with excitement. "Of course, Sotheby's will take a percentage, but you can be very pleased with the remainder."

"Oh, I will be, I'm sure," I said. "But, Diane, who was bidding on the phone?"

"We'll never know, but it had to be a private collector of some sort. But whoever it was did us a wonderful favor—the sampler was going to go for forty-five and he got it up another seventeen thousand dollars."

"Yes, and I can use every penny of it." After heartily thanking Diane for all she'd done and suggesting that she hurry home, I hung up the phone with a much lighter heart and a considerably less-burdened mind.

Later, though, as I was telling Sam about the auction, I wondered aloud about the identity of the private collector who had so adroitly pushed the museum to a record-breaking bid.

"Sam," I said, little flashes of suspicion darting through my mind, "would that be something a sociopath would do? I mean, it would have to be somebody who had convinced Sotheby's that he could back up his bid, and it would have to be somebody with the gall to impersonate a wealthy bidder—if it wasn't a wealthy bidder to begin with—and somebody who could melt away scot-free if he happened to win the bid."

"You're thinking what I'm thinking?" Sam asked.

"Well, I wouldn't put it past him to be *able* to do it, although why he'd *want* to is beyond me."

"Maybe," Sam said in a musing sort of way, "maybe he was paying Mattie's estate back for that cellarette he took—if he took it."

"Oh, my goodness, you think?" I sat bolt upright at the thought. "That would mean I'd have to rethink everything I ever thought about him—if it was him."

Sam laughed. "Then again, maybe he just enjoys fooling people, seeing how far he can go without getting caught."

"If that's the case, I'd say he's gone pretty far. Nobody's caught up with him yet, and I kind of doubt anybody ever will." I stopped and thought about the man I had assumed was Andrew F. Cobb, thinking of his slight build, his roughened hands, and his sly, ingratiating smile. "If it *was* him, it's as if he's a wandering mischief maker, stealing a little here and there, disturbing the atmosphere wherever he goes, and having his own fun, sometimes at the expense of others, and occasionally, for no particular reason, for their benefit."

Amused, Sam said, "You make him sound like another Loki—if that's who was doing the bidding."

"Well, whoever," I said, unfazed by Sam's reference to some mythical character. "I'm beyond looking a gift horse in the mouth, whatever name he uses."

The day finally arrived, some months later and after several days of tutelage by Mr. Sitton, when I could trot around to the several beneficiaries, handing out checks like John Jacob Astor passed out dimes to the masses.

LuAnne was elated to receive her check. "Oh, my! At last I'm going to have some Christian Louboutins—I just love those red soles, and I've never been able to afford them. Bless Mattie's heart, I know she'd love for me to have at least one pair."

"I'm sure she would," I said, with only a slight roll of my eyes.

Mildred smiled—a little sadly, I thought. "I think I won't cash this. I'm going to frame it, just to remind me that Mattie was thinking of me even though I rarely gave her a thought. We never know what people really think of us, do we, Julia?"

Callie Armstrong laughed her head off. "Is this real? Five thousand dollars? I can't believe it. Mattie is going to send half my brood to camp next summer, and I'm going to bless the day I met her."

Hazel Marie cried, then with tears streaming down her face said, "Oh, Miss Julia, this is just the sweetest thing. Who would've thought that Miss Mattie was so wealthy and so generous with it?"

"I'll tell you all about it, Hazel Marie," I said, "when I get through with my rounds. Believe me, *nobody* would've thought it."

Norma Cantrell, the pastor's receptionist, looked at her check, sniffed, and said, "Well, this is a surprise. Guess you never know about people, do you?"

Carl at the Shell station wiped his hand on his greasy coveralls before accepting the check. He looked at it, then at me, then blinked several times. "Is this right? The amount, I mean?"

"Yes," I said, "she wanted you to have five thousand dollars for taking such good care of her car."

He stood staring at the check until it started shaking in his hand. Then he covered his face with his other hand, turned away from me, and murmured, "'Scuse me, I got to call my wife."

That's one, I thought to myself as I left the Shell station, *who can really use the money. Good for you, Mattie.*

When I passed her check to Sue Hargrove, she stared at it almost as long as Carl had. Then she smiled. "I certainly didn't expect this, so most of it will go to the Boys and Girls Club. I'll save enough to buy a dozen or so petits fours. Come for tea tomorrow, Julia, and we'll eat them all in honor of Mattie."

I should've waited until Roberta Smith got home to hand over her check. She nearly disrupted the entire library when I caught up with her behind the reference desk. "Five *what*!" she almost shouted, her eyes bulging. "Is that really five *thousand*? Oh, Julia, do you know what this means? I'm going to *England*! I'm going to walk where Jane Austen walked, actually *walked*! Oh, bless Miss Mattie's heart. Oh, this is wonderful!"

I left before I was told to leave.

Helen was her cool, composed self as she accepted her check.

She thanked me for it, then thanked me for asking her to help Diane, then thanked me for things in general—all very low key with no apparent emotion. Then, as I turned to leave, she began to cry.

It seemed to take forever to track down Junior Haverty, the bag boy at Ingles grocery store. By this time of the year, he was back in classes at the high school, and I'd been tempted to leave his check with the grandmother with whom he lived. I'm glad I didn't. I would've missed the absolute disbelief and joy with which it was received, although he couldn't quite place Miss Mattie Freeman.

"Well, see, I take groceries out for all kinds of ladies," he said. "The old ones, you know, and I'm so busy loadin' up their cars and puttin' the sacks just like they want them that I don't ever get a good look at anybody. But, man, I can't believe this." Then he turned and yelled, "Hey, Grandmom! Guess who's going to Chapel Hill next year!"

The rest of the bequests—excepting one—were easy enough to distribute. I wrote checks to the PEO scholarship fund, to the local library, to the county Humane Society, and to the Shriners hospital, making sure each recipient knew that the checks came from the estate of Mattie Cobb Freeman. Then I put them in the mail—registered and insured.

That left the church.

Chapter 50

"Norma," I said as I walked up to the receptionist's desk outside Pastor Ledbetter's office. "I apologize for not calling for an appointment, but I know the pastor is eager to see me, so . . ."

"He already has a full day," she said, covering the desk calendar with her arm. "I can give you an appointment sometime next week. What day would you suggest?"

"*Today.* This *very* day." I leaned over her desk. "Norma, if you don't tell him I'm here, I'm going to make an appointment for six months from now, and if that happens, I seriously doubt that you will be here then. Believe me, he is waiting with bated breath for my arrival."

"Oh, well, in that case . . ." She bestirred herself to write a note, then rose from her chair. "Please have a seat for just a few moments. He's on the phone, but I'll give him the message." She slipped into the pastor's office, apparently gave him the note, then returned to her desk to begin shuffling a few papers around.

I sat and waited. And while I waited, I smiled to myself at the memory of the phone call I'd received a few months previously. The caller had been Zeb Benson from Benson's Jewelry on Main with news of the value of Mattie's jewelry. To tell the truth, I'd almost forgotten that I'd left it to be appraised, so it had been a pleasant surprise to be reminded.

Zeb had somewhat reluctantly purchased all of Mattie's jewelry, saying that he'd been thinking of offering a few vintage items for sale. "And I guess," he'd said with a sigh, "I could start by offering these pieces—see how it goes, you know." Then he brightened at a new thought. "Perhaps some of Mrs. Freeman's friends will be interested in a purchase. Something to remember her by, you know."

I assured him that it was an excellent idea, but refrained from buying anything myself.

So an additional check from Benson's Jewelry on Main had been added to the estate's account from which I was making disbursements.

Norma looked up as the light on her phone went out. "You may go in now," she said in a tightly formal voice.

So I did and greeted the pastor, who, as I'd suspected he would be, was more than eager to see me. I had forewarned him the week before that the disbursement of Mattie's bequests was in the works, so he knew why I was there.

"Miss Julia!" he cried, jumping up from his executive chair and coming around the desk to greet me. "How good you're looking these days. Whatever you've been doing certainly agrees with you. Have a seat. Here, sit right here, and let's get down to business. Summer will be here again before we know it."

He almost, but not quite, rubbed his hands together. I sat, opened my pocketbook, and withdrew an envelope.

"I'm sure you know what this is," I said as he eyed it. "I'm sorry it's taken so long to settle Mattie's estate, but we had to wait for auctions to be held and paperwork to be done, as well as making sure that everything was done legally and aboveboard. But here it is, Pastor, Mattie's bequest to the church."

He took the envelope, slit it open, and drew out the check. When he saw the amount, his eyes got large and a flush swept over his face. "Oh, my . . . uh, goodness," he said. "Thirty thousand dollars! We'll have the church air-conditioned before you know it. This is, indeed, manna from heaven."

"Well, I'm not sure of that, Pastor," I said, dreading to rain on his parade. "As I've already told you, Mattie *specified* how she wanted that money to be used—and she didn't include an air-conditioning unit. It's to go for new paperback hymnals, and color-matched pew cushions, carpet, and choir robes."

"But, Miss Julia, we're in dire straits here. Don't you recall how uncomfortable the services were this past August?"

Well, yes, I did, but they'd been uncomfortable not just because of the lack of air-conditioning. However, I wasn't about to open that can of worms. Pastor Ledbetter, contrary to the inclinations of most aging fundamentalists, was becoming more and more open-minded to the redefinition of centuries-old commandments and admonitions—all in the cause of increasing church membership. He'd become ready and willing to jump onto any pop culture bandwagon that came along, but, to my way of thinking, if the church became just another wide-open social group, why bother with it?

"I do recall, Pastor," I said, "but it's my duty to remind you of what Mattie wanted. I've discussed this matter with Mattie's attorney, and he tells me that my responsibility ends when I turn over to you the designated amount. Which I've just done. What you do with it—after being informed of her wishes—is entirely up to you and the deacons." I stood up, preparing to take my leave. "All I can say, Pastor, is let your conscience be your guide."

That took some of the wind out of his sails, but if he expected me to agree with him on how the money was to be used, I couldn't do it. Mattie had ruled and governed my life ever since she'd gotten sick and died on us these many months past, and I wasn't about to let anybody else off the hook at this late date. He could do as he pleased, but it wasn't my business to make him feel better about going against Mattie's wishes, especially since following Mattie's wishes had constricted my days for so long.

"Oh, Miss Julia," the pastor said as I moved toward the door. "I believe Mrs. Conover mentioned to me some while ago that Mattie had not only left the church a specific amount, she'd indicated that any monies left after all the other bequests were filled were to come to the church as well."

"You're absolutely right," I said, brought up short by my short memory. "I was about to forget that there was some left over and that it does, indeed, go to the church." I opened my pocketbook and removed a change purse. Handing it to him, I said, "This is what Mattie had in her pocketbook—it comes to a total of four dollars and eighty-five cents and is what is left over in her estate. So if you use the large check for air-conditioning, this might purchase a few paperback hymnals."

His face fell when he unsnapped the little purse and looked inside at the four dollar bills and a scant handful of change. "Yes," he said, sadly, "perhaps a few."

"Mattie wasn't a wealthy woman, Pastor, and I'm sure she did without a lot of nice things that she would've liked to have had. Yet she wanted what assets she had to come to the church. Use them well, Pastor. And now, thank the Lord, my duties are done."

Then I went home.

"Oh, Sam," I said, leaning against him as we sat together on the sofa in the library—our second favorite place to be. I had just told him of my meeting with Pastor Ledbetter, as well as my doubt as to what he was going to do with the sizable check I'd handed to him. "It's all over. I can hardly believe it. I won't know what to do with myself tomorrow. I've done nothing but muddle through the tangles of Mattie's estate for so long that I'm now at a loss."

"I expect you'll find something to do. Think of this: you said you wanted to give something special to Etta Mae Wiggins. You could go shopping for her."

"I've already ordered her the Fantasy Goddess of the Arctic Barbie. It's a limited edition."

Sam's eyebrows went up. "And she'll like that?"

I nodded. "She'll love it."

"Well, okay, but you might want to also order a tombstone or a marker for Mattie's grave and . . ."

"What!" I jumped straight up from the sofa. "You mean I

should've done that, too! I never even thought of it. And I've spent all the money, or not spent it, but handed it out. Why didn't Mr. Sitton tell me? How could I have forgotten such a thing. It should've come off the top before any disbursements were made. Oh, Sam, what am I to do? I've failed in my job!"

Just as I had been ready to pat myself on the back for the professional way I'd executed Mattie's will, here this had to pop up to remind me of how poorly I'd actually done it.

"This is a *mess!*" I cried, wringing my hands to keep from pulling my hair out in despair. "I can't believe I've been so slack. Of *course* there has to be a marker, but not a tombstone, Sam. Not a big granite block with angels or little lambs on it. No, that wouldn't be suitable. Mattie wasn't a little lamb sort of person. I think a simple bronze marker with her name and her birth and death dates with maybe a brief Scripture verse or something."

"Sit down, honey," Sam said, reaching for me. "Don't beat yourself up over it. If Mattie made no arrangements for a marker, she may not have even wanted one."

"Oh, that's a thought, Sam," I said, whirling around toward him. "She may have already chosen one and paid for it—she did for everything else about her funeral. *Whew!* Wouldn't that be a relief! I'll check with the Good Shepherd Funeral Home first thing tomorrow. It could be that LuAnne has already ordered it.

"But, Sam, if Mattie didn't make arrangements for a marker— I mean, maybe she forgot just as I did. So if she didn't, I will just do it myself." I plopped down beside him, fully confident that I could redeem my thoughtlessness by selecting, ordering, and installing a suitable marker for Miss Mattie Freeman, and paying for it as well.

"That," Sam said with an approving smile, "would be an admirable thing to do. And an appropriate one, too. Then you can surely put *paid* to your duties as her executor and her friend."

"Friend, ha!" I said, stirred up again. "*No* one would saddle a friend with what Mattie left with me. I tell you, Sam, I don't want to execute another will for either friend or foe for as long as I live, and I certainly don't want to be buying gravesite markers for everybody and his brother! Do you know what those things cost?"

Sam shook his head. "No."

"Well, I don't, either, but it won't be cheap. But let's not talk about what friends do for friends. Mattie remembered everybody she considered her friend in her will. But not me. All she left me was one big mess, and after devoting night and day to her affairs for months, I have to pay to have her grave marked. I'll tell you, Sam, it's a good thing that I'm a Christian—I'd be really upset if I wasn't."

Sam pulled me over to him, put both arms around me, and whispered softly, indulgently, "Julia, honey, you are a mess. What am I going to do with you?"

So, since he asked, I told him.

Miss Julia Weathers the Storm

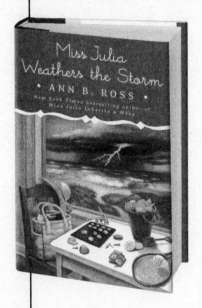

Miss Julia and her friends and family take a big group trip to the beach, including six-year-old Latisha, who is searching for seashells when she discovers some valuable treasures that have washed up from a strong storm off the coast. As the storm nears, the crew heads back to Abbotsville, and it appears that the three strangers they met on the beach—who seemed a bit too interested in Latisha's treasures—have followed them back to their sleepy town. In yet another highly entertaining installment in the series, Miss Julia must rely on her quick wit and strong will to once again save the day.

VIKING